"LOGAN...I LOVE YOU. YOU KNOW THAT, DON'T YOU?"

He let his hard-held breath escape. "Yes," he whispered.

"I know you're afraid to love me. But I'm not afraid."

"Oh, God, Rosalee, I'm not afraid for myself but for you!"

"Don't be afraid for me. I'm a grown woman. I know what I want. I want you, Logan. I'm shameless for saying so, but I want to be with you, stay with you."

"I'd marry you in a minute if I thought it was a chance that I might not ruin you . . . any thread of hope we'd be able to live in peace. In the end it would destroy you!" His voice shook as a flood of despair knocked at his heart.

"I'm not convinced of that. I've waited for you all my life. If you love me, even half as much as I love you, you'll not turn me away. I'm asking you to take me in all the ways a man takes the woman he loves," she whispered . . .

"Five stars! Dorothy Garlock is to historical romantic fiction what Elizabeth Barrett Browning is to the love sonnet!"
—*Affaire de Coeur* on *Restless Wind*

"For those who like their romances emotionally complex and brimful of grit, Garlock holds the reins masterfully."
—*Publishers Weekly*

BOOKS BY DOROTHY GARLOCK

After the Parade
Almost Eden
Annie Lash
Dream River
The Edge of Town
Forever Victoria
A Gentle Giving
Glorious Dawn
High on a Hill
Homeplace
Larkspur
The Listening Sky
Lonesome River
Love and Cherish
This Loving Land
Midnight Blue
More Than Memory
Nightrose
Restless Wind
Ribbon in the Sky
River of Tomorrow
The Searching Hearts
Sins of Summer
Sweetwater
Tenderness
Wayward Wind
Wild Sweet Wilderness
Wind of Promise
With Heart
With Hope
With Song
Yesteryear

DOROTHY GARLOCK

Restless Wind

WARNER BOOKS

An AOL Time Warner Company

WARNER BOOKS EDITION

Copyright © 1986 by Dorothy Garlock
All rights reserved. No part of this book may be reproduced in any form or by any electronic or mechanical means, including information storage and retrieval systems, without permission in writing from the publisher, except by a reviewer who may quote brief passages in a review.

Cover design by Diane Luger
Cover art by Mike Racz
Handlettering by Carl Dellacroce

Warner Books, Inc
1271 Avenue of the Americas
New York, NY 10020

Visit our Web site at www.twbookmark.com.

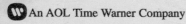 An AOL Time Warner Company

Printed in the United States of America

First Printing: June 1986
Reissued: June 2002

10 9 8 7 6 5 4 3 2 1

For my sisters,
Mary Bruza,
because she faces what comes and never looks back
and
Betty O'Haver,
for all that she is, and for all she means to me

Author's Note

The town of Junction City is a fictitious name for Loveland, Colorado, a beautiful city just east of the Rocky Mountains, as I imagined it would be had it existed at the time of this story.

All the persons in this book are fictitious with the exception of historical figures such as Colonel J.M. Chivington, a former Methodist minister. As commander of the Military District of Colorado he was responsible for the deaths of five hundred Indians, mostly women, children and old people in a deed known as the Sand Creek Massacre. However, the people in my story could have lived in the Colorado Territory in the late 1860's where the Indians, a people considered less than human by some of the whites, and who were dispensable because they were an obstruction in a stream of insatiable dreamers, lost their world, and are no more!

Dorothy Garlock

Chapter One

The sound of rain dripping on the dirt floor woke Rosalee from a sound sleep. The roof had sprung a leak! She sat up on the edge of the bed and slipped her feet into her shoes. It was so dark she could not see the lamp or the matches, and groped around, hands outstretched. She found the match and drew the head along under the table top, held the flame to the wick, and turned it low before replacing the glass chimney. When she finally located the leak, she set a bucket under the drip.

A low moaning wind swept around the corners and under the cabin eaves. The drops of rain fell slowly and heavily, beating against the tin roof and splattering against the window. The night was so black she could see nothing but her own reflection in the small pane of glass. Not even a flash of lightning broke the darkness.

She wrapped her arms around herself as a chill crept over her skin. How gloomy and still this stone cabin was! She looked at the yellowstone chimney and fireplace and was

1

tempted to build a fire. The clock on the mantel told her it was several hours until dawn, yet she was reluctant to blow out the lamp and return to the double bunk where her younger sister slept. She glanced at the ladder leading to the loft where her brother had his bed.

"Poor Ben. Only fourteen and so much responsibility."

Ben had come in after dark tired and wet. All he had to show for his day's work was a tough, wild steer he had rousted out of the brush. Tomorrow she would help him mark it with their Rolling S brand and add it to their small herd. With any luck they would gather enough unbranded stock to buy supplies for another year—if they could get them to the rail head.

Drip, drip, drip. Rosalee eyed the bucket, grateful the leak was not in the roof above where Ben slept. She was wide awake now. She held up her gown and went across the hard-packed earthen floor to listen at the hide covered door leading to the lean-to. Her father was snoring peaceably. She glanced down at Charlie, the big, brown, mongrel dog that lay with his rear against the outside door, his heavy jowls on his paws and his eyes on her.

The cabin was built of native stone taken from the bluffs behind the house. It consisted of one large room and a lean-to that served as her father's room. It had a peaked roof, with a loft at one end of it. There was a large fireplace, a square table, a double bunk attached to the wall, two chairs and two benches. Shelves along the walls above the sheet-iron cook-stove held the cookware, and pegs for the clothing lined the opposite wall. Three years on a dirt floor! How her mother would have hated it! They had always been poor, but until now they'd had a house with a wooden floor.

Rosalee flung the long, thick braid of light brown, sun-streaked hair back over her shoulder. There would be no money this year to buy planks for flooring. Every dollar would be needed for food and for shells to hunt meat for the table and, if necessary, to protect this little spot they called home.

Her father had been a dreamer, a drifter. A thousand acres of preempted government land and this cabin were all he had to show for a lifetime of work. He had worked hard—when he worked. He was a man skilled at both the carpenter's and mason's trade, but he never stayed in one place long enough to build anything permanent for himself. Now he was as dependent on Rosalee and Ben as was their ten-year-old sister, Odell.

Rosalee stood beside the table and thought about when they had first come to the Colorado Territory three years ago. The land had lain empty, lonely and still. The last town had been twenty miles behind them. In all that distance they had not seen another ranch or a line shack or a fence . . . not even a horse or a cow. She had not been able to suppress her disappointment.

"What did you expect for four hundred dollars?" her father had said testily when they rounded a point and saw the cabin tucked close under the shoulder of a hill.

Rosalee's heart had shriveled within her. Before her was the solitary building, squat and bare, without a shed or pole corral. Only the tall trees kept it company in all this vast space.

"It's ours—bought and paid for," Grant Spurlock had said proudly.

Drab and barren, it was a roof over their heads. Rosalee knew how he felt. It had been two years since they had lived in anything other than a wagon, two years since they had buried her mother back in Missouri. She had been just sixteen and Ben eleven when they came to this place. Despite being constantly alert for marauding Indians seeking revenge for the Sand Creek Massacre, they had built a pole corral and a log shed for their stock, spaded up a kitchen garden and dug an irrigation ditch from the spring. Ben had milked the cow, chopped wood, and cared for the horses. They had branded their twelve head of cattle and turned them loose on last year's growth of long bleached grass.

Grant Spurlock had seen his new home through blurred vision, and a few months later he was totally blind. In the middle of the night when she opened her eyes to total darkness, Rosalee realized how helpless and terrified her father must have been when he first lost his sight. He had adjusted far better than she had expected he would. He spent his days carving animals and birds from blocks of wood. Rosalee thought it a miracle that the talent for creating such beautiful things never presented itself until he lost his sight. In the evenings he taught sums to Odell and Ben, and dredged his memory for bits and pieces of knowledge to pass along to his children.

Rosalee suddenly became aware that Charlie was on his feet and was standing stiff-legged and alert, his nose pressed to the door and his head tilted in a listening position. It was deadly quiet. She couldn't hear anything except the rain on the tin roof and the drip of water as it splattered in the bucket. A low, rumbling growl escaped from Charlie's throat.

"What is it, boy?" Rosalee whispered. "Has one of those mangy steers wandered into my garden?"

The hair on the back of Charlie's neck stood up and he growled threateningly. His paws dug at the door sill.

"What is it, Rosalee? What's wrong?" Ben called from the top of the ladder.

"Charlie thinks something's out there."

"If Charlie thinks somethin's out there, somethin' is!" Ben scrambled down from the loft. "Soon as I get hold of the rifle, douse the lamp."

Rosalee grabbed her dress and pulled it over her head before she blew out the lamp. Without the light the room was pitch dark. She blinked several times and felt her way past the table and along the wall to the window. Charlie was digging urgently at the door, whining his frustration at not being able to get out.

"There must be an animal out there or Charlie wouldn't act like this. Maybe it's a bear."

"It's more'n likely a two-legged bear. One of them Clayhill riders wanderin' around, drunk as a skunk." Ben edged up beside his sister to peer out the window. "We been gettin' a lot of company lately," he added with a hint of disgust in his voice.

Rosalee strained her ears, but still couldn't hear anything.

"Hello the house." The voice reached them over the racket Charlie was making.

"Sshh . . . Charlie," Ben commanded. "I told you it was one of them no-goods."

"Hello the house."

"Who are you and what'a you want?" Ben called, and Rosalee wished his voice didn't sound so boyish.

"A traveler with a sick woman. I saw your light."

"A traveler with a sick woman, my hind foot!" Ben snorted. "It's one of them drunk no-goods wantin' to get in outta the rain."

Rosalee tried to make out a shadow in the darkness, but the night was too black. "Tell him to come up to the window and show himself," she whispered. Then, "Make Charlie be still, I can't hear."

"I'll bet a biscuit he's got a dog out there or Charlie wouldn't be so crazy to get out."

"What's goin' on out there, Rosalee? What's all the racket about?" Grant called from the lean-to.

"A stranger, Pa. Says he's a traveler with a sick woman."

"Ha! Likely story. Keep the door barred."

"Hello the house. I mean you no harm. I'll hand my gun

in if you open the door." The man's voice broke on a raspy cough.

"What if he really does have a sick woman, Ben? We've got to find out." Rosalee tried to see into the darkness outside the window, but to no avail. "Tell him to come up to the door. I'll light the lamp and you hold the rifle ready. But first tell him as soon as we open the door Charlie'll be all over him like a dirty shirt."

"We've got a mean dog," Ben called.

"Tie him up. My dog will kill him if he attacks."

"Make your dog stay back. Come up to the door. I've got a rifle on you. Light the lamp, Rosalee, and put that rope on Charlie."

"You know I can't hold that dog."

"Then hold the rifle and I'll hold him."

Rosalee waited for a minute so her eyes could adjust to the light, moved over and took the gun from her brother's hands.

"We're gonna open the door," Ben called. "Hand your gun in."

They heard a whine outside the door and a voice giving a command. Then a rap sounded on the door.

Charlie lunged and growled. "Be still, Charlie." Ben yanked on the rope holding the dog and slowly lifted the heavy bar from the door.

Rosalee waited in an agony of suspense. What if there was more than one man out there? They could push their way into the cabin and there would be no way she or Ben could stop them. Ben pulled the door open wide enough for the light to reach out to the man who stood there. He was holding his six-shooter by the barrel, butt forward. Ben reached out, took it, and swung the door open wider.

The man's huge, wet frame filled the doorway. He wore a buckskin shirt with the tail outside and belted about the waist. Fringed leather pants and knee-high moccasins encased his legs. His flat-crowned hat sat straight on his head and water dripped from its brim. Thick, black hair hung to his shoulders and his deep-set eyes were licorice black. A full mustache, shaped in a wide downward curve around his mouth reached almost to his jaw. High, prominent cheekbones and skin the color of copper proclaimed his Indian blood.

"I'd be obliged if you'd allow me to bring my mother in out of the rain." He waited, his gaze going from Ben to Rosalee.

Rosalee read the Indian breeding. It registered in the slightest widening of her blue-green eyes. "Your mother?"

"She's on a travois. I'm trying to get her to a doctor."

"It's twenty miles to town and there's no doctor there that I know of. Bring her in. Ben, do something about that dog." Rosalee put the rifle on the pegs. Ben backed into a corner, holding Charlie's rope in one hand and the man's six-gun in the other.

The man disappeared from the doorway and they heard him giving sharp commands; then he was back with a blanket-wrapped bundle in his arms. As he stepped into the room, the water ran in rivulets onto the dirt floor from the bundle he carried and from his own clothes.

Rosalee had shaken Odell awake, and now she moved hastily out of bed and crossed over to sit wide-eyed and scared on the bench beside the table. The man stood hesitantly until Rosalee came to him and peeled the wet blankets away from the still form in his arms. She nodded for him to lay the woman on the bunk.

"What's goin' on?" Grant came in from the lean-to. He had pulled on his britches, but his feet were bare.

"The woman is sick, Pa. It's all right. You can go back to bed."

"All right? Why'd you let them in for? She could have the cholera!"

Rosalee's eyes flew to the man's face. He shook his head and somehow she believed him.

"It isn't the cholera, Pa."

The man dwarfed her. He stood silently, seemingly unaware that the water that dripped from his clothes was forming a mud puddle around his feet. His eyes questioned her—or were they daring her to voice her surprise that the woman he was asking her to care for was an Indian? He turned his head and coughed. It came from deep in his chest.

"I'll take care of her. You'd better get out of those wet clothes or you'll be sick, too."

"Thank you, ma'am. Is it all right if I put my horses in that corral I saw out back?"

"Horses?"

"A mare and a foal. I'll tie my stallion out under that big cedar and the dog will watch him." He coughed again.

"Do you want Ben to do it?"

"No, ma'am. The dog wouldn't let him close to the horses."

"There's a lantern beside the door."

"Thank you, ma'am, but I don't need it."

He went out the door and Ben, dragging Charlie on the rope, came over to peer down at the woman on the bunk.

"She's an Indian!" he hissed.

"Sshh . . . don't tell Pa. You know how unreasonable he can get."

"But . . . Rosalee . . ."

"She's a human and she's sick!" Rosalee whispered. "Shut up about it and tie up that dog. Ben," she said over her shoulder, "build a fire. Odell, don't just sit there! Put your dress on over your nightgown."

Rosalee turned her attention back to the woman. Somehow the man had managed to keep her dry. She was so thin she scarcely made an indentation in the cornhusk mattress. Her cheeks were wrinkled, flushed and sunken. Her eyelids fluttered and her breath came rapidly. She moved her hands restlessly. Only a few strands of her once dark hair showed among the gray. She looked old, very old. Rosalee pulled off her moccasins. Her feet and legs were hot.

"She's burning up with fever. Odell, put some water in the washpan and bring me a cloth." Rosalee opened the cloth shirt the woman was wearing, but closed it when she saw it was the only garment she wore. The long, butternut dyed skirt was dry, so she wrapped it around her legs and covered her with a blanket.

She was bathing the woman's face with a damp cloth when a rap sounded on the door before it was pushed open. The man stood beside the door, his saddlebags over his arm. Rosalee glanced at him.

"If you have anything dry to put on you can change in the loft."

"How is she?"

"She's burning up with fever. How long has she been sick?"

"About a week. I brought her down from Wind River Canyon."

"A week? Has she eaten anything?"

"Not for a couple of days. I'd be obliged if—"

"Odell, get up and heat some milk," Rosalee said sharply. "And put some sugar and a biscuit in it."

"Who are ya, man?" Grant demanded. He had found his way to his chair beside the fireplace.

The stranger eyed him and Rosalee waited. Grant made no effort to turn his face toward the man and she saw the dark eyes flick from her to her father and back to Ben, who still held the six-gun.

"Name's Logan Horn. The woman's my mother." He threw

the words out like a gauntlet. His face showed no emotion at all, but his eyes bored into Rosalee's.

"Grant Spurlock, late of Independence, Missouri. Ever been there?"

"Once or twice." He tried to suppress a cough. "I'm making a mud puddle, ma'am."

"It'll dry as soon as the fire gets going. Go on up to the loft and throw down your wet clothes. If you don't have anything dry to put on, wrap yourself in a blanket."

"I've got dry clothes." He took off his hat and hung it on a peg beside the door, sat down on the bench, and pulled off his wet moccasins.

Rosalee sat on the edge of the bunk and bathed the woman's face. She was very sick and pitifully thin. Her breath came in gasps. Rosalee's heart contracted at the sight of her ravaged face. Odell brought the cup of milk and Rosalee tried to spoon some of it into the woman's dry, parched lips, but it ran down the side of her chin. Finally, Rosalee had to give up. The only other thing she could do was squeeze water from a cloth into the woman's mouth. It was a slow process.

When Logan Horn came down from the loft he was wearing duck trousers, a cloth shirt, and low-cut leather moccasins. He spread his wet clothes on a bench beside the fire and came to hunker down beside the bunk.

"She'll die," he said softly. He gazed intently at his mother's still face.

"Oh, no! Maybe . . . not," Rosalee said, but knew he spoke the truth.

"She'll die," he said again and the back of his fingers stroked the hair at her temple. "She was only waiting for me to come and I came too late."

"If we can break the fever . . ." Rosalee's voice trailed off.

"No."

"We can't just give up and let her die!"

"She wants to die. It's her time. I shouldn't have taken her from her people."

"Then why did you? The trip and the rain . . ."

"I was angry. They had cast her out because all the men in her family were dead and she had no one to bring meat to her lodge."

"I've heard that they do that. It's mean and cruel."

"It's their way of surviving. She understood." He turned his face away and coughed.

"You're sick, too. Pa's got a dab of whiskey."

She spoke to the back of his head, then continued to look at him when he turned his face once again to look down at the woman on the bed. She noted the smooth broad expanse of forehead; the black-lashed, hooded eyes beneath strongly arched brows; the straight nose, wide mouth; the thick, faintly waving hair that framed a wholly arresting face that demanded attention, but gave away nothing at all.

Logan was aware the girl was studying him. She had been kind; kinder than he had expected a white family to be after being roused in the middle of the night. Yet she made him self-conscious, and he shifted his feet and turned his body at an angle away from her.

"I'm so sorry there's nothing I can do for her." She wanted to cry for the big man and his pathetically thin mother.

He turned back as if surprised by her words. His eyes were two mirrors of misery. "You have given her a place to die. She would not have asked even that of you."

Tears sprang to Rosalee's eyes and he turned his gaze away from them. As she moved from the bunk and carried the washpan back to the shelf, she whispered to her father that the woman was dying and then urged Odell up the ladder to sleep in Ben's bed. Charlie had settled down beside the door and Ben had placed the six-gun on the mantel beside the clock. She suggested to Grant that he go back to bed, and after awhile he did. Ben sat in Grant's chair and was soon asleep.

Rosalee moved quietly. She added more wood to the cookstove and ladled water into the black iron teakettle. When it boiled, she opened the can with their precious supply of tea, put two pinches in the crockery pitcher, filled it with boiling water, and sat a wooden plate on top of it so it would steep.

Logan Horn was sitting on the edge of the bunk. He held one of his mother's thin hands in his. He was angry at himself. He had waited too long to come back for her. While he was fighting to free the slaves, his mother's people had been massacred at Sand Creek. She had fled north with her relatives to the Yellowstone. It had taken him two years to find her.

Morning Sun, his mother, was once the beautiful daughter of Running Wind, a Cheyenne chief. A white man had married her in an Indian ceremony; it had been his means to get her into his bed, to use her during his short stay with her people. When he was ready to leave, he divorced her. He "threw her away" at a tribal ceremony called the Omaha Dance. Playing the irate husband, he danced alone with a stick in his hand. He struck a mighty blow on a drum with the stick, threw it into the air, and shouted, "There goes my wife." Morning Sun had felt much shame at being discarded in such a manner.

Someday soon, Logan vowed silently, he would look into the eyes of the man who hadn't wanted him, the man who was ashamed he had slept with a squaw and gotten her with child, and he would kill him.

"Mr. Horn." Rosalee stood beside him with the mug of whiskey-laced tea in her hand.

Logan's mind jerked back to the present. There was a burning ache in his throat that had nothing to do with the raw, raspiness that had plagued him for days. It was as if he was traveling down a dark narrow path through a region of devastation. *Mister Horn*. This slip of a girl was the first person to give him that respect since he came into the Colorado Territory. Singly, few had dared to call him "dirty half-breed" or "red ass." They were braver in numbers, and he had endured their insults in stony-eyed silence, steeling himself against the animosity in the eyes turned on him.

He knew now he would not remain passive in the face of insult ever again. Unless he planted his feet and asserted his rights, he would be trampled into the ground by the "civilized" people who had massacred hundreds of helpless women, children, and old people at Sand Creek.

He took the mug from Rosalee's hand. "Thank you."

She pulled the bench up beside the bunk and sat down. Somehow she felt her presence was welcome. The man sipped the tea in silence.

"What is her name?" Rosalee whispered.

"Morning Sun. She was once the most beautiful girl in her village. My grandfather, Running Wind, said he had been offered many horses for her."

"But she chose your father?"

"Yes."

The word was softly spoken, but Rosalee felt it was bitter in his mouth. She sat silently and waited for him to finish the tea.

"I remembered her with smooth skin, laughing eyes, and dark hair that hung to her knees. She was beautiful and sparkling. I didn't recognize her when I found her. I went to the village and asked for the mother of Deer Horn, daughter of Running Wind, sister of Tall Horn, after who I was named. She had been without a lodge for months, eating the food that was thrown to the dogs. She fell to her knees weeping. I vowed she would be warm and have all she could eat for the rest of her life. I've taken care of her for only two short months. It is little enough to do for one who gave me life."

Rosalee looked up to see the sparkle of tears on his thick lashes. She looked away quickly and blinked back the moisture from her own. The woman on the bed moved restlessly, her eyelids fluttered and opened. She saw only the man who sat on the edge of the bed. He leaned forward.

"My mother . . ."

"You are still with me, my son?"

"For the rest of our days, Mother."

"It is good to be with you while I wait for the night wind to carry my spirit along the Hanging Road to the abode off *Heammawihio*, the Wise One Above." Her eyes were bright and watchful. "There is a thing I would say to you." She lifted her hand, trying to reach his face. He took it in his and carried it to his cheek. "My son," she said weakly. "My son, greatest of them all. I can hear you weeping. There are too many tears, too much hatred, too many ashes behind you."

"What do you mean?" he asked in a hushed voice.

Morning Sun's eyes were strangely bright. "The death song rises from every rock, every blade of grass and drop of water in all this vast land. Our land was once the place of warm sunlight and endless song. Now it is a land of tears. The Indian and the *Wasicun* have wounded it. Do not run away. Stay and heal it. Touch the joy of life, my son."

"I intend to stay, my mother. Is this not the place where you gave me life?"

"My son. My beloved son. I hear you. I know the path you walk is not easy. I would see you walk with a sense of beauty and a compassion for life. The *Wasicun* and I gave you life. Do not despise the one who is your father. He cannot help being what he is anymore than you can help being what you are."

"Don't ask that of me, my mother. For I have vowed that someday I will kill him."

A half smile curled her lips. "No, my son. Killing is the

refuge of cowards and my son is not a coward. Show your father that you are the better man and he will die a thousand times."

"I will think on this, my mother."

"I see your heart, my son, and seeing it has warmed my own. When the time comes you will do what is right."

A film glazed her eyes, but there was fearlessness in her face. She knew she was dying, but the knowledge of it held no terror for her. She had walked too long beside the Spirit People to fear joining them. She was confident she would live forever among her long-lost loved ones.

Logan knew his mother was slipping away from him to walk in the darkness forever without him. He saw her lips open, but no sound came from them. In the silence she went on talking soundlessly. One of her hands groped for his and fastened on his wrist. A tremor passed through her body, then her life ebbed away.

Rosalee had moved away from the bed when Morning Sun began to talk. She stood, now, with her back to the bunk, her hands on her cheeks. There are no easy deaths, she thought, and her mind flashed back to her mother's death while giving birth to her sixth child. Death was cruel, agonizing, gut-crushing. She turned back to Logan Horn. He sat on the bunk, his mother's hand in his, his eyes riveted to her face. Had the woman closed her eyes in death, or had her son closed them? Rosalee moved to stand beside him and placed her hand on his shoulder. He looked up. Her eyes were a mirror of tears.

"I wish there was something we could have done."

He nodded. "You did more than I expected a *Wasicun* to do. It was dry and warm here, and she could see my face. I thank you."

"I'll take care of her, if you like."

"I'd be obliged. I have her ceremonial dress." He tucked

his mother's hand beneath the blanket and stood up. The tin roof rumbled as the restless wind passed over it. Logan lifted his head and raised his eyes to the ceiling. "Good-bye, my mother," he whispered.

Chapter Two

Logan Horn sat at the table and drank the hot tea while Rosalee washed and dressed his mother's body. Soon after the woman had breathed her last, he had gone outside and stayed for a long while. When he returned he carried a package wrapped in an oiled slicker. It contained a beaded dress of soft leather that had once been white but now was yellowed with age. He laid it on the end of the bunk beside worn, white moccasins and a feather necklace and turned away.

By the time dawn streaked the sky the wind had carried the rain clouds away. Everything looked fresh and clean, but the ground was soggy underfoot.

Logan brought the mare from the corral and attached the travois. After commanding the dog to sit at the mare's head, he returned to the cabin for his mother's blanket-wrapped body. Ben and Rosalee followed him into the yard.

"I'd be glad to come along, Mr. Horn." Ben stood awkwardly on first one foot and then the other and spoke in hushed tones, acknowledging the presence of death.

"Thank you for the offer, but this is something I need to do alone. I'd be obliged for the use of your ax."

"You're welcome to it," Ben said, and went to get it from the woodpile where the blade was sunk in a log to protect it from rust.

Logan secured his mother's body to the travois with a rope and saddled the spotted stallion. He picked up the mare's reins and turned to the silent pair.

"I thank you for taking us in and for all you've done, ma'am." He mounted the horse and put his fingers to the brim of his hat. Rosalee went to him and thrust a cloth-wrapped package into his hand.

"A few biscuits and some meat." She met his downbearing gaze with the same air of assurance she had maintained the night before.

"Thank you."

"Are you familiar with the country, Mr. Horn?"

"Yes, ma'am. I've been through here before."

"There's a beautiful spot to the west, just beyond that line of fir trees." She lifted her arm and pointed toward the mountains. "It's on a high plain. It's peaceful and calm and I don't think anyone ever goes there but me and Ben."

"Is it on Clayhill land?"

"No. I don't think the land has been taken up. The Clayhill ranch is north and west of here."

Logan narrowed his eyes and looked toward the place she had pointed out. "I'll head for the line of firs."

"It's a two-hour ride."

"I'm in no hurry."

He brought his eyes from the hills and looked down into the girl's upturned face. From the first he had been comfortable with her. Her low, sweet voice was like the gentle music of a brook. Her eyes had come from the sky and looked into his, unclouded by suspicion, hate, or fear. Her skin was golden from the sun, and her hair was thick and heavy with small tendrils dancing around her face. The wind caught at her dress and whipped it out behind her. She was tall and thin and swayed like a reed. Rosalee was unlike any woman he had ever met; soft, pretty as a buttercup, calm, sensible, and compassionate.

Logan had no name for the feelings that flooded him as he looked into the woman's delicately drawn features. Even with tension drawing his nerves tight, he could only marvel at this girl who could take on a man's responsibilities yet remain totally a woman. She was the strength of this family. She and the boy were carrying a heavy load.

There was a curious stillness between Logan and Rosalee—a waiting, uneasy silence that deepened and pushed them farther apart. Only her sky-blue, thick-lashed eyes and the faint color that lay across her cheeks betrayed the fact that Rosalee was not completely at ease.

"I'll be back." Something like a smile crossed his face as he continued to study her thoughtfully. Then, he put his fingers to the brim of his hat and his heels to his mount and moved away. The mare followed with the foal at her side. The travois carrying the beloved body of his mother bounced gruesomely over the uneven sod. The wolf dog, sniffing the ground, moved out ahead of the stallion.

Rosalee's eyes followed him, but he didn't look back.

Logan sat in the fast-fading light, as motionless as the wild hills that surrounded him, rough, old, and hugely somber. His thoughts drifted over the solemn silence, the bold peaks and the windswept canyons. This was a land that had charmed his soul, a land that could not be ignored, a land that punished, but also rewarded vigilance. The golden air, the halcyon silence and the unravished panorama quivered with promise. This was a good land, and here he would stay.

The sun was gone. The scarlet fingers of dusk faded and the moon rose swiftly to cast a mellow light over the plain. Logan sat beneath the scaffold that held his mother's body. He felt a restless stirring and knew the unfed hunger of a lifetime would not let him go. He had to see the man who had sired him, the selfish bastard who planted his seed in a beautiful, young woman and then carelessly discarded both her and her child. No, he had not merely discarded them. He had ruined Morning Sun, divorced her in such a way that no other man would have her.

Logan stood and leaned his forehead against the pole that supported the platform. All the days and all the years came together and were the same, and all rushed toward this moment. Time stopped, then fell away and hung motionless in the great void. Even the wolf dog and the horses seemed to sense the eerie quality of the time and place and were quiet.

He mounted the stallion, whistled for the dog and the mare, and made his way steadily through the night. It came to him that he had reached a crossroads but there was never the slightest doubt which path he would take. What really mattered was that he could not turn back, nor did he want to.

At sunset Rosalee walked away from the cabin and, her hair stirring in the breeze that swept the valley, she stood alone beside the trail and looked toward the west. She never tired of the evenings. She loved to watch the soft sunlight change the color of sky and mountains. The air was cool and fresh with the smell of cedar if it was sweeping down from the mountains, or with the smell of sage if it came from the plains.

When she was young, Rosalee thought, everything seemed easy, and life was forever. She had spent a lot of time dreaming about the kind of life she wanted. She had not imagined it would be so hard, and so . . . lonely. There had always been a man in her dreams, one whose face kept changing, but who was very much in love with her and ready to die for her. She had wanted to meet him someday. Cowboys and drifters had stopped by the cabin now and then when they heard about an unmarried woman living there, but she had not the slightest interest in any of them. They were hunting for a woman, any woman.

It wasn't, she thought, that she was looking for a man who owned a wide stretch of land, with cows and a ranch house with more than two rooms. It was more than that. She was a woman with a woman's love to give, and she needed someone to reach out for it. There was an emptiness within her, a yearning that had to be fulfilled.

When the light was gone she went back to the house. She had worked hard today as she worked everyday. Ben had his chores to do and was away from the cabin most of the day. It was Odell she worried about. She was at a formative stage and needed stimulus for her mind. She was quick, imaginative, outgoing, and she more than any of them needed to be with people.

Grant was still angry because Logan Horn was a breed and the woman he brought into their home was an Indian. He had sulked all day, refusing to work with Odell on her numbers and showed not the slightest interest in the smooth piece of pine Ben brought down from the bluff behind the cabin.

Rosalee loved her father dearly, but simply couldn't understand his prejudices. In Missouri he had despised the Yankees and the hill people. She had no doubt that had they gone farther south he would have despised the Mexicans, and farther west it would be the Chinese.

"Papa went to bed." Odell was drawing a design on the dirt floor. "He's still mad."

"Maybe he'll be over it by morning."

"Why does he hate Indians?"

"I don't think he hates them. He's heard about the bad things some of them have done and he forgets that there are bad people among all the races."

"That Colonel Chivington was bad. He made the soldiers kill all those babies at Sand Creek."

"Yes, he was bad. I'll never understand why he thought children, women, and old people were a threat. The government should be deeply ashamed for what he did. Who can blame the Indians for seeking revenge? Thank God things have settled down."

"Mr. Horn didn't look like a savage. And he didn't talk like one. I ain't never seen a Indian with a mustache before."

"He was only part Indian. He said his mother was once the most beautiful woman in her village."

"Pa said that didn't make no never mind. He said breeds was the worst kind. I wish I could've talked to Mr. Horn."

"It wasn't the time for idle conversation. He was grieved over his mother. If he comes back again, you can talk to him."

"Pa won't like it."

"We'll have to handle that when the time comes. Now you get to bed. Tomorrow is wash day."

"Rosalee . . . how long before we can go to town?" There was a wistful longing in the child's voice.

Rosalee went to her, sat down in the chair and pulled her onto her lap. "In about a month. We may have word from the store in Denver by then."

"Do ya think the store man'll want Pa's birds?"

"I'm hoping he will. We sold two of them in Junction City and the stage driver promised to take a couple of them to a store in Denver."

"Are we awful poor, Rosalee?"

"We've got more than some people, honey. We've got a

place to live and we've got each other. In some ways we're rich."

"Huh? You're funnin' me."

"No, I'm not. I've got you. I wouldn't trade you for all the money in the world."

Odell gave her a gap-toothed grin. "Then you ain't got no more sense than a pissant."

"Ladies don't say pissant."

"Wasn't nobody to hear but you. I say it sometimes to the friend in my head. I named her Mary after that pretty woman we met in Junction City."

Rosalee swallowed several times and hugged her little sister to her before she spoke. "I'm sure Mrs. Gregg would like that."

"Will I be pretty when I'm growed?"

"You're pretty now. When you're older you'll be so pretty we'll have to build a fence around you, is what we'll do," Rosalee teased. "Now, you get to bed. Ben's already snoring up a storm."

"Will ya tell me the story about the princess?"

"Not tonight, lovey. I'm going to sit out on the step and churn. We've got enough cream skimmed off the milk to make us a nice bit of butter. You'll have some in the morning with flapjacks."

The breeze coming down from the mountains was cool. Rosalee sat on the steps, a shawl around her shoulders, and listened to the night sounds. A squirrel scrambled about in the branches that extended out over the cabin and a dry twig fell to the tin roof. Far away a coyote called to his mate, and her answer echoed down the hills. She heard the faint stirrings among the horses in the corral, and sometimes one would stamp or blow dust from his nostrils. These familiar sounds accompanied the slush, slush, slush as she rhythmically moved the wooden dasher up and down through the milk in the churn.

These were the lonely hours for Rosalee, when at last she could let down from the work of the day. A time when she could feel the night wind in her hair and could look at the bright, silent stars. Her thoughts, as they had done throughout the day, fixed firmly on Logan Horn. She refused to admit she was disappointed he hadn't come back today. She half expected to see the ax at the woodpile when they woke in the morning. Through the darkness, his coppery face emerged and hung suspended before her eyes.

The last look he'd given her had held a hunger that, even as naive as she was, she could not fail to recognize. It was a look so very unlike the stern, expressionless face he had presented from the moment he had arrived at the cabin. At that moment she had felt a tingling run down her spine, and a fluttering sensation in her groin. She was sure he was aware of the turbulent feeling his look had inspired. She hoped to God he had turned away before the flood of scarlet washed up her neck to flood her face. Just thinking about it caused the skin on her face to warm.

To still her thoughts she began to sing to herself, as she did sometimes, her voice just a breath of a whisper.

"Lord Lovel he stood at his castle gate,
A combing his milk-white steed;
When along came Lady Nancy Bell,
A wishing her lover good speed, speed, speed,
A wishing her lover good speed."

It was comforting to Rosalee to sing the English ballads her mother had taught her. To her they were old, familiar friends.

"Charlie is my darling, my darling, my darling,
Charlie, he's my darling, the young chevalier."

The dog, lying with his jowls on her foot, lifted his head when he heard his name. It had been Ben's idea to name the mongrel puppy after the young chevalier in the song. She always took Charlie with her when she was outside the cabin at night. He heard every strange sound and several times he had alerted her to a rider coming toward the cabin and allowed her time to get inside. She reached down, patted his head, and continued her song.

She wasn't sure when she became aware that Charlie was sitting very still, looking off toward the west. When she did, she gripped a handful of the long hair around his neck and ceased the movement of the dasher so she could listen. She couldn't hear anything, but she could tell by the way Charlie tilted his head that he did.

"What is it, boy? Is someone coming?" Charlie looked at her and began to wag his tail. "Is it *him*?" The dog's tail wagged harder and he strained against the hold she had on him. "Are you wanting to play with that strange dog? He may not be friendly this time." She had to turn him loose if she was going to pick up the churn and go inside the cabin.

The instant he was free of her grip, Charlie was off and running. Rosalee stood on the step and watched him. He was clearly visible in the moonlight; then he disappeared in the shadows, and she heard his bark of welcome. It was *him*! She had not really thought it was anyone else. Charlie was delighted that his friend had come back. What should she do? Should she go inside and let him leave the ax and be on his way, never to see him again? If she stayed would he think she had been waiting for him? For a long moment she continued to stand there, her eyes fastened to the break in the trees, an alien feeling in the pit of her stomach.

He came riding out of the shadows and into the moonlight. The wolf dog and Charlie frolicked around him. When they got too close to the foal, the mare whinnied and spun around in position to lash out with her hind legs. The dogs ignored her, ran around each other, reared up, and nipped at each other's throats. Rosalee thought the wolf dog was wonderfully patient with Charlie, who was little more than a pup and full of youthful enthusiasm.

Rosalee scarcely had time to note that the travois was no longer attached to the mare and that she had a pack on her back before Logan Horn was riding into the yard. Her hand sought the dasher and she began to move it up and down, unconsciously seeking to provide a reason for being on the step. Her eyes clung to his face. He was wearing the buckskins, and the flat, round-brimmed hat was pushed back to his hairline.

"Evening, ma'am. I've brought back the ax." He pulled the stallion to a halt not ten feet from her, dismounted, and lifted the ax from a loop on the saddle. "I'm much obliged for the use of it. It would pleasure me to cut some wood in payment."

"That won't be necessary," Rosalee said sharply. "Folks need to help one another when they can without expecting something for it."

"I'm not used to asking for help, ma'am. It galled me to have to knock on your door." His voice was cold and flat.

"Why? I'd not have hesitated to ask you for help if my Pa had been sick."

"You're not a breed, ma'am."

"How do you know that? I'm English and German. That makes me a breed. The Indians, the Mexicans, and the Chinese are the only people in the West that aren't a mixture of some nationality or the other. You're obviously very sensitive about your blood, Mr. Horn. I'd think you'd—" She cut off her outburst as though a hand had been clamped over her mouth, and flushed to the roots of her hair. She stood there staring at him, wondering why in the world she had let her tongue run away with her.

"You'd think I'd . . . what?" He leaned on the ax and looked at her. The stallion had begun to snort and toss his head. Horn turned, gathered the reins in his hand, and walked toward the woodpile.

She heard him sink the blade in the log and fully expected him to mount up and ride away, but he tied the horse to a stump and came back. She was working the dasher briskly up and down, although she was sure the cream had turned to butter.

"I haven't had buttermilk in years."

She had expected him to say anything but that. The tension went out of her and she breathed deeply. "Would you like some?"

"I have a cup in my saddlebag." His tone was lighter, friendlier.

"Have you had supper?"

"I had the biscuits and meat you gave me at noon. That'll hold me till morning."

"You can have more of the same. This time you can have butter on the biscuits."

Rosalee didn't wait for him to answer. She slipped quietly into the cabin and felt her way to the workbench and quickly stacked a plate with biscuits and meat. Her fingers groped for a spoon and she went back outside. He had gone back to his horse, slipped off the bridle, and fashioned a rope halter so the animal could crop the grass beneath the pine tree where he had tied him the night before. She went to him, thankful they would be away from the cabin in case her father should awaken.

"Give me your cup and I'll get the buttermilk."

She went back across the yard to the churn, dipped into it and brought out milk and butter. When she turned he was standing beside the stump, holding the plate and watching her. Some of the milk sloshed onto the ground and she laughed. The sound floated to him lightly on the breeze. He thought it was as musical as the bells in the church in Saint Louis.

"If you'd come sooner you could have had supper with us."

"I don't think your pa would have liked that."

She flinched as if his words were razor sharp. After a hesitation she sat the cup on the stump and turned her face away. "How do you know? He didn't say anything."

"He didn't have to."

"It's because he's blind and he's afraid for us."

"Don't put a different name to it. I knew this morning, when the little girl whispered to him that my mother was an Indian, that he was angry because you had taken us in. I expect you got a dressing down for taking in an Indian *buck* and a sick *squaw*."

"I'm sorry you were made to feel unwelcome."

"It's a thing I've gotten used to. There are men who hate other men and wish them dead simply because of the color of their skin. Your pa's one of them. He was brought up to believe that if you're not white you're just so much dirt to be trodden underfoot."

"Please don't talk like that," Rosalee said in a stricken voice. "My mother tried to explain it to me once. She said some people have got to feel superior to someone because they have this feeling of worthlessness inside them. My pa's had that feeling all his life because he never thought he'd accomplished much. I don't understand it, and I suspect he doesn't understand it either. It's what he was taught. I'm trying to teach Ben and Odell that we are all God's creatures and there are the good and the bad among all of us." She gave her head a little shake. "Do you believe me?"

"I believe you. Unfortunately, you're among the minority." He took the cup from the stump and nodded his head. She sat down and he squatted on his heels beside her and stuffed a biscuit in his mouth. "You make a mighty good biscuit."

"I should. I've made a million of them. They'd be better if you smeared them with butter." She handed him the spoon. "Dip it into the milk and you'll find some floating around. Tomorrow I'll dip out the butter and work the milk out of it."

His slow smile altered his face and gave warmth to his stern features. "Fresh butter? I've not had fresh butter for a long time."

Rosalee laughed softly, suddenly strangely at ease with him. "Sometimes we don't miss a thing until we get it again."

He gave a thoughtful nod, his gaze wandering over her slim body. They sat in silence while he emptied the plate. He turned his head to look at his animals, gave a low whistle, and the wolf dog came to him.

"Watch the girls, Brutus." The dog trotted away to hunker down not far from the mare and the foal. He ignored Charlie, who still had play on his mind.

"Is that his name? Why did you name your dog after a murderer?"

Logan chuckled in surprise at the question. The sound was so unexpected that Rosalee almost forgot what she asked.

"Why not? Brutus lived and Caesar didn't. My Brutus is a survivor. I got him from a trapper who mated a timber wolf and a mastiff bitch. His wolf blood is predominant. He can almost follow the scent of a bird in flight. He's loyal and smart and doesn't seem to require the friendship of any living creature except me and the horses. What more can I ask?"

Rosalee's thoughts were in total confusion. Logan Horn

was an educated man. There was more to him, much more, than any man she had ever met. For the space of a dozen heartbeats she sat there regarding him in thoughtful silence.

"You're a very strange man, Mr. Horn," she whispered wonderingly. The pulse at the base of her throat beat frantically. She had the feeling that this was a very important moment in her life.

"You wouldn't think so if I was all white," he said quietly. "I think of myself as a man, with needs just like any other man."

"I would still think you're different," she insisted.

"I could say the same for you. I've not met many women in the West that knew Brutus killed Caesar. And none in an isolated place such as this."

"My mother was a schoolteacher before she married my papa. How long have you been away from your mother's people, Mr. Horn?" She held her breath during the silence that followed. Had she been too bold? Would he tell her to mind her own business?

"A long time. I was six years old when my uncle came back to the village to get his Indian wife and daughter. He persuaded my mother and my grandfather to let me go with them. I would be educated and sent back to help my people."

"And were you?"

"I was educated to the point that I almost forgot who I was. Then the war came along. I served for four years. During that time, facing death everyday, I found myself."

She caught the faint sound of an indrawn breath. "You haven't talked about yourself for a long time, have you?" she asked in a thoughtful murmur. "Did you miss your mother?"

"At first I had Dancing Flower, my uncle's wife. He named her Louise and insisted that I call her that, but I thought of her as Dancing Flower. She died, then her daughter died, and there was only me and my uncle."

"How old were you then?"

"I was eight."

"Poor little boy. Did you cry?"

"The white part of me cried, the Indian part didn't."

In spite of knowing the danger of probing farther, Rosalee was compelled to say: "Your uncle must have loved you."

"I guess he did in his own way. I went to good schools . . . for a while. Then I was taken out and tutored privately. You see, the people who send their children to exclusive academies don't want them sitting in the classroom with an Indian. At first I thought there was something wrong with *me*. Later I asked my uncle about it."

"Did he tell you?"

"No. It was then I realized that he never really looked at me." A deep undertone in his voice revealed the pain from long ago. "My uncle had a deep sense of responsibility for me, but that was all. He and my father came West with John Fremont in '42 and were made welcome in my mother's village. They spent the winter and each took an Indian wife. When it was time to move on my father divorced my mother, but my uncle promised to return and he did. He tried to make up for my father's callous attitude toward my mother and me by seeing to my education and making me his heir when he died."

"Did you ever see your father again?"

"No. He and my uncle had a falling out. Both were wealthy Englishmen. My father stayed in the West. My uncle lived out his life in Saint Louis."

"Is Horn your father's name?"

"It's my name. I was born in a Cheyenne village and named Deer Horn by my grandfather. My uncle named me Logan after we went to Saint Louis. He didn't want to enroll me in school with a name like Deer Horn."

Rosalee became self-conscious about the questions she was

asking. Looking into his eyes, she voiced the thought tha.
came to her. "I've been rude. I'm sorry I've asked so many
questions."

"I wouldn't have answered them if I hadn't wanted to,
he said in a direct way. "You're an easy person to talk to
Miss Spurlock."

Rosalee was mildly surprised by his statement. Another
question bubbled on her lips, but she held it back. For a long
minute they looked at each other, half smiling.

"My name is Rosalee."

"It's a musical name."

There was a long silence during which he never ceased to
watch her. Finally, she voiced the question she had been
holding back.

"Was your mother heartbroken when your father left her?"

"Yes. She had great pride and was ashamed. My mother
was part Spanish. Running Wind, her father, took a Spanish
captive for a wife. Her name was Carlotta de Vega, but he
called her White Cloud. She came to love him very much
and bore him two sons and a daughter. When she died my
grandfather transferred all his love to my mother. He said she
was as beautiful as my grandmother and had all her endearing
qualities."

"Then you have as much Spanish blood as Indian."

"I'm not ashamed of my Indian blood," he said curtly.

"I'm sorry. I didn't mean..." Her voice trailed off.

"That it made me seem a little less Indian in your eyes?"

"No! I meant that it explained...the way you look." She
sat in an agony of embarrassment and suspense, expecting
him to mount up and ride out.

In the tense silence, Logan's voice sounded unnaturally
loud. "How come the land to the west isn't filed on?"

Relieved, Rosalee thought a moment before she answered
"The Clayhill ranch is to the north. Mr. Clayhill has used

that range for a long time. There's been people on it, but they never stay."

"How come you're here? Hasn't he tried to run you off?"

"We only have a thousand acres. He has sixty thousand. I don't know why he leaves us alone when he has run others off the land. His drovers harass the small landholders." Rosalee tried to keep the antagonism she felt for all things Clayhill out of her voice.

"Have you met him?"

"When we first came here he came by and talked to my pa. He had about twenty riders with him. He's not been back since. His drovers come by now and then and Ben runs into a Clayhill hand every once in awhile. I think they've had orders to leave us alone. The Haywards, the Smithfields, and the Cranstons came about a year after we did. They're from Kentucky and are homesteading in the hills to the east. The Parnells have a place out there somewhere. I met Mrs. Parnell in town once. And you always have to have a couple of rotten apples in the barrel. The Cranes and the Barkers are shiftless and haven't even tried to clear their land."

"Will your pa object if I leave the mare and the foal here for a few days?"

"He might, but he'll get over it. Ben and I will look out for them."

"Aren't you going to ask where I'm going?"

She looked at him quickly and saw that he was smiling. "I suspect," she mused, returning his smile, "that you're referring to all the questions I've asked. You've asked a few yourself." When he continued to smile, she said, "I'll not disappoint you. Where are you going?"

His laugh was deep and soft and he gazed at her so long a swift new wave of color filled her cheeks. She wondered if he could see it in the moonlight and if he could hear her heart pounding. She wanted to press her hand to it to stop its mad gallop.

"I'm going to town and buy that land."

Rosalee took a slow breath while the import of his words sank in. Finally she said, "You're going to buy *that* land?"

"That's what I said. I knew when I rode over that land today and found a place to build my mother's scaffold that here's where I'd stop and here's where I'll stay. Will you mind having a breed for a neighbor?"

"That's not even worth an answer and you know it!" she said with cold formality. "Besides, it isn't us you have to watch out for. It's Mr. Clayhill. He won't like it at all."

"There's nothing he can do about it if I buy the land."

"There's plenty he can do about it. He's got more than twenty men working for him and most of them will do whatever he tells them to do regardless of what it is."

"Where're your boundaries?"

"Our land borders the Clayhill ranch on the west. It runs east to the canyon and I don't know how far south."

"No matter. I can tell by looking at the map at the Federal Land Office."

"You're really going to do it?"

"If the land hasn't already been bought."

"But . . . you don't know Mr. Clayhill. He's always used that range and he's got some tough, mean men. They'll not let you stay."

"Does that bother you?"

"Of course it does. I don't want you . . . killed!"

"He'd go that far, huh?"

"He's used that range for twenty years. He'll not want to give it up. Logan . . . ah, Mr. Horn, you'll have more trouble than one man can handle." Rosalee got to her feet. He picked up the plate and the spoon and stood towering over her.

"Maybe," he said solemnly. "But it's something I've got

to do." He put the plate in her hands. "Thank you for the supper and for the information. I'll put the mare and the foal in the corral. Will it be all right if I leave my pack in the cow shed?"

"Of course." She turned and looked up at him. She was a tall girl, but he towered above her. "Mr. Horn . . . as long as you're going to town, will you buy a bag of peppermint sticks for my sister? I'll give you the money before you leave in the morning."

"It would be my pleasure to buy the treat." He stood looking at her. He wanted to tell her that he had thought about her every minute during the ride back from the high country, that she was nothing like any woman he had ever known; she was warm and gentle and lovely. He couldn't say any of those things to her yet. He would have to move cautiously. "Good night, ma'am. Thanks again for the supper."

Chapter
Three

Logan woke before dawn, saddled up, tied up his bedroll, and rode out. Brutus sprang past to take his customary position out in front of the horse. The stallion was impatient and Logan let him run until his sides heaved, something he wasn't able to do when the mare and the foal were with them.

He rode northeast, following the trace, anxious to reach the town twenty miles away. He had a lot to think about. He hadn't realized how much he had missed congenial company. He tried to put the woman out of his mind and fasten his thoughts on what lay ahead, but they repeatedly darted out of control and returned to her. He muttered an oath in self-contempt. "You've been too long without a woman, you stupid sonofabitch. Just because she had more human qualities than you've seen in a *Wasicun* for a long while doesn't mean she'd cotton to you!"

He reached Junction City a couple of hours after sunup. He pulled his mount to a halt on the edge of town, checked the Colt strapped to his waist, then walked the handsome, spotted stallion down the main street. He steeled himself to accept the jibes and the stony-eyed hostility he would encounter as he moved down the street amid horses and wagons. A cur came out to challenge Brutus, who trotted close beside the stud. Brutus's bared fangs and the low growl were enough to send the cur back between the buildings. Logan had been here months back and remembered the dusty street, the unpainted wooden buildings, and the loafers who sat in front of the saloon.

He rode up to the rail in front of the town's only eatery, dismounted, and tied the reins. Brutus stood close beside him on stiff legs. The hair stood straight on the back of his neck. The dog didn't like being in town.

"Stay with the man, Brutus." The dog looked up at him, then obediently moved over beside the horse's front feet and hunkered down.

Logan mounted the steps and crossed the board porch. He had just reached the door when it swung open and three tall, dusty, young drovers came out. They were laughing and joshing each other, but the minute they saw Logan they turned their attention to him.

"Well, now. What've we got here? Do you fellers see what I see?"

It was the old familiar scene, one that never changed; but today marked a new phase in Logan's life, and he felt not the slightest tinge of humiliation. Tempering the anger that swept over him was a feeling that was almost pity for the poor bastards who, in their misguided judgment, thought it elevated them a little higher to step on his pride.

"I think what we've got here is a red ass. Howdy, red ass! Don't you know you can't eat in here with white folks? We ain't got no stomach for stink." He put his hand to his mouth, patted his lips, and let go with a war chant. "Hey . . . a . . . a . . . heya!"

Logan's face never changed expression as he walked steadily toward the door. When he came alongside them, his hand flashed out and fastened on the cowboy's shirt, then he hauled him off his feet and slammed him up against the wall.

"You need to learn some manners. You put that filthy name to me again and you'll wish to God you'd never set eyes on me. I'll tear the tongue right out of your stupid head!" The rage that burned in him boiled out. He slammed the young cowboy against the wall several more times before he released him to sag to the porch. "Now, get out of my way, buzzard bait! Go crawl back into the hole you came out of!"

He glared at the two other men and then deliberately put the point of his shoulder against one of them and spun him halfway around as he strode into the eatery.

Logan passed between the tables only half filled with diners and took his seat at the far end facing the door. The people in the room couldn't help hearing the commotion on the porch and they stared at him in hostile silence. Logan placed his hat on the chair beside him and ran his hands over his face and hair, then let them rest in his lap while he breathed deeply to calm himself. There were times when he was shaken by his rage. He seldom allowed his control to slip, but when it did, it frightened him. He knew that if either or both of the other men had made a move, he would have killed them. The realization that he was capable of a spur of the moment killing, after being so sickened by it during the war, filled him with dismay. He tried not to think about what had happened on the porch and concentrate on getting his stomach settled to receive the food—if he was served any.

"What'll ye have, mister?" A heavyset woman, her dark hair parted in the middle and pulled to a tight bun on the back of her head, called from the back of the room.

Logan turned. Her face was flushed from the heat of the

stove and she fanned it with the tail of the apron wrapped about her waist.

"Whatever you have ready, ma'am."

"Hungry, air ya?"

"My stomach was slapping my backbone all the way to town."

"Ha, ha, ha..." The fat woman laughed and her belly bounced in rhythm. "I'll fix ya up a bait of steak and eggs."

"You gonna cook fer a Injun, Mable?"

The surly voice cracked over Logan like ice. He swiveled to see who was speaking. The man wore dirty range clothes and had a week's growth of whiskers on his face. His pale, watery blue eyes were filled with hostility. Logan stared at him. He almost felt sick to his stomach. Would he have to kill him? The thought had just popped in his mind when the woman's loud, angry voice filled the room.

"Yore gawddamned right, I'm gonna cook for him! I ain't put up no signs that says 'cause yore an Injun, or a drifter, or a shit-eating polecat, like ya are, Shorty Banes, that ya can't eat here. His money's good as yores, his manners is better. If'n you can't hold yore tongue, ya can haul yore ass outta here!"

"Hit don't seem right," the man protested angrily. "Hit's not decent to be a eatin' alongside a redskin."

"What'a you know 'bout what's decent? If'n ya was atryin' to be *decent*, you'd'a took a bath afore ya et! The stink of sweat 'n whiskey ya carry 'round's enuff to turn my stomach. This here's my place 'n hit seems right to me to feed 'im. I can do as I want to. If'n yore gonna keep on arunnin' off at the mouth, Shorty Banes, ya'll get the backside of a skillet. I ain't takin' no orders from you or nobody on how to run my own place! Ya can shut yore mouth or git, 'n I ain't arepeatin' myself!"

The man grumbled, turned his back, and hunkered over

his meal. Logan pressed his lips together to suppress a smile. The world suddenly seemed brighter.

By the time Logan finished his second cup of coffee, the room was cleared. The woman, Mable, came out of the kitchen and stared at him with bright, blue eyes.

"Ya done et all that? Hit was the biggest slab a meat I had 'n hit's gonna cost ya two bits."

"It was worth every penny of it. Coffee's the best I've had since Saint Louis."

"I don't keep the grounds aboilin' more'n a week. If'n ya do, it'll be so bitter ya might as well drink boiled acorns." She snorted in disgust. "Ya goin' to be stayin' 'round here?"

"I'm thinking of it."

"Keep a sharp lookout for the Clayhill men. That Shorty Banes is one of 'em. There ain't no law here. It's ever' man fer hisself."

"I realize that. Does Clayhill own the town?"

"He'd like to think he does. He ain't got no say about my place or the mercantile, but runs 'bout ever'thin' else."

"I guess that includes the Land Office," Logan said dryly.

"Shore as hell does. A few people slipped in a year or so back 'n got set up there in the hills. Ain't been nobody since. He strong-arms that Land man. Adam Clayhill means to hang onto what he's got 'n he'll take what he ain't got if'n he takes a notion."

"What about his family?"

"He went back East 'bout ten or twelve year ago 'n come back aparadin' his new family through town jest like they was somethin' to see. The girl ain't nothin' but a snot. She comes to town actin' like she owns the place. They take the stage to Denver, 'n from what I hear they lord it over folks down there, too. The boy ain't too bad. Folks kinda liked him, but he's gone off some'eres and ain't been 'round fer quite a spell."

Logan sat quietly and listened. There was more, much more, he'd like to know about Adam Clayhill, but he couldn't bring himself to ask.

"Don't guess he had no kids a his own," Mable was saying. "Leastways, I ain't ne'er heard a none. He sets a store by that gal. The way she carries on she needs her bottom blistered, is what she needs."

Logan put his money on the table. "Are you sure that's enough? I must have eaten six eggs."

"Hit's plenty. Come again. I like to see a man what puts away his vittles."

"Thank you, I will. Where's the Land Office?"

"At the end of the block. Next to the general mercantile."

"Thanks. I need to go there, too."

He paused on the porch and stood staring off down the street. For the first time he wondered if he was acting wisely or like a damned fool. What he was going to do might start a series of events that could lead to a lot of killing. He felt the weight of the money in the belt around his waist, shrugged his shoulders, and stepped off the porch and into the dusty street. He had come too far to back down now.

When Logan pushed open the door to the Federal Land Office, a bald, round-shouldered man who sat at a desk against the wall looked at him for an instant and then turned back to the papers on the desk.

"What'a you want?" he growled.

Logan crossed to the counter and placed his palms on the dusty surface. "I want to see the land map." His voice was smooth against the unfriendly silence.

The man gave no sign of having heard. He shuffled papers, dipped his pen into the inkwell, and wrote on a paper. Logan's palm slapped against the counter top. The man jumped as if stung and replaced the pen with exaggerated patience.

"I said I want to see the land map and I want to see it *now*!" Logan's voice was flat, angry.

The man turned and faced him. Red with fury, he stared while he waged a silent battle with himself. His wavering eyes took in the smoldering look of anger in the eyes of the man who was plainly a breed. He noted the broad shoulders, the hard, lean length of him and his stance. The Land Officer wasn't brave enough to stand up to this man. Self-preservation won over pride. He got slowly to his feet when Logan shifted his.

"This here's a government office, and I'm a government official. I'll thank you to show some respect," he said with a show of bravado.

"Respect! Goddamn you!" Logan snarled. "I wanted to see the land map. That's what you're here for, you . . . bastard! Get it or I'll put a hole in your damned head." He stepped close to him, towered over him. The man reached behind him, brought out a long cylinder, and held it between them. Logan snatched it from his hand, unrolled it, and took it to the counter. When the man started to walk past him to the door, Logan's arm shot out and stopped him. "You're not going anywhere. Take hold of the end of this map and weight it down so I can look at it."

"I . . . need to go out back."

"I don't care if you piss in your pants. You're staying here until I finish my business." Logan's eyes quickly scanned the map. He was familiar with the territory, familiar with maps. As a captain in the Illinois Regulars he'd scanned many maps and made instant decisions. He noted the location of the Spurlock ranch and the land of the nesters to the east. He tapped the map with a double-jointed forefinger that turned toward his thumb. "How many acres in this section, starting here?" He placed his finger at the beginning of Clayhill property and traced it south to the river. He looked up to see the man's eyes riveted on his crooked finger. "Look at the map, goddamn you! How many acres in this marked off section?"

"That's been spoken for." The man cast a despairing glance toward the door.

"It's government land. It isn't marked sold on the map. If you don't have the deed I'll catch the next stage to Denver and you'll be without a job." He stared down at the man, his face closed like a trap.

"I . . . got the deed."

"Get out the papers. I want to see the legal description."

"I—"

Logan grabbed the front of his shirt. The man stared up into a face rigid with anger and his tenuous resolve broke.

"I'll . . . get it."

Logan let go of his shirt. The man made a move toward the door and then, thinking better of it, went to the desk and drew out the papers.

"How many acres?" Logan hovered over him.

"Thirty thousand."

"Thirty thousand at twenty-five cents an acre. I'll count out the money while you fill out the papers."

"Mr. Clayhill ain't goin' to like it."

"You'd better stop worrying about *Mr. Clayhill* and start worrying about *Mr. Horn*. I'm here and he isn't!" Logan shoved the trembling man down in the chair. "Make the deed out to Logan Horn."

When he had finished counting out the money, Logan shoved it across the counter. He then strapped his considerably lighter money belt around his naked waist, pulled his tunic down over it, and buckled on the heavy gunbelt. He snatched the papers from the clerk's hand, and after carefully scrutinizing them to see if they were in order, he folded them, tucked them inside his shirt, and went out the door.

A wagon was drawn up beside the porch of the general

mercantile. Logan glanced at the supplies loaded in the wagon bed. It occurred to him that he should get his wagon and supplies now in order to avoid coming to town later.

He paused in the doorway of the store to allow his eyes to adjust from the bright sunlight to the darkened interior. It was filled to capacity with goods. Barrels of flour, sugar, salt pork, salted fish, and cornmeal crowded the aisles; jugs, tools, rope, and harnesses hung from the rafters. When his eyes became accustomed to the light, he saw a woman standing beside a table of bright yard goods. She wore a blue dress and a stiff-brimmed sunbonnet. Logan put his fingers to the brim of his hat and the woman nodded in response.

"Howdy." The clerk was a big, red-faced man with thin gray hair. He spoke politely to Logan, then looked past him to the woman. "You decided on anything, Mrs. Parnell?"

"Not yet. You go ahead and wait on your other customer, Mr. McCloud. I'm waiting for Cooper."

"Well, now. What can I do for you?" The man looked him straight in the eye and Logan almost sighed with relief. He'd dreaded dealing with another belligerent person.

"I need a wagon and team to haul supplies before I can think about buying them."

"You come to the right place. I own the livery and I've got several wagons out back. Step out and see if any of them suits you. Don't have any mules, but I've got a good team of bays."

"I don't think I'd take a mule if you gave him to me. I developed a powerful hate for the stubborn creatures while I was in the army."

"Soldier, was ya? What side was ya on?"

"Illinois Regulars."

"You don't say? I come out here from Springfield, myself. If you see anything you want out back, walk on over to the livery and take a look at that bay team. They're sound. Not more'n eight years old." The man gave him a teasing grin and a wink. Logan smiled his understanding of the joke. In Illinois you never admitted to a horse being over eight when you sold him.

When Logan returned, he asked the price of the team and the wagon. The price the man quoted was reasonable, and Logan nodded in agreement. While the man found his helper to hitch the team to the wagon and bring it out front, Logan made out a list of supplies he would need.

The woman moved up to the counter with a bolt of goods in her hand, and Logan politely moved aside. She was tall, with soft, beautiful blue eyes and wisps of light hair that framed her face beneath the bonnet. Her face had age lines at the corners of her eyes and on each side of her mouth. She was not a young woman, but her skin was smooth and soft and her smile pleasant.

"You go ahead and make out your list. I'll just put this down on the counter. I have plenty of time. I'm waiting for my son."

"I can't seem to think, right offhand, what all I'm going to need," Logan said, and looked around the store. He had the peppermint sticks at the head of the list. He looked up to see the woman staring at his crooked finger. He flexed it and frowned. This was the second time today someone had looked long and hard at his finger.

The store man returned and Logan gave him the list.

"I'll make out a bill of sale for the wagon, harness, and team. You might need it."

"I'd be obliged. I need to send off a letter. Do I leave it at the stage office?"

"Leave it with me. I'll see that it gets on the stage to Denver."

"Thanks. Do you sell paper and envelopes?"

"Not to someone I'm planning on getting as much money out of as I am you. Here . . ." He reached under the counter for a tablet and an envelope. Logan grinned, moved down to the end of the counter, and began to write:

Mr. James Randolph
Randolph House
Denver, Colorado Territory

I'd be obliged if you would wire Springfield and tell Wagner, Spillman, Landers, Hinkle, Henderson, and Tigeman that jobs are waiting for them. They're to come to Junction City and ask directions to the Spurlock ranch. The Spurlocks will tell them where to find me.

I'm in the market for two thousand head of cattle if the price is right. You can write in care of the general store here in Junction City.

Logan Horn

He sealed the envelope, addressed it, and handed it to the storekeeper. "Add the cost to my bill."

"Don't worry about that. I'll have my hand deep in your pocket by the time I fill the list and add on the team and wagon." He selected a shovel from the group that stood against the wall and picked up a couple of ax heads. "Mind telling me where you're fixing to settle?"

"I don't mind. I bought some land out beyond the Spurlocks."

"Out beyond the Spurlocks? Would that be the range Clayhill grazes?"

"I've heard it mentioned that he does. My cows will be on it now."

"Wheeee . . . I'm thinkin' there's goin' to be hair in the butter when Clayhill finds out."

"I wrote to a friend about finding me some cattle. I'd appreciate it if you'd hold my mail here for me."

"I do it all the time. I hold all Mrs. Parnell and Cooper's mail. How are you amakin' out, Mrs. Parnell? Cooper still aplannin' on getting him a fancy stallion and goin' in the horse business?"

"He's afiguring on it. It may not be for a year or two. We've still got a lot to do out at our place."

"I would make you acquainted with your almost neighbor if I knew his name. My name's McCloud."

Logan held out his hand. "Logan Horn." The man grasped it firmly.

"This here's Mrs. Parnell. She and her boy have a spread back up in the hills beyond where the Kentucky people settled."

Logan tipped his hat. "It's nice to make your acquaintance, ma'am."

"The same here, Mr. Horn."

"Here's your team and wagon." Mr. McCloud went to the door and looked out. "Pull 'er up here, Virgil," he called. "He's goin' to load up."

"I'm going to add a few more things to the pile before you add it up. Mrs. Parnell, I'd be obliged if you'd pick out a piece of dress goods for a little girl about this high." He held his hand to his waist. "Her hair is light and her eyes . . . I'm afraid I didn't notice."

"It sounds like Odell Spurlock. I've met her and her sister."

"That's her name. Her folks were mighty kind to me a few days back."

"I know just the piece." Mrs. Parnell pulled a bolt of bright yellow from beneath the other material. "This would be pretty on Odell, especially if you got a length of yellow ribbon for her hair."

"Thank you, ma'am. Cut off whatever Mrs. Parnell thinks

will be needed, Mr. McCloud, and add the ribbon and a tablet and pencil to the bill. I'll load the things you've listed."

On his second trip to the wagon he glanced down the street and saw the Land Office man standing in the sunlight talking to another man. They watched him as he tossed the tools in the wagon. On his next trip he noticed three or four men had bunched around the Land Office man. They were all looking at him.

Logan cursed under his breath. Goddamn! Would it ever be over?

When he came out of the store again he was carrying a sack of flour on his shoulder and the men were standing beside his wagon. Shorty Banes, from the restaurant, was with them. Logan took time to wonder why he was called Shorty. He was big. Perhaps an inch shorter than Logan's six-feet, two-inches, and he was heavy. His head sat on his broad shoulders like a bull's. The men beside him ranged in size from average to tall, but none was as powerfully built as Shorty Banes. Logan paused, looked each man in the eye, and then shouldered his way through the pack to put the sack in the wagon.

"Do you reckon he thinks he's agoin' to stay on that land, Shorty?"

"Even a stupid Injun ain't that dumb."

Logan's muscles bunched. It wasn't going to be easy, he thought.

"I ain't never seen a redskin that was worth doodle-squat in a man-to-man fight, did you, Shatto?"

"I ain't never seen one worth the powder it'd take to blow 'im ta hell."

Fury began to swell the veins in Logan's neck.

"I wonder what he'd do if'n I took my pig sticker and cut a slash in that flour sack?"

Logan dropped the sack in the wagon and turned to face

his tormentors. "Why don't you try it and find out? May be that you're all mouth and no show."

One of the men reared back and let out a loud guffaw. "Shorty, I'm athinkin' the red ass is a askin' fer trouble."

"What's on your mind? I'm busy." Logan felt cold and tight for all the burning rage that threatened to boil up and out of him.

"Don't get sassy with me, Injun." Shorty Banes looked into eyes that were cold and ugly. Something about the big Indian bothered him. He didn't run true to form. The man was ready to take them all on. It showed in the way he stood easily balanced, his legs planted wide apart, his right hand hovering within easy reach of the pistol belted about his hips.

"Well . . . If you're going to jump me, come on. I can kill two of you easy enough. Cowards usually run in packs," Logan said with a sneer.

"You gonna take that off him, Shorty?"

"Watch yore mouth! You talk big fer an Injun with no backup."

"He's got backup, Banes." The voice came from the end of the porch. Logan glanced at a tall, whiplash thin man with a dusty hat tilted back on his heat. He was leaning casually against the wall of the store.

"Stay outta this, Parnell. Mr. Clayhill ain't turned loose on you yet, but he will."

"I'm sayin' you're not goin' to jump the man like a pack of dogs. He's got backup. If you want a go at him, go ahead I'll keep the rest of the varmints off his back."

Logan looked Shorty Banes in the eye. "Are you afraid to take on an *Injun*, Shorty? I'll make it anyway you want guns, fists, or free-for-all."

"Take 'im on, Shorty. Tear down his meat-house!'

Logan smiled when he saw the big, angry man fumble with the buckle of his gunbelt. This was better than he expected. He never doubted his ability to beat another man in a fair fight. During the war, as a recreation, he and his men had practiced the Oriental way of fighting. He was gifted with uncommon speed of hand and foot, steadiness of nerve, and had the ability to shoot instinctively, if necessary, to protect himself.

Shorty shoved his gunbelt into the hands of one of his friends and stepped off the porch. Logan placed his hat and his gunbelt in the wagon and moved out into the dusty street.

"All right, Injun. I'm gonna learn ya it ain't p'lite to mouth off to white folks."

He swung suddenly, a vicious backhand. Expecting the burly man to attack with swinging arms, Logan sidestepped easily, and Shorty stumbled off balance.

"What's the matter, horseshit? Can't you find me? I'm right over here."

Shorty roared and moved in fast, swinging both hamlike fists. Logan met his rush with a blow to Shorty's throat with the side of his hand, whirled and hit him alongside the head with the bottom of his foot, whirled again and kicked him in the stomach. *Swish!* The air went out of Shorty's lungs. He staggered back and shook his head.

"Had enough?" Logan taunted. "I warn you, white trash, I can kill you with these hands and feet."

In a furious rage, Shorty lowered his head and charged. A blow grazed the side of Logan's face and he evaded another. He sidestepped to avoid being caught in a bear hug, aimed a blow to the back of Shorty's neck, then spun around and kicked him in the groin.

Shorty let out a howl and fell to his knees holding his privates. He was doubled up with pain. In less than a minute the fight had been taken out of him, and Logan wasn't even breathing hard.

"You stupid sonofabitch! I could've kill you easily if I had wanted to. Next time, I will. You tell that old bastard you work for that I've bought that land and I'm going to hold it Tell him to get his herd off! A month from today I'll shoot every goddamn cow I find on *my* land!"

Logan strapped on his gunbelt and put on his hat. Shorty's cronies bunched around him and lifted him to his feet. Logan moved up onto the porch. "I'm obliged to you," he said to the slim, sandy-haired man, and held out his hand. "The name's Logan Horn."

"Cooper Parnell. That was some kind of fightin'. You're right handy with your feet."

Logan grinned. "I learned that from an Oriental I met during the war. Takes some practice, but anyone can do it. It comes in handy when you go up against someone that outweighs you by fifty pounds."

"You sure clobbered Shorty. He won't be forgetting it. Watch your back."

"Thanks, I will."

When the wagon was loaded and the bill paid, Mr. McCloud held out his hand to Logan. "You're welcome in my store anytime. I'm not beholdin' to Clayhill. If the time comes that I'm not my own man, I'll burn the sonofabitch down and go back to Illinois. Good luck, young feller."

"It looks like I'm going to need it."

"By the way, there's a canvas under the wagon seat in case it rains." He looked at the cloudless sky. "Don't much look like it now, but you can't tell come sundown."

Logan climbed up on the wagon seat. He didn't care much for driving a team, but this time there was no help for it. He slapped the reins against the backs of the bays, and they moved off up the street toward the eatery where his horse and dog waited.

Mable came out on the porch while he was tying Mercury behind the wagon.

"I see ya got ya a outfit, 'n I see ya had trouble already with Shorty Banes. Ha, ha, ha . . . You shore took him down a peg. He ain't goin' to be adroppin' his britches fer a spell. Hit's goin' to make him madder 'n a rained-on hen. Watch yourself, now."

"I'll do that." Logan removed the saddle from his horse, put it in the back of the wagon, and tied the horse behind. "I hope you won't have any trouble with Clayhill riders on my account."

"Don't you worry none about that. This here's the only eatin' place in town. They ain't goin' to go hungry even fer Clayhill. Say . . . that's his girl over there agivin' ya the eye. Old Clayhill'll get a first-hand report of the goin's on. She's a bitch, is what she is . . . Why there was a time when . . ."

Logan only half heard what Mable was saying. He was looking at the woman in the handsome buggy across the street. She was lovely, and her clothes were some of the finest he had seen. She was dressed all in white from the high-button shoes to the wide-brimmed hat set atop high-piled blond curls. A black boy was driving the buggy and two mounted men lounged in their saddles behind it. The woman was staring at him and . . . smiling.

Never before had Logan received such a bold, admiring look from a woman. Her stark, naked gaze roamed over him leisurely and gave him the sensation of being slowly undressed. He shifted on the seat in acute embarrassment.

"I'll see you the next time I'm in town, ma'am."

"Say, mister . . ." Mabel added, "if'n ya want to stop some'ers fer the night, ya might want to stop at Mary's. She's a widder woman 'n lives 'bout five or six miles out. House is painted up nice and she's got flowers. She does doctorin' 'n such. Got a girl or two if ya need yore ashes hauled."

"I remember seeing the place. Thanks."

He watched Brutus size up the team of bays, then move

on out ahead. Logan put the team in motion and followed. When he passed the buggy he glanced at the woman. Her eyes were still fixed on him. She was openly amused and he saw her eyelid droop in a flirtatious wink. He ignored her. Clayhill's stepdaughter was as dangerous as a keg of gunpowder in a forest fire.

He drove out of town, ignoring the stares of the loafers in front of the saloon and the people on the street who paused to gawk. He didn't see any sign of Shorty Banes and his cronies, but he had the uneasy feeling that he might be watched by a dozen pair of eyes. The feeling stayed with him until he was on the open road.

Chapter Four

A stillness hung over the timbered benchland—a quiet so complete that the dull sound of the horses' hooves and the wagon wheels rolling over the thick, yielding mat of pine needles faded into nothingness. The glow of elation Logan felt when he stuffed the deed to the land in his shirt had died a trembling death in the wake of his troubled thoughts.

Despite his bravado in town, he knew he might have bitten off more than he could chew. It would be weeks, even months before the members of his old army platoon arrived, although he supposed they had already left Illinois and might even be in Deadwood by now. They would have kept in touch with James Randolph, the only other survivor of the group who fought together during the War Between the States, and he would relay the message.

He thought about his land. The grazing was good; there was timber for buildings, an unlimited view that he liked, and plenty of good water. Moreover, there was a maze of

canyons to the south, mountains to the west, and his nearest
neighbors were the Spurlocks.

Uncle Henry would approve of the way his money had
been spent, Logan mused. Invest in land and cattle, he had
advised. The day of making a fortune in the fur trade will
soon be over. Logan's face creased in one of his rare, sudden
grins. His uncle would have gloated over the fact he had
bought the land out from under Adam Clayhill.

He was traveling up the valley beside a busy stream, the
jingle of the harness echoing on the air. The wagon rocked
on steadily, making him feel lonely and turning his thoughts
inward to settle on Rosalee Spurlock. From the first he had
felt the difference between her and the other women he had
known, and he had known a few of them intimately. He
admired her steadiness of will, her deep-rooted integrity, her
womanliness, and her ability to speak frankly. He found himself responding to those qualities rather than her startling
beauty. He doubted that she was even aware she was a beautiful woman.

Logan could feel the swelling in his groin as he thought
about her. He was a man of strong sexual hungers and didn't
regard this physical change in his body as a sign of love. The
only thing he knew about love was what he had read in the
classics. He knew he wanted it someday when he was ready
for it, but with all the trouble ahead of him this wasn't the
time. Yet he was lonely and longed to have someone of his
own. He envied the men who were deeply rooted. He craved
permanency, craved it with an urgency intensified by his years
of seeking it. This was where he would sink his taproot. He
would not let events conspire to uproot him again.

He jolted along on the wagon seat and wryly reflected that
there was more than a modicum of truth in the adage having
to do with the inadvisability of man living alone. This thought
brought him up short! Good Godamighty! What was he think-

ing? In this part of the country it was unthinkable for a white
woman to marry an *Indian*.

Logan was brought back from his dark thoughts by Brutus's odd behavior. He was turning his head to the left and
to the right, then back to look at him, alerting him to an
unfamiliar scent. Logan was at once on guard. The trail had
wound away from the stream and was passing between high
boulders and scrub cedars that afforded plenty of concealment.

On a sudden hunch, Logan unbuckled his gunbelt, lifted
his tunic, and dipped into his money belt, taking all the gold
except for a few coins. He reached under the wagon seat for
the canvas and hid the gold in the folds. He hastily rebuckled
his gunbelt about his waist and moved the rifle to lay across
his lap.

Brutus, with his nose to the ground, moved rapidly ahead.
Suddenly he turned and came back. He barked, and the startled team, nervous and excited, picked up speed. Logan pulled
back on the rein with his feet braced against the footboard at
the front of the wagon.

Three things happened simultaneously and they all registered vividly in Logan's mind. A shot blasted the stillness,
Brutus dropped in his tracks, and a loop appeared directly
ahead of him and he ran headlong into it. He felt the rope
clamp his upper arms to his sides in a viselike grip while he
was clawing for his rifle. He was jerked from the wagon seat
and the breath went out of him when he hit the ground. The
vision of a thousand faces filled with unreasonable hatred
flashed before his eyes as a cloak of darkness covered him,
lifted, covered him again, and was slowly swept aside so he
could see that he was ringed in solidly by mounted men.

With his arms pinioned, Logan felt for his gun and found
an empty holster. He was defenseless, but through blurred
vision he saw it lying on the ground a few feet away. He

rolled over on his stomach in an attempt to reach it, but was jerked viciously as the rider with the rope looped about his saddlehorn gigged the horse. The animal jumped sideways and backed up as if he were holding a steer. The encircling rope tightened and Logan was hauled helplessly over the rocky ground. He tried to protect his face and head by holding it up, but by the time the horse was pulled to a halt his hands and arms were numb from the tight rope and his face bloody from the sharp stones.

"How'd ya like that, redskin?" Shorty Banes leaned from the saddle and spit. "I aim ta learn ya a lesson, *boy*. We'uns don't cotton to Injuns acomin' in here what don't know their place. Hear?"

"He ain't so full a piss 'n vinegar, now, huh, Shorty?" Logan glanced at the man who spoke. He was the same one who had taunted him at the store: tall, gaunt, hooked nose, and small mouth. He reminded Logan of a buzzard.

"I hear tell ya got ya a good supply of cash on ya. Guess ya think that makes ya good as a white man. Where'd ya git it?"

"That's none of your goddamn business." Logan's eyes shifted back to Shorty. He pulled himself to his feet and loosened the rope. He clenched and unclenched his fist in an effort to get the blood circulating again.

"Ya better not be gittin' mouthy with me, Injun."

Logan looked at the other three riders. The hooked-nose one, called Shatto, was leaning on his saddlehorn, grinning down at him, a stream of tobacco juice running out the side of his mouth. He didn't look too smart; he'd follow Shorty's lead. The other two were younger. One shifted his eyes away from Logan's direct gaze; the other lounged indifferently in the saddle, a twig in the corner of his mouth. Logan jerked the rope up over his head and Shorty gathered it in.

"I ast ya a question, red ass. Where'd ya git the gold?"

"And I answered, you crazy bastard! I said it's none of your fuckin' business."

"Yo're short on brains, redskin. Ya ain't got no backup now. Ya answer me or I'll put a slug in yore stinkin' red belly."

"I inherited it from my uncle." Logan was impotent with rage, but spoke calmly.

"I ain't never heard of no Injuns ahavin' that kind of money," Shatto said and spit a stream of yellow tobacco juice that dribbled down Logan's shirt.

"My uncle was white." It took all of Logan's self-control to ignore the insult. His fury had mounted to the extent that he was almost sick from holding it in.

"Well, what'a ya know. Yore pa musta been horny as hell ta poke his pecker in red meat." Shorty laughed and drew a long, thin blade from a sheath in his saddle. "What'a ya say, boys, 'bout us adoin' a little cuttin'? Let's make us a gelding outta this here stud."

As soon as the words registered in Logan's brain, he flung himself straight at Shorty. A wild, piercing cry of rage tore from his throat. He made a grab to jerk him out of the saddle and felt the stinging pain of the coiled rope across his face. Instinctively, his hands went to his eyes and a booted foot that connected with his chest knocked him to the ground. Instantly, he was buried under an avalanche of striking, kicking men. He heaved and bucked, using every ounce of his strength, and spilled them away from him. But he couldn't get enough air in his lungs and one leg was bent under him. He couldn't get to his feet! Blows from the booted feet connected with his sides and the coiled rope continued to rain blows on his back and head. He tried to crawl, but was kicked to the ground while the rope blazed fire across his back.

Was this the end? Would he die here, kicked to death by this scum? He grunted under the lash of the rope as it came down across his back like a white, hot flame, but that was the only sound he made. He lifted his head and opened his lips to curse his tormentors, but no sound came. The hate-filled faces wavered and danced dizzily before his eyes. His mind commanded him to get to his feet and fight, but his body, on fire with pain, refused to obey.

From somewhere in the darkness he heard Shorty say, "Turn the fucker over. He's goin' to git what's acomin' fer what he done to me."

Logan felt hands working at his belt, then his pants were pulled down, his privates exposed. He tried to lift his head, but a booted foot held it to the ground. With frantic eagerness to protect himself, he sought to roll over. Something was wrong with his legs and his chest felt numb. It was his last coherent thought. Lights exploded in his head and he fell through a great, black hole.

"I ain't got no stomach fer this, Shorty. Ya said we'd whop the shit outta him and take his money. Ya didn't say nothin' 'bout acuttin' his nuts."

"Christ, Frank! He ain't nothin' but a gawdamned Injun. Give me yore knife, Shatto. I lost mine some'ers."

"I ain't awantin' none of this, Shorty," Frank insisted. "Kill 'im, if'n ya want to, but I ain't fer cuttin' 'im. That'd get folks riled, even if'n he is a Injun."

"Ya ain't got nothin' ta say 'bout it! I ain't even ortta a let ya come along, ya wet-eared sonofabitch! Get ta hell outta the way!"

"All I wanted outta this was that stallion. Shit! That's horseflesh!" Pete said.

"Ya crazy bastard! Ya can git hung for stealin' a horse!"

"Shut up, Frank!"

"Shit!"

"Do yore cuttin' 'n let's go!" Shatto said.

"I figur'd on takin' that stallion," Pete insisted.

"That shows that all yore a usin' fer brains is that stick ya got atween yore legs. I'm atellin' ya, I ain't ahavin' no part in horse stealin'."

"A buggy's acomin'!" Shatto let loose a string of swear words. "Looks like Mrs. Gregg's."

"Shitfire!"

"We better git the hell outta here if'n we wanta do any whorin' at her place!"

"I can't find my knife," Shorty grumbled.

"Ta hell with it. C'mon!"

Shorty Banes mounted and turned his horse toward the still figure on the ground. "Stomp the sonofabitch!" he commanded. The horse hesitated, then jumped over Logan, and took off on the run.

Logan struggled against the awful darkness that pressed down on him. He fought against it until his eyes opened slowly to more darkness. Fear enveloped him. Was he dead? Where was he? He tried to move and the agony of pain tore through him. He lay perfectly still, his eyes open wide. He was alive.

Slowly, his thoughts assembled, sorted themselves out, and he remembered.

"No!" The strangled cry burst from his throat. He tried to move his hands to his groin, but his arms felt as if lead weights were attached to each hand. "Noooo . . ." he said again, and the word was a sob in his throat.

A light moved near him. He rolled his head toward it. It was then he realized he was in a bed and his head was on a pillow. The light came closer until it was so bright he had to shut his eyes against it, but not before he saw that it was a lamp and a woman carried it.

"So you're awake."

Logan opened his eyes and tried to focus them on her face. "Did they . . . did they . . . cut me?"

"No. You've still got all your parts."

For a space of a dozen heartbeats he stared at her soft, pretty face, not knowing that tears gushed from his eyes and ran down over his torn cheeks.

"What's wrong with me?" he whispered. "My jaw feels like it's broken."

"I don't think it is. I felt it before it had time to swell. You've got some bruised or broken ribs and your back is torn up pretty good. It would have been a lot worse if you hadn't had on that buckskin shirt."

"I thought the bastards were going to kick me to death."

"I was on my way to town when I saw your team and wagon. One of the men was going through it and the other three was standing over you. They left in a hurry. I didn't get to see them, but I recognized a horse or two."

"I know who they were," he said wearily. "Did they take my money belt?"

"You didn't have a money belt on you when we found you, but we found money in your wagon when we unrolled the canvas to cover your supplies. It's in your saddlebags."

"Thank you, ma'am."

"My name is Mary Gregg."

"I passed here on the way to town. The flowers . . . and things . . ." He closed his eyes for an instant, then opened them wide. "My horse?"

"He's all right," Mary said quickly. "He was a handful to deal with, but we got him into the corral. Josh, the man who works for me, has an eye for a good horse. He said he's one of the finest he's seen, even if he is as ornery as a polecat."

"He doesn't like anyone near him but me and Brutus. Oh, God! The sonofabitches killed Brutus!"

"Brutus?"

"My dog. I remember now. They . . . shot him."

"We didn't see him, but we wasn't looking for him, either."

She dipped a towel in the washpan beside the bed, wrung it out, and laid it over his discolored face. The cool dampness laid its soothing touch over his burning skin. His voice came to her muffled by the cloth. "Thank you, ma'am."

Mary looked down at the man's battered, swollen face and anger welled up in her. She gently smoothed the tangled hair off his forehead.

"Do you want something to drink? I've got whiskey."

He rolled his head on the pillow. "No, but . . . thanks."

She drew a chair close, sat down, and continued to lay the cool cloth on his face. Here was a man, a real man. He had as fine a body as she had ever seen; rangy, muscular, hard. Beneath the smooth skin of his chest and arms were ridges of muscle, put there by hard work. His stomach was a flat, hard plain, and his manly privates, which had been exposed to the sun when they came upon him lying in the trail, were huge, as was fitting a man his size.

Mary removed the cloth and dipped it in the water. She looked closely at the still face with the thick brush of black eyelashes lying on his cheeks. He had Indian blood; the high cheekbones and sculpted nose told her that. His midnight black hair was soft, wavy and clean. He was a man anyone would turn to look at a second time.

The minutes passed; Mary changed the damp cloth. She thought he was sleeping. Suddenly his eyes sprang open.

"My papers!"

"They're safe, Logan Horn. The deed to your land is in your saddlebags under the bed."

"Thank God! And . . . thank . . . you!"

"Go to sleep. You've nothing to worry about." She gave his big, hard hand lying on the bed a squeeze with her soft one. "Try not to move around. I've got a coat of salve on your back."

"Ma'am, I couldn't move if the house was on fire," he mumbled, and was almost instantly asleep.

Mary turned the oil lamp down low and continued to sit beside him until Minnie, a thin, flame-haired girl came to the door.

"Ain't he waked up yet?"

Mary stood and picked up the lamp. "He woke up and now he's gone back to sleep again."

"Dud Simms just left. I never said anything 'bout him bein' here, Mary. Honest."

"I knew you wouldn't if I asked you not to," Mary said kindly. "I hope Clara and Hannah will keep quiet, too."

"Clara's got Billy Hopper in there. Him 'n Dud was the only ones to come by tonight."

Mary Gregg was a full-bodied woman in her early thirties with soft brown hair and a pretty, unlined face. Her skin was smooth and white. She never allowed the sun to touch it if she could help it. Her cheeks were rosy without the use of the rouge her girls used, and her lips red. She kept herself immaculate at all times.

Mary had come to the territory as a bride. She and her husband had filed on government land, but pressure from Adam Clayhill had caused her husband to give it up. After he died, Mary took a couple of unfortunate girls under her protection after they had been run out of another town. The need to make a living forced her to open her own place. She never had more than two or three girls at one time, and they stayed until they found some cowpoke or drifter to marry them or they left of their own accord. One of them had married a mule-skinner by the name of Josh Hamilton and stayed on to help her run the place. Meta was a fine cook and Josh took care of the outside chores.

As far as anyone knew, Mary Gregg had never personally serviced any of the men who came to her house. She demanded that her girls be treated kindly and that they never be forced to do anything against their will. It was said that she was one of the richest women in this part of the territory.

"Dud told me 'bout what happened in town today. He said a Indian rode in with a pisspot full a gold and bought up range old Clayhill's been usin'. I'd like to see the old bastard's face when he finds out." Minnie looked to see what effect her words had had on Mary, because everyone knew of her intense hatred for Adam Clayhill. Mary's expression never changed and the disappointed Minnie continued. "He said the Indian got in a fight with Shorty Banes 'n cleaned his clock before he could say scat. Dud said Shorty was madder 'n a hornet 'cause the Indian kicked him in the nuts 'n he thought his ruttin' days was over! Ha, ha, ha . . . I wish they was. He's like a hog! He ain't never goin' to use me no more," Minnie said with a toss of her red head.

"All you have to do is say the word, Minnie, and he'll not get through the door again. You know that."

"You reckon *that's* the Indian he was talkin' 'bout?" She jerked her head toward the bedroom door. "Whoeee! I don't care if'n it was him or not that kicked the shit outta Shorty. I'd open up fer him . . . anytime!"

"Humm . . . You stay out of his room unless he asks for you. Hear?" Mary said in a no-nonsense voice. Then, "Let's see if Meta's got some fresh coffee. She'll want to hear about what went on in town today, too."

Rosalee brought her arms up out of the warm suds and looked off toward the east as she had done a dozen times in the last hour. There was no movement on the trail or on the horizon. She glanced around for Charlie and decided he had gone off somewhere with Ben.

She put her hand to the small of her back and straightened. She was tired. At daybreak she had brought the iron boiling pot from the cowshed. She had half filled it with water, carried from the spring in the cliff behind the house, and built a fire under it. The first batch of clothes were drying on the bushes and the rope she had stretched from the corner of the house to the oak tree beside the corral.

The late May sun had some heat to it in the middle of the day, and Rosalee wiped her face on the end of her apron and pushed the hair back from her eyes.

"Where's Odell, Pa?" she called.

"How'd I know?" Grant had been surly for several days. Periodically, he went through days of depression when he felt useless and helpless. He sat on the step and whittled on a long stick.

"It's time for nooning," Rosalee said as she approached him. "Shall I bring yours out here?"

"Suit yourself."

The inside of the cabin was dim and cool compared to bright sunlight. Rosalee glanced quickly around for her sister. Odell, lost in thought, sat in Grant's chair.

"What are you doing in here when it's so nice outside?"

"I hate it here, Rosalee," Odell blurted. "Pa's a grouch and there's nothin' to do." Her pixie face puckered as if she would cry.

"Pa will get over it, honey. In a day or two he'll be chipper as ever. And as far as something to do . . . the clothes are dry. You can bring them in while I fix up a bite to eat."

"All you ever do is . . . work! I hate it here. I'm going to live in a town when I grow up! And I'm going to have books, a pretty dress, and real shoes." She covered her eyes with her hands and began to sob.

"Oh, honey!" Rosalee lifted her out of the chair and sat down again with the child on her lap. She hugged her and pushed the hair back from her tear-wet face. She understood her feeling of loneliness and despair and longed, with all her heart, to make life more enjoyable for this little girl who was more like her child than her sister.

"I know how you feel, honey, really I do. I would like all those things, too. But we can't have them. We've got Pa to take care of. Mama would want us to take care of him and try to make him happy. Think how he must feel, being blind and having to depend on us. You're his only joy in life now. When he's going through these bad times we've got to be patient with him."

"He . . . told me to go away 'n stop yappin' at him."

"I'm sure he didn't mean it. He probably had a lot of thinking to do."

"And he said he'd be better off dead than the way he is."

"He didn't mean that, either. What would we do without Pa to tell us stories in the wintertime?"

"I've heard 'em all."

"So have I, but I like to hear them again."

"He'll get all riled up when Mr. Horn comes back to get his horses. He said he wasn't havin' no damn half-breed ahangin' 'round here." Large blue eyes looked at Rosalee, and when tears appeared she tried to blink them away.

"Maybe he'd like Mr. Horn if he talked to him," Rosalee said patiently, though she knew it wasn't true. Her father was so like so many others who'd never stop to consider that this land had belonged to the Indians and that they were the intruders.

Odell lifted the hem of her dress and wiped her eyes. Rosalee felt the tears rising in her own throat. She hadn't realized the depth of her little sister's loneliness or the intense feeling of rejection the child suffered at the hands of their blind father when he was in one of his black moods.

"Do you know what we're going to do?" Rosalee said

lightly and happily. "When we finish the washing, we'll play a game of hide-and-seek. Then tonight we'll cut a body for your doll out of the scraps of Ben's deerskin. Pa made such a beautiful doll head, it's a shame she doesn't have a body."

"Oh, Rosalee! Could we?"

"Of course we can. And I've been thinking about something else, too. When Ben goes over to the Haywards' you can go along with him and stay a few days. Mrs. Hayward said you were welcome anytime. She said one more youngun among her five would be no trouble at all. You can play with Sudie May and Polly. By then we'll have your doll ready and maybe even a dress for her."

"How'll you get 'round Pa? He won't want me to go."

"I'll talk him into it."

Odell's face brightened and an infectious smile shifted the lines of her mouth upward. "Oh, golly! Oh, golly! I love you, Rosalee." She threw her arms around her sister's neck and hugged her. "But what if Pa—"

"Don't think about that! Think on the good side." She lifted the child off her lap. "But first things first. We've got to fix the meal and finish the washing. Then we'll play."

"You was goin' to work in the garden."

"Oh, fiddle! I can work in that old garden anytime. It's a lot more fun to play hide-and-seek," Rosalee said lightly, and was rewarded by a gleam of pure pleasure in her little sister's tear-wet eyes.

Grant remained in his black mood all afternoon. Rosalee anxiously watched the trail for Logan, although she was sure it would be late evening, and possibly not until morning, before he returned. She wasn't sure what her father would say to him. He could be cruel and cutting in his remarks if he felt strongly about something. She dreaded his bringing up the fact that Logan was a breed.

When she thought of Logan Rosalee felt a surprising, overwhelming burst of happiness. Even now, as she played hide-and-seek with Odell, she could see his sudden smile behind her eyelids when she closed her eyes. It made crinkly lines around his eyes and deepened the indentations in his cheeks, making him look surprisingly boyish. She blushed at her thoughts, then chided herself to keep her mind on the game. She picked up her skirts and ran to hide behind the cowshed. This was her last turn at hiding; the sun had gone behind the mountains in the west, and soon it would be time to start the evening meal.

Hunkered down behind a pile of logs, Rosalee could hear Odell coming along beside the corral fence. She stopped to call to the foal and the mare nickered softly. The mare continued to nicker even after Odell had gone into the cowshed. It suddenly occurred to Rosalee that the mare had heard another horse. She stood and moved to the end of the corral where she could look down the trail.

Four horsemen, galloping their mounts, came from between the break in the trees. Rosalee felt no alarm. Riders came this way several times a month. The trail from here on was rough and hazardous, but it was a shortcut to the Clayhill ranch. She called out to Odell.

"Someone's coming, Odell. I'll have to go to the house." She walked rapidly in order to be beside her father when the men arrived. "I'm here, Pa."

"Who is it? Sounds like three or four horses." Grant had moved his chair out into the yard. He poked the stick he'd been whittling on in the ground beside it and folded up his pocket knife.

"There's four of them, and they look like Clayhill riders." She squinted her eyes. "They're Clayhill men. A couple of them have been here several times before." Rosalee didn't like the man they called Shatto, or Shorty Banes. But she hadn't told her father that. She had not seen the other two men before.

"Howdy, ma'am. Mind if we water our horses?" Shorty leaned back in the saddle and grinned at her.

"Go ahead. But you just crossed the creek a ways back."

"We did? I didn't see no creek. Did you, Shatto?"

"Naw. I ain't seen no creek since we left Junction City," he said in a foolish attempt at humor.

"We'd be obliged fer some supper, bein's on how it'll be a spell afore we get ta the ranch." Shorty edged his horse closer.

"I'm afraid I don't have anything prepared," Rosalee said curtly.

"Coffee, then?" Shatto asked, and spit in the dirt of her flower bed.

Rosalee looked at their leering faces and felt a sudden chill. They had never been this bold before. She moved over and placed her hand on her father's shoulder.

"We're out of coffee."

"Water your horses and move out." Grant spoke for the first time.

"Ya reckon they ain't goin' ta be friendly, Shatto?"

"Hit don't appear to me that they is," he said, and flung his leg up over his saddle horn. "Yore a right sightly woman, ma'am. Ain't yore name Rosalee?"

"It's Miss Spurlock to you." She could feel her father's body tremble beneath her hand and she patted him reassuringly, hoping to keep him calm.

"She's a uppity one, ain't she, Shorty?"

"C'mon. Let's water our horses and go." The man who spoke was younger than Shorty and Shatto. He had a growth of thin, blond whiskers on his pimpled face and he held such a tight rein on his horse that the animal danced and fidgeted.

"Shut up, Frank. I wanna visit with the purtty woman."

"Shorty, you'd better not—"

"I said, shut up, Frank. If'n yore in such a gawdamned hurry, ride on out. Ya ain't been nothin' but a pain in the ass all day, anyhow. All ya do is yap, yap, yap."

"Ya ain't ortta talk like that in front of a lady," Frank insisted angrily. "Ain't that right, Pete?"

"He can talk any way he wants. Hit makes me no never mind."

Grant was trying to rise from the chair, but Rosalee's hand pressed him down. However, she couldn't keep him from blurting out angrily, "Water yore horses and git the hell outta here!"

Shorty let go with a loud guffaw. "What'a ya goin' ta do if'n I ain't a mind to, old man?"

Rosalee could feel the rage in her father, and when he sprang to his feet her hand on his shoulder was as nothing. There was something deadly here! Fear squeezed her heart. She remembered Ben had set the rifle just inside the door this morning. She made a move to go to the cabin, but Shorty spurred his horse to cut her off.

"Ya changed yore mind 'bout gettin' us some supper?"

Rosalee didn't answer. She stepped sideways and went around the horse. Shorty slid from the saddle on the other side and flung his arm across the doorway.

"Shorty," Frank called. "Me'n Pete's goin' on. Ya'll had better come, too."

Shorty ignored him. His loose lips parted in what he considered a flirtatious smile, showing yellow teeth. "Ya don't want me ta go, now do ya?" he said in a soft, purring voice.

His words shocked and sickened her. She moved back and he followed, backing her into the horse. She was frightened now, but determined not to show it.

"I certainly do want you to go. Mr. Clayhill wouldn't be

pleased to know you're here making a nuisance out of yourself."

"What's a nuisance? Does it mean a . . . stud?" He jerked his pelvis toward her in an obscene way, grinning all the while.

Rosalee's face flamed with embarrassment and fear. She looked wildly about, then quickly turned and started back toward her father.

"Yore woman's agettin' away, Shorty. Want me ta get 'er for ya?" Shatto didn't wait for an answer. He jumped his horse toward Rosalee. "Wha . . . whoo!" he shouted.

Rosalee was halfway across the yard when he grabbed her beneath the arms and pulled her up against his thigh. "I got 'er," he shouted gleefully. "And I'm agoin' ta get me a kiss 'afore ya can 'ave 'er."

"Let me go!" Rosalee screamed, and fought the hands holding her.

"Get your filthy hands off her, you low-life scum!" Grant yelled.

She heard her father's cry of rage. Frantically, she turned her head so she could see him. He charged forward, the pointed whittling stick in his hand. He jabbed ahead of him viciously, hitting nothing. Shorty laughed and spun toward the sound. Now all the men were laughing at the blind man stumbling around in the yard.

Shorty darted behind his horse. "Who . . . eee! Ya better watch out, Shatto. He's agoin' ta git ya," he taunted.

Grant lunged toward the sound. He jabbed with the stick and struck the saddle. He drew it back and with all his strength he jabbed again and the sharp point of the stick went into the soft mound between the hind legs of Shorty's horse. The animal screamed in pain, whirled and lashed out with his hind legs. Both of them connected with Grant's body. One struck him in the chest, the other beside the head. He was flung into the air. When he hit the ground he lay grotesquely limp and still.

"Pa!" Rosalee screamed. The arm holding her loosened and when her feet hit the ground she was running. "Pa... Oh, Pa!" The side of his head was crushed. She knew immediately that he was dead.

"You stupid sonofabitch!" Frank yelled. "Ya've done it, now. Ya'll get run outta the country fer messin' with that woman. And ya done got 'er pa killed. I ain't had no part a this. C'mon, Pete."

"Go on, ya lily-livered bastard. 'Twas his own doin'," Shorty shouted. He was chasing after his still-bucking horse. He caught him, gave the reins a hard jerk, and hit the animal up beside the head with his fist before he mounted. "Let's get ta hell outta here. Crazy old fool got what he had acomin'." He put his heels to the horse and took off on the run. Shatto looked down at Rosalee and her father, spit a stream of tobacco juice in the grass beside them, and followed Shorty.

Rosalee was only vaguely aware the men had left. She knelt beside her father, numbed with shock. Ten minutes ago she had been playing happily with Odell. Now, her pa was dead, his blood seeping into the ground where he lay.

Odell! She had forgotten about her little sister. She stood, looked around, and saw the girl running toward her from the corner of the house. Rosalee ran to meet her and gathered her in her arms.

"Rosalee! What's wrong with Pa? What'd those men do to him?" She tried to wiggle out of Rosalee's embrace. "I wanna see Pa."

"No! Don't look at him! The horse . . . kicked him and he's . . . dead! It happened so fast. Oh, Pa!" She fell to her knees with her sister in her arms and sobbed.

"I saw it! Pa was trying to help you, Rosalee!" Odell began to scream. "Pa! Pa! Pa!"

Chapter
Five

Rosalee covered her father's body with a blanket and sat beside him, holding Odell in her arms. The weight of grief pressed down on her. Only she, Odell and Ben were left from a family of eight. First they lost two brothers, then a baby sister and Mama. Now Pa was gone. He had been cantankerous at times, and opinionated, but he had also been loving. He'd loved his wife and he'd loved his children. Pa died trying to help her! If only she hadn't cried out when the man grabbed her! A black wave of hate flooded her heart when she thought of the men who had laughed and jeered as he stumbled across the yard.

It was almost dark. Ben came riding into the yard whistling a tune. He had a young deer thrown over his saddle and Charlie loped alongside him.

"What are you sitting out here for?" he asked when he saw his sisters sitting in the grass. "What..." He slowly dismounted, knowing something was wrong, instinctively knowing that something had happened that couldn't be changed. "Rosalee . . . what'er you doin' out here, and what's . . . that?"

"Pa's dead." Rosalee reached for his hand and pulled him down beside her and Odell. "Pa's dead, Ben."

"He . . . can't be . . . What happened?"

Rosalee put her arm around him and pulled his head to her shoulder. "He was kicked by a horse, honey. But there's more to it than that. You've got to help me with him. Odell and I waited for you." Sobs tore at Ben's throat, but he was trying to be manly and hold them back. "Go ahead and cry, honey. Odell and I are all cried out for the time being."

Ben let the tears flow, and after awhile, still in shock, he went to the shed and came back with a flat board. He and Rosalee rolled their father's body onto it and carried him into the house.

"What'll we do, Rosalee? Shall I ride over to the Haywards? They'll come, and so will the Cranstons."

"It'll only take you an hour. Why don't you wait and leave at first light? Oh, Ben! I don't know if I . . . can take care of him like I should! His poor head! I don't want to remember him like that."

Ben came to her and put his arms around her. He was half a head shorter than his sister, but his young body was strong from hard work.

"I'll help you. Pa wouldn't want us to remember him . . . like that, either. I'll get that good shirt of mine and we'll wrap it about his head like a bandage. We'll put his black pants on him and his good shirt. Just keep thinkin' about what Pa would tell us to do. He'd say for us to hold up our heads and do the decent thing."

They laid their father out on the bunk where a few nights ago Logan Horn's mother had lain. They dressed him and set a candle on the bench beside him. Odell went to sleep, but Ben and Rosalee talked through the night. Ben was for riding over to the Clayhill ranch and reporting the men to Mr. Clayhill.

"Let it lie, Ben. He wouldn't do anything to them. They would say it was an accident, which it was. But it was an accident they caused to happen."

"I don't think Clayhill knows or cares what his men do. I've met up with his foreman a time or two. He's not like the hands. He 'pears to be a cut higher. He might do somethin'."

"I wouldn't count on it, Ben. We've got to think about what we're going to do now."

"We'll stay on here. There's nothing else we can do."

"I know. But I worry about Odell. If Mrs. Hayward will take her home with her, I'm going to let her go and stay awhile. She gets so lonesome here, and now without Pa . . ."

"What about you, Rosalee? Don't you get lonesome, too?"

"Of course I do. But without Pa and Odell to look after, I'll ride out with you for awhile. Maybe together we can get a few more cattle and we'll drive them to Junction City. We could use the cash money."

Ben left to take the news to the neighbors as soon as dawn streaked the eastern sky. Rosalee went with him to the corral to get his horse. Logan Horn's mare and foal came to meet her. During the long night she had thought of him once or twice and wondered what the future held for him as well as for Odell, Ben, and herself.

"I'll be back as soon as I tell 'em about Pa. It'll take awhile for 'em to load up." The tragedy seemed to have steadied Ben. He went about what he had to do calmly. "I skinned out the deer I got yesterday. It's a little 'un, so you might as well roast the whole thing. There might be nigh on to thirty people here if they bring all the kids. You and Odell put on your good dresses, Rosalee. As soon as I get back I'll start to rig up a table in the yard. We'll do this up right so Pa'd be proud."

"Oh, Ben! Go on before I start bawling again. And Ben . . . when you come back you'd better tie Charlie up. He's not used to being with so many kids and he might bite one of them."

"I don't think he'd do that, but he'd be grabbin' off a hunk of that deer meat if he got a chance."

The Haywards and the Cranstons arrived by mid-morning. They came in wagons loaded with food they had hastily gathered from their storehouses: smoked ham, hominy, dried beans, honey, freshly baked bread, and apple jelly. Shortly before noon Mr. Smithfield and two of his sons rode over on horseback carrying a basket of fried apple pies. His wife was ailing, he said, but she sent her condolences.

Lottie Hayward climbed down off the wagon seat holding her baby in her arms and the rest of the children spilled out the back of the wagon. She gave the oldest one a quilt to spread on the grass under a shade tree and cautioned each one to be quiet out of respect for the dead.

"I'd better not see a smile or hear a titter till we're in the wagon 'n away from here," she said sternly, and waited for a chorus of, "Yes, Maw."

The children, all dressed in their best, obeyed and tried to conceal their excitement. Lottie left the sleeping baby in the care of Polly, the oldest child, and went to where Rosalee and Odell stood beside the door greeting their guests.

"Hit's just about the awfulest thing I ever did hear of," she said, shaking her head sadly. "Yo're just little orphans, is what ya are!" A few tears squeezed from between her eyelids and she blinked them away. She hugged each of the girls. "Now tell me what to do. Where'll I put the vittles I brought? I'll swan to goodness, we're agoin' to have a bunch to feed!"

"You didn't need to bring anything, Lottie," Rosalee exclaimed.

"Why I did so! Landsakes! What's neighbors fer?" Lottie Hayward was a big, square-built woman with large hands and feet. It was said she could plow as well as her husband. The lines of her homely, weathered face were arranged somberly to fit the occasion, and she talked in a muffled whisper as if she were afraid she would disturb the dead.

"Odell, why don't you go sit on the quilt with Polly and Sudie May? Lottie will help me now. And so will Mrs. Cranston when she gets the baby to sleep."

"No. I'll help you, Rosalee. Pa'd . . . want me to help."

"All right, honey. If you want to."

The men fashioned a coffin for Grant from the planks that Ben and Rosalee had been accumulating to floor the cabin. It was a crude affair, but Rosalee lined the box with her mother's best quilt. After her father was placed in it she put a faded pink cloth rose from one of her mother's hats in his hand. Ben wanted to bury him on a knoll at the corner of their land and Rosalee agreed. They walked behind the wagon carrying the coffin with Odell between them and the neighbors walking quietly behind.

The burial ceremony was brief. Rosalee asked Mr. Hayward to read a scripture from her mother's Bible, and they sang a chorus of "Rock of Ages." When it was over, Ben stepped forward and used two of his precious supply of nails to nail the lid of the coffin in place. Odell started to sob when they lowered the coffin into the ground and the men began shoveling in the dirt.

Rosalee led the mourners back down the hill to the cabin. She thought about how comforting it was to be with people at this time. Then her thoughts turned to Logan Horn, and she remembered the sadness on his face the morning he lashed his mother's body to the travois. He had gone through this alone except for the little help she had given to him. Where was he? she wondered. Why hadn't he come back?

A burial or a wedding was almost the only occasion to bring neighbors together. It was a chance to visit and exchange news. The men were anxious to know about the handsome, blooded mare and the foal in the Spurlock corral. Rosalee left it up to Ben to tell about Logan Horn stopping at their place in the middle of the night with his dying mother. She could tell that Ben was enjoying having the men's rapt attention and she was proud of him for stating so matter-of-factly that Logan's mother was an Indian and that he had taken her body into the hills to build a scaffold according to the custom of her people.

She watched her neighbors for signs of prejudice, but if they had any they kept them concealed. She wondered what they would think if she told them Logan had gone to Junction City to buy the range Adam Clayhill had been using all these years. She hadn't even told Ben that news. Her eyes strayed once again down the trail toward town. Something had gone wrong or Logan would have been back for his horses by now.

By the time the neighbors made ready to leave in order to be home before dark, Rosalee had told the circumstances leading to her father's death a dozen times. She named the men from the Clayhill ranch.

"That there foreman, Case Malone, seemed like a good sort of a feller. He come by one time 'n said they had stock on the range 'n if 'n we let 'em be, they'd let us be, 'n they have."

"They ain't bothered us none," Mr. Cranston said. "I heard tell he ain't been foreman but fer two, three years. Injuns killed the other'n. Guess he was meaner than a rattler. I don't know where this 'un come from, but he ain't no fool."

"You plannin' on astayin' here, Miss Rosalee?" Mr. Hayward asked.

"Of course. Our land is paid for. This is our home and now our pa is . . . buried here."

"Well now, you just be mighty careful of them fellers 'n any other drifter what comes by." He shook his head. "My, my . . . it used to be a woman's worry was the Injuns, 'n a man, even if he was at the bottom of the barrel, would die aprotectin' 'er. Times is achangin'."

"Don't worry, Mr. Hayward. I'm going to keep the rifle handy from now on. I appreciate you and Lottie taking Odell home with you for awhile. You make her mind and help with the work. She needs children to play with. It'll help keep this off her mind for awhile."

"We're jest proud to have her. If'n ya'll need any help you jest holler. It ain't but a hour's ride over here."

The children were in the wagons. Odell sat between Sudie May and Polly. She tried not to smile, to show her excitement, but her eyes gleamed. Ben and Rosalee kissed her good-bye.

"Mind Lottie and help with the baby. Ben and I will ride over next week and see if you want to come home."

Lottie set a basket in the wagon. "You keep the rest of the honey, Rosalee. I see ya've et all yores . . . No, I don't want the rest of that ham. Keep it fer yoreself 'n Ben. I'll take a hunk a that deer meat, if'n yore sure ya can spare it. Silas can't make the time to hunt like he ort to."

"Keep the bread 'n the hominy, Rosalee," Mrs. Cranston insisted. "I got aplenty at home."

"Thank you all. I don't know what we'd have done without you."

The women hugged Rosalee. The men, after they shook hands with her and Ben, climbed up on the wagon seats and put the teams in motion.

"Bye, Rosalee. Bye, Ben," Odell called.

"Don't ya worry 'bout 'er none. We'd jest be proud fer 'er to stay fer quite a spell. I forgot to ask ya, Rosalee, if'n ya want some tater eyes to plant. If'n ya do, send Ben over." Lottie turned around to wave.

"We've got plenty, Lottie, but thanks." Rosalee and Ben waved at Odell until the trail turned and the wagon was out of sight.

"It'll be more lonesome than ever without Odell and ... Pa," Rosalee murmured.

"I'll turn Charlie loose." With his hands in his pockets and his head bowed, Ben walked toward the cowshed.

After the chores were done, Ben lay down on the bunk and went to sleep. Rosalee covered him with a quilt because the night was cool. She flung her shawl around her shoulders and went out to sit on the step. So much had happened since Logan Horn had pounded on their door in the middle of the night.

Charlie came to lie down at her feet and she stroked his shaggy head. Rosalee sat, not moving, her jumbled thoughts twisting and turning like a tumbleweed driven by a brisk wind. Pa was gone ... poor Pa. He'd not been the same after Mama died. He'd loved her so much.

Rosalee watched the break in the trees leading to the trail to town and a thought came to her mind that made her heart freeze: The Clayhill riders! Had they met up with Logan and killed him?

The Clayhill ranch house was ablaze with light as it was every evening at this time when Della Clayhill was at home. It was a big, square, two-storied, white frame house with a wide, railed veranda on three sides, surrounded by a white picket fence that no ranch hand dared to step within without being invited. The long, narrow windows on both the upper and lower floors were decorated with elaborately carved woodwork. Stained glass panes adorned the upper part of the windows as well as the double doors that opened onto the veranda. It was said to be one of the most elegant houses in the Colorado Territory.

Della loved the house with its Persian rugs, voluptuous, velvet draperies and ornate Victorian furniture, but hated its location. Since her mother had died five years before, she had spent as little time here as possible. It was a boring, savage land, and the people here were equally boring. But if she was going to stay in the good graces of her stepfather, she had to divide her time between the ranch and Denver.

Lately Della had begun to worry that Adam might marry again. He had made several trips to Denver to visit a widow not much older than herself. The thought of sharing her inheritance with another woman was not something Della liked to think about, and she had given considerable thought to the idea of getting Adam to marry her. He was still a vigorous man and the thought of sleeping with her stepfather was rather intriguing. She had often wondered why her mother had detested the physical side of her marriage to Adam. He was big, strong, demanding, had an explosive temper, and could be exceedingly cruel at times.

Della had been eleven years old when her mother married Adam ten years before. Even then she had adored him and spent as much time with him as possible. She was not an outdoor type of girl. She hated the smelly outbuildings on the ranch, the wind blowing her hair, the hot sun making her sweat. Being inside the lovely house was more to her liking. She became adept at bossing the servants, which irritated her mother but amused Adam. Some days she would spend hours standing at the window waiting for him to come in. She loved to sit on his lap and wiggle until his *thing* got hard and he would lift her off and take her mother up to the bedroom.

Her sixteen-year-old brother, Kain, had detested him. He and Adam never got along and Kain left the ranch two years after they arrived. He kept in touch with his mother until she died. Since then, nothing had been heard from him.

Della knew she was beautiful. She gazed into the long

mirror beside her dressing table and tucked a strand of her blond hair in place. She was of average height and very slim. Many men had enjoyed encircling her waist with their two hands. Her breasts were fully rounded, her nipples large. Her eyes dropped to them and she was pleased to see how they jutted against the thin, white muslin of her gown. She almost always wore white with a touch of pastel. Impulsively, she lifted the skirt of her dress and yanked off a petticoat. She ran her hands down over her belly and lower to see if her pubic hair was visible through the white gown. It was, but not nearly as much as she would have liked. At least there was nothing between *her* and the dress. She tucked a fresh sachet between her breasts and left the room.

Adam will still be angry, she thought as she went down the carpeted stairs. She had told him about the half-breed buying the range as soon as she had returned from town. He had exploded with a fury that she had seldom witnessed before. The foul language that spewed from his mouth was downright exciting. Just thinking about it and the way he had picked up a heavy goblet and flung it at the wall sent delicious quivers down her spine. He had walked the floor and cursed for an hour before going into his office. He had not come out for dinner and she had dined alone.

The house was quiet, she observed with a smile. The servants were keeping out of the master's way. He had been known to knock one of them off their feet when he was in a terribly foul mood and they had not anticipated his wishes correctly. Della had no fear of him. Papa Adam had always been gentle as a lamb with her.

Adam had left the door to his office open, but the red velvet door draperies were pulled. In this way he could hear what was going on in the house and yet have his privacy. Della pulled aside the drapes and stood framed in the doorway. Adam sat at his desk, a sheaf of papers in his hand. Della watched him through lowered lids. His white hair was thick and sprang back from a broad forehead. She knew he was proud of his hair and proud of the white mustache he kept trimmed to perfection. He was a big man with wide shoulders and long arms. His waist had thickened over the years, but it was not unattractive. The buttons on his shirt were undone and a mat of reddish-brown hair sprinkled with gray was visible.

"Papa Adam..." Della made her voice velvety soft and looked at him with a quiet, childlike sweetness.

"Della, honey, come in. Did I scare you when I went on my rampage?" He rolled back his chair and stood up.

"Noooo..." Della moved across the floor swiftly like a child seeking comfort. Adam automatically opened his arms and she went into them. "Are you still angry?"

"Your gawddamn right I am! I can't wait to get my hands on that stupid fucker who sold my land! He knew I was going to buy it as soon as I sold the herd. He'll wish, by Gawd, he'd had tin around his asshole when I get through with him. He won't be able to shit for a month. The scrawny prick let the land go to a cunt-screwin' half-breed!"

Della could feel him tremble with rage. She snuggled her face against him, opened her mouth and blew her warm breath on his chest. She loved it when he forgot himself and said the dirty words he used when he was talking to the men. She snuggled against him for a long moment and decided he was so worked up over the sale of the land that he didn't even realize she was there. It irked her. She didn't like being ignored. She raised her head and kissed him on the chin.

"Oh, now, it can't be all that bad. Come and sit down and let's talk about it." She tugged on his hand, led him to the big leather arm chair and pushed him down into it. She sat down on his lap and put her arms around his neck. "This is the way I used to sit on your lap when I was a little girl," she whispered. "Remember?"

"I sure do." He chuckled. "You were as soft and cuddly as a snub-nosed puppy."

"A puppy! Puppies are ugly."

Adam laughed. "You? Ugly?" He laughed again. "Honey, you were the prettiest little thing I ever saw. You still are."

"Do you think so, Adam?"

"I sure do. Don't I spoil you rotten? Don't you have everything you want?"

"Not everything."

"Just name it, honey. I'll get it if I can."

She kissed his chin and wiggled her bottom firmly against the soft mound beneath it. "What are you going to do about that Indian? Where do you suppose he got the money?"

"Stole it. He's probably got a price on his head down south and thought he'd come up here and buy some respectability."

"He's awfully good looking." Della knew her words would rile him, and she wasn't disappointed.

"What the gawddamned difference does that make? He's a fuckin' blanket ass! He'll haul his ass off that land and out of the territory or I'll nail his red pecker to a tree! I've used that range for twenty years. I'm not giving it up to anyone, especially not to a stinkin', dog-eatin' savage that don't know his ass from a hole in the ground."

In his agitation Adam's hand had found the side of her rounded bottom and pressed it against his growing hardness. A pleasing, familiar feeling began to crowd the thoughts of the Indian from his mind. When she was a little girl he'd used her soft, little bottom to get himself aroused so he could make it with her cold, prim and proper mother. She didn't have on as many clothes now as she did then. He looked down his long nose and into the neck of her dress. The soft mounds of her breast were pressed together and her nipples were hard little knots that his fingers itched to touch.

Adam knew Della was not the sweet, little innocent that she pretended, at times, to be. He had seen her flirt with the men, had seen her on occasion rub against them. It had amused him to see her get them steamed up and then walk away and leave them. She tilted her head and their eyes met. Slowly, the pink tip of her tongue came out and made a slow pass over her upper lip and then came to rest at the corner of her mouth. It stayed there while they looked deeply into each other's eyes. What she was sitting on was rock hard now, and they both knew it.

"I'm your . . . papa," he said hoarsely.

"No, you're not. My papa died or my mother wouldn't have married you."

"You've been like my daughter."

"This doesn't feel like you're holding your daughter?" Her fingers slid down between them and she moved her hip to make room for her hand to grip him.

"Good gawdamighty!" The breath exploded from his lungs.

"You're awful big, Papa Adam," she whispered, but continued to hold his eyes with hers. This was the most thrilling game she had ever played and she was determined to get the most out of it. His angry outbursts had set her blood dancing and created an ache between her legs. "I've always loved you." Her words were uttered breathlessly, and his eyes moved to her lips that remained parted, showing a pink tongue moving back and forth over the edge of her small white teeth.

"You know what your doin', don't you? You've done it before." A spurt of jealousy made him want to shake her.

She laughed softly. "You're not the kind of man who wants a quivering virgin."

"Don't start something you'll not finish, girl," he said harshly.

"What would you do to me, Papa Adam, if I moved my hand and . . . got off your lap, and . . . went up to bed and locked my door?" She spoke slowly, her eyes sparkling and mischievous.

He looked at her for a long moment and suddenly realized that it was inevitable that this happen. It had been building for years. He had wanted her in this way since she was twelve, but the feeling hadn't surfaced until now.

"I'd break your gawddamned neck!" he said viciously.

Peals of soft laughter came from Della's lips. "I'd love it, Papa. Really I would."

"Don't call me that!" He put his mouth to hers, crushing her lips against his teeth, crushing her against him until the breath left her body.

Through the pounding of blood in his ears he heard the clang of the bell on the veranda. He lifted his head to listen as Samuel, the black servant, opened the door. There was a low murmur of voices and then muffled footsteps coming down the carpeted hallway.

"Mastah Clayhill, suh." Samuel's voice came through the heavy draperies that covered the door. "Mastah Malone is heah."

"Gawddamn!" Adam whispered the curse under his breath, then called out, "Tell him to wait in the parlor."

"Yas'suh."

Della laughed softly after Samuel's footsteps had receded down the hall. "I don't think Case has been in the parlor before."

Adam pulled her arms down from around his neck and with his hands beneath her knees moved her feet to the floor. "It's important or Case wouldn't come to the house."

Della stood up and Adam got to his feet. Their eyes met, hers smiling, his smoldering. His nostrils were extended as he took air deep into his lungs. She stood close to him and ran her fingers lightly over the bulge in his pants.

"You'd better wait awhile before you call Case in. He might get the idea you're smuggling . . . fence posts."

A slow smile spread over Adam's face. "You horny little slut! You've been this way all the time!"

"I love it when you talk like that!" she said and gripped him hard.

He removed her hand from him and stepped back. "Get out of here so I can get myself in shape to talk to Case."

"Are you sure you don't want me to help you get rid of *that*?" Her eyes flicked to his crotch and up again, laughing into his eyes.

"Later."

"Whatever you say . . . Papa."

"You . . . gawddamned little bitch!" He reached for her and she moved quickly to the door, laughing silently back at him.

Della slipped between the drapes and ran lightly up the stairs to her room. She closed the door and leaned against it. It had been so easy! Adam would be an exciting lover and she knew just how to stir him to anger. She'd have him eating out of her hand and she wouldn't even have to marry him. This way she would be free to see who she pleased, and do as she pleased while she was in Denver. As Mrs. Adam Clayhill her activities would be carefully scrutinized, but this way . . .

Adam could scarcely believe what had happened. Della had always treated him affectionately, but he'd had no idea she was so attracted to him. He had watched her little bottom round out and her breasts grow. She was a stunningly beautiful woman. He had bought her pretty clothes, paid for her to attend a good school, and later furnished her a house in Denver. She had been away from the ranch much of the time during the last few years, and he had missed her. She'd started it, by God, he mused. Once he took her he'd sure as hell not share her with anyone else!

Adam rubbed his hands together and reached into his desk drawer for a cigar. Cecilia, the Mexican girl he had brought to the ranch on the pretext of helping in the kitchen, had furnished him with a variety of pleasures. She was a hot-blooded little bitch, but she was afraid of him. Violence and anger had always stirred him to passion. It was then that he wanted it most. It was the same with Della. She wanted him to curse at her, say filthy words. He chuckled as he thought of how her eyes had brightened when he called her a slut. She might even enjoy being knocked about a bit. He looked down at himself and laughed out loud. He'd have to get his mind off the thought of spanking her bare little butt if he was ever going to talk to Case.

He sat down, leaned back in the chair and blew smoke rings into the air. After awhile he rolled his chair up to the desk and bellowed for Samuel to tell Case to come in.

The minute Case Malone walked through the door Adam knew he was angry. Case had been recommended to him two years ago when his foreman of fifteen years was killed by the Cheyenne. He'd often wondered why Case had come to Colorado. He was a Texan and had been a Texas Ranger for several years. He was good with the men, good with the stock, but so straitlaced he was a pain in the ass at times.

"What's happened, Case? I can tell you've got your back up about something." He motioned to a chair, but Case stood in front of the desk with his hat in his hand.

"I wanna fire four of the men."

"What for?"

"They stopped at Spurlock's place on the way back from town. They got to foolin' 'round 'n one of 'em grabbed Miss Spurlock. She screamed 'n her pa went at 'em with a sharp stick he'd been whittlin' on. Durin' the fracas he poked it in Shorty Bane's horse 'n the animal kicked him to death."

"Well, what the hell did he think he could do? He was blind as a bat," Adam said irritably.

"He was *atryin'* to protect his daughter."

"It's too bad he got himself killed, but I don't see it as any reason to fire four good men. We're short-handed as it is."

"I've told the men repeatedly to stay away from the small ranches 'n farms. They'd no business at the Spurlock's place," Case insisted.

"They didn't hurt the woman, did they?"

"No, they didn't hurt her, they only caused her pa to be killed." Case didn't even try to keep the sarcasm out of his voice. "They disobeyed orders."

"We're going to need all our hands. Tell them I'm going to knock off half a month's pay."

" 'N that's all?"

"That's all." Case spun on his heel and started for the door. "Case, we've something else to discuss."

Case turned slowly and looked at the big man puffing the cigar. "Yep," he said slowly, "I think we do."

"I suppose you've heard that a stinkin' breed shoved enough gold in the hands of that spineless agent at the Land Office and paid for the south range."

"I heard."

"I've intended to buy that range for the last couple of years. My cash money has been tied up, but I'll have enough in a month or two. We need that range. I want that redskin off that land. Understand? I've already sent word to the Land Office that the sale is not to be recorded. The Indian can pick up his money on his way out of the territory."

" 'N if'n the man insists on his right to buy government land the same as you did?"

"Then shoot the bastard or hang him. I don't care which '

"I'll not be part of runnin' a man off'n his land. I told ya that when I come here. Accept the fact he stepped in and bought it when ya didn't."

Adam got to his feet so fast it sent his chair crashing back against the wall. "Don't be giving me any of your gawddamn advice! You work for me, by Gawd! If I say for you to get rid of that red sonofabitch, you get rid of him, or else flag your weak ass off my ranch!"

"Then I'm no longer aworkin' for ya, Mr. Clayhill. I worked for the law too long to start breakin' it now. I'll be off'n yore land by sunup." Case walked rapidly to the door, then angrily threw back the drapes and passed through.

"Don't you turn your back on me, gawddamn you! I've paid you good wages. You walk out on me and you'll wish to Gawd you'd kept your mouth shut and followed orders. I'll blacken your name so you'll never get another job in this territory or any other." Adam followed Case down the hall to the door. "My say carries weight with the Cattlemen's Association," he threatened.

Case turned with his hand on the knob of the door. "Do as ya please. I'd not work another day for a sonofabitch like ya if'n I was starvin' to death."

"There's plenty of men to fill your job," Adam yelled as Case yanked open the door and stepped out on the veranda. "You watch your back, you sanctimonious blister. You Texans think you're so gawddamn special, but you're nothing but a bunch of spineless pricks!"

Case wheeled and his gun leaped into his hand so fast Adam never saw the move. "Ya watch yore *mouth*, Clayhill, or ya'll find yoreself aclawin' sky." He spoke in the same unruffled voice, but every word struck the astonished Adam like ice. Case had moved in an easy, uncoiling motion. He stood in a half-crouch, his eyes pinpointed on Adam's, his face expressionless, his eyes cold.

Instinctively, Adam knew he faced a killer. Case would shoot him where he stood. It was a side of the man he'd not seen before. Case Malone was a gunslinger, there was no doubt about that. He backed slowly into the hall and slammed the door shut.

"Della!" he roared. "Della!"

Chapter Six

Logan sat up on the side of the bed and reached for his buckskin breeches. The roosters in Mrs. Gregg's barnyard had started their morning chorus an hour earlier. Now, he could hear someone stirring in the kitchen. He had to clench his teeth to keep from groaning as he stood to pull up his pants and fasten his belt. His body was a mass of welts and bruises. The skin on the side of his face, where Shorty had struck him with the coiled rope, was as raw as a piece of fresh meat, bruised and swollen. He put his hand up to touch it and winced. He finished dressing, picked up his hat, his saddlebags, and left the room.

At the bottom of the stairs he followed the noise of ashes being shaken down from the grate in the cookstove until he reached the kitchen door. A lamp sat in the center of a cloth covered table and a woman stood at the stove.

"Ma'am..."

"Oh, my Gawd!" Frightened, she whirled to face him. "It's you! You just about scared the wind 'n water outta me!"

"I'm sorry. I want to speak with Mrs. Gregg before I go. Do you mind if I wait here until she comes down?"

"You're in no shape to be out of bed, much less tryin' to fend for yourself on the trail. Mary'll tell you that." She pulled a chair out from the table. "Sit down. Coffee will be ready in a minute and meat and eggs a minute after that. Josh is doing chores. He'll be in by the time it's ready." She was a plump, pleasant-faced woman with dark brown hair streaked with gray.

"Thank you, ma'am."

"I'll swear to goodness you're the most polite feller we've had here in a coon's age." She set a loaf of bread and a board on the table and placed a knife beside it. "Cut yourself off a slab of that bread and tell me if it isn't the best you ever ate. Mary is the breadmaker around here. None of us can top her and we've about quit tryin'."

Logan tried to smile, but the swollen part of his face wouldn't allow it. He sliced the bread and smeared it generously with butter. The butter brought his thoughts back to Rosalee.

"I heard snatches of talk last night, Mrs. Hamilton. I heard someone say something about Mr. Spurlock being killed."

Meta Hamilton shook her head. "Some of the loudmouths that come in here think they're still herdin' cows. I'll swear. Mary told them to tone it down." She removed a round lid on the stove with the poker and set the coffeepot down in the hole. "Mr. Spurlock was blind, poor man. Seems like some Clayhill riders stopped by the house and was ateasin' his daughter. Mr. Spurlock heard her cry out and tried to get to her." Meta went to the pantry and returned with a slab of bacon. "Well, anyway, he had a sharp stick and he poked it in one of the horses and it kicked him to death. Now, isn't that awful? Those Clayhill riders are gettin' bolder and bolder. They think they can do about as they please, 'cause there's no law here to speak of. The bunch that stopped at the Spurlocks' won't be comin' 'round here any more. Mary knows who they are and she'll put the cabosh on that."

"Did they mistreat Miss Spurlock?" Logan's dark face showed no emotion at all and he used the same courteous voice, but his insides were convulsing with anger.

"Not that I heard of. Of course, it was a Clayhill drover telling it. He said they were just funnin' with her and she got scared and screamed." Meta turned the meat that was beginning to sizzle in the big iron spider.

"And when did this happen?"

"They were telling it last night, so it must of happened the day before that. Do you suppose it was the same bunch that jumped you?"

"I'll know after I talk to Miss Spurlock." Logan's stomach had been growling as he came down the stairs. Now, his appetite had almost left him.

"Logan! What are you doing out of bed?" Mary's voice came from behind him and he got painfully to his feet.

"Mornin'. I'll be leaving, but I wanted to speak with you and thank you."

"You're welcome to stay."

"I appreciate it. But I left a mare and a foal with the Spurlocks, and I think I'd better get on out there and see about them."

Mary sat down at the table. Her dress was fresh, her face newly scrubbed and powdered. Her soft, brown hair was neatly piled high on her head. "Did Meta tell you what happened at the Spurlocks?"

"She told me."

"I'd like to ride out there with you and pay my condolences to the family."

"You're welcome, ma'am. But it may not be safe."

Mary laughed softly. "I'll be safe, Logan. Being in the

business I'm in assures that. Drovers, drifters, and even out-laws don't want anything to happen to this place. The only trouble would be with the renegade Indians and they only attack at night." She looked into his eyes, her smile both mischievous and knowing.

In spite of his anger, anxiety, and swollen face, Logan returned her smile. "How many renegade breeds have you met, ma'am?"

She looked at him, her eyes twinkling. "How many ren-egade madams have you met, Mr. Horn?" The question brought a dark flush to his face and she burst out laughing. "Don't answer, Logan. I *am* a madam and my social status in this town equals yours. We'll have a few good friends, but the majority will look down their noses at us."

Logan held his coffee cup in his two hands and stared unseeingly at the cuts on his hands and wrist. After awhile he spoke in a thoughtful, careful way.

"I've been thinking, ma'am. I need a safe place to leave some papers." He looked inquiringly from Mary to Meta.

"You can speak freely in front of Meta and Josh. They're my family. We look out for one another." Meta came with the coffeepot and filled their cups and Mary smiled at her fondly. "I'd never have made it without them."

"Josh and I feel the same. It's like she was our own daugh-ter."

"Daughter?" Mary laughed. "Meta! We're the same age."

"That makes no never mind. How many eggs, Logan? Josh eats three."

"That will be fine," Logan said and lifted his coffee cup to his lips. It was difficult for him to sip the coffee and the cup felt as if it weighed a ton. "I was thinking, ma'am, about the deed to my land and the receipt for the money I paid. The agent will hold off sending the gold and the notice of the sale to Denver until he hears from Clayhill. Until the sale is recorded I'll have no legal claim if I can't produce the papers."

"Adam Clayhill will do everything in his power to run you off that land. If you don't leave, he'll try to kill you. Oh, he won't do the job himself. That isn't Adam Clayhill's way. He'll hire it done."

"I'm going no place at all. I own the deed to that land and I'm staying."

"That brings up something else. There's bound to be a good deal of speculating about where you got the money to buy up a large chunk of the territory. Folks around here don't have much cash money. They'll be curious and . . . suspicious."

"I figure they'd think I stole it. Fact is, I inherited it from my uncle. He owned a fur trading business and several large barges that took trade goods from Saint Louis to New Orleans. He also owned the boats that took the trade goods to the eastern ports. When he knew he was dying, he liquidated his assets because he knew I had no interest in the business. He left his money to me and advised me to invest in land and cattle."

"Why did you come here? Why not Texas, Arizona or the Wyoming Territory?"

"I was born here. My mother was here."

Mary put a generous amount of cream in her coffee and stirred it thoughtfully. "You mentioned your missing money belt that first night. I have one that belonged to my husband. You're welcome to it."

A glint of amusement showed in Logan's gaze. "That was a hunch that paid off. I left one coin in the belt they took off me." He looked down at his cup and when he looked up his eyes studied her gravely. "I'll not forget what you've done for me, ma'am."

"You owe me nothing, Logan. I was on my way to town."

She reached across the table and touched his hand. "I have an iron safe here. I'd be glad to keep your papers."

"I'd be obliged. I was going to ask you that and if you'd keep my gold, too. It's the money for my herd. I have stock certificates and money in an eastern bank, but if a cattleman is going to sell he'd want cash money."

"I'd be glad to keep it for you, Logan. Of course, there's no guarantee it will be here when you come for it. But if your money is stolen they'll take mine, too."

"Then we'll cry about it together," he said and pushed his plate back.

"You didn't eat your meat," Meta scolded.

"I hardly ever leave anything on my plate, ma'am. But I'm having a hard time chewing right now." He stroked the side of his face. "I came pretty near to getting a broken jaw."

"There's no big hurry for you to leave, Logan." Mary pushed back her chair and stood up.

"I thank you. And I want to pay for my bed and board." He stood and reached for his saddlebags that hung on the rack beside the door. He stood still for a moment as the room swayed, then righted itself.

Mary took in Logan's drawn expression and the way he held onto the back of the chair. "Are you sure you're all right?"

He nodded. "I'm right enough."

"If you insist on going, I'll drive you in the buggy and Josh will drive your team."

"I must go." He placed several gold coins on the table. "The gold is very little for what you did for me, ma'am."

"I didn't do it for money. Put the coins back in your poke and I'll put it in the safe along with your deed and bill of sale," Mary said in a no-nonsense voice. She took the poke and the papers from his hand, slipped the coins inside, and left the room.

"Josh is usually in by now." Meta turned worried eyes to the door. "What'a you suppose is keeping him?" The door opened and a stocky man with gigantic shoulders and iron-gray hair came in. "There you are, sugar," Meta said. "Give me that milk bucket and wash up. It's a good thing I didn't start your eggs. Guess you know this is Logan. You almost broke your back agettin' him up the stairs."

Logan looked at Josh but made no move toward him. It had become habit with Logan since he'd been in the West to wait before extending a hand lest he be rebuffed. Josh's face broke into a lopsided grin and he stepped forward, his hand outstretched.

"Howdy. I didn't think you'd make it to yore feet fer a week. Ya was shore stove up."

"I'm sure obliged to you. I was wondering how the women got me up the stairs. Now I know."

"Mary pressed one of the . . . ah, visitors into helpin'," Josh said with a broad grin. "I didn't do it by myself."

"How come you're late, sugar?"

Josh put his arm about his wife and patted her bottom. They were both short and square and about the same height.

"There was a wolf hangin' 'round the barn this mornin'. I first spotted 'im by the corral. He slunk off, 'n after milkin' I saw 'im again. I got my gun 'n looked for 'im, but never got a sight on 'im."

"Well, my, my! Do you think he's after a calf?"

"He looked pretty gaunt, but I reckon he could drag down a calf."

Logan put on his hat. "Thanks for the breakfast. I think I'll go on out and try to get limbered up a bit."

"Go easy, now," Meta called. "Josh'll come help with the team when it comes time to hitch up."

Logan walked away from the house. The morning air felt good on his hot face, but didn't do much to clear the buzzing in his head. He looked around to get his bearings, then moved toward the corral, not daring to hope the wolf Josh talked about was Brutus. He'd not had another glimpse of the wolf dog after he'd seen him drop in his tracks ahead of the team. Mercury's shrill whinny broke the morning stillness and he waited impatiently for Logan to reach the pole fence.

"It's good to see you, too, man. We came through this better than I thought we would." He rubbed the nose of the big Appaloosa affectionately. "Have you seen anything of the boy? I figure if he's alive he'd follow your scent."

Logan went to the end of the corral and whistled two short blasts. His eyes anxiously scanned the brush on the hillside. He whistled again and waited. Almost immediately he heard a faint whine from a pile of straw inside the corral, and Brutus, moving slowly, came toward him.

"Christ! Am I glad to see you!" Painfully, Logan got down on one knee. The dog lowered his body to the ground and crawled to him. The top of his head was encrusted with dried blood. "You got creased a good one, didn't you, boy? I'll bet you've had the granddaddy of all headaches. I've had a few aches, myself. But the three of us are back together now, and we'll go on out and get the girls. Our time will come. We'll get a chance at the bastards who did this to us." He stroked the underside of the dog's jaw while he talked and Brutus whimpered and licked his hand.

When Josh brought out the team to hitch them to the wagon, Logan was there to help. At times the pain in his side took his breath away and he would have to pause and lean against the side of the wagon. Josh watched him and saw his pain, but didn't say anything. He decided the man had a stubborn streak a yard wide and it would get him killed, sure as shootin'. For a lone man to try to hold thirty thousand acres of land when a big gun like Adam Clayhill wanted it was pure tomfoolery. Any number of men would shoot him in the back for a hundred dollars. Josh admired his courage, but still thought he was a fool.

Logan sat on a stump, Brutus at his feet, and watched Josh hitch a pair of matched bays to a light buggy. He was hot, his head felt as if someone was pounding on it with a hammer, and he ached from the top of his skull to the tips of his toes. Through the haze of pain one thought persisted. He wanted to get out to the Spurlocks and see Rosalee again. Just remembering her gentle features and quiet serenity gave an uplift to his spirits. He had reached out for someone through the lonely emptiness of his life the night he knocked on her door, and she had welcomed him. He had shared more of himself with her during the few hours they spent together than with anyone else before. Now she would be grieving for her pa. He wanted to see her, be with her, and comfort her as she had comforted him.

Mary came out of the house with a large-brimmed hat on her head and a cloth-covered basket in her arms. She set it in the back of the buggy and made room for another that Meta carried.

"I've brought food for a noon meal," she announced.

"In that case you'd better be hungry," Meta said. "She's got enough there to feed ten men and two mules!"

Mary's quick laugh rang out with throaty vibrancy. "You ride with me, Logan. This buggy's an easier ride than the wagon."

"My dog won't be able to make it unless I can figure a way to get him in the back of the wagon. I tried, but I'm not up to liftin' him."

"I can do it," Josh said, and made a move toward Brutus. The dog backed away and bared his teeth.

"Don't touch him," Logan said quickly. "He's touchy, especially now, when he's hurtin'. I think, maybe, he could walk up a plank if we let the tailgate down." He lowered the end of the wagon and Josh carried a plank from the barn. Logan led Mercury to the end of the wagon and tied him. "Come on, boy. Come up here and stay by the man." Slowly and painfully Brutus obeyed. Logan made a place for him to lie on top of the sacks of grain and the dog settled down, but watched every move he made. Logan stroked his jaw. "I know it goes against the grain to ride, but you can do it this time. Rest and you'll be all right in a day or two," he murmured. "The man'll be right here with you."

It took almost every ounce of Logan's strength to get in the buggy. He offered to take the reins, but Mary already had them clasped firmly in her gloved hands; she knew how to handle the team and loved to drive.

"It's a beautiful morning," she said, then lapsed into silence.

Logan sat upright, or leaned forward with his elbow resting on his thigh. He couldn't decide which hurt most: his back, his ribs, his buttocks, his jaw, or his head. By the time they were halfway to the Spurlocks' he was almost out of his head with fever and fervently wishing he was anywhere except where he was.

Mary glanced at Logan from time to time. His face was ashen and she knew he was suffering excruciating pain. His nostrils flared and he closed his eyes against the torment. She didn't bother him with conversation, but concentrated instead on keeping the bays in a smooth trot, and soon they were a good mile ahead of Josh and the plodding team.

Rosalee came to the door to throw out a dishpan full of water and saw the buggy coming. It was Mary Gregg. Somehow she knew she would come as soon as word of her father's death reached her. Rosalee was aware that Mary ran the local brothel, a fact she had kept from their father. The news had been whispered to her by one of the town's matrons after she and Mary had talked in the mercantile. A week later, Mary drove out to the ranch, and before she got out of the buggy she asked Rosalee if she knew who she was. Rosalee had nodded and said, "Come in and try a slice of honey cake." They had been good friends ever since. Odell adored Mary, and Mary always remembered to bring her a treat when she came and spent some time talking just to her.

Rosalee wiped her hands on her apron, smoothed her hair with her palms, and swiftly whipped off her apron to turn the clean side out. She stood in the yard beside the door and waited. There was someone with Mary, but it didn't look like Josh. Then the realization hit her that it was Logan in the buggy beside Mary. She felt her face grow hot and her heart thumped painfully.

Mary pulled the bays to a slow walk to calm them down before she brought them to a halt. Logan swayed dizzily on the seat beside her. Only sheer willpower kept him erect in the seat. Rosalee moved away from the house, her eyes going from Logan to Mary.

Logan looked at her with fever-dulled eyes. Her face blurred, came into focus, then blurred again. "Rosalee, I . . . came back," he murmured.

"He's been hurt," Mary said. "I was afraid he'd faint before we got here."

"How bad?" Rosalee tried to speak casually, trying to deny with her tone how shaken she was.

"He was beaten—cruelly! Now all of a sudden fever has set in. He's burning up. Stubborn mule! He was determined to come out here."

Logan's unblinking eyes remained on Rosalee's face. She stood beside the buggy, her hand on the side of the seat.

"I was afraid . . . they'd killed you." She almost choked on the words.

"They almost did!" Mary was beside her. "I don't know

if he can get out of the buggy. We'll have to wait for Josh. He's driving Logan's team."

It hadn't even occurred to Rosalee to wonder how Logan came to be with Mary. It was enough that he was here. She looked back down the trail. The wagon wasn't in sight yet, and even Ben wasn't here to help. He had just left to check on their small herd.

"Logan, listen to me . . . Do you think you can get down if I help you?" His hand lay on his knee. She covered it with hers without thinking about it.

He turned his hand over and clasped hers so tightly she almost winced. "Just . . . help me."

"I will. I'm strong, Logan. Put both your feet over the side." She kept her eyes on his face and saw the pain when he moved. "Slide off the seat and lean on me."

"I'll . . . hurt you."

"No. I'm afraid I'll hurt you."

"It's his ribs and his back," Mary said and reached up under his arm to give him support. "Try not to touch his back. Oh, I forgot his buttocks! How has he been able to sit all this time? Come on, Logan. We'll get you inside so you can lie down."

His knees buckled slightly when his feet hit the ground, but he stiffened them. "I'm sorry," he murmured.

Rosalee lifted his arm up and over her shoulder. "Lean on me and let's go." Mary went ahead of them into the cabin. "There's clean bedding on the bed, Mary. Turn back the quilt."

Logan remained erect and let Rosalee guide him. She led him to the bunk and he sank down.

"Don't lie down, Logan," Mary said. "We've got to get your shirt off so I can tend to your back. Oh, you foolish man! Why didn't you stay at my place a few more days?" Rosalee paled when she saw the bloody welts and torn skin.

"Bless his buckskin shirt," Mary murmured. "Without it his back would be ribbons."

Mary's voice reached Logan from some far distant place. He was eased down on his side and didn't recognize the grunt he heard as having come from his own throat.

"Take off his moccasins, Rosalee. We've got to get his britches off, too. His buttocks are torn up almost as bad as his back. You'll have to help me. You'd think a fallen woman would be able to manage that alone, wouldn't you?" she said without humor.

After they had stripped the dark giant of a man, they covered him with a quilt. Then Rosalee hurried to the spring for a bucket of cool water and Mary went to the buggy for her basket of supplies. Josh and the wagon were coming over the rise.

"I don't know how he managed to sit in the buggy," Mary said. She had folded the quilt back so she could apply a coat of salve to his buttocks. She covered them with a clean cloth and went to work on his back.

"He's burning up with fever," Rosalee said with a worried frown and placed a wet towel on his forehead.

"When I finish here I'll make some sage tea. That will help take down the fever. Logan, are you awake? You need to drink water or the fever will burn you up inside. Bring a dipper of water, Rosalee. Stubborn Indian," Mary fumed. "He's got to be thirsty, but he wouldn't ask for anything!"

Logan gulped the water so greedily that part of it ran down the side of his mouth. He lay back down and Rosalee put the damp towel on his face. There were a million questions floating around in her mind, but they would have to wait.

Josh's square bulk filled the doorway just as Mary finished covering Logan's back and pulled the quilt up over his shoulders.

"I figured this's why you was in such a all-fired hurry," Josh said. "He was 'bout to keel over afore we left."

"He never let on at breakfast that he wasn't doing fine. But I should've known when he didn't eat much."

"That dog of his'n won't let me near the stallion. I put the gate down 'n he jumped off the wagon, but he just sits there 'n bares his teeth."

Rosalee went to the door and looked out. "Logan probably told him to stay. Brutus," she called. "Brutus, come." The dog looked at her. "Come, Brutus. Come see for yourself that Logan is here." Slowly, the dog moved around the side of the buggy. He put his nose to the ground and sniffed, lifted his head and looked at the doorway. He came cautiously to the door, then stepped over the sill and went to the bunk. He put his nose against Logan's face and a high, keening whine came from his throat. Logan didn't move. He had fallen into a deep sleep. The dog sat down. He looked from Rosalee to Logan and back again.

"He's been hurt, too! Look at the blood on his head."

"How will we get him out of here?" Mary asked.

"I shouldn't have called him in." Rosalee took a cautious step toward the bed, expecting to hear a growl coming from the massive throat. When none came she took another. "Brutus, stay with the girls," she said firmly, remembering the orders Logan had given him the night before he left to go to town. The dog stood and looked at her. "Stay with the girls, Brutus." He went to the door, looked back at the bunk, and went out.

"Phew!" Mary gave a sigh of relief. "Who are the girls?"

Rosalee smiled. "A mare and a foal. Logan left them here in our corral."

"I'd hate to tangle with that sucker," Josh said. "And I'd hate it aplenty if'n I had to shoot him."

"Bring in the baskets, Josh. And we should get Logan's

wagon of supplies out of sight. I'd not put it past Clayhill to send someone over here to put a torch to it." Mary paused and caught her lower lip between her teeth. "Oh, Rosalee. I meant to tell you how sorry I am about your father as soon as we got here, but it didn't seem to be the right time. And then we got busy with Logan..." Her voice trailed away.

"Thank you, Mary. I understand. So much has happened in just a few days that my mind is in a total whirl."

"Where's Odell?"

"She went home with the Haywards after the burying."

"That will be good for her. She'll be with other children. Oh, here's your brother. Hello, Ben."

"Hello, Mrs. Gregg. What's going on, Rosalee? Whose wagon is that?" Ben's worried voice came from the doorway.

Rosalee placed another cloth on Logan's head. "Let's go outside and I'll tell you."

Mary and Rosalee followed Ben into the yard. A man walked a big buckskin horse around the corner of the house. For an instant Rosalee froze when she recognized the Clayhill ranch foreman. He put his hand to the brim of his hat and nodded.

"I met up with Mr. Malone down by the draw. I invited him to noon with us."

There was a long silence after Ben spoke. The man sat still in the saddle, waiting. The black hatred for everything Clayhill came rushing back to Rosalee. Clayhill men were responsible for her father's death, and she didn't doubt that they were also responsible for what had been done to Logan. She would not feed one of them in her home! She opened her mouth to say so when Mary spoke.

"Hello, Case. Going somewhere? I see you've got your bedroll and your saddlebags are full."

Rosalee realized then that his eyes had not left Mary's face since he came around the corner and saw her.

"Hello, Mary. I thought I might amble on back to Texas. There don't seem to be anything here to hold me."

Chapter
Seven

"You've got the same reason you had when you came here
two years ago, Case—your job with the mighty Mr. Clayhill," Mary said with heavy sarcasm.

"I don't have a job."

"You quit? Now, why did you go and do a thing like that?"

"We had a difference of opinion." His drawling response
came to her like a soothing hand and she hid her relief with
light banter.

"Well! It's about time, Case Malone!"

Rosalee didn't understand why Mary was so agitated. Her
cheeks were flushed and she held her chin at a defiant angle
as if she were defending herself. Case leaned casually on the
pommel of his saddle and watched her without a flicker of
impatience on his face or in his voice.

"I'm right sorry about what happened to your pa, ma'am,"
he said to Rosalee.

She nodded with polite coolness, but didn't speak.

"Get down, Mr. Malone." Ben broke the silence that followed and darted an angry look at his sister for not extending the invitation. "Get down and make yourself to home."

"You're welcome, Mr. Malone," Rosalee said reluctantly. She had to back Ben's invitation, although she desperately wished the man would ride on. He had surely seen Logan's horses in the corral and he would know the team and wagon didn't belong to them. Their wagon was behind the house.

"Thank you, ma'am. I'd like a drink of water if it's not a bother."

"And while you're about it, Case, you might want to see some of Clayhill's handiwork," Mary said and led the way into the house.

Rosalee groaned inwardly. What in the world was Mary thinking of? She walked stiffly into the house and went to stand at the head of the bunk where Logan lay.

Ben and Case Malone came into the cabin and Ben, anxious to make him feel welcome, motioned him toward the waterpail and the dipper that hung on the wall.

Case drank thirstily, then hung the empty dipper on the nail. "That was mighty good. Thank you."

"Come take a look at Logan Horn, Case. I'm sure you've heard about the *savage* who had the unmitigated gall to buy land Clayhill has been using all these years. It took no less than four Clayhill riders to do this to him. If Josh and I hadn't come along, Shorty Banes and the riffraff that rides with him would have beaten him to death. That's not all; beating him senseless wasn't enough! They had pulled down his britches and exposed his privates. We got there just in time to prevent them from castrating him."

The breath Rosalee took into her lungs was sharp and quick. She held it for a long time and it finally came out in small puffs. Her face was the picture of flagrant outrage, her beauty highlighted by the high color in her cheeks and the sparkle of unshed tears in her eyes.

"The sons of bitches!" Case looked down at the man on the bed and cursed.

"It was Shorty Banes. That pie-eye of his has been tied to my hitching rail so many times I'd recognize it a mile away. They stole Logan's money belt when they saw us coming and took off like they were shot out of a cannon. You see, Case, everyone wants to stay on the good side of the woman who runs the whorehouse, even scum like Shorty Banes."

"Gawddamnit, Mary! Hush up talkin' like that!"

"It's true, Case."

"You don't have to put words to it!"

"Mary doesn't have to mince words around me, Mr. Malone. I've known from the first what goes on in the house between here and town." Rosalee darted a warning look at Ben to keep quiet.

Mary laughed. "It isn't your tender sensibilities that bothers Case, Rosalee. But let's forget about that for now and spread out a meal. Case, you and Ben carry the table out under the shade tree. Meta fixed up a basket and we can pretend we're on a picnic. There's no need for us to stay in here and disturb Logan. That man's been to hell and back again. He needs some peaceful sleep."

Meta had sent fresh bread and wild strawberry preserves, boiled eggs, cold, sliced ham, and fried pie made from dried peaches. Ben enjoyed the meal. Rosalee often accused him of having hollow legs when he sat down at the table. Josh and Case ate heartily, Mary ate very little, and Rosalee scarcely anything. Her mind was on Logan and her stomach was in too much of a turmoil to accept the food.

When the meal was over, Mary lingered at the table to talk to Case and Ben took Josh to where Grace, their old cow, was staked out to feed. The cow had been limping for the last few days and Ben wanted Josh to look at her foot.

Rosalee excused herself and went into the cabin. She was grateful for this time alone with Logan. His forehead was still hot and he moved restlessly on the bunk. She dipped a cloth in a pan of cool water and bathed his hot face. He had pushed the quilt down to his waist. The golden tone of his arms, chest and ribs were marred with large purple bruises and raised red welts. Her heart gave a painful twist when she looked closely at the raw, swollen side of his face. For a moment she wanted to cry. Instead she blinked furiously so she could study his face while there was no one around.

It was the same face she remembered—well shaped, the chin stubborn, the jawline obstinate. A stubble of beard covered his cheeks. Dark, straight brows over wide-set eyes looked as if they had been painted there with a paintbrush. She wished she was bold enough to trace their line with her fingertip. She held the wet cloth to his puffed, skinned cheekbone. "Oh, Logan," she breathed. "Your poor face!"

Heavy lashes lifted and she was looking into his eyes as dark as midnight almost as soon as the words left her mouth. Their faces were a mere foot apart. "Rosalee . . . Rosalee . . ." Her name came from his lips on the fragment of a breath.

"I didn't mean to wake you."

"You didn't."

"Are you thirsty?"

"I feel like I could drink the spring dry."

Rosalee brought the dipper rimming full of water. He raised up on an elbow and she held it to his lips while he drank. When he finished it his head sank wearily to the pillow. He caught her hand before she could move away.

"I'll get more water—"

"Don't go."

She sat down on the bench.

His lips moved and she had to lean close to hear what he was saying. "Stay with me . . . for awhile."

Rosalee swallowed hard. He was holding her with his dark, feverish eyes. A flush tinged her cheeks.

"Are you feeling any better?"

"I think so. I'm sorry to come in on you like this. And I'm sorry about your pa."

She nodded and looked away from him, then back. "Mary is still here. She's going to make sage tea to help break your fever," she said for the want of something to say. He didn't say anything, just watched her with those great dark eyes. "You're going to be all right. You'll stay here with me and Ben until you're well again."

"I shouldn't be here. I'll bring my trouble down on you." His hand squeezed hers hard. "But I wanted to come . . . wanted to see you again."

"I'm glad you came back," Rosalee whispered shakily. "I wanted to see you. I was worried about you." Their eyes were locked, establishing a communication that didn't need words. They shared their desire to be together again naturally, with no awkwardness between them.

Fathomless eyes looked into blue-green ones for a long time while his thumb absently stroked the back of her hand. Logan's gaze moved over her calm, composed features to the dedicated arched brows and hair the color of a young fawn. It was pulled straight back from her forehead, gathered at the nape of her neck and braided in a long loose braid that hung over her left shoulder and down over her breast. He gazed at her face as if to etch it in his memory, then wearily closed his eyes. "You're so . . . peaceful."

Rosalee felt the tears welling in her eyes again. She placed her other hand over the hand holding hers and gently stroked the skinned knuckles. His hand was long and slender and the forefinger on his left hand turned toward his thumb at the first joint. She wondered if it had been broken and healed stiffly, but no, he flexed the joint when he curled his fingers around hers.

She raised her eyes to his face and saw that he was watching her again through half-closed lids. She looked back at him, her gaze unwavering. Rosalee was suffused with the warm glow of happiness; content beyond measure to be with him, holding onto his hand, taking care of him. It seemed to her that she had lived all her life just to reach this point in time.

"I'll leave . . . come dark."

She shook her head. "You'll stay here until you're well."

"They'll come looking for me. I don't want to meet up with them here. You and the little girl—"

"My sister went home with the Haywards, our neighbors to the east. Where will you go, Logan? How can you hope to hold that land by yourself?"

"I have men coming—good friends who don't think of me as anything other than a man. We'll hold the land. I'm going to make them my partners, help them get a start so they can bring out their families. Clayhill won't run us off."

"But they'll kill you before your men get here!" Rosalee cried in a distressed voice.

"Don't worry, little Rose. There's a maze of canyons on my land. Although I wasn't raised an Indian, I have all the survival instincts of one. They'll not find me until I'm ready to be found." His eyes closed. "I'll rest here awhile, then I'll go."

"You'll not leave here until you're fit," Rosalee said staunchly. "If the Clayhills come they'll face three guns instead of one. I can shoot and so can Ben."

His eyes opened and he looked into hers with something like amazement in their depths. When he spoke it was slowly and carefully. "You'd do that for . . . me?"

"Of course," she whispered fervently. "Wouldn't you do it for me?"

The sound of Mary's voice reached her from the doorway. "Rosalee . . ."

She stood and Logan dropped her hand. "Try to go to sleep," she murmured to him. "I'll be back." She could feel his eyes on her. At the door she looked back and they were closed.

"Riders coming," Mary said urgently as soon as she stepped outside the door. "The old bastard himself is leading the pack."

Rosalee reached inside for the loaded rifle that stood beside the door since the day her father was killed. "Logan will try to get up," she said anxiously. "He won't let us face them alone. What'll we do?"

"We're not alone. We've got Josh and . . . Case."

There was a proud tone to Mary's voice and Rosalee turned her gaze from the approaching riders to look at her. Her eyes were on Case. He stood with his back against the side of the house, one leg bent at the knee, the bottom of his booted foot flat against the wall. He lounged there casually, his hat pulled low over eyes that were focused on the riders, twirling a twig between his fingers as if he hadn't a care in the world.

Rosalee darted another glance at Mary. "I'd not count on him," she said briskly.

The sight of the big, white-haired man sitting majestically on the rapidly approaching white horse sent a floodtide of anger through Rosalee. Her hate for this man who controlled so many lives in this valley was powerful and frightening. It bubbled up from her toes, flooding each vein with unrestrainable force. All the pent-up fury she had pushed back since her father's death broke loose as she moved to the middle of the yard and lifted the rifle to her shoulder.

She stood waiting, a slender girl in a faded blue dress

The breeze was behind her, pushing her skirt against the backs of her legs and lifting strands of hair from the top of her head to swirl around her face.

"Stop right there!" she shouted before they reached the house yard.

She scanned the faces of the six men who pulled their horses to a halt behind Adam Clayhill. Shorty Banes and Shatto were not among them, but the two young drovers that had accompanied them the night they caused her father's death were there.

"You're not welcome here," she called in a voice made shaky by her anger. "Get off our land."

Several of the men hooted with laughter. "Feisty, ain't she?" The man who spoke spit a stream of yellow tobacco juice in her direction.

Ben moved up alongside of her, lending her his support. She was never more proud of him.

"Now see here. I don't want any trouble with you," Adam bellowed. "I came by to tell you I'm sorry about your pa."

"You're so sorry you've still got the men who caused his death working for you. I'd say you're the one whose *sorry*," Rosalee said bitterly.

"You watch your mouth, girl. I let you stay here because I felt sorry for you. I should have known better." He took his agitation out on his horse and yanked on the reins. His mount danced halfway around and back again.

"You've *let* us stay here?" Rosalee said in a cold, sarcastic voice. "That's very generous of you, considering we bought this land from the government and our deed is recorded in Denver."

"I was the first white man to come to this valley and I stamped it as mine. I drove off the stinkin' redskins and I drove off the riffraff, the scum who follow the trailblazers to a new land and feed on the strong." He lifted his fist and shook it toward the western range. "I'm not backin' up a foot, hear! I never would have let you settle in here, but your pa told me he'd be blind and you'd be moving off in a year or two. I was doin' him a favor. I'll do another, now he's dead, and pay his kids twice what he paid for the land. Pack up and be off this property by sundown tomorrow."

"You'll not get this land at any price."

"She shore talks big, boss," a lanky drover said, and leered at her openly.

"Gawddamnit, girl! I'll not offer again."

Adam had been surprised to find Case Malone at the Spurlock ranch. The men told him he had left the bunkhouse at first light and he had expected him to be in Junction City by now. His eyes flicked to his horse, the bedroll behind the saddle, and the bulging saddlebags. From the looks of the table in the yard, the local *madam* had brought food to the bereaved family and Malone had been invited to stay. He'd seen her slink inside the cabin as they rode up. The bitch didn't have the guts to face him! When he finished with the Indian he'd run her out of the country, too. He should have done it long ago.

Adam decided the girl was all bluff and that Malone had no interest in this. He might be a sanctimonious bastard, a drifter and a gunslinger, he reasoned, but he'd stayed alive for a long while by using common sense. He was smart enough to know when the cards were stacked against him. Adam wasn't quite sure about the mule skinner who worked at the whorehouse, but if he had any brains at all he'd not go against seven men. Adam calculated the risk, kicked his horse, and moved in.

"Stay back!" Rosalee said sharply. When Adam continued to walk his horse toward her she aimed the rifle between the front legs of his mount and fired. The impact of the bullet hitting the ground sent sharp, stinging clods of dirt up under the horse's belly. The frightened animal reared and almost upset a startled Adam.

"I said, stay back!" The recoil, when she fired the rifle, spun Rosalee off balance for an instant, but she recovered quickly and recocked the gun.

"Damn you to hell, girl!" Adam roared after he brought his horse under control. He quieted the animal and reassessed the situation. Case Malone was standing at the end of the house. He looked relaxed and loose, as if what was going on was of no concern to him. Although his better judgment told him it was dangerous to goad the man, Adam's pride compelled to do so. "What are you doing here, Malone? You figure on getting a job ramroddin' this outfit?"

"Maybe," Case said evenly.

The Clayhill men laughed loud and long. Most of them were glad to see the last of Case Malone. He'd driven them hard, been relentless in seeing to it they put in a day's work for a day's pay. He allowed no abuse of any animal and was intolerant of mistakes. For awhile he'd had the full backing of the old man, but gradually Clayhill had seen the light and suddenly Case was gone. Several of the men sitting their horses behind Adam had given more than one thought to putting a bullet right between Case's shoulder blades.

Pete, the young drover who had been at the house with Shorty Banes the night Rosalee's father was killed, moved his mount close to Adam's and they talked in low tones. Adam jerked his mount around and moved him to the side so he could see the corral.

Rosalee took a long, slow breath to steady herself. The drover had spotted Logan's horse!

"Who does that Appaloosa belong to, girl?" Adam demanded.

"That's none of your business." Rosalee spoke in a low, controlled voice, but every word came out sharp as a dagger.

"Are you hiding that half-breed? Is he holed up in there?" he demanded.

"That, too, is none of your damned business!"

"Gawddamn you to hell! You're going too far! If that buck's in there, I want him! Hear!" he shouted and almost strangled on his anger. His face turned a deep, dark purple-red and for an endless moment he stared at the cold-eyed girl, aware, for the first time, of the lethal hatred in her face.

A bushy-faced man spurred his horse up beside Adam's. "We can get 'im outta thar, Mr. Clayhill, if'n ya jest say the word," he said eagerly.

"You just try it, and Clayhill dies!" Rosalee centered the rifle on Adam's chest.

Mary's voice cut into the tension between them. "And I'll send a few of you to hell right along with him."

Adam looked past Rosalee to where Mary stood in the doorway of the cabin with an old buffalo gun raised to her shoulder.

"Stay out of this!" he said roughly. "You've got no business butting in."

Case was in the range of his vision. He was still standing beside the house, twirling a twig in his fingers. The mule skinner had lifted a rifle from the buggy. He stood with his finger on the trigger and the barrel pointed to the ground, but Adam knew it could be raised in a split second.

Adam's cold, blue eyes swung back and bored into Rosalee's. She met them unflinchingly. "You'll regret this," he snarled. "You'll not always be backed by a whore with a buffalo gun. You tell that breed he'll wish to hell he'd died in a tepee before I get through with him."

"Ya better watch who you're acallin' a whore, Clayhill." Case's soft slurry voice had steel in it. "Put that name to her again 'n I'll kill ya."

Adam was startled, but to cover it he laughed nastily. "Well

what do you know. So that's the way the wind blows."
His eyes roamed over Mary, then looked back at Rosalee with
the same chilling contempt. His lips beneath the white mustache twisted in a sneer. The knowledge that there was nothing
he could do at the moment but back off was a corrosive acid
inside him. The only weapon he had was insults, and he
brought one up out of the acid pit inside him and spewed his
venom at Rosalee. "Do you want to be fucked so bad you'll
let an Indian buck straddle you? There's nothing lower than
a white woman who'd get on her back for a piece of red ass.
You should have let my boys know when you were in heat.
They'd have been glad to service you." His cold, steel blue
eyes bored into hers, then suddenly he laughed. "This ought
to make for some pretty good talk in town, huh boys?" He
wheeled his horse, and then wheeled back. "Tell that Indian
bastard to haul his red ass out of here while he's still got an
ass to haul. As for you, split-tail . . . you'd better pack up and
get. I'll be back to burn the Indian stink out of this place!"
He spurred his horse cruelly and the animal leaped to a run.

Rosalee still held the heavy rifle to her shoulder. Every
nerve in her body urged her to tighten her trigger finger and
shoot him out of the saddle. The insults had shaken her to
the very roots, but she refused to allow his cruel words make
her kill. She looked at her brother and saw that his fists were
clenched and there were tears of frustration in his eyes.

"If I'd a had the gun, I'd a killed him."

Ben's distress calmed her. She smiled at him. "Words can't
hurt me, Ben. That was the only weapon he had left, and he
dipped down into his dirty mind to find something to try to
hurt me." She handed him the rifle. "That thing's heavy. You
hold it the next time we have callers."

"I didn't think you were ever going to speak up and say
anything, Case." Mary stood the heavy, old gun on the stock
and leaned on the barrel. "This old thing isn't even loaded

and I don't think it would fire if it was. I just snatched it off the wall."

Case laughed and shook his head with admiration. "I'd a swore you wasn't bluffing, Mary girl."

"I knew Josh's gun was loaded, and I was *sure* you'd come through in a pinch," she said with a saucy toss of her head.

"I'd a backed ya. Ya know that, but it don't pay to show yore hand till ya have to," he said quietly.

Mary looked at him for what seemed an endless moment, then turned to Rosalee. "Come on in. I've had the devil of a time keeping this *wild Indian* in the cabin. The only thing that kept him here was the fact you were right in the line of fire and would be the first to be hit if he as much as stuck his head out the door. He's been gnashing his teeth and pawing the floor."

Logan had put on his breeches. He sat on the bunk, leaning over to one side, taking as much weight off his buttocks as possible. He raked his fingers up over his forehead and through his hair in frustration. His eyes fastened on Rosalee's face with such compassion that she knew he had heard every word of Adam Clayhill's insults.

"Case, meet Logan Horn. I bet this is the first time in his life he's had to hang back and let other folk front his trouble. Logan, meet Case Malone. He was Clayhill's foreman for a year or two. He was in earlier when you were asleep." Mary made the announcement and waited.

Rosalee was grateful for Mary's chatter. She needed time to get her thoughts together. Standing just inside the door, she saw the skeptical look cross Logan's face before it closed off and became devoid of expression. He had never looked more Indian than at this moment. His features were as bland and cold as marble. He straightened his back, holding himself stiffly erect. Rosalee wondered where he got the strength. An hour ago he could scarcely hold up his head to drink. She felt his tension and waited anxiously to see how Case would react.

"Howdy," Case stepped forward and held out his hand. "It goes against the grain ta have to lay back, don't it? But I learned durin' the war pride don't keep a bullet from puttin' a hole in yore head. Don't get up." He grinned. "I've seen fellers go through a Texas tornado and come out lookin' better'n you."

Logan hesitated for only a second, then extended his hand. Rosalee could see him relax his iron control and her shoulders slumped with relief. Mary had known how Case would react! And Case Malone had endeared himself to her for life!

"Howdy. I've not been in a Texas tornado, but I've been in a Tennessee cyclone."

"Put 'em both in a poke 'n ya couldn't tell the one from the other."

"You and Mr. Malone sit down and talk to Logan, Ben. I'll get a cold jug of milk from the spring." Rosalee pushed her brother toward the men.

"Ma'am," Case said quickly. "What happened out there in the yard wasn't no play. When that old man said he'd be back he meant it. Stay near the house, near that rifle, unless yo're planning on moving out."

"We're not moving out," Rosalee retorted firmly.

"I'll get the milk, Rosalee. Mr. Malone's right. Pa was sure as shootin' we didn't have enough land for Clayhill to mess with, but seems Pa was wrong. The bastard was just bidin' his time."

Rosalee was proud of the way Ben spoke up. He had grown up a lot during the past few days. He had been her support and her comfort. She gazed at him with love in her eyes.

"That goes for you, too, son. Take the rifle when ya leave the house, 'n take yoreself a good look 'round afore ya step out the door. Keep yore eyes amovin' in a circle ahead of

ya. When ya get back we'd better have us a little talk." Every
eye in the room focused on Case. Rosalee's were wide with
surprise, Ben's serious, Logan's flat and observing, and
Mary's—she was looking at Case with her heart in her eyes.

Josh, standing in the doorway, was taking in the scene in
his own quiet way. "Case is right, Ben. Ya better get used ta
keepin' a eye peeled. Yawl jest throwed down on a full deck."

It was warm in the cabin even with the front and the back
doors open so the breeze could circulate. Rosalee insisted
that Logan lie down. He only lifted himself up to drink cup
after cup of the sage tea that Mary was sure would break his
fever. Ben and Josh carried the table back inside, and while
they were out watering the stock, Mary unpacked her gift of
food and arranged it on the shelves. Rosalee kept her ear
tuned to the conversation between Logan and Case.

"Illinois Regulars."

"Texas Volunteers."

"I run up against them once."

"Ya think Custer'll clear the plains a redskins like he claims
he will?"

"The bastard'll try."

A soft laugh. "You, too?"

"Me and half the Union Army. I'm surprised he hasn't
been shot in the back."

Rosalee and Mary exchanged smiles. "They seem to like
each other," Mary whispered.

Later, after Josh and Ben came in, Mary brought up the
subject that was foremost in their minds.

"Rosalee, you and your brother and sister can't stay out
here alone. I would take you home with me, but it wouldn't
be a proper place for you."

"Ben and I will stay here. We have no choice. Our sister
is over with the Haywoods and they will keep her until it's
safe for her to come back home. If we did accept Mr. Clay-

hill's offer to pay us twice what our pa paid for the land, we'd be no better off because there would be no other land in this valley to buy. What would we do? Where would we go?"

Josh spoke up. "It's like Case said, miss. Old Clayhill don't fool around. If'n he wants this place he'll do what it takes to get it, 'n there ain't no law to stop 'im. If'n nothin' else, he'll turn that pack a dogs loose 'n they'll be smellin' 'round here day 'n night. There ain't nobody there now ta hold 'im in line." He jerked his head toward Case. "Ya won't be able to poke yore head out the door." He looked guardedly at Mary, but her eyes were on Case.

Rosalee glanced at Logan. He had his Indian face on again, but she could see his fists clench and unclench and knew the anger that was eating him inside.

"How many acres ya got here?" Case sat with his chair tipped against the wall. The sunlight coming through the open door shone on the gray hair at his temples and the squint creases at the corners of his eyes.

"A thousand acres, is all," Ben said.

"Yore land borders this'n?" Case addressed his question to Logan.

"Partly along the western boundary, all along the southern."

"Guess ya know ya got the best grazin' in the valley," Case said with one of his rare grins.

"I figured it," Logan said. "I saw some of the stock that had been grazing on it. Why didn't Clayhill buy up the range? It would only be common sense. With more and more people moving west, how could he hope to hold it?"

"I think he was agoin' to, but he got his money tied up in fancy houses 'n trips to Europe for that girl of his. And he'd used the land for twenty years for nothin'. He figured it was his 'cause he was the first white man to ranch here.

He got a mite careless 'n you slipped in 'n laid down the gold. He kept a big thumb on that Land man. He shore thought he had the range in his pocket."

"No one stood up to him ten years ago when he cleared the valley of what he called nester trash!" Mary said quietly.

Case's eyes flicked to Mary. He took the makings for a cigarette out of his pocket and rolled it slowly, wet the paper with his tongue, and lit it. "Are ya interested in takin' on a foreman, Miss Spurlock?"

Rosalee's mind was stunned to blankness by his words. Her eyes flashed to Logan's. There was nothing in his that gave her a clue as to what he was thinking.

"You must be funning, Mr. Malone. We only have twenty head. Hardly enough for Ben to take care of."

"In another year you might run more if Logan lets you use some of his range. If I'm agoin' to be 'round here awhile, I might as well be doin' somethin'." While he spoke he was looking at Mary.

"I thought you were going back to Texas." Mary spoke casually, but Rosalee noticed a small catch in her voice.

"Yeah. I said there wasn't nothin' to hold me here, but I guess there is." He lifted his shoulders. "It's as good a place as any."

"Case Malone!" Mary exclaimed. "You said there was no place as good as Texas." She was smiling and there was a faint deepening of color at the base of her throat.

"I guess I lied 'bout that. I ain't exactly what ya'd call a saint, ya know."

A flutter of an idea crossed Rosalee's mind as her eyes went from Mary to Case. Then it struck her strongly that there was a current of understanding that flowed between them. Was Mary in love with him? She tucked the thought away in the back of her mind to bring out and examine more closely another time.

Logan raised up on an elbow. His fever was breaking and bead of sweat stood out on his forehead. "What kind of offer are you making her, Malone?"

"Well, now, let me see. There's no need of cash money changin' hands. Ben 'n me'll work the place for the time bein'. After things've toned down some, I'll bring in five hundred head and graze 'em on yore land. Yore pay will be my know-how on how to get ya set up in the ranchin' business. I take it yore short on experience and long on book learnin'. I'm the other way 'round. I figure we'd hitch together."

"We can't pay you, Mr. Malone," Rosalee said firmly. "Ben and I are lucky to graze twenty head and they stray off to the good grass."

"Ya can pay me bed 'n board, ma'am."

Logan and Case were studying each other; each, with his own thoughts, making decisions that would affect their lives for years. Case left his proposition hanging in the air and waited. Finally Logan spoke.

"You know, I've got to get the hell out of here. I can't take the Spurlocks with me and I can't fight Clayhill from here." He spoke slowly and only to Case. "You'll stay here, stand between them and Clayhill?" Case nodded. Logan leaned back and rested his head against the wall. "It's a deal, Malone. Take him on as foreman, Rosalee. And Case, when the time comes, I'll be grateful for your advice. I'll need an experienced man to show me the ropes and you can take your pay any way you want it: cash, cows, or shares in my ranch."

"Suits me fine."

"I'll put it in writing if you want."

"Handshake's good enuff for me." He let the front legs of

his chair down to the floor and unfolded his long length to get to his feet. "Ma'am, where do I throw my bedroll?"

"Hard-Case Malone! You're an . . . unpredictable man," Mary said, but she was smiling.

Chapter
Eight

Mary and Case walked away from the house while Josh hitched the bays to the buggy. Mary wore her wide-brimmed hat and stood with her back to the late afternoon sun.

"Case..." She placed her hand on his arm and he immediately covered it with his. "Why did you decide to stay and help them?"

"May be that Clayhill reminds me of a story my pa told 'bout a feller that came to Van Zandt County back in the forties. He had a mouth on 'im like Clayhill. He hogged the range 'n the water 'n tried to stomp out the homesteaders till my granddaddy got his craw full. But the time he was through with that ol' boy he'd pulled in his horns and hightailed it out of the country. Guess I'm like my granddaddy. I got a craw full of Clayhill."

"He'll not pull in his horns until he's dead! I told you what he was like when you first came here. It sure took you long enough to see that I was right."

"I knew ya was right all along, Mary honey. He just hadn't done nothin' up to now, 'n it was a job."

"You don't need a job, Case. Damnit! You and Hank have just as much land as Clayhill. Go home before you get yourself killed!"

"I come for ya, Mary. I'll not go home without ya."

Mary looked up into his quiet face. There was no mistaking the love that shone from his eyes.

"We've gone over this a hundred times. I'll never go back to Texas. Word of what I've become would spread like a prairie fire. I'm used to the role of the scarlet woman here, but I'd rather be dead than embarrass my family or yours."

"Then I'll just have to stay here."

"I'll not marry you, Case—ever. Go home. Find . . . someone else." She lowered her head so the brim of her hat covered her face. He lifted the floppy brim and looked into her misery-filled eyes.

"Ya might as well ask me to cut off my arm. I won't ask ya again why ya married Tom. I reckon it was 'cause I'd been gone so long and I never come right out 'n told ya my feelin' for ya."

"Tom was a good man, Case. He always treated me well."

"He didn't take care of ya like I'd've done. But that's water over the dam. If ya won't come home with me, I'll stay here with you."

"You can't stay here indefinitely. You've been gone almost two years! It isn't fair to Hank."

"Hank's runnin' things just fine."

"It isn't fair to Logan to let him count on you to help him get started," Mary argued. "It may take years for things to smooth out here. You can't stay that long. And Case . . . you could be killed! Clayhill would think no more about ordering you killed than he would smashing a bug. He's that kind of man."

"I'll be here if you are, Mary. I shoulda bought that range myself 'n brought up some Texans to hold it. I never even thought 'bout it. I had other things on my mind." His eyes roamed her face lovingly.

"I'm going to worry myself sick about you," Mary threatened in a tight voice.

A smile crinkled the lines around his eyes. "I'm right glad to hear it."

"Case! What am I going to do with you?"

"Ya can marry me. Close that house down, burn it, let Meta and Josh have it. I'll—"

Mary turned and walked rapidly toward the buggy. Case walked beside her, his hand on her elbow. He helped her up onto the seat, his eyes anxious.

"Take care of yourself, Case."

"I'll get my horse 'n ride a ways with ya."

"There's no need for that. We'll not be bothered. Clayhill is smart enough to know that he doesn't have a man who would harm me and jeopardize his visits to my house. That may not be exactly true after I post a blacklist naming Shorty Banes and company," she added dryly.

Mary saw the pain flick across Case's face before a cloak of impatience covered it, and she wished she'd had the good sense to keep her mouth shut. She could see a muscle twitch in his jaw as he ground his teeth together in frustration.

"Keep a lookout, Josh. I'll ride to the top of the bluff yonder. If I see anythin' ya ought to know, I'll fire a couple a shots." He looked at Mary with bleak eyes, squeezed the hand that lay in her lap, and stepped back. "I'll be out to see you in a few days."

The springs on the buggy yielded to Josh's weight. He flicked the backs of the bays with the reins and swung them in a wide arc around the yard and headed them toward town.

"Bye, Mary. Bye, Josh," Rosalee called from the doorway.

Ben, holding Charlie by the collar, waved.

Mary waved back, let her eyes linger for a moment on Case's face, then looked straight ahead. The team seemed to sense they were headed home and stepped lively down the trail. In half an hour they had left the hills and were on the plain. The sun was a red ball above the horizon before they spoke. It was Josh who broke the silence between them.

"That man loves ya a powerful lot."

"Don't you start in on me, Josh! I know how he feels and there's nothing I can do about it."

"You love him, don't you?"

"Of course I love him. I can't remember when I didn't love him. Our parents grew up together, we grew up together. Oh, God, Josh! I've made such a mess of my life and now I'm ruining his."

"Why didn't ya marry him in the first place?"

"Because I was sixteen and stupid. Case went back East for a year and I was lonely. I got caught in the hayloft with Tom Gregg. Nothing happened, but my parents insisted that I marry him." Mary sighed remembering her mother's anguish. She had to do the *decent* thing. She had to marry poor, spineless Tom Gregg or else be in total disgrace. "We married and came out here," Mary added slowly. "Case came home and went to war."

A lump rose up in her throat that she found difficult to swallow. She had forgiven her mother long ago for forcing her to marry a man she didn't love. But she knew in her heart that, had her mother lived, she would never have forgiven *her* for what she had become.

She listened to the jingle of the harnesses and the thump of the horses' hooves and tried to wipe out the painful memories of the past.

*   *   *

Rosalee was putting the leftovers of the noon meal on the table for supper when she heard the pounding hoofbeats of a running horse. She went to the door just as Case pulled his horse to a quick stop beside the woodpile where Ben was chopping kindling for the cookstove. He spoke to the boy, then dismounted and came to the house.

Logan, alert when he heard the horse, lay on the bunk with his eyes on the door. He raised up when Case came in.

"Can ya get on yore feet, Horn? We gotta get ya and Miss Spurlock outta here. I took a look 'round with my glass from the top of the bluff. There's a dozen men squattin' 'round a cookfire 'bout four miles off to the west. I figure it's Clayhill's bunch 'n they'll be acomin' in to get ya tonight. More'n likely they got orders to burn out this place."

"Tonight?" Rosalee's heart stumbled, then beat hard against her ribs. "He won't burn us out. That was just a threat," she scoffed weakly.

Logan sat up on the side of the bunk. "Good God almighty!"

"Miss Spurlock'll drive ya in the wagon. I know it galls ya to run, but like I said afore, pride don't shield ya when the bullets fly. There's a place south and east where ya can hole up. I don't think the Clayhills know 'bout it. Leastways it wasn't spoke of. I'll start ya off and tell ya how to get there. It'll take a couple a hours in the wagon. Ya should make it before dark. Gather up food, blankets, 'n what ya need to get Logan on his feet, ma'am. Ben's hitchin' up the wagon."

"Ben can drive the wagon. I'll stay here."

"No, ma'am. That won't do. There'll be just me astandin' between you 'n them. Men in a pack is worse'n a pack a dogs."

"But . . . Ben is just a boy." Rosalee began to fill a basket with the food Mary had brought.

"That's it. He'd be a heap safer'n you if we're caught."

"He's right, Rosalee." Logan was standing with his palms on the table to support himself. "Goddamn! I'm sorry I brought this down on you."

"It would've happened anyway. If you and Mr. Malone hadn't come Ben and I would've had to face it alone. Mr. Clayhill wants this land. He thinks if we stay others will come."

"What about the people with land toward the east?" Logan asked.

"They're over the ridge," Case said. "I doubt he'll go after farmland. It's range he wants. He's afraid it'll be taken up."

"Do you think they'll burn the house, Mr. Malone? Mama's trunk . . . Pa's wood carvings . . . Odell's . . ." Rosalee's voice trailed away. She took a short breath and turned her face away from the men so they wouldn't see the tears that sprang to her eyes.

"It's a rock house 'n the roof won't burn. It'll take 'em a spell to get it started and I won't be sittin' on my hands."

"Take Rosalee and Ben to Mrs. Gregg, Malone. I'll stay here. He wouldn't be coming here but for me!" Logan said desperately.

"With that kinda thinkin' how'd you Yankees win the war? One, even two against a dozen is more'n I want to tackle. It's no disgrace to back off and pick yore time." He picked up a pillowcase and stuffed it with the wood carvings on the mantel. "Where's yore ma's trunk?" Rosalee nodded toward the lean-to. He ducked his head beneath the low door, went inside, and came out with the trunk. He set it beside the door.

Ben drove the wagon up to the front of the house, tied the reins to the brake handle, and jumped down. Rosalee met him at the door and put her arms around him.

"I don't want to leave you here, Ben."

"Mr. Malone explained it to me. It's the only thing to do.

You go on, now. He's helpin' us the best he knows how and we do what he says. What's Mama's trunk doin' here?"

"Put it on the wagon, son, along with this bag of your Pa's birds. If the worse comes, ya'll have 'em." Case turned to Logan. He had put on his shirt and moccasins. His face was wet with weak sweat. "Ya got some good horse flesh. Will the mare 'n foal trail?"

"They'll follow the stallion. How's my dog, Ben?"

"He been in the corral all day. I took him a pan of water and part of a rabbit Charlie caught, but he wouldn't touch it until I left."

Logan walked to the door carefully, balancing himself with a hand against the wall. "I'll whistle for him or you'll not get near the horses."

Case was throwing things in the wagon. Pushing the blankets and the food under the canvas stretched across the bed. "Ben said ya got a pack in the shed. I'll get it. Ben, go hitch up yore wagon. While I'm agettin' yore sister headed out right, load up what ya can 'n light out for Mary's. If they see ya they'll think yore pullin' out like Clayhill said."

Logan whistled a couple of short blasts, and soon Brutus came around the corner of the house with Charlie bouncing around him, wanting to play. The big wolf dog ignored him. Logan leaned against the side of the wagon.

"Are you up to working, boy? You'll have to keep the girls in line, see to it they don't fall behind or stray off." Brutus whined and got down on his belly, but kept his eyes on Logan's face. The gash the bullet had laid across the top of the dog's head was clean and wet. Logan glanced at Charlie, who sat with his head cocked to one side and his tongue lolling. "He did a good job, Brutus. You're in fine shape. Given time I think you could make a man out of that kid."

Rosalee had been so busy flying around the cabin gathering up things to take with her that she hadn't had time to think.

She stood in the doorway and looked back at the home that had been hers for the past four years; the hated dirt floor, the small glass window that furnished their only daylight during the long winter months. Would she ever see it again? Mama's clock! She took it from the mantel and wrapped it in her cloak and extra dress. Odell's doll head! Where was it? She ran to the lean-to and snatched it from the shelf.

"Ma'am," Case called urgently.

Logan was on the wagon seat, sitting on a feather pillow. Rosalee had wondered how in the world he had managed to climb up there. She put her foot on a spoke in the wheel and sprang up into the wagon and sat down beside him. She crossed the long shawl around her shoulders over her breasts, tucked it beneath her thighs, and picked up the reins. Mercury was tied to the back of the wagon and the mare and colt stood nearby. Case came out of the cabin with the water bucket crammed with things from the kitchen shelves and an arm full of bedding from the lean-to. He threw them into the back of the wagon and mounted his horse.

"We're runnin' outta time, ma'am. Move out."

Rosalee looked for Ben to kiss him good-bye, but he and Charlie were not in sight. "Bye, Ben," she called. "Bye. Stay with Mary till . . . I come back." Her eyes were swimming with tears and her voice shook, but she held her chin up and sailed the whip out over the backs of the team with far more force than necessary to get them moving.

The horses strained at the harnesses, then the wagon moved to swing out and around her vegetable garden and past the low-branched oak tree Odell liked to climb. Rosalee kept her eyes straight ahead. Things near and dear to her were being torn from her grasp and there was a clammy, sick feeling in the pit of her stomach.

Case took the lead and set a fast pace. It took all of Rosalee's strength and concentration to handle the team. She turned once to look at Logan after they left the yard and veered off to the east to cut across open range to reach the edge of the timber. He was sitting on one hip, leaning heavily on the arm he had flung across the back of the wagon seat. His face muscles were taut, his eyes hooded, and his lips pressed tightly together. He flinched from the jolt as a wheel of the wagon passed over a rock. Rosalee knew he was suffering from bruised or cracked ribs as well as the open lacerations on his back and buttocks.

The land they were traveling through was lush and beautiful. On one side of them was a thick grove of stately pines and beneath their branches was an abundance of ferns and wild flowers. On the other side, the valley spread out in a sea of rich green grass that would stroke the belly of a horse as he passed through it. Rosalee could hear the plaintive call of the mourning dove and the happier sound of a bobolink. Another time, she would have enjoyed just being with Logan. Now, they followed Case silently, each wrapped in their own thoughts.

The sun had completed its journey across the sky. In the southwest a purple cloud bank appeared. A cool breeze drifted down from the mountains, rippling the long grasses and stirring the upper branches of the pines where the birds were settling for the night. Case came back to ride beside the wagon and speak with Logan.

"The canyons are ahead. Have ya been through here before?"

"No, but I knew they were there."

"'Bout a month ago I run onto some Indian houses built in the cliffs. Don't look like there's been anyone in 'em for a long time. If we get ya there ya could hold off a army with a couple of good rifles."

"My mother's people know of the place. They say the Navajos and the Utes killed the cliff dwellers over a hundred years ago. They also speak of a spring that's hot the year round. The Cheyenne think it's a sacred place and never go there."

"I hope ya don't agree with 'em, cause that's where we're agoin'. I never heard the place talked of at Clayhills, but that don't say they don't know 'bout it."

"They can track us there easy enough."

"I'm countin' on that cloud bank yonder. A good rain afore mornin' would wipe out the signs. Anyhow, I don't know of a man in that outfit that could track a herd a jackasses down a muddy road," he added dryly. "At the end of this bluff there's a boulder that sets out makin' for a passage through what appears to be solid rock unless yore up close. It's rough 'n it'll jar the hell outta ya for a ways. Go on down to the flats 'n ya'll see the cliffs off to yore left."

"I'm uneasy about Rosalee being here. She should have gone with her brother. What if I come down with more fever and can't protect her?"

Case grinned. "She don't have two left hands. Ya shoulda seen the shot she put between the legs of Clayhill's horse."

"You should've taken her to Mrs. Gregg," Logan said stiffly.

"I'd a died tryin'. But what if they'd a cut us off? If they didn't kill her while they was atryin' to kill me, they'd a done worse." Case's face took on a wintry expression.

"What you did was right, Mr. Malone." Rosalee spoke up firmly. "Don't worry about me, Logan. I never thought I could shoot at a man, but I can now if I have to."

"I'll scout 'round 'n see how things are shapin' up afore I come back," Case said. "Ben'll be all right at Mary's, ma'am, and I'll ride over to the Haywoods' 'n let 'em know what's goin' on."

"Thank you, Mr. Malone. Tell . . . Ben not to worry and tell Odell I'll come to the Haywards' as soon as I can."

"I'm obliged to you, Malone, for what you've done," Logan said sincerely.

"I took yore measure, Horn. If'n I'd a found ya lackin', I'd a had Miss Spurlock take her chances on gettin' to Mary's." Case's steely eyes bored into Logan's black ones. A silent message passed between them; one understood by both men.

Logan nodded. "As I said, I'm obliged."

"I'll try 'n make it back in a day or two." Case brought his horse to a stand to turn around. "Don't blow no head off till you see who it is." A slow smile drew little wrinkles in the corners of his eyes. He put his hand to the brim of his hat. "Ma'am," he said, and wheeled his horse. "There's a overhang down there ya can get under fer the night. Ya won't have no time to get on the cliff afore dark," he said over his shoulder and spurred his horse into a gallop.

Rosalee was overcome with sudden shyness. She was acutely aware that she and Logan were alone in this vast land, one depending on the other for survival. She tried to put aside all thoughts and concentrate on getting the wagon through the opening and down over the rocky trail to the floor of the valley. Her arms ached from pulling on the reins to keep the team from going too fast. She sensed the agony Logan was enduring. When they reached the bottom and the land leveled off she glanced back to see if the mare and the colt were still behind the wagon.

The valley had cliffs at one side and a jagged row of tree-topped hills on the other. When the cliff dwellings were visible she darted a glance at Logan. He was staring straight ahead, holding himself stiffly erect. Sweat no longer dampened his face, and she noticed a quiver in the buckskin-clad shoulders. He was getting a chill!

Rosalee snaked the whip out over the backs of the horses and urged them into a brisk trot. Darkness was approaching rapidly when she finally found the overhang Case said would shelter them for the night. Her first effort to get the wagon under the protective covering failed, and after shooting an apologetic glance at Logan, she moved it out, swung the team in a wide loop, and came in from the opposite direction. This time the back hub of the wagon wheel almost scraped the wall of the cliff. She pulled the team to a standstill and twisted the reins around the brake handle.

"I have to unhitch the team before dark, Logan," she said gently. "Are you all right?"

He nodded. "Turn Mercury loose. Brutus . . . will watch." He spoke through clenched teeth to keep them from clicking together.

Rosalee leaned over the seat, reached under the canvas for a blanket, and wrapped it around his shoulders. "I'll fix you a place to lie down as soon as I can."

It was almost dark by the time she had the team staked out for the night. When she returned to the wagon, Logan was lying on the ground wrapped in the blanket she'd put around him. As she pulled the cornhusk mattress out of the wagon she silently blessed Case for thinking about it. Working swiftly, she made a bed between the wagon and the rock wall. The constant flutters of lightning that worried the sky in the southwest told her it would rain before too many hours passed.

Rosalee knelt down beside Logan. He was lying on his side with his head on his bent arm. "I've made a bed behind the wagon, Logan. Come and lie down on the mattress and I'll get more blankets."

He stirred and pushed himself to a sitting position, then rolled over on his knees and got to his feet, leaving the blanket on the ground. He braced himself against the side of the wagon.

"I'm sorry . . . Rosalee."

"Come lie down," she urged.

"The horses?"

"The mare and the foal are with Mercury. I told Brutus to stay with the girls and he went with them. I'm surprised that he obeys me."

"It's instinct. Wolves are family oriented. To him, you're my mate," he murmured.

Rosalee felt a sudden soaring sensation inside her, as if joy had come dropping down out of a cloud. It was startling, yet so suddenly wonderful she felt giddy with happiness. His mate! The words skidded to a halt in her brain and throbbed there for endless moments. To mate with a man meant the right to comfort him, to give him love, shield and protect him, take him into her body and nourish the seed he planted there.

"It's going to rain. I'll build a fire back next to the cliff after I tie the canvas over the wagon." The words came automatically when she spoke. Everyday, impersonal words that her mind conjured up to crowd out exciting, impossible thoughts.

"I'm glad the merchant put in the canvas. I'd forgotten about it." Logan, too, spoke words that were of no consequence, and not at all connected with those in his mind.

He reached for her hand and squeezed it tightly. In the back of his mind there had always been a picture of a woman who would walk beside, not behind him. The face had not been distinct, but her character had been. Now the face of this sweet woman would forever be etched in his memory, even though she'd not be the one to walk beside him. He loved her too much to subject her to the scorn of being wed to a breed.

Loved her? The realization sank into his mind like a stone. Yes, by God! He loved this white woman with all his heart!

Chapter
Nine

Logan clung weakly to the wheel of the wagon. His back felt as if it were on fire and his knees and thighs throbbed from the stomping they had taken. He was unable to draw a deep breath, and through all this, his stomach growled with hunger. He had believed he'd suffered the ultimate pain when he took a bayonet in the side during the war. That pain had been concentrated in one spot. Now, he hurt all over. Goddamn the scum who did this to him! They'd pay for it and for what they'd done to Rosalee!

"You'll not get your strength back standing there," Rosalee said firmly. "You've got to rest and eat. Tomorrow we'll make camp in the cliff house. From there we'll be able to see the whole valley. Lie down. I'll get you some food as soon as I cover the wagon."

Logan eased his aching body down onto the mattress and Rosalee covered him with a blanket. He watched her as she foraged beneath the canvas for what she wanted, piled it next to the cliff, and lashed the top securely to the wagon bed.

She worked swiftly and efficiently, with no wasted motion. He liked to watch her as she moved. Her body seemed to flow from one position to the next.

Rosalee had been careful to leave a pie-shaped space between the wagon and the cliff. Now, she hung a blanket over the wagon wheel and built a small fire in the narrow area. Logan's eyes followed her graceful movements. His admiration for her increased; not only for her beauty, but for her mind. She had planned well. The fire wouldn't be seen even if Clayhill's men did stumble into their valley. Here was the woman he'd dreamed of all his life; and now that he'd found her, he had nothing to offer her.

Rosalee nourished the small blaze until it caught and burned steadily, then set water to heat for the sage tea Mary said Logan must drink. She went to the end of the wagon and looked off toward the southwest. The lightning flashed frequently and now she could hear the faint rumbles of thunder in the distance. She prayed it would rain. Rain would make it more difficult for Clayhill's raiders to find them and might prevent them from burning her home. She closed her mind against the pain of that thought and went to hunker down beside Logan.

"Don't go to sleep, Logan. You've got to eat something."

"I'm not asleep. You must be worn out. It's been a hard day and driving that green team was no easy job. Sit down here beside me."

The light from the fire caused sinuous shadows to stir over his dark face and Rosalee could feel the movement of his eyes over her. The pitch blackness outside the small circle of light closed around them like a great dark blanket wrapping them intimately together.

"I'll get the food basket." Rosalee rose stiffly to her feet and moved toward the fire. Her body was shaking as if with a sudden chill. As she knelt before the fire to pour the sage tea into a drinking cup, her heart quickened and her legs suddenly grew weak with a trembling awareness of this man and the thought that within this small space they had made a home for the night.

When she returned to him, Logan had moved to the far edge of the mattress to make room for her. She sat down with her legs folded beneath her and delved beneath the cloth covering on the basket. She brought out a piece of meat and a biscuit, put the two together, handed them to him, then fixed one for herself. They ate in silence. When Logan finished his meat and bread she gave him another without him asking. When he leaned up on an elbow to drink she handed him the cup, then took it from his hand when he finished. She felt good watching over him, handing him his food, letting him rest. His face was relaxed and he was eating as if he were truly hungry.

Lightning forked overhead, followed by a crash of thunder. Rosalee pulled the shawl more tightly around her shoulders. The air was cold and smelled of rain. The lightning came again, followed by sharp cracks of thunder and a puff of wind that rippled the canvas on the wagon.

"We may be getting more than a rain," Rosalee murmured.

"Are you afraid of storms?"

"I didn't mind them in the stone house, except for the noise. There's nothing noisier than rain and hail on a tin roof." She smiled, remembering.

"I took shelter in a sod house in Nebraska one time during a storm. I was surprised at how quiet it was. There's a lot to be said for a good sod house."

"They'd be warm in the winter."

Rosalee sat quietly beside him, listening to the sounds of the approaching storm. After an exceptionally loud crack of thunder, she spoke again.

"On our way out here from Missouri, we came through

Nebraska and Pa spotted a black cloud with a funnel hanging down. It looked as if it was coming right at us, so he whipped up the horses and we turned down into a gulley. We got out of the wagon and lay down in a low spot. We heard a big wind pass over us. Later we saw where trees had been torn up by the roots. It scared me when I thought of what it would have done to us in the wagon."

"Why did your pa pull up stakes and come out here?"

"Oh, I guess he thought if he left the place where Mama died he'd not hurt so much. He didn't care much about anything after she died. And when he couldn't see anymore he lived in the past. Sometimes he called me Nettie—that was my mother's name. He said my voice was like hers."

"It must have been hell for him."

"It was. Mama died giving birth. Pa blamed himself. He said it was his fault. But Mama wouldn't have blamed him. She loved him too much." It didn't seem at all strange to Rosalee to be discussing this intimate subject with Logan. She reached over and pulled the blanket up over his shoulder. "Mary brought fried peach pies when she came out today. I put one back for you." She laughed. The sound was light and musical and very feminine. "Ben is at the age where he eats everything in sight."

"He's steady for a boy his age. I reckon he had to grow up in a hurry."

"He did. He's only fourteen and he's been doing a man's work for four years. He's smart, too. I taught him and Odell to read and cipher. Mama was a schoolteacher before she married Pa, but I think I told you that."

"I don't care. Tell me again. I like to hear you talk."

"I'm talking too much, is what I'm doing. You need to go to sleep. Mary said rest and sage tea would put you on your feet." She paused. "She did say for me to put more salve on your back and that you should take off that buckskin so the air could get to the sores."

"I've got a cloth shirt and pants in my pack." He threw the blanket back and started to get up.

"Is the chill gone? Did the tea warm you?" With a hand on his shoulder, Rosalee pressed him down.

"It sure did. I'm sweating, now."

Intermittent drops of rain, pushed by the wind, hit her face as she worked at the end of the wagon to get to Logan's pack. It was heavy and she was breathing hard by the time she dropped it beside the mattress. He had removed his shirt and was on his knees feeding small sticks to their dying campfire. The flames licked at the wood, caught, and flared. He turned and the light flickered on his naked back. Rosalee had to choke back words of rage when she saw his lacerated flesh. That one human being could be so cruel to another was beyond her understanding.

"I'll see about the team while you change," her whispered voice trembled.

"Don't go. It's . . . raining. I'll change pants under the blanket."

Rosalee went to the edge of the overhang and stood with her back to him. Logan had seen the hurt in her eyes and the way her lips parted with a sob of pity when she'd seen his back. As he dug into his pack his thoughts troubled him. Rosalee was a sweet, proud woman who was capable of giving her heart and soul to the man she loved. Beset by loneliness, he'd longed for such a woman. His eyes drank in the sight of her straight back and proudly held head. What would it be like to be free to ask her to share his life?

It was agony getting out of the buckskin pants and into the cloth ones. His knees felt as if he'd never be able to grip the sides of a horse again. He was sweating from the effort by the time he lay down on the mattress and called her name.

The rain came in a steady downpour, urged on by a chilly wind. Rosalee was thankful for the overhang and for the supply of wood she had been able to gather for their fire. She worried about Ben. Was he safe and dry at Mary's? Did Odell miss her and want to go home? Had Clayhill's raiders burned the house and barn? And was Case Malone out in this torrent somewhere, sitting beneath a thick pine?

Logan lay on his stomach, his arms at his sides, his face turned toward her. On her knees beside him, Rosalee lifted the dark, glossy mane of hair that lay on the back of his neck and moved it to the side. It felt clean and soft between her fingers and they were reluctant to leave it. She folded the blanket down to his hips and gently applied a layer of salve to the wounds on his back. She watched his face for a sign that she was hurting him, but he didn't as much as flicker an eyelash. When she finished, she took a clean cloth from Mary's medical basket and spread it across his back.

"That feels better," he murmured with his eyes closed.

"We've got to put it on your . . . bottom."

"No, I won't ask you to do that."

"You don't have to ask. I insist. Unbutton the front so I can pull your pants down," she said stiffly and prayed he couldn't see the color of her face. Oh, Lord, she thought, he'd seeped into her heart and there was nothing she wouldn't do for him, and do gladly.

Logan lifted his hips to reach the buttons on his pants. God, it hurt to put pressure on his knees! While his hand was there he pulled his sex from between his thighs and up to hide the treacherous organ beneath his belly. Even now, with the feel of her fingers in his hair and her cool hands on his bruised and throbbing flesh, he could feel it swell with desire for her.

The skin of his buttocks was a tawny gold beneath the welts and bruises. The wounds had opened during the jarring ride from the ranch and she was sure they were more painful than the ones on his back. She carefully applied the soothing salve and covered them with a cloth.

"Will you be cold if you leave your shirt off for the night? We have extra blankets." She pulled the soft cover up and around his shoulders, repacked the basket, and set it aside.

Logan turned on his side. He could never remember anyone taking care of him like this. During the war he'd stayed in a home to recover from his wounds, but the members of the household were hostile to him. He never knew if it was because of his Indian blood or if it was because he was a Blue Belly.

"I'll not be cold, Rosalee. But you're shivering. Wrap a blanket around yourself and sit here beside me."

"You must drink what tea there is left. I'll let the fire die down. We'll need the dry wood we have to start one in the morning." She handed him the cup and waited for him to drain it.

"Rosalee, I don't know of a delicate way to say this, but . . . I'm about to float away on a sea of sage tea!"

She giggled softly. "I was wondering about that." She pulled an oiled slicker from his pack. "Put this over your head. Follow the wall to another little overhang. The rain is letting up a bit."

While he was gone, Rosalee slipped out the opposite end of their camp and into the darkness. She relieved herself and returned, wiping the rain from her face and hair. While there was still a faint light from the dying campfire she tidied the camp, placing their supplies back against the wall and covered them against the possibility of a quick wind change that would whip the rain in under the overhang.

When Logan returned she was waiting for him. She took the wet slicker from his shoulders and hung it over the wagon wheel. He eased himself down onto the mattress. He removed his moccasins and tilted them on the sides so the soles were exposed to the warm coals of the fire.

"Rosalee, Rosalee." He repeated her name as though trying to taste it. "You're truly an exceptional woman. How did I find you in all this vast country?" He lay back and pulled the blanket up over him. "You've been doing for me all day and I know you're tired. Get a blanket and lie down here beside me. As far as propriety is concerned . . . to hell with it. It's too wet and cold for either of us to sleep on the ground."

Rosalee stood in an awkward silence broken only by the steady beat of the rain hitting the ground and an occasional distant roll of thunder. She did not argue with him. She took off the damp shawl, sank down on the edge of the mattress, and removed her wet shoes. Her feet were cold and she tucked them up under her skirt and pulled the blanket up over her. She lay with her back to him, her head resting on her bent arm, and felt the pounding of her own heart in her throat and temples. This morning she never even imagined she'd be alone tonight with Logan Horn, the breed who had come to her door with his dying mother. And here she was, lying with him on her own mattress, miles from another human being.

"Your braid is damp." His whispered words came to her out of the darkness.

She reached to pull the braid over her shoulder and her hand encountered his hand. The touch caused a fluttery feeling to erupt in her stomach. There seemed to be nothing to say, although she searched her mind for words. A shiver of pure physical awareness of him chased a strange sensation up and down her spine.

"What are you thinking about?" His whisper reached her ears again. She could feel a gentle tug at the back of her head and knew his hand was still on the thick braid.

"I was wondering if Ben was all right." Emotion weakened her voice as she grasped for something to say.

"He'll be all right at Mrs. Gregg's." His words came slow and reassuring. Then, "I saw the way she looked at Malone. They mean something to each other."

"I think so, too. Mary has been my friend since we came here."

"How did that come about, considering . . ."

"Ben and I never let Papa know . . . about the house she keeps. He had feelings about things like that."

"Yes. I can see that he would." There was a long silence, then he asked, "What do you think?"

"About what?"

"About the house Mary keeps?"

"I try not to think about it. I know that Mary doesn't do . . . it herself, although she would still be my friend if she did. She keeps a good place for women who were going to be in that . . . business anyway." She paused, wondering if he thought it strange that she was discussing this with him. "I first met Mary in the mercantile. She helped me pick out dress material for Odell. After she left, one of the town women whispered to me that she was a *scarlet* woman. She said she was telling me this for my own good."

He chuckled. "Every town has a few people who take it upon themselves to judge the morals of others. Do you think she was telling you for your own good?" he queried softly.

"Oh, no. I knew better than that. She didn't care about me. She thought she was elevating herself above Mary by pushing her down into the mud. Mama always said to look out for someone who tells you unpleasant things about someone for your own good."

"She was perceptive. I think I would've liked your mother." There was a small silence while Rosalee's heart released a flood of happiness. "What would your mother have thought about me?" His low-voiced query hung in the air.

While she was thinking about the question, the image of

her mother's calm face flashed before her eyes. "She would've withheld judgment until she got to know you. She believed it was what was on the inside of a man that counted. She often chided Pa about his prejudices."

Rosalee could feel the rhythmic movement of his hand as he stroked her braid. She lay very still, afraid even the slightest movement of her head would cause him to move his hand away. With her eyes tightly closed she pictured his face, unreadable as the face on a stone sculpture. She wondered if he would ever share his innermost feelings with anyone. Suddenly, she wanted to see his firm lips spread with a smile, his dark eyes laughing, his stoic features relaxed, and above all, she wanted him to feel the happiness of knowing he was loved and wanted. The silence became so long she thought he had gone to sleep. Finally, his hushed voice came to her ears.

"You're tense, now. Are you afraid of me?"

His words brought her head and shoulders around. "Of course not!" She waited, and when he didn't speak, she said, "Should I be?"

"No! Lord, no!" he groaned as if adrift in a sea of misery of his own making. The whispered words caused her heart to make a frantic leap.

"I'm not afraid of you, Logan, and I never have been." She laid her head back down on her bent arm. "From the moment I saw you standing in the doorway, all wet from the rain, taking the chance you'd be turned away because of your Indian blood, I wasn't afraid. But I knew today what Case meant when he said he'd taken your measure. I wanted to tell him then not to worry, but I didn't know how to put it into words." She spoke softly, with her eyes closed.

His fingers left the thick braid and clasped her shoulder as though he were clinging to a lifeline in an open sea. The hunger to be near her, to touch her, had been with him since he'd ridden into the hills to find a resting place for his mother. This woman was every sweet dream he'd ever had rolled into one. He would gladly give ten years of his life to be free to pull her against his chest, nuzzle his face in her hair, and fall asleep with his arms around her.

Thoughts whirled about Rosalee's brain like wind-whipped tumbleweed. His hand that gripped her shoulder made her feel weak and liquid inside. She knew if he pulled, just the slightest bit, she would turn to him. But his hand didn't pull; the fingers slowly relaxed and left her. She wanted to cry.

"Are you warm?" he asked, and tucked the blanket closer about her neck.

"Yes. Are you?"

"Yes. Get some sleep."

"The rifle is behind you and your handgun is under the head of the mattress."

"I know. I saw you put them there. Don't be afraid to go to sleep. Brutus is out there. He'd let us know if anyone comes near."

Rosalee rolled over onto her back and raised up. "I forgot about him! He'll be wet and hungry."

Logan laughed softly. "Lie down. He's all right. The horses will be under a good stand of thick pine, standing with their tails to the wind. Brutus will find a dry spot under the brush to wait out the storm."

"But he'll be hungry."

"I don't coddle him. He does his own hunting. I don't feed or take care of him. He doesn't *belong* to me. He stays with me because he wants to. That's the way we both want it."

His fingers touched her arm and moved down to wrap around her hand. The slender fingers offered no resistance when he laced them with his. It was a waiting moment for both of them. Then he inhaled as deeply as his cracked ribs would allow and let the air escape slowly from his lips. The thoughts in his head were transformed into words that rushed out of his mouth without him scarcely realizing he was saying them.

"Let me hold your hand, sweet Rosalee. It is all I can ever have of you!" There was pain, anguish, pleading in his voice.

"Logan—"

"Sshh . . . don't say anything. This is the first night I've spent on land that's mine and I'm glad you're with me."

Chapter
Ten

Rosalee did not speak or move after Logan's whispered words. They kept going through her mind: "I'm glad you're with me." Tears ran down her cheeks, and she cried silently for a lonely little boy, and for a big, lonely man caught between the white man's world and the Indian's. He held her slender hand in his large, calloused one, and sometimes he clenched it so hard she thought the bones would break, but she didn't draw it away. The urge to banish his loneliness was a compelling force dragging at her.

At first her body was as taut as a bow string. She was physically and mentally exhausted, but gradually she relaxed and listened to the soft sound of Logan's breathing. Finally she fell asleep, holding tightly to his hand.

Later she woke, chilled, her muscles tense, her skin prickled with fear. She didn't know what had awakened her. Logan's hand no longer gripped hers tightly, but they were still joined. Then she heard the wind sweeping through the empty cliff dwellings above them, moaning like a woman in pain.

She thought of what Logan's mother had said the night she died about the night wind coming to take her spirit along the Hanging Road. Far away a coyote called to his mate, and her answer echoed down from the hills.

A poignant loneliness possessed Rosalee and she turned her head toward the man who lay beside her, wishing with all her heart she could move close to him and his arms would welcome her.

"It's only the wind in the cliff houses." His whisper came out of the darkness to reassure her, and his fingers tightened on her hand.

"I thought that's what it was. It sounds so lonely."

"You're cold. Turn over and move your back toward me. We'll warm each other."

"I could get another blanket out of the wagon."

"It'll be morning soon. Turn over." He released her hand when she moved.

It seemed like a dream to Rosalee. He lifted the blanket covering him and spread it over her, but left the thickness of her blanket between them. His arm was a pleasant weight across her body and his hand, once again, found hers. She felt the warmth of his breath on her neck and wondered if he could feel the thumping of her heart. She was sure she'd never sleep, but she became deliciously warm and relaxed and sleep finally claimed her.

When next she awakened, only the thin material of her dress was between her back and his chest. His arm held her tightly to him and his face was against her hair. She had never been this close to anyone other than Odell when they snuggled together during the long, cold winter nights. This hard, warm body that curled around hers sent a tide of tingling excitement through her. She didn't dare move for fear of waking him. She lay perfectly still while the red fingers of dawn crept across the eastern sky, and listened to the birds in the willows, chirping their morning greetings to each other.

"You can lie awfully still. Are you sure you're not part Cheyenne?" His voice was deep and soft, close to her ear.

"You . . . were playing possum!" she accused.

"Uh huh. So were you."

"I didn't want to wake you. Do you feel better?"

"I won't know for sure until I move."

"You're about to find out, because I'm going to get up. We've got a lot to do this morning."

"I don't think I want to find out."

"Coward!"

"You'd call a man a coward when he's down?" There was laughter in his voice.

"Sure. I'm no dummy. I know you can't catch me if I run."

"Are you going to?"

"Going to what?"

"Run?"

"Not until I put my shoes on." She threw back the blanket and sat up. His arm slid from around her. She kept her back to him because her lips would not stop smiling. "Brrr . . . it's cool this morning," she said while lacing her shoes. "And the sky is clear. Do you think we should risk a fire?"

"I think so. The smoke will hit the top of the overhang and scatter out. Coffee will taste mighty good."

Rosalee smoothed her hair back with her two hands and put her shawl around her shoulders before she stood and looked down at him. His sunken cheeks, covered with a shading of dark beard, brought his high cheekbones into prominence. His facial lines were so strong, so thoroughly masculine. His mustache, curved down the sides of his mouth, gave him a fierce look. But now his eyes and his lips were smiling in unison and there was nothing fierce in the look he gave her. She studied him leisurely, thankful to be standing above him. Was she crazy? she thought. Why was she so happy when her home and family had been wrenched from her?

"Yes, I think you feel better today," she teased when she finally spoke. "But you'll not be breaking any wild broncs for awhile."

He laughed with sheer exaltation at her reference to his injured bottom. "You'd win a bet on that, little Rosalee."

She built a small fire and made coffee while Logan dressed and walked out into the early morning light to look around. The sky was clear with the promise of a warm summer day. He looked down the valley and could see Mercury and the mare standing in the tall grass. Near the camp he saw where Rosalee had stretched a rope between two trees and fastened the bays to it with a slide loop so they could feed. He smiled with newfound pride in the ability of the slim, quiet woman.

Above him were the abandoned cliff dwellings. He studied them for a long while, appreciating his long ago ancestors who had built their homes of rock and adobe and stacked them, one atop the other, like three stairsteps. A ramp, wide enough for a single horse, led to the first level. His mind, trained from his war experience, realized the place could be made almost impregnable. Who and what had caused the demise of a people capable of building this structure? Was it sickness? Or were they a peaceful people, killed by the warlike Navajos and Utes?

Logan turned back toward the camp beneath the overhang. This was his land, now. He would not be driven away. He would stay here, by God, and defend his right to it!

They sat on the mattress and ate what was left of the meat and biscuits and drank the hot coffee. When they finished, Rosalee dug into the basket and brought out the fried peach pie. She gave it to him with a shy smile. Their smiling eyes locked as they remembered her saying she had hid it from Ben. He took a huge bite and held it to her mouth for her to do the same. She chewed slowly without tasting, not realizing that the happiness in her face caused troubled thoughts to creep into Logan's mind.

He didn't want this sweet woman to give him her heart. It would surely break when subjected to the taunts and insults she'd receive as the woman of a breed. He had to get her back to the *Wasicun* before word got out that they'd been alone and dirt was thrown in her beautiful face—before she was shunned and insulted by her own kind. He loved her too much to cause her that kind of pain.

His dark face closed down as if he had suddenly put on his Indian mask. Only his eyes, searching her face, showed movement. Rosalee knew instinctively that his thoughts concerned her. A chill touched her. Her blue-green eyes probed his dark ones for a reason for the sudden change of mood until he got slowly and painfully to his feet.

"It's almost sunup. I'll get the horses and we'll move camp." He strapped his gunbelt about his hip and picked up his hat. "I'll bring Mercury and tie him here where he can see down the valley. He was mountain bred, with strong survival instincts. He'll let us know if there's a horse a mile away."

Rosalee stood. She was almost afraid to speak. Without understanding why, she was convinced that he had firmly put distance between them. Had she been too forward? Did he suddenly realize she had lost her heart to him and this was his way of letting her know her love would never be returned? The thought drove a painful wedge in her heart. She had been a fool to think he might care for her just because he'd said he wanted to see her again. He had been hurt and sick when he came back to her. She felt tears burn her eyes and turned abruptly to put out the campfire.

"I'll hitch up the team and move the wagon closer. We'll have to hide it, anyway." She spoke over the sob in her throat and was quite pleased with the way the words came from her lips.

Rosalee didn't hear Logan leave, but she knew he had gone. She straightened and watched him walk toward the stallion and mare. He whistled several short, shrill blasts, and the horses began moving toward him. She had wanted to ask if he was up to the work necessary to move the camp, but his attitude forbid any personal conversation between them. She thought about what he'd said about Brutus and realized the same applied to him. He wasn't a man to be coddled. He didn't *belong* to her. If he stayed with her it would be because he wanted to.

Logan cut two stout willows and fashioned a travois for the mare to pull. An hour later, most of the contents of the wagon were piled in one of the rooms in the cliff house. Rosalee was fascinated by the strange ruins of which she had previously heard nothing. She found fragments of pottery, some of it black and white, some orange, some red. There were smoke-blackened firepits, arrowheads, and other evidence of the people long gone. All of these things gave her some idea of the people who had lived in this place, loved here, died here.

Using the mare and the travois, Rosalee brought wood up the ramp and stacked it in one of the rooms. The foal, curious and playful, frolicked along behind them. She sniffed at Brutus, lying in the shade beside Mercury, then raced away with her tail in the air. Rosalee envied the carefree young colt. She was secure in the knowledge her mother would see to it that no harm came to her.

Rosalee watched the stallion for a sign the keen eyes had seen something he did not understand.

"His eyesight and hearing are far superior to ours," Logan

explained. "His ears will swivel and twitch. He'll lift his head and sniff into the wind and become restless. If that should happen, send Brutus for me."

Logan led the team to drink at the stream and hid the wagon among the thick willows. Exhausted, he leaned against a bolder out of sight of the cliff house and mopped his face with a damp cloth. His legs trembled with weakness. He had seen Rosalee look at him sharply and then away when he made the last staggering trip up the slope leading the mare. He knew she was concerned for him and hurt by his cool treatment. God above! What else could he do? There was the rest of the day and tonight and possibly tomorrow and the next day to get through before Malone came for her. She had worked doggedly since early morning, and now, without being told it had to be done, she was trying to remove all trace of their camp beneath the overhang.

When Logan came up the ramp, Rosalee was standing on the ledge, her hand shading her eyes as she looked back toward her land. The breeze pushed her skirt against her legs and her lifted arm pulled her dress taut to outline her soft, rounded breasts. An ache to claim her for his own, to build his life around her, gnawed at him. He stood completely still, watching her, fighting the emotions that threatened to shake him from his rigid conviction. He wiped his sweating palms on his thighs and continued up the ramp. If Rosalee saw him she gave no indication.

He turned in the doorway of the room where they had piled their gear and stood for a long moment, staring at her. She had made him welcome when he needed someone so desperately, and she had come with him willingly to this lonely place. It was a strange feeling to be trusted so implicitly. Was it *her* trust in him that had stirred him as nothing had? Was it his need to protect and care for someone other than himself that had aroused this feeling in *him*? Another thought crowded into his mind while he tried to analyze why this particular woman had come to mean so much to him: Just as the maternal instinct is strongest in a woman, the instinct to protect is strongest in a man. Love, he decided, must be a combination of all these feelings.

They ate the evening meal in silence. Logan led the horses up the ramp and into the cliff house. Brutus lay on the ledge and Logan sank down on the mattress and was almost instantly asleep. Rosalee made a pallet for herself on the other side of the room. Too tired to sleep, she stared into the darkness and listened to the sounds made by the horses stabled in the other room. When she finally dropped off, her sleep was deep and dreamless. She awakened when Logan led the horses back down the ramp.

Breakfast was another meal with only civilities exchanged. When it was over Rosalee went to sit on the ledge where she could see both ends of the valley, and Logan sorted through the supplies he'd bought at the mercantile. He methodically stacked the foodstuff in a tin larder, the tools in a corner, the ammunition and rifles just inside the door. He set aside the package containing the yellow dress goods and the candy sticks he'd bought for Odell until he finished, then he took them to Rosalee.

"A woman in the store in Junction City said this would do for your sister."

Rosalee looked up at him, her eyes never wavering from his, and accepted the package. She opened it and ran her fingertips over the soft yellow material and the shiny, satin ribbon. Odell had never had anything so fine. She felt a rush of homesickness for her little sister and her eyes filled with tears. She kept her head bowed, hoping he wouldn't notice.

"Thank you. Odell will think she's a princess in this."

"I wanted to get something for you, too, but . . . I didn't think it would be . . . I didn't think you'd accept anything."

He stood awkwardly, looking down on her bent head, cursing himself for fumbling for words.

"No! No, I couldn't accept . . . anything. You don't owe me or my family . . . anything." Her trembling fingers continued to stroke the material.

"I think I do."

"Well, you don't," she said firmly.

"I owe you and your family for taking me and my mother into your home. And I owe you for standing between me and Clayhill when I was laid up," he said stubbornly. Why the hell wouldn't she look at him? "But that wasn't why . . . I wanted to give you something that—"

She jumped to her feet, blazing with anger, her teary eyes glaring into his. "I don't want anything from you! You don't *owe* me anything! You don't owe me a damn thing!" she shouted. "I would've done as much for a cur someone was going to shoot, and . . . don't you forget it, Mr. Logan Horn!"

In the stricken silence that followed they maintained that grotesque pose, their eyes locked, ungiving.

"I don't understand why you're angry," Logan said in a voice that shook.

"This is why I'm angry!" She shoved the package against his chest and he grabbed it before it fell to the ground. "My sister doesn't need your . . . charity, and that goes for me and Ben, too!" She was breathing hard, her soft, young breast rising and falling as she blurted her words. Tears of anger and homesickness rolled down her cheeks, but she held her head high as if they were not there. She smoothed her hair in a swift gesture and turned away from him.

Dumbfounded, Logan watched her walk into the room, her movements stiff and jerky, her face averted. He was still standing there, holding the package in his hand, when she came out with her extra dress over her arm and a cloth knapsack in her hand. She passed him, her head tilted in a proud, defiant way, and went down the ramp.

"Rosalee . . ." Her name was almost a groan as it left his lips. She ignored him and a worried frown covered his face. "Rosalee!" he called again, this time in sudden accusing anger. "Where the hell are you going?" She had reached the bottom of the ramp and whirled to look up at him. His words had struck up an answering fire in her.

"I'm not going to try to walk out of here, if that's what you're thinking. I may be a lot of things, but I'm not a fool! I'm going down to the stream to bathe, and after that I'm going to sit and wait for Case Malone to come get me."

"I don't want you down there by yourself."

"*You* don't want?" His words caused her temper to run out of control. "Let me remind you, Mr. Horn, I'm entitled to the same consideration you give Brutus. I don't belong to you and if I stay with you it's because *I* want to. Right now, I *don't* want to!"

Logan watched her mouth spilling out the angry words. She stood glaring up at him with eyes that looked like bits of blue-green ice. He could see the heaving of her breast, and the thought of the sweet softness he'd felt brush against him during the night being touched by another man made his skin grow icy and his heart throb with agony.

"Goddamnit, Rosalee! There'll be all kind of vermin combing these canyons looking for me if Clayhill pu~ ⸱ a price on my head. You could come across one of them, or a bear, or a cougar. If you insist on going I'll have to go with you."

"No!" She dug into the knapsack and brought out an old handgun. "I can protect myself, and . . . from you, if necessary."

Her cold, blue-green eyes did battle with his smoldering dark ones. She was breathing deeply, erratically, like someone who had run too far, too fast. She knew her last words were unfair, but didn't wish them back. They made up a little for the humiliation of being rejected after she had so blatantly shown her feelings for him. She tilted her chin haughtily and walked away with as much dignity as her trembling body would allow. It wasn't until she'd rounded the boulder and was out of sight that she allowed her shoulders to slump and the tears of defeat to roll down her cheeks.

Rendered numb by the scene's climax, Rosalee passed through the high boulders and down into the valley shaded by cottonwoods, box elder, ash, and into the willows that grew thickly along the stream. In deep despair, she stared dully at the ground and walked on, not noticing the small flocks of birds that took flight ahead of her, the buzzing june bugs, or the young deer that paused, head up, alert, then took off on the run, white tail high. She came to the stream and saw that walking would be easier if she went upstream, and followed the bank along a well-worn animal path.

One time she paused and looked back the way she had come. How could she have been so stupidly naive? How could she have fallen in love with a man who came in out of the night, out of the storm, and looked at her with great, dark, lonely eyes. She had simply handed him her heart. Logan had read her actions as clearly as if she had put them down on paper. He knew she had fallen in love with him and felt sorry for her! She groaned aloud at the humiliating prospect of going back to face him, but she would have to endure it. There was nothing else she could do. She fought an almost overpowering urge to take one of the bays and go home as she pictured that isolated haven. The only thing that stopped her was the thought of Clayhill's raiders. If they killed her, Odell and Ben would have no one.

The small green valley lay still in the lazy afternoon sun, a faint heat emanating from the white rocks that lined the stream. She walked on, uncaring of the distance, and beads of sweat lined her forehead and dampened her armpits.

She came to a small waterfall that rustled faintly as it cascaded over the rocks and lost itself in widening ripples on its journey downstream. There she stopped and listened to the silence. Never had she felt such stillness, never had she felt so alone. All this land, she thought, was haunted by memories; memories of long-vanished people and of the Cheyenne, who thought this was a holy place—and hers.

She decided to bathe beside the waterfall rather than in the pool above. Her thoughts tormented her while she removed her shoes and stockings and slipped her dress over her head. She stood in her shift, then stepped out of it with a natural grace and with no shrinking at her nakedness. One of her greatest pleasures was bathing. Often she could wash the worries from her mind while she scrubbed her body and hair. From her knapsack she took a small bar of soap and went to the water's edge.

Rosalee trailed her foot in the water, fully expecting it to be as cool as the mountain spring at home. The water was warm! In fact, it was almost hot! Was this the hot spring Case had mentioned? It had to be. The shock of her discovery sent a flood of excitement through her. Logan would be so pleased that it was on his land! She couldn't help being glad for him.

She walked out into the warm stream and sat down. The water came up to cover her breasts and her thick braid floated behind her as the water swirled around. After awhile the warm moving water served to work off the tension and she stood to soap herself. Her body was lithe and strong, for since childhood she had worked alongside her father, and later, alone or with Ben. After lathering every part of her body she unbraided her hair and sank down again.

It was so pleasant in the water she stayed there until the skin on her fingers wrinkled. She came out of the pool and stopped at the edge to wring the water from her hair. Using her soiled dress for a towel, she dried herself, then dressed and sat down on a large rock to continue rubbing her hair and combing through it with her fingers. She felt wonderfully clean and sat absently pondering the miracle of the hot spring.

Abruptly, she was startled out of her lethargy by the scream of a wildcat. The sound was not especially close, so it didn't put her in a panic, but it caused her heartbeat to quicken. She picked up the pistol and held it in her lap. Behind her was the cottonwood, the ash and the pines. To her left was the thick willows and across from her the red, rocky cliff. She shaded her eyes with her hand and scanned the great, tilted slabs of rock for movement. She had heard the scream of a cat many times and had on occasion glimpsed one in the distance. It was reassuring to remember hearing Mr. Haywood say, the day her father was buried, that it was rare for a cat to attack a person unless cornered.

Minutes passed slowly without a sound or a movement and her uneasiness passed. She shook her hair vigorously to dry it and bent to put on her shoes. Thick, light brown tresses, shiny clean with sparkling highlights, fell to her hips like a shimmering curtain. Impatiently, she looped the strands behind her ears so she could see.

"Yeeeow!" The primitive cry of the cat came from across the stream and it was so close Rosalee jerked herself erect and gripped the pistol. Seconds—or was it hours?—passed while she scanned the rocky ledges. The silence pressed down on her. She reached for the knapsack and was about to get to her feet when a voice, low and calm, came from behind her.

"Don't move. I don't want to shoot if I don't have to."

Logan's voice! Thank God! She sat ramrod straight, looking straight ahead. Apprehension squeezed her lungs until she couldn't breathe.

"Where is it?" she whispered shakily when she could find the breath to speak.

"Across the stream and to the left about ten feet up, moving this way."

"I see it. Oh!" She couldn't hold back the low cry when the cat paused, facing her, its yellow eyes gleaming, and let out a piercing scream.

"Sit steady. I've got him in my sights, he'll either spring when he's directly opposite you or he'll go on."

The large, slick cat moved with effortless grace over the ridges and rims of the slanting cliff. It came to the ledge that hung over the water and made a sudden stop. The tawny brown cat froze in immobility with its head jutted forward. His long, sweeping tail hung close to the powerful hindquarters, his yellow eyes glared fixedly on the intruder beside the stream. A shattering blast exploded from its huge mouth the instant before it bunched its muscles and sprang. The body arched and stretched, front paws reaching out. The sharp crack of the rifle was no louder than a small pop to Rosalee's stunned senses. The bullet found its mark and the cat plunged straight down into the water.

To Rosalee, it was like a dream played in slow motion. The only move she made was to lift her arm to her face and cringe. She was only vaguely aware when Logan rushed past her to go to the water's edge. He held his rifle, cocked and ready. When he was sure the cougar was dead he turned to her.

"Oh, blessed God!" The words came from a stiff, dry throat. She jumped to her feet to run to him, but the stern disapproval on his face stopped her.

"Move," he said harshly. "The sound of that shot will carry five miles in these canyons." His words hit her like a blow between the shoulders.

Without giving her a second glance he trotted off down

the animal path that ran alongside the stream. Too shattered by what had just happened to be able to do anything, she obeyed without question. Her limbs came alive and she stumbled after him. He was angry! He was very angry, and regret for her inconsiderate action washed over her like an icy wave.

Swiftly and silently, Logan moved down the trail ahead of her and it took all her concentration and strength to keep the distance between them from widening. The dark stains on his shirt told her the wounds on his back had opened and she knew he was suffering from weakness, but his stride never faltered. Nor did he look back to see how she was faring.

Her head throbbed painfully, but the worse pain was in the back of her mind, reminding her that she had been foolish to disobey Logan. If he had not followed she would be dead now! He had followed to make sure she was safe, and by firing the rifle he might have revealed their hiding place to those who wanted to kill them.

Chapter
Eleven

Rosalee's heart was racing. Blood rose in her face, burning her skin, beating at her throat by the time they turned to go up the incline to the cliff house. She held her soiled dress over the long, loose hair that fell down her back to keep it from snagging on the brush as they hurried through it.

Logan stopped behind a boulder to survey the valley before he strode out in plain sight, and Rosalee's legs, being so long in motion, didn't stop until she ran into him. Satisfied that their hideout hadn't yet been discovered, he moved out again and she followed. Without looking back at her, he ran to where he had staked Mercury, jerked on the rope holding him, and led the stallion up the ramp.

"Brutus!" he called sharply. "Get the girls." The dog leaped to obey.

Rosalee ran up the ramp behind the horses and reached the ledge in time to see Logan leading the stallion into the empty rooms. The mare and foal followed and Brutus stood at the doorway. Rosalee shaded her eyes with her hand and looked toward the opening they had passed through several days before. The only movement was a soaring hawk, white billowing clouds being pushed by a brisk wind, and the gentle waving of the high grass in the lowland.

"That blue dress is like a banner against this red rock," Logan said from behind her. "You'll have to put on the other dress or stay inside." He was carrying adobe bricks from the ruins and piling them along the edge of the ledge.

Rosalee went inside, unbuttoning the front of her blue dress on the way. She changed dresses hurriedly, and without combing her hair, braided it in one long rope and tied the end with a string she took from her pocket. Knowing she was wrong to have wandered so far after Logan had warned her not to go to the stream was like a sharp pain in her heart. She owed him her life. If he'd not followed to make sure she was safe she'd now be a meal for the cougar! Reaction made her legs tremble violently and lights danced before her eyes. She put a hand out to the wall to steady herself, waited a moment, and went out into the late afternoon sunlight.

Brutus lay at the end of the ledge. Rosalee didn't take time to wonder if he had been ordered to watch or if he was just resting there. She went into the ruins and carried brick after brick to the ledge where Logan was building a barrier to use in case they were fired on from the ground. He didn't speak to her, but his eyes found her face each time he put a chunk of adobe in her hands before he picked up one in each of his and carried it to the ledge. The wall rose slowly. Finally, when it was large enough to crouch behind, Logan stopped and wiped the sweat from his face with the sleeve of his shirt.

"Do you think they'll come?" Rosalee asked, looking off toward the west where the sky was awash with crimson.

"They'll come. They know we're somewhere in the canyons and sooner or later they'll stumble onto the opening and come into the valley." He wiped his face again. "I want to be ready for them."

They looked steadily at each other. He held her with his eyes as firmly as if he held her with his hands. A flush tinged her cheeks, but her wide, blue-green eyes never wavered.

"I'm sorry," she said miserably, and tried to hold the frayed ends of her nerves together so she wouldn't cry. For a space of a dozen heartbeats they regarded each other in utter silence.

"I think we both learned something," he said with less than his customary stolid reserve.

"You had a right to be angry with me."

"Enraged is a better word. It scared the living hell out of me when I saw that cat. All I could think of was what if the gun misfired."

"I owe you my life. Thank you." She dropped her eyes to her clasped hands, scratched and bleeding from carrying the bricks.

He reached out and took them in his, turned them palms up, and rubbed his crooked finger over a long, bloody scratch.

"You should have gloves," he murmured. "I've got a leather pair in my pack. They'll be too big, but better than nothing."

"What I need is another bath," she said, watching his finger slide over her palm. Her eyes flew to his and a surge of hot blood flooded her face. He was thinking of her standing naked beside the stream!

"I'll not say I didn't see you," he said with a laughing glint in his eyes. "I saw a lovely wood nymph come up out of the water and it was worth everything I've endured since I came West." His smile broadened when a new wave of color tinged her cheeks. "You're even prettier when you're embarrassed."

"Logan!" She expected to feel mortified, and was surprised that she was only mildly embarrassed. "You were . . . watching me!"

"Uh-huh. But I was watching for the cat, too," he said with a chuckle. His amusement at her self-consciousness was something he did not try to hide.

"I should be mad at you!" A faint, tingling thrill passed through her and laid its fleeting change across her face. Her laugh was free and warm. "But how can I be, when you saved my life?"

"In some parts of the world, when you save a life, that person belongs to you, body and soul." The serious words caught her off guard.

"Is that so?" She was almost incapable of coherent speech or thought, conscious only that her hands were still clasped in his and that he was looking down at her through half-closed lids.

"Do you know what that means?"

"That you own me?"

"And you me."

"But . . . I didn't save *your* life," she protested huskily. "Mary did."

"I doubt that Shorty Banes would have killed me, although I probably would have wished that he had. Clayhill *meant* to kill me, still means to."

"I don't want to think about that." She pulled her hands from his and turned away only to turn back with a glowing smile on her face. "I forgot to tell you . . . the pool I bathed in was *hot*! I'm sure the hot spring Case told us about is in the larger pool above. It's on your land, Logan! If you build your house near it you can pipe hot water to the house! I've heard it can be done."

His smile answered the radiance on her face and not the news she gave him. He thought, as he feasted his eyes on her, that this was no coy miss who used flirtatious guile on a man. She was a woman, with all the feminine instincts, but open and natural with her feelings. He had seen more beautiful women, but none that had the inner glow of this lovely creature.

"Rosalee, Rosalee..." Her name came from his lips like a caress. He laughed. It wasn't a chuckle, but a real laugh. "I'll never be able to keep you away from that pool, now!"

She laughed with him, scarcely aware of anything but the big, dark man smiling down at her. Her eyes slid over his relaxed features, his smiling eyes, his tall, loose frame. Her heart began to pound with a new rhythm as they hungrily eyed each other.

"I wish you could soak in it, Logan. It would heal your poor back and take the soreness out of your ... arms and ... legs." She finished with a strange tremor in her voice.

"I'd like that, but it's a luxury I can't afford right now." He rubbed his fingers over the stubble on his chin. "I'd like a shave, but that's got to wait, too."

"I used to shave my papa," she whispered between spasmic breaths.

"I keep a sharp razor. I'd have to make certain you're not mad at me before I turn you loose with it." His eyes teased her.

Rosalee was agonizingly aware of the man at her side during the long silence that ensued, and finally said the first thing that came to her mind. "Do you think they'll come tonight?"

"If they do, it'll be before dark. I don't think they're foolhardy enough to wander around in the dark looking for an Indian." His slow smile drew little wrinkles at the corners of his eyes and she knew he spoke half in jest, half in earnest. Almost imperceptibly, the look on her face altered, leaving it creased with a worried frown.

"Oh, Logan! I don't want you killed! Give up your claim to this land and ride away."

"I'll not be driven off my land like Clayhill drove the

Cheyenne off theirs. This time it will be an Indian who will do the driving out." He took a slow breath, wanting to make things clear to her. "I paid out good money for this land. My title will be watertight once the deed is recorded in Denver." His voice softened. "Don't worry, little Rosalee. I can back up my stand."

"But how? You're only one man against many."

"One small hole in a dike will grow bigger until the dike crumbles. Clayhill has had things his way long enough. I intend to be the small hole that causes his downfall." He put his hands on her shoulders. "You shouldn't be here. If Malone doesn't come tomorrow or the next day, I've got to figure out a way to get you to Mrs. Gregg."

His dark gaze searched her blue-green, distressed eyes. She was as full of pain as he. A sense of helplessness threatened to destroy his determination to keep distance between them. He stared gravely at her for a long moment, then let his hard-held breath out like a sigh and his hold tightened painfully.

"There's only a couple of hours of daylight left. If they don't come through the opening by dark we're reasonably safe until morning. When the moon comes up we'll walk down to your pool. It may be the last chance we'll have for awhile."

Her face brightened. "The warm water will help your back and your sore muscles. I know it will!"

That brought a slow smile to his lips. "Then you'd better get me something to eat so I don't keel over on the way," he drawled.

Darkness came and, shortly after, a half moon rose above the cliffs. Logan rose stiffly from his vigil at the end of the ledge where Rosalee had brought him a hearty meal of fried, smoked meat, pan gravy, bread and strong coffee. Together they led the horses to the grassland below and staked them out so they could eat during the night hours.

Rosalee insisted he stay below while she returned to the room to get her soap and clean dress. She took a clean shirt from Logan's pack and held it to her cheek for a moment before she ran lightly down the ramp to where he waited.

Constantly alert, he paused to look and listen before he took her hand and they walked down through the willows toward the stream. This new intimacy with Logan was like heady wine to Rosalee. They seemed to know each other's needs, read each other's thoughts. He didn't have to say, "take the rifle"; she automatically reached for it and held it while he led the bay team to the stream to drink. She helped him move them deeper into the willows.

They walked, side by side, up the path toward the pool. The sky was clear and stars blossomed overhead. An owl hooted, bull frogs croaked in the backwater of the stream, and far away the faint sound of a lonesome coyote reached them. Rosalee banished all troubled thoughts from her mind and gave herself up to the enjoyment of being with the man with whom she wanted to spend the rest of her life. Her mother had said that when she met her true love she would know him. She thought happily that her mother, wherever she was, could look down and know that she'd found him. Once she stumbled on the uneven ground and Logan took her hand, drew it into the crook of his arm, and pressed it to his side. She was sure she had never been so happy and so content as she was at that moment.

"Logan . . ." She tilted her head until her cheek brushed his shoulder. "What did you mean when you said we both had learned something today? I know what I learned. What did you learn beside the fact that I can be headstrong and unreasonable?"

"You admit it, huh?" He chuckled softly and it seemed to her he pressed her hand tighter to him.

"I don't like to admit I was wrong, but there's no help for it."

"Among my people, when a woman disobeys she gets a beating. Will it make you feel better if I whack your bottom with a willow switch?"

"You . . . wouldn't!" She drew the word out and peered up into his face to see if he was teasing. A soft, throaty laugh came out of the darkness. "Logan . . ."

"Next time I'll not even stop to think about it."

The thought that they'd be together so there would be a next time caused her heart to jump out of rhythm. They came to the place where she had bathed. The body of the cougar still lay half in and half out of the water. Behind them something scuttled into the brush. The night was alive with sounds, and Rosalee unconsciously moved nearer to Logan. He placed the rifle within easy reach and pulled the dead animal out of the water.

"He's a big one." He took a thin blade from his boot and began removing the pelt.

"I'll always think about him crouched there on the ledge. I was never so scared in my life." A new awareness of her danger struck her so forcibly she trembled violently.

"It's over, and a valuable lesson has been learned. This is a hard, rough country, Rosalee, and you have to be prepared for the unexpected. A man out here can't afford to make many mistakes." He worked swiftly, the blade making sure slashes. When he finished he spread the pelt out on the rocks, skin side up so it would dry. "I'll pull the carcass into the brush and in a week's time the scavengers will have taken care of it."

"He's too big! You'll hurt your ribs." She tried unsuccessfully to keep the revulsion from her voice. "I'll help you."

His arms went around her and pulled her against him. "Rosalee, Rosalee . . . I've never met a woman like you before." He breathed the words into her hair.

"Is that good . . . or bad?" Her voice caught and she kept her face pressed to his shirt, loving the feel of his arms around her, wanting it to last as long as possible.

Logan was certain now that he held a special place in her heart and his own began to clamor with the desire to hold her, caress her, take comfort in the fact he was loved. He had to hold back for his own sake as well as hers. She had no acquaintance with blind hatred, ugliness. The taint of being a breed's woman would crush her bubbling spirit. He closed his eyes and pressed his lips against the smooth strands of her hair. Once committed there would be no going back. In time she would come to hate and resent him. He shuddered. The thought was like a knife blade twisting in his guts!

"Both good and bad," he said lightly, and stood away from her. "Let's get this beast out of sight so we can enjoy our bath."

Rosalee knew he had been as shaken as she had been by their close contact. She had felt his heart pound against hers, had felt his lips in her hair, and the trembling of his hands as they moved on her back. He wanted her. Somehow she knew he had the same craving for her love as she had for his, but he was determined to keep a barrier between them because of his Indian blood. He was holding himself in restraint, and all she could do was wait unless she was the one to destroy the barrier.

They each took a leg of the cougar and dragged it some distance from the pool. Rosalee had to steel herself in order to touch the animal, and was immensely relieved when Logan signaled they had gone far enough.

"I don't want to shock your modesty, but I'm about to

strip and get into the pool," Logan said when they came back to the water's edge. He began to take off his shirt.

"I won't look if you won't," she said daringly. Then, to cover her embarrassment, added, "I'll wash your shirt before we leave." She glanced at him. He had pulled off his knee-high moccasins and was unbuttoning his pants. She turned quickly and stood with her back to him. His soft laughter came to her out of the darkness.

"Don't forget . . . I haven't promised . . . anything!" he teased, and she heard him splashing in the water. "This is hot! Oh, it feels good. Come on in, Rosalee."

"Not till you promise." She tried to keep the giggles out of her voice.

"I saw you this afternoon. Have you grown something new since then?"

"That was different. I didn't know you were watching me."

"You won't be sure, now. I may tell you I'm not looking when I am."

"That would be cheating!"

"Yeah."

Happiness sang in Rosalee's heart. She turned and searched for his dark head above the water. "Turn around," she called.

"I'm turned."

"Logan Horn! I can see your teeth gleaming in the moon-light. I know your mouth isn't in the back of your head!"

He let out a shout of happy laughter and she wished she could see his face. Quickly, she pulled her dress over her head, dropped her shift, and sprinted into the water.

"You've got a mole on your backside, Rosalee," he called.

"Oh . . . you!" She knelt in the water until it came up to her neck, then moved into the deep part of the pool. "I'll not let you use my soap if you don't behave," she threatened.

"Are you going to wash my back?"

"It's too deep for me out there."

"Can't you swim?"

"I can't even float!"

"I'll teach you someday . . ." His voice trailed off. "The water is hotter near the falls."

"Isn't this wonderful? Do you think the water is this warm in the wintertime? Imagine taking a bath with the snow on the ground!" The moon was lost momentarily behind a wandering cloud and she felt a moment of panic when she couldn't see him and he didn't speak. "Logan . . . where are you?"

"Here, near the falls."

"I couldn't see you."

"I can see you."

"I'm going to get out. If you want the soap, you'll have to come get it." Silence. After deep listening, where she heard only a chorus of hoot owls and the splash of the water cascading over the falls, she called, "Logan . . . don't scare me." He came up out of the water beside her, shaking his dark head and pushing the hair back from his face with his two hands. "Oh! My land! You're like a fish!"

He held out his hand and she put the soap into it. The water came to her armpits, covering her breasts. He stood beside her, working the lather into his hair, then over his face, shoulders, and arms. His eyes never left her face, and hers clung to his. They didn't speak; the silence spoke for them. They both were acutely aware the other stood naked a few feet away, and both of them wanted desperately to reach out to the other. Rosalee stared longingly at his broad shoulders, at the width of his chest, and the hardness of his arms. How would it be if he reached for me? she wondered. She could feel the force of his intense gaze and her heart thudded painfully. Her love for him grew another measure, and tortured her. He wants to, she thought. He wants to reach for me, to hold me.

But he didn't. He held out the soap and she took it from his hand. He dived beneath the water and she hurried out of the pool and into the shadows where the cool air washed over her damp, warm body. After she dressed, she moved away from the place where his clothes lay, and knelt down to wash her dress and his shirt. She kept her face averted when he came out of the pool and didn't turn until she was sure he had dressed.

They walked back down the path, he carrying the rifle and she their wet clothes. Unspoken in both their minds was the thought that this was likely to be the last peaceful night they would spend together. It was only a matter of time until Adam Clayhill and his raiders found them, and Case was sure to come tomorrow or the next day.

Rosalee felt a frantic need to lighten the mood, but nothing lighthearted occurred to her, and in the end she said, "Did the warm water help your back?"

"I'm sure it did. It took the stiffness out of my muscles, too." The very quietness of his voice told her his thoughts were elsewhere and she made no further attempt at conversation.

A deep silence settled over the night, isolating the calls of the night birds, the crickets, and the faint rustling sound of a packrat scurrying through the dried leaves on his nocturnal wanderings.

Brutus was waiting for them when they rounded the boulder below the cliff house. Logan spoke to him in a low tone and Rosalee went past them up the ramp. Her heart was as heavy as lead in her chest. She added a few twigs to the coals of the cookfire, and in the faint light of the blaze she laid out the cornhusk mattress and a blanket for Logan. She made a pallet for herself on the other side of the room, completing it as the fire died, leaving the room in darkness. After she removed her dress, shoes and stockings, she crawled under the blanket wearing only her shift and let the tears roll from her eyes.

Logan stood outside the room, fighting a silent battle with his own thoughts. It seemed to him he had searched through a lifetime of emptiness, reaching for something to hold onto, only to have it crumble to nothing in his hands. Up until now he had faced the discouraging fact it would always be this way. The Indians accepted him; the whites did not. Had he not been schooled and reared among the whites, his life would have been less complicated. The irony of it was, he felt more white than Indian, and he now couldn't accept the Indian way of life.

Inside the cliff house was all he'd ever dreamed of having—a sweet, soft woman to love and take care of, one who would love him in return. Forces beyond his control were closing in on him. He felt it like the chill of winter. Would their coming find him competent to stand against them? He sighed deeply. He did not know.

Rosalee knew when Logan came through the doorway. "Your bed is over by your tack," she said softly. He didn't answer, but soon she heard the scraping of the rifle barrel as he stood it against the wall.

"Go to sleep. Brutus will let us know if anyone comes." He spoke slowly, tiredly. The dry cornhusks made a rustling sound when he lay down.

She lay on her back, staring up into the darkness, seeing how he looked, his great strong body, dark eyes, copper-colored skin, and his one concession to vanity, the full mustache, shaped in a wide downward curve around his firm mouth. She wondered how the mustache would feel against her face. Her breath became heavier, and a hunger for him that was like a pain went from her lips down into her loins, centered there and pulsed. She had wooed him by doing for him; she had loved him in secret, yearning for him to turn to her. He was companionable, his great, dark eyes eternally watching her, but beyond this he would not go. She wanted to submit to him and comfort him with her woman's sweetness. It would never happen, she thought desperately, unless she made it happen.

She came to a sudden decision, threw back the blanket, and slipped from her bed before she had time to reconsider her action. Her shift fell to her knees when she stood in the cool darkness, consumed by shame for what she was about to do, her body flaming, her damp braid hanging down her back. She knew exactly where he was, and she sensed his dark eyes on the whiteness of her body. She walked barefoot across the hard-packed floor and knelt down on the mattress. A sense of helplessness threatened to send her scurrying back to her pallet, and she said the only thing that had any meaning for her in this endless moment.

"Logan . . . I love you. You know that, don't you?"

He let his hard-held breath escape. "Yes," he whispered.

"I know you're afraid to love me. But I'm not afraid."

"Oh, God, Rosalee! I'm not afraid for myself, but for you!"

"Don't be afraid for me. I'm a woman grown. I know what I want. I want you, Logan. I'm shameless for saying so, but I want to be with you, stay with you."

"I'd marry you in a minute if I thought there was any chance it might not ruin you . . . any thread of hope we'd be able to live in peace. In the end it would destroy you!" His voice shook as a flood of despair knocked at his heart.

"I'm not convinced of that. I've waited for you all my life. If you love me, even half as much as I love you, you'll not turn me away. I'm asking you to take me in all the ways a man takes the woman he loves," she whispered shamelessly.

"I *can't*, Rosalee! I've thought about it until I'm half out of my mind . . . trying to convince myself that after awhile you wouldn't come to resent being married to a breed." His voice was hoarse with pleading. "I can't ask you to endure the snubs of your neighbors and friends. You'll not be accepted anywhere, Rosalee. I know, I've lived with that reality all my life."

"I want to be with you, live with you. Be your mate in all things. You're what matters to me." She waited in an agony of suspense. "Do you love me? I've got to know!"

"God, yes! I love you with every drop of blood in my body, I love you with all my heart and soul, whatever that may be. There's no question in my mind about loving you, my sweet and beautiful girl! The problem is—"

"Hush! Hush!" she said joyously, and lifted the blanket and launched herself into his arms.

A moan slid out of him and his arms closed around her and pulled all her whiteness into the curve of his great, hard body. She lifted her arms, encircled his neck, and wound her fingers in his damp, dark hair. For an endless time he held her clamped to him, hurting her with his desperate hunger to feel every inch of her, breathing hard into her hair. Then his mouth covered hers, ground and bruised and lifted.

"My darling girl! I love you so much!" he whispered, between frantic kisses. "I love you, love you . . ." The words trailed off as his mouth traced the pattern of love on hers.

She gloried in the closeness of their bodies. It was as if she had been on a long journey and, at last, she was home.

Their lips caught and clung, released and smiled against each other, caught again. They were kisses of newly discovered love. They laughed lowly, intimately, joyously, and their fingers moved over each other's faces; hers lingering on the stubble on his cheeks.

"Logan." His name came sweet and shivering from her throat.

"I wish I'd shaved. I'll scratch your sweet face."

"I don't care. Just keep kissing me. Your lips are soft, not at all what I expected."

The laugh bubbled up out of his throat and he rolled so she was on her back and he was hovering over her. "You're more than I ever dreamed of." His lips covered her face, moved down her smooth cheeks to her lips that waited, warm and eager.

"Your mustache is soft," she whispered after a long deep kiss.

"I'll get rid of it if you want me to."

"No. I want you to stay as you are."

"I'm not sure how to love you," he groaned, breathing hard. "I'm afraid I'll hurt you."

"You'll not hurt me." She squirmed against him and he hugged her tighter. "Do people love each other with their clothes on?" she whispered. The warm safety of his arms was heaven! She felt as if she could ask him anything.

"Some do."

"Are we going to?" Her hands slid carefully down his back to the waist of his pants.

"No, by God!" He held her face in his hands, kissing her eyelids, the curve of her cheek, her mouth. His tongue traced the outline of her lips, slipped in between and stroked the edge of her teeth. He felt her tremble beneath him and raised his head. He knew he had to be gentle, but it took all his self-control to keep his passion in check. The thought that this sweet woman had never known another man filled him with a strange emotion. He had never been with a woman this innocent. He prayed he could make it beautiful for her.

"You're trembling," he whispered. "Don't be afraid. This kind of love is for giving and sharing. I'll try to be gentle ... but I'm so full of love for you."

"I could never be afraid of you. I'm just ... excited." Her mind whirled giddily.

He moved away from her for a moment and she brazenly slipped out of her shift. He was back, leaning over her, drawing her, naked and beautiful, against him. She was shattered by the sheer pleasure of lying naked beneath him, but the pleasure had just begun, as she discovered under the roaming caresses of his lips. In a frenzy to caress him, her hand found a ridge on his back.

"Your poor back! Your ribs!" she cried in an agonized whisper.

"It's all right, sweetheart." His answering whisper breathed past her ear. "It's nothing compared to the pain of wanting you." His hand moved over her body from shoulder to thigh, caressing the flat plain of her belly, and then moved to her breast. He cupped it in his hand, squeezed it gently. "Ah . . . how I've wanted to feel this softness." He lowered his head and buried his face between the soft mounds. His hair, soft and clean, lay caressingly on her bare flesh. "Rosalee . . . to be with you like this is . . . heaven."

She felt a sharp thrill as his lips tugged at her breast and hugged his shaggy head to her. Her fingertips roamed over his smooth shoulders and neck, lightly fingered his ear, and plunged into his thick, dark hair.

"Your skin is so smooth."

"So is yours," he whispered against her flesh. "You smell good, feel good."

"So do you."

"I like the way you taste, the way you look, the way you are with me—soft and sweet." His lips moved up and tingled across her mouth with feathery kisses. Her breast filled his palm. His strong fingers stroked and fondled as carefully as if he was holding a precious life in his hand. His lips left hers and he gulped for air.

She couldn't speak. Her palms slid over muscle and tight flesh as if she had to know every inch of him. He advanced his pelvis against her thigh, deliberately letting her feel his elongated hardness. It was firm and throbbing against the thigh pinned between his, his need a tumulting pressure in his groin that verged on actual pain. She wasn't frightened of it, despite the things her cousins back in Missouri said about the dreadful, hurtful thing a man put inside a woman. She wanted it, welcomed it, and was awed by this giant of a man who trembled beneath her touch and yet demanded nothing she was not willing to give.

"Darling . . ." The word came from her like a sigh. His masculine scent filled her nostrils. She felt the wetness of his tongue on her breast.

"I'll hurt you when I come inside you. You know that?"

"I know it and want it—"

His hand moved down her belly and into the soft hair between her thighs, his fingers felt the wetness and moved into her mysterious moistness. Rosalee gave a small strangled cry. Tremors shot through her in rocketing waves. She grabbed the thick wrist of his hand resting on her belly and pulled the exploring fingers from her body.

"Oh . . . Logan! Darling . . ." It was a quivering whisper.

"Did you like that, sweetheart?"

"Yes, yes! Oh, yes!"

"That's only part of it, my love." A low groan came from him and he gently spread her thighs. He supported himself on his forearms and moved between them. He lay still for a moment and rained tender, soft kisses on her face. "I like the feel of your breasts against my chest, your heart beating against mine." He whispered words of love against her lips.

He took her mouth in a hard, deep kiss, but the kiss wasn't enough. Only by blending together could they even begin to appease the hunger they had for each other. He lifted his hips. Her hand burrowed between his belly and hers to guide him into her.

"Oh . . . my love!" She arched against him in sensual plea-sure.

"I'm so big! I know I'll hurt you! Oh, God! I don't know if I can stop!" His cheek was pressed to hers, his words came in an agonized whisper.

"Don't stop, love! Don't stop—" His concern brought tears that rolled down her temple to his. He felt them, turned his head and caught them with the tip of his tongue, then found her lips and kissed her with lips wet with her tears.

He made a sudden move with his hips and Rosalee felt a small, sharp pain which was nothing compared to the intense pleasure of being filled by him. He stopped when he felt the proof of her virginity give way beneath his battering. His kisses became even more tender.

"Oh, Logan! You're completely inside me! How wonder-ful!"

He raised his head and rested his forehead against hers. She was a constant surprise, a constant joy. "You were made to be loved . . . and cherished!" he whispered. "I pledge my love and my life to you, sweet Rosalee."

"And I to you, my wonderful man."

"I wanted to do this the night we sat by the woodpile. I'd feel myself begin to swell and I'd breathe deeply and say, Oh, God, don't let me scare the hell out of this sweet woman. I ached for you tonight in the pool—all of your sweetness just a foot away and I didn't dare reach for it." He murmured love talk in her ear and moved gently in her body, trying desperately to hold back his own release until he'd made sure she'd experienced the supreme pleasure.

The spasms of exquisite feeling that followed were like a gorgeous dance throughout her body. At times it was like a gentle wind caressing her wet, nude body. At other times it was like an enormous wave crashing over her. The whole world was this man joined to her, his sex at home in the cavern of her body, deeply implanted, moving gently, throb-bing, caressing, loving. She arched her hips hungrily and he wildly took what she offered. It was an ecstasy too beautiful for mere words. It was a joyous eclipse into time.

Rosalee was not really aware when it ended. When she returned to reality, Logan was leaning over her, his weight on his forearms. Her arms were around his neck, her breast pressed firmly to his chest.

The sweet familiar smell of his breath and the light brush of his mustache against her face brought a small inarticulate sound from her. She tightened her arms and her body, holding him inside her warmth and hungrily turned her mouth to his. Her hand moved to his tumbled, thick hair, and fondled the back of his neck lovingly.

"Are you all right, love?"

She laughed softly, caught his lower lip between her teeth and bit gently. Her hands moved down to where they were joined, enjoying the feel of where he disappeared into her body.

"You've brought me something very new, my Indian brave. We have done something wonderful together. So this is mating," she said with something like awe in her voice. "I am filled with you. I think I shall always feel empty without you there."

His breath caught and he couldn't say anything. He was still fully extended within her. A mighty gust of passion surged up, rocked them, enveloped them in a swirling, translucent world where nothing existed but the two of them and the ecstasy they shared.

Long afterward, lying face to face, they held each other. Her head rested on his arm, hers was curled about his chest, her palm flat against his back.

"I tried to keep control, but it slipped away and I lost myself in you."

She smiled against his mouth. "I never imagined it would be so all-consuming." She stretched lazily, her thighs sliding through his hair-roughened ones. "I feel so . . . good."

He cuddled her against him. "Go to sleep, love," he murmured.

Hours later, with Rosalee sleeping soundly in his arms, Logan tried to still his troubled thoughts. He had tried. God! How he had tried! He placed soft kisses on her forehead and she mumbled sleepily and snuggled closer.

"Oh, my sweet woman," he whispered. "What have I done to you?"

Chapter Twelve

After his confrontation with Rosalee, Mary, and Case Malone, Adam Clayhill rode away from the Spurlock ranch in a rage. Anger unfailingly turned his face a mottled crimson. He was a large, raw-boned man with a powerful frame. When he was angry, he struck out brutally. Now, his spurs stabbed his luckless mount again and again. The gelding's powerful haunches propelled it forward into a hard run and dust spurted under its hoofs as it sought relief from the punishing jabs. Within two miles Adam had outdistanced the other riders. The wind beating against his face failed to cool his temper; and when he looked behind him and saw that he was alone, he hauled his blowing horse to a halt so suddenly the mount reared and plunged to the side.

The men rode up, but kept a distance between themselves and their violently angry boss.

"What the hell you sitting there for?" Adam roared. "Get your big, stupid asses on down to the draw and out of sight; come night, flag it back there and burn the sonofabitch down!

If the Spurlocks are in the house, so be it. The slut's no better than the gawddamn stinkin' red ass! Burn it!" he shouted. "If there's one fuckin' stick left you can collect your pay and haul your asses off my ranch. I'll have no man working for me who can't take orders. Hear me?"

The men moved restlessly. Frank Gerhart, the young drover who had been with Shorty Banes the day Grant Spurlock was killed, hung back when the rest of the men rode off down the draw. It had gone against his grain when Banes and Shatto beat and stomped the Indian. It wasn't that he cared about the goddamn Indian, he rationalized. The bastard should have stayed on the reservation. It was just that he'd not realized what scum he was riding with until they hauled out the stick between his legs and started to cut his nuts. Jesus! If they'd do that to the Indian, they'd do it to him if he crossed them. And then there was the matter of the blind man. Holy Christ! Poor bastard! He was only trying to protect his daughter. Frank wanted no part of burning the girl out. He'd hired on as a cowhand, not a raider! But how was he going to get out of it?

"Mr. Clayhill . . ."

"What the hell you hanging back for?"

"I got a pain in my gut 'n a runnin' off at the bowels. I don't know if'n I kin sit a saddle much longer."

Adam's hard gaze fixed on the young rider, and fresh anger poured out of him. "You chicken shit! You don't have a pain in the gut! You got no guts! Get the hell off my land, get the hell out of the territory, you gawddamn, squeamish Indian lover! Shorty said you were a pain in the ass! If you hadn't dragged your feet the bastard would have been dead by now, or wishing he were."

Frank's eyes fell under the older man's glare. "If'n yore firin' me, I'll collect my pay and git."

"A man who *quits* in the middle of the month gets no pay.

Collect your tack and hightail it." Adam's tone conveyed his contempt, and his hard blue eyes studied the young cowboy as if seeing him for the first time. "Be gone by the time I get to the ranch, or by Gawd, I'll bury you there." He wheeled his horse in the direction of a roundup camp. He'd send Banes and his crew to the Spurlock ranch in case there were any more yellow bellies in the bunch. First Case Malone and now this whining bastard! Good Gawd, where were the men with blood and guts like Chivington who drove the damn savages onto the reservations where they belonged?

Frank spurred his horse and took off on the run. He was glad it was over. It was only the second or third time he'd even talked to Clayhill. The crotchety old bastard had showed his ass good at the Spurlock's. It wasn't right for him to treat Miss Spurlock like a slut. Frank reasoned that he might have strayed down sinner's path, but he didn't hold with talking filthy man-talk to ladies, and he didn't hold with cutting, killing, and burning. By God, he wasn't a murderer!

Frank didn't know exactly where he'd go, or what he'd do. He'd spent the last of his money in town thinking he had almost a month's pay coming. He'd not press for it. That old bastard wasn't above having him gunned down, and Shorty Banes would do anything to stay in good with the old man. It was best to collect his tack and ride out. He'd work somewhere for beans and bread until he could land another job. Anything was better than getting sucked into a mess like this. He didn't want to tangle with that Indian, and he didn't want to tangle with Case Malone. Somebody was going to get killed before this was over, and he was going to make sure it wasn't him.

When Frank rode past the white, wood fence that surrounded the big ranch house, he was surprised to see Della Clayhill come through the gate and call out to him.

"Cowboy . . . come here."

Frank reined his horse. "Yes, ma'am."

"Didn't you ride out with Mr. Clayhill to look for the Indian?"

Della looked into the young rider's eyes, then slowly let hers wander over his face and settle on his lips before she smiled. It was a trick she used when she wanted to beguile a man into thinking what she wanted him to think and telling her what she wanted to know. It worked almost every time with those whose positions were inferior.

"Yes, ma'am."

"Well? Did you find him?"

"Yes, ma'am."

"Is that all you can say? Come now—you're far too handsome to not be able to talk to a woman. I bet you have to fight them off of you when you go to town." Della laughed up at him and placed her hand on his leg. "Are you going to tell me what happened or do I have to pry every word out of you?"

"Nothin's happened yet, ma'am. The Injun's at the Spurlocks. The girl wouldn't let yore pa at him. Guess he's pretty stowed up."

"Stowed up? What happened to him?"

"Wal, now . . . yore pa knows 'bout it. He even knowed Mrs. Gregg had took him to the Spurlocks. Shorty had a setta with the Injun in town 'n him 'n Shatto wanted ta waylay him. They beat the livin' daylights outta him. They'd a done more, but Mrs. Gregg come and we scattered."

"What more were they going to do? Were they going to kill him?" Della asked sharply.

"No, ma'am. I don't reckon. They was agoin' ta . . . agoin' ta . . . ah . . ."

"What were they going to do, for Christ sake!" Della's patience was wearing thin. Besides, she had come out into the sun without a hat and could feel the heat on her face. She'd be sure to get a freckle or two out of this, but it would be worth it if she could find out anything more about the handsome brute who'd been constantly in her thoughts since she saw him in town. His black eyes had looked straight into hers. She had known exactly what he was thinking, what he wanted. . . .

"They was agoin' ta, ya know, do what they do ta make a . . . gelding."

"Cut his balls? Holy shit!" The words exploded from Della's mouth. "If the sons of bitches had ruined him I'd have personally shoved a hot poker up their asses and reamed them out good! The stupid bastards!"

The change in her face was almost as shocking to Frank as her words. The sweet smile slid away an instant before her lips spat out the vulgar words. Her eyes glittered with a cold light and her nostrils flared.

Frank gaped. She reminded him of a small, deadly snake, coiled and ready to strike. He'd been brought up to believe ladies were something special to be protected and revered. He'd not heard the cheapest whore say the things this *lady* was saying. Disillusionment pressed down on him. He wanted to move on, to get his things and leave this ranch forever, but hesitated to put his heels to his horse because her hand on his leg had tightened.

"Why did you come back?" Della demanded curtly.

"Mr. Clayhill will tell ya. I come fer my tack."

"Why? Did he fire you?"

"Yes." Frank left off the "ma'am" deliberately. She didn't seem to notice.

"What happened at the Spurlocks?"

"Nothin'. Miss Spurlock held us off with a gun. Yore pa backed down."

Della hooted with laughter. "I bet he liked that! He'll be

fit to be tied by the time he gets home. Is he staying there with her?"

"Who . . . ma'am?"

"The Indian, you fool! Is he living at the Spurlocks?"

"I'm athinkin' nobody'll be livin' there fer long. Yore pa give orders ta burn 'em out." Frank's young voice was tight and thin and disapproving, but Della was so taken up with her own thoughts she didn't notice.

"Good! That'll get rid of her!"

Frank looked at her cold face and wondered how he could ever have thought she was a lady, a real lady. He nudged his horse and headed the animal toward the bunkhouse.

Della's hand slid absently from his thigh when the animal moved away. Her mind was utterly absorbed in thoughts that had nothing to do with the young cowhand. She had to find a way to reach the Indian. Why was Adam in such a goddamn hurry to get rid of him? What difference did a few weeks or a few months make to him? She was pleased with the way she'd been able to manipulate Adam. They'd had a good tumble in bed, and she had no doubt that within a few days or weeks she'd have him ready to do whatever she wanted. But holy shit, he was fifty years old! Once or twice and he was all through. Just thinking about lying with the half-breed, being impaled by his rigid maleness, caused an undulating heat inside her. She'd heard Indians were the best at the game of sex; all primed like a stud looking for mare in season. She was determined to find out for herself if it was true.

A short while later, his personal belongings and his bedroll tied behind his saddle, Frank left the ranch. He wanted to put as much distance as possible between him and anything that had to do with the Clayhills, and especially Della Clayhill, the old man's stepdaughter.

* * *

When Case Malone left Rosalee and Logan after pointing out the entrance to the valley of the cliff dwellers, he took a different route back to the Spurlock ranch. The single track ran through thick stands of cedar and pine, and topped out on the plateau. He rode swiftly toward the Spurlock ranch, and as he came nearer, dropped down into the long, green valley, his approach masked by junipers.

Case's face gentled when he thought of his reason for being so far from Texas and the likelihood he would make the Colorado Territory his home. "Mary." Her name slipped unnoticed from his lips, and he gave himself up to his favorite pastime—daydreaming about her. Lovely, proud Mary. He was thirty-eight years old and he had loved her all his life. He had wanted her when she was fifteen, but had gone away to give her time to grow up. When he returned she was married to Tom Gregg. The crushing hurt had sent him on a two year spree, then to war. He came home to an empty life and had joined the Texas Rangers. When he heard she was widowed, he came looking for her to take her home.

Mary would never go back to Texas. He knew that now, but what the hell! Home was Mary. When he came to Junction City and found his love the madam of a whorehouse, he had been shocked. But he could see now how that could have happened. Mary had forever been the champion of the underdog. In order to support herself, Mary had provided a place for the women to ply their trade. It had never entered Case's mind that Mary was active in the business other than that it was her house and she set the rules. He had to smile when he thought of the courage it must have taken for Mary to undertake such a venture. Her upbringing had been so rigid he'd sometimes wondered if her mother was bucking for sainthood. He knew one thing for certain: he was going to marry that woman. He'd waited long enough while she dilly-

dallied, thinking she was a scarlet woman and not good enough
for him.

Drawing up at the crest of a low hill, Case scanned his
back trail. He sat on his horse for a moment, studying the
terrain before and behind him with a careful eye. It was
growing late and the sun was already behind the mountain.
The softness of the evening was settling over the valley, and
the air was cooler.

He thought of the Indian, Logan Horn. He was a man.
He had to be to buy up that land knowing what he had to
face. Case took pride in the fact that he could take the measure
of a man in a matter of minutes. It came from long practice;
dealing with cowboys, drifters, and every type of man imag-
inable during the war. He had learned quickly which ones he
could depend upon to stand beside him when the going got
rough and which ones would turn tail and run. Horn would
stand. He might die standing there, but he'd stand.

The girl would be safe with Horn. Case thought about it
carefully. It was clear that she was smitten. She could hardly
keep her eyes off the man. A man as well educated and as
affluent as Horn must have known a vast number of women
back East who wouldn't have cared about his Indian blood.
He might think Miss Spurlock backwoodsy even though she
was a pretty woman. Case frowned. In this country any white
woman who took up with a breed would have a tough row
to hoe. He may have made a mistake throwing them together,
but what else could he have done?

Taking his time, he let the big horse work his way through
the junipers. A wild turkey gobbled and scurried into the
underbrush. Case drew cool air deep into his lungs, air touched
with a faint scent of sage and—something else. Smoke! He
kicked his horse into a run and didn't pull up until he was at
the edge of the timber and had a clear view of the Spurlock

ranch. The bastards had fired the house and were working on the barn and the outbuildings!

Case pulled his rifle from the boot. Damn! He hadn't expected them to show up until dark. His eyes quickly scanned the scene for a sight of Ben. Thank God the boy was gone. The only thing that moved beside the raiders were the chickens who ran, flew low, ran again, and squawked until used for target practice.

Case dismounted and led his horse back into the trees, then squatted behind a boulder. The inside of the house was in flames, as were the barn and sheds. There was nothing he could do about that now. He scanned the faces of the men. He knew them all as the most unsavory of the lot he had tried to whip into a decent ranch crew. Case picked his target and looked down the barrel of his rifle. He set his sight on Shorty Banes, lowered it and fired. The bullet hit exactly where he wanted it to hit—the toe of Shorty's left foot. The raiders, all except Shorty, dived for cover behind their horses. He fell to the ground holding his foot and screaming with pain.

"I could've killed ya, ya bastard," Case yelled. "That was fer what ya did to Horn."

"That you, Malone? Ya ruined my foot!"

"I shoulda ruined that thing atween yore legs! That's where yore brains are."

"Ya gawddamned Injun lover! I'll git ya fer this!" Shorty got to his feet and tried to hop toward his horse.

"Stay where ya are or the next one goes in yore head! Hear? Listen ta me, ya yellow-bellied, worthless scum! Nobody but a bunch of lowdown sons of bitches'd burn out a woman 'n a kid! There's not a man among ya that's got the guts ta come out 'n face me!"

There was a moment's silence. "It's Clayhill's orders," one of the men yelled.

"'N yore followin' 'em like a pack of dogs after a bitch

in heat," Case shouted. "This land 'n Horn's was bought 'n paid for, all fittin' 'n proper. Clayhill's buckin' the United States government on this, 'n anybody who backs him is a party to it. The soldiers from Fort Collins'll be down here like a shot when they hear 'bout it."

"Sheeit! Tell that ta the fellers behind the barn, Malone." There was a chorus of loud guffaws. "Clayhill's got em in his pocket. Ya better clear out 'n take that red ass with ya. The old man'll hunt ya down 'n have yore hide."

"Horn ain't nothin' but a gawddamn breed, Malone. Why're ya stickin' yore neck out fer him?"

"If'n shit was brains, Malone, you'd rule the world!"

"Ya plannin' on gettin' ya some of that ass when the Injun gets done with it, Malone?"

"Ain't no Texas man I ever heared of that'd take on a white woman after she's been humped by a Injun."

The men were getting braver with their taunts.

"Ah . . . he ain't wantin' no red ass's leavin's. He's gettin' his from that uppity whore what thinks her shit don't stink." Coarse, loud laughter followed the remark.

Fury tore through Case, shutting off his breath. He took a deep breath and forced himself to be calm. He coolly took aim on the foot of a man hiding behind his horse and fired.

"Eeeoow!" The screech was loud and long. The horse jumped and ran when the man fell to the ground. "It warn't me what said it!"

"'Scuse me," Case said politely. "Maybe it was that other shithead standin' behind the roan." He fired again. The bullet found its mark and the man yelled.

"Gaawwd! It warn't me! I ain't said nothin'!"

"Then Shorty must be doin' all the talkin'. The rest of ya crow bait mount up. If'n I see one a ya again, start grabbin' iron, 'cause that's what I'll be doin'. Ride out—west, where I can see ya." One of the men went to help Shorty, and Case called out, "Leave Banes. Better yet, stand 'im up 'n spread his legs. I wanna see if I kin geld 'im with this rifle. I'm athinkin' the sight's off a hair."

"Good Gawdamighty!" Shorty yelled. "Don't leave me with the bastard!" He crawled on his hands and knees toward his horse.

Case fired and Shorty's hat flew off his head. "By God, this sight *is* off. I wasn't aimin' to ruin a good hat!"

The men mounted and took off at a surging run, leaving Shorty Banes silhouetted against the flames of the burning buildings. Black smoke drifted up from the smoldering haystack beside the shed and disappeared into the darkening sky.

"Git to walkin', Shorty, less ya want a bullet in the other foot." Tired of the game, Case wanted to end it.

"Gawddamnit, Malone! I cain't walk!" Shorty whined.

"Then crawl, ya bastard!" Case put a bullet into the ground in front of him. "Move, or I'll kill ya where ya stand 'n leave ya fer the buzzards!"

Shorty began to crawl toward the west and Case lowered the rifle and watched him. It was more than the sonofabitch deserved, he thought. But he'd never killed a man who wasn't shooting back.

Case had watched Shorty crawl the length of a good lariat when a sound behind him caught his ears. His hand dropped to the butt of his gun and he turned, listening. Each rock, each tree, each shrub was studied with particular care, making allowance for the gloom, contours, distances. He sat hunched, the side of his arm resting against the boulder. After several minutes he moved away from the rock. At that instant, he heard the click of metal just as he was struck by a wicked blow on the shoulder. He heard the other shot as it struck him and searing pain tore through his side. He grabbed wildly for his gun as he tumbled backward. It took all his will to lie still and wait. He held his fire until he saw the shadowy shape of a man come from behind the bushes and approach him. He lifted the gun and aimed instinctively. The sharp, splitting crack that sliced the silence was his own shot. The bullet went into the man's head from beneath his chin and he was dead before he fell.

Through the heaving, roaring blackness, Case fought to stay conscious. Who else was out there? Was the bushwhacker a Clayhill rider? Eleven men rode out from the Spurlock ranch, and they hadn't had time to circle around. Whoever he was, the bastard had got his, but he'd caught it good himself. Case felt the wetness of blood against his skin. His hand clung to the one real thing in his tilting world, his gun. His eyes seemed very heavy and he blinked them slowly. He knew he was going to pass out. His last thought was of Mary. Mary, his only love . . . he'd come, like he said. He'd not die and leave her.

Case fought his way back to consciousness and lay very still, trying to locate where he was. He was lying on his back in the open. The black of the sky above him was broken by flickering lightning and thunder rolled in the distance. Memory returned. Memory of shots that came out of the darkness. He'd let himself be bushwhacked! Pain racked him. He couldn't focus his eyes clearly, but someone was leaning over him. He tried to lift the gun, but it was too heavy. He waited for the inevitable.

"Gawd, Mr. Malone. Ya ain't dead?"

"I don't think so. Is that you, Ben?"

"No. It's Frank. Frank Gerhart."

"If ya come back to finish me off, git on with it."

"I ain't with 'em, Mr. Malone. Mr. Clayhill fired me. I went back to the ranch to get my tack 'n was aheadin' for town. I saw what was agoin' on 'n stayed up there in the rocks. I thought it was over till I heard the shots over here."

"Who was the backshooter?" Case gasped.

"'Twas Shatto. Ya killed 'im."

"He wasn't with the bunch that fired the house."

"The old man might a sent him out on his own."

"A backshooter's lower'n a snake's belly!" Case gritted. His mind told him he must move, but his muscles refused to obey.

"Where'd ya git it, Mr. Malone?"

"The shoulder 'n side. F—etch my horse and get a blanket before I sh—ake myself t'death." His head throbbed and his shoulder and side tortured him with every beat of his heart. Icy chills racked him.

Frank wrapped the blanket around him. "I'll help ya anyway I kin, but I ain't no good a'tall at takin' out bullets."

"Young Ben Spurlock headed for town about sundown. He's drivin' a team 'n got a cow tied on behind the wagon, so he's not making much time. Tell him where I am 'n to come back with the wagon. If you miss him, go on to Mrs. Gregg's and tell her what happened."

"I'll do it, Mr. Malone. I'll get help fer ya. Is there somethin' else I can do afore I go?"

"Leave me a canteen. I got a powerful thirst."

The water ran out the side of his mouth, but some of it went down his throat, giving him some relief from the thirst. After he finished drinking, he lay wrapped in the blanket and drifted in and out of sleep. When he was awake he tried to keep the thought from his mind that the young drover might ride off and leave him there to die alone. He dozed and woke up thinking he had to get to Mary. She would be expecting him. He struggled to get to his feet, but his weakness was too great and he fell back. His head seemed to explode and he sank down into a pit of blackness.

What was happening to him? The pain in his shoulder was agonizing, and his side burned like fire. He was moving. The jingle of the harnesses told him he was in the wagon. Frank had come back! He was on his way to Mary. Mary would know what to do. His head throbbed and he shook with chills despite the blankets. His thirst seemed without end, and he remembered from somewhere that thirst usually accompanied a heavy loss of blood. He closed his eyes, wishing the blessed darkness would claim him, and it did.

Josh stood beside Mary and held the lantern while they waited for the wagon. Mary's heart had felt like a lump of lead in her breast ever since Frank Gerhart had pounded on the kitchen door and told her that Ben Spurlock was coming in with Case and that he was badly wounded. Dread kept Mary rooted to the spot in the yard. She was scarcely aware of the wind pushing the lightly falling rain against her face. Finally, she heard the wagon coming, and Josh walked out to the edge of the yard and held the lantern to guide Ben to the door.

When Mary saw Case she put her hand to her throat. "God in heaven!" she exclaimed. "What—" Her words died when she saw his shirt was soaked with blood and his face was white beneath the tan. He was unconscious, but rolling his head from side to side. A hoarse croak came repeatedly from his lips. Mary pulled herself together and began issuing crisp orders. "Get a board to carry him on. Meta! Get my bed ready!"

Case was taken to her room and lifted gently out of the rain-soaked blankets and onto the bed where Mary and Meta went to work removing his blood-soaked clothes. Josh came in with a basin of hot water and a stack of bandages.

"I . . . can't do it, Meta," Mary wailed. "The bullets went through him, but there are pieces of cloth in there that have got to come out and I . . . can't. Oh, God! For the first time in my life I can't do what I know has got to be done."

"You don't have to, love." Meta pushed Mary down into a chair. "Sit right there. Me 'n Josh'll do it."

Mary sat beside the bed and stroked Case's forehead and the dark, silver-streaked hair at his temples. She leaned over, kissed his lean cheek, and whispered in his ear, "You'll be all right, darlin'. You're home with Mary. I'll take care of you. Lie still. They'll finish soon. Oh, Case, darlin', how could I have ever thought I could send you home and never see you again!"

Josh and Meta worked together, first washing and digging out all the foreign matter from the wounds and then washing them with liquid made from boiling cliff rose, a remedy Mary learned about from a Cheyenne woman. The wound in his shoulder was less serious than the one in his side where the bullet had scraped across the top of his hip bone. The gaping flesh was black and blue and the wounds looked bad. Josh smeared them with a jellylike salve, and he and Meta wrapped Case in bandages.

When they finished they brought hot bricks wrapped in cloth and packed them around his shaking body before covering him with blankets. Mary sat beside him and spooned whiskey into his mouth. She talked to him and her voice seemed to have a soothing effect. His body stopped shaking and his head ceased to roll.

It was well after midnight before Mary laid her head on the pillow beside his and closed her eyes.

Chapter
Thirteen

Several days went by before Mary was sure that Case would live. After the chills left his body, fever set in. She sponged his body day and night, but his fever soared. In his delirium he told of being sunk into a black pit where demons, laughing with glee, played on his body with torches and hot pitchforks. He called repeatedly for Mary. She bathed him, fed him, crooned to him; held his head to her breast and begged him to live. She left his bedside only to take care of her bodily functions.

One morning she noticed small beads of perspiration forming on his temples. Almost afraid to believe the fever was breaking, she wiped his damp forehead with a dry cloth and waited. Soon the forehead was damp again, and she buried her face in the pillow beside his head and gave herself up to a storm of weeping.

When Case opened his eyes, he was looking into Mary's face. His brain was too numbed to know where he was. Fog drifted before his eyes and his body felt suspended in a vacuum. He felt no pain and moved his arm, thinking he might be dead. If he was, he decided, Mary was with him, so it was all right.

"You big, dumb galoot! You scared me to death!" Mary's scolding voice was trembling, but she was smiling, too.

"I love ya, Mary girl," he croaked.

"I love you, too. I've loved you all my life." Tears rolled down her cheeks.

"Tears for me?"

"No. I'm just so mad at you for getting yourself shot!"

"I don't hurt anywhere."

"Course not. Folks say I'm better than any doctor around. I learned about it from an Indian woman." Relief was making her giddy.

With supreme effort, he forced himself to stay awake. "Clayhill burned . . . out the Spurlocks. I was too late—"

"You almost got yourself killed!"

"I never figured to git it from a backshooter."

"Sleep now. When you wake up I'll feed you some beef tea and you can tell me what you want done. Ben is here and I've given Frank Gerhart a job. But we can talk about it when you wake up."

"I dreamt ya was kissin' me."

"It wasn't a dream." She placed her lips on his dry ones and kissed him gently. "Get well so you can hold me," she whispered with a ragged breath.

"I won't never leave ya, Mary."

"If you even try, I'll . . . break your leg!" She clasped his hand in both of hers.

That brought a slow smile to his lips. "Or come at me with a old buffalo gun?" he said on the drowsy edge of sleep.

Mary nodded, blinking back the tears. He lay with his eyes closed, breathing shallowly, and his hand went limp in hers.

"Try to sleep a little," she said close to his ear. "I'll be here."

* * *

From Ben and Frank Gerhart, Mary pieced together the story of what had happened at the Spurlock ranch. She asked Frank to stay on and Josh fixed sleeping quarters for him and Ben in a corner of the barn.

Later that evening, when she, Meta, and Josh retired to the back of the house to leave the front part for the girls and their "company," she broached the subject of closing the house.

"I'd give the girls some money and put them on the stage to Denver if I didn't think we'd be better off letting things stand as they are. Most all of Clayhill's cowhands have been here at one time or the other. I think they'd balk if he ordered them to burn us out."

Meta and Josh nodded in agreement. "There ain't another place like this'n in fifty mile," Josh said. "Them drovers've got used to bein' pleasured. They ain't gonna want to give it up."

"The men that come here are treated fairly and I've doctored more than a few of them," Mary said. "There won't be much said about Case killing Shatto. It's Shorty Banes he'll have to look out for. Frank said Case made him crawl out of rifle range to where one of the men waited with his horse."

"That ain't agoin' to set good, but Case can handle Shorty."

"I'd say that being humiliated in front of the other men hurt more than getting shot in the foot."

Josh shook his shaggy head. "Clayhill ain't agoin' to back down. He'll set a feller on Horn like he done Case. If'n Horn stays, more'll come."

"How about the Kentucky farmers beyond the east ridge?" Mary asked. "Do you think they'd help Logan?"

"Why should they? As long as Clayhill leaves 'em be, they'd have no call to deal themselves in."

"Case won't give up now that Clayhill sent a backshooter

after him and burnt out the Spurlocks," Mary said firmly. "I know him well enough for that. He might have let Logan fight his own battles, but not now."

"That Indian bit off a chunk to chew," Josh said.

"Why do you call him 'that Indian'?" Mary asked suddenly.

Josh looked at her in bewilderment. "'Cause that's what he is. Ain't no mistake about him being a breed."

"I don't call you 'that Irishman,' and there's no mistake about you being Irish."

"But that ain't the same thing." His ruddy face reddened even more. "I like him, but—"

"But he's an Indian," Mary said wearily. "Your remark reflects the attitude almost everyone has. It's strange. Logan Horn is an intelligent, educated man who could help develop the territory, yet people will shun and despise him because of his Indian blood. Texans felt the same way, to some degree, about the Mexicans after the Alamo."

"It ain't agoin' to be easy fer him," Josh admitted.

"No. It's not going to be easy for any of us until Clayhill is forced to pull in his horns and realize he doesn't own this part of the world and everything in it because he was the first white man to settle here," Mary said bitterly.

Meta gave her a questioning glance. Mary seldom allowed her hatred for Adam Clayhill to show. Meta and Josh were the only ones who knew the depth of that hatred. After being responsible for her husband's drinking himself to death and leaving Mary destitute, Adam had wanted her for his mistress. When she refused he had blackened her name until the only recourse left to her was to open this house.

"I'm going to send Frank to the Parnells' to ask Cooper to come over," Mary said after a long, thoughtful silence. "I hear he stood up for Logan in town when Shorty and his bunch jumped him. I've got a big favor to ask him, and after the week I spent at the ranch taking care of his mother, I don't think he'll turn me down."

"Mary! I ain't never knowed of you to call back a favor." Meta's eyes mirrored a slight rebuke.

A hard, determined mask slid over Mary's face. "Don't put me on a pedestal. I can fight dirty just like anyone else when I'm cornered. Adam Clayhill will get what he deserves as sure as my name is Mary!"

Case woke up at noon the next day. The first thing he saw was Mary sitting in a chair beside the bed, her head tilted back, her eyes closed.

"Ya look tired."

Startled by the suddenness of his voice, Mary leaned close to peer into his face.

"How do you feel?"

"Weak as a newborn kitten."

"You can eat as soon as I've shaved some of those whiskers off your face."

He lifted his hand to his cheeks. "Good Lord! How long have I been here?"

"Almost a week. In all that time you haven't had anything but beef tea and sugared whiskey."

They looked at each other for a full minute. Whiskers roughened his jaws, his lips were cracked and peeling, and there were deep caverns beneath his cheekbones; but his eyes were clear, and they roamed Mary's pale face and fastened on her trembling lips. Concern showed in his steel blue eyes.

"Ya've wore yoreself out." His fingers touched her cheek.

"No such thing!" She closed her eyes and bent to kiss his lips. "I've never taken care of you before. But don't go and get yourself shot so I'll have to do it again. Next time I'll turn you over to Josh," she threatened.

While she was feeding him a thick chicken and dumpling

stew, she told him she had sent Frank to the Parnell ranch to fetch Cooper.

"We've got to trust someone to get Logan's money receipt and deed to Denver to have it registered. No doubt Clayhill has told the Land Office man here to hold the money and not record the sale. It's only a matter of time before he starts hunting for the deed."

"What do ya know 'bout Parnell?"

"Enough to know he resents the tight hold Clayhill has on the territory and everyone in it. Cooper tends to mind his own business, but he stands up for what's right. Sylvia, his mother, despises Clayhill. She never says why, but it's there in her face when his name is mentioned."

"I told Rosalee I'd be back in a day or two 'n bring her here. If Clayhill's men find her and Horn and kill 'im, you know what'll happen to her! After bein' out there alone with Horn all this time they'll assume the worst 'n not have a shred a respect fer her."

"Oh, fiddle! You forget Logan's an Indian. He'll not be easily cornered," Mary snorted. "He'll take care of Rosalee. I'd bet my life on it. I saw the way those two looked at each other. They're in love. Any man who would go through the agony Logan went through to get to her has got to be in love." She wiped his chin with a napkin. "Had enough?"

He grinned. "Will ya stay if'n I keep eatin'?"

"Till it comes out your ears." She jabbed a heaping spoonful into his mouth.

"I wish I could sit up 'n drink that coffee," he said after he swallowed.

"Well, you can't, and that's final."

"That's not all I'm awishin'."

"Case! A couple of days ago you were almost dead and here you are trying to get me in bed with you."

"I've waited a long time." He looked at her with a consuming tenderness in his eyes.

"So have I, darlin', so have I."

She leaned down to kiss his cheek, but his head rolled so that his lips found her mouth. What started out to be a gentle kiss became something entirely different. His hand found the back of her head and pressed her lips to his with surprising strength.

There was no haste in the kiss. Slow, sensuous, languid, he took his time quite deliberately, and every move of his lips increased the deeply buried heat in her body. Their breaths mingled when he released the pressure and she raised her head. She was filled with a driving physical need which drummed through her veins like thunder. She felt as well as heard the hoarse sound he made in his throat.

"I'm agoin' to marry ya," he said thickly. "I've been awaitin' . . . forever."

"Case," she groaned against his neck. "Oh . . . Case—"

"I'll take ya back to Texas, if'n ya want to go, Mary. But I'd rather stay here 'n build our own place. This is raw, new land, like East Texas was when my grandpa went there. He built his own place 'n I want to build ours."

"We don't have to make a decision about that now," Mary said gently. "Sleep for awhile. Frank should be back with Cooper sometime this evening."

"Ya could lay here beside me." His eyes teased her.

"Oh, no! You're going to have to be satisfied with this." She placed soft kisses on his face and stroked the hair at his temples. "Case, darlin', I've been a fool to let what others think keep me from you. I know what I am, and I've done nothing to be ashamed of. If you're willing to accept me on those terms, I'll be the best wife I know how to be."

"We've . . . wasted so much time." Weak, unashamed tears rolled from the corners of his eyes.

Their kiss was long and sweet and full of commitment. When it was over, Mary picked up the tray and Case's eyes followed her to the door. She turned, her eyes bright with her own unshed tears, and her heart lifted from the lonely place where it had held itself during the past ten years.

He wanted to tell her that he had loved her for as long as he could remember, and that every conscious moment while he lay soaked in his own blood waiting for Frank and Ben to come for him, he had thought of her. He wanted to say that she was the warmest, gentlest, loveliest woman he'd ever known. He wanted to explain to her that he didn't know soft words, that he'd never said them to a woman, but he had a heart full of love for her and that he'd die to keep her safe.

It was pure heaven to know he was loved by the woman he'd loved all these years. Case wanted to stay awake and enjoy his new happiness, but his eyelids drooped wearily and he slept.

The kitchen and Mary's living quarters were separate from the rest of the house. When the three girls who were currently in residence came to supper they were dressed as modestly as if they were dining in a preacher's home. After the evening meal they would retire to their rooms and put on their gaudy evening attire. The "guests" were entertained in the parlor before being taken to the rooms upstairs. A minimum of three drinks was served to each man, and Josh was always there to take care of a rowdy if Mary's quelling words from the doorway failed to take effect.

Frank and Cooper Parnell arrived just as Meta was putting supper on the large kitchen table and she added two extra plates. Mary saw three pairs of eyes hone in on Cooper and wanted to slap three faces.

"He's mine," Minnie whispered.

"We'll see about that." Hannah tossed her auburn curls and opened her blue eyes wide to ogle him.

"Shut up and behave," Mary snapped as she passed behind them. "Hello, Cooper. You and Frank wash up and come to supper."

Cooper was a tall, sandy-haired man in his mid-twenties, with powerful shoulders and an amazing quietness about him. The muscles of his shoulders, arms, and thighs bulged his buckskins, although he gave an overall appearance of being whiplash thin. His hips were lean and he wore a gun strapped below his waist, as did most men. But Cooper wore a bowie knife, too. Both knife scabbard and gun holster were tied down.

Mary had come to know the Parnells quite well. Two years ago his mother had come down with a severe case of influenza, and Cooper had come to Mary in the middle of the night to ask her for help. She had gone home with him during a raging snowstorm and stayed at the Parnell ranch for a week working around the clock with Cooper, applying hot onion poultices to Sylvia's chest and giving her a few drops of ipecac syrup every few hours. Sylvia survived, and she and Rosalee had become her only women friends.

Mary looked at Cooper, remembering his tender devotion to his widowed mother while she was ill. She had thought about playing Cupid between him and Rosalee, but the opportunity had never presented itself. Now it was too late. Rosalee was in love with Logan.

Ben sat at the table beside Frank and ate with gusto. His eyes went often to the three girls who sat opposite him and he hung on every word they said. Mary began to wonder if she had been wise to bring a fourteen-year-old boy in contact with the girls whose profession, no doubt, fascinated him.

The meal itself was enjoyable. Dishes were passed with utmost politeness after Mary said grace. Ben's table manners were good, and Cooper's faultless. Frank, not used to eating on a cloth, spilled food beside his plate and poured his coffee in his saucer to blow on it. His face reddened and his feet moved in an embarrassed shuffle when he burned his fingers and spilled the coffee in his plate.

Hannah managed to edge close to Cooper as she and the other two girls carried the dishes from the table while Meta served a bread pudding with thick cream. She ran her fingertips across the knuckles of his hand and gave him a conspiratorial wink. The message was clear. She would take him by the hand and lead him upstairs, given any encouragement at all. Cooper merely grinned at her.

Mary followed the girls out of the kitchen and closed the door. On her face was the pained look of a mother faced with irrefutable proof of her daughter's waywardness.

"Hannah, I will not have you soliciting business in my part of the house. You know the rules. You can abide by them or leave. Cooper is here as *my* guest. Until he goes out that back door and comes in the front, keep your hands off him. Is that understood?"

"Yes, ma'am." Hannah lowered her eyes, but not before Mary saw resentment in them. "There ain't been hardly nobody here fer a week," she complained.

"That's the way it is in any business. You can't expect the place to be crowded every night. You came here with the only dress you owned on your back, riding behind a cowhand who gave you a ride from town. If you want to leave you can take all your clothes and I'll give you a hundred dollars extra besides the money I'm holding for you. Josh will take you to the stage in the buggy. Make up your mind what you want to do."

Hannah looked down at the toe of her shoe peeking from beneath her floor-length skirt. "I'll stay."

"All right. There's something else I want to make clear. Ben Spurlock looks older than fourteen, but that's how old he is. At that age he's naturally curious about you girls. Stay away from him."

"How about Frank?" Clara asked, and Mary was surprised to see her blushing.

"Frank can do as he pleases on his own time. Right now he's broke, dead broke. That's why I gave him a job. That, and the fact that he helped Case. If one of you wants to take him upstairs without pay, that's your business; but don't serve him drinks unless he pays. That's my business."

After a chorus of "yes ma'ams," Mary went back to the kitchen and fixed a tray to take to Case.

Cooper sat in a chair beside Case's bed and Mary sat on the edge.

"That's it in a nutshell, Cooper," Mary said. "I've got the papers, but if Adam Clayhill gets his hands on them before they're recorded, there's no proof Logan paid for that land."

"I was going to Denver in a week or two; I'll make it sooner." He grinned, his teeth showing white against his tanned face. "It'll be my pleasure to put one over on Clayhill."

"Thank you, Cooper. I knew you'd help." Mary adjusted a pillow behind Case's back. "Adam has grown overconfident. He's not run into men the caliber of you, Case, and Logan," she said proudly.

Cooper was a peace loving man, yet there was something in him that gloried in a good battle. There was also in him a fierce resentment against those who abused their power and a strong streak of rebellion ever ready to well up and defend the underdog.

"I've got a letter here for Horn. McCloud gave it to me when I came through town. I'll leave it with you. It's from a James Randolph of Denver."

"I'll see that he gets it. I've a feeling he'll bring Rosalee in as soon as he can."

There was an insistent rap on the door. Slightly irritated

by the interruption, Mary got up to open it. Josh beckoned her out into the hallway.

"Adam Clayhill and four of his men rode in. They're tying up out front," he said in an urgent whisper.

"Out *front*? He knows my quarters are at the back of the house. He'd go there if it was me he wanted to see. Who's with him?"

"Dud Simms, Billy Hopper, 'n two I ain't never set eyes on afore."

"If there's trouble, Josh, I don't want Case to be in on it. He's so weak he can hardly stand."

Mary went quickly down the hall and opened the door leading to the wide foyer. Minnie and Hannah came out of the parlor just as the outside door was flung open so hard it struck the wall, bounced, and hung open. Adam and his men crowded into the hall, hats pushed back on their heads, spurs jingling as they raked against the table legs and carefully polished woodwork.

"Take your pick of the girls, boys. I'm payin'!" Adam bellowed, and slammed down a fistful of coins on the table, his eyes on Mary, examining her from head to toe.

"Yeeewhooo!" One of the strangers shouted and threw his hat at the ceiling. "I'm atakin' this'n." He grabbed Minnie around the waist and flung her around. Her feet hit the door and it crashed against the wall again.

"You're not welcome here." Mary spoke calmly, but firmly. "Take your men and leave."

"Leave? This here's a whorehouse, isn't it? Me and the boys came to get our ashes hauled." He took off his hat and sailed it across the room. "Bring out the whiskey, *madam*," he commanded. His cold blue eyes pinned hers.

The instant the cowboy set Minnie on her feet her hand flashed out and slapped him across the face. "Get yore hands off me, damn you!"

The cowboy hooted with laughter. "Eeeewhooo! I like 'em fightin', bitin', 'n scratchin'! I'll take this'n, boss. Where's yore room, honey?" He grabbed her arm in a hamlike fist.

"It's up to you, Minnie," Mary said. "You don't have to take him to your room if you don't want to."

"I don't want to! He's dirty as a hog. If I take one, it'll be Dud." She shook his hand from her arm and stood away from him.

Stung to anger by her blunt refusal, the cowboy threw back his head and spat out, "Yo're shore uppity for a whore. Ya think I ain't good enuff?"

"Yore not *clean* enough," Minnie said angrily.

"I told you to haul out the whiskey," Adam demanded. "We've come to have a party, didn't we, boys?"

Mary lifted her chin and a fierce defiance glittered in her eyes. "I said for you to leave. My girls don't entertain marauders, backshooters, and trash!"

"Speaking of trash, *madam*," Adam sneered. "I'm taking you. I'm goin' to find out if what's between your legs is as pretty as what's on your shoulders."

The insult brought a flush to Mary's cheeks, but she lifted her brows and looked at him coolly. "*Mister* Clayhill, what I told you a long time ago when I rejected your offer to set me up for your personal . . . pleasure, still holds. I can't see you for dirt! You're an insult to the human race."

Her scorn cracked like a whip across his pride. His shaggy gray head jutted forward and he gritted out viciously, "You gawddamn bitch! Who are you callin' trash? You, runnin' a whorehouse; you, openin' your legs for every drifter who comes by; you, takin' up with a red ass! That's trash!" He pointed his finger in her face. "You've got Malone here, haven't you? He killed one of my men and crippled three more. I'm not sittin' still for it. You tell him he isn't in Texas, he's in *my* territory and I'll see him hung!" He reached out and grabbed her by the arm.

"Get your hands off Mrs. Gregg." Cooper Parnell's voice came from behind Mary.

"Are you dealin' yourself in?" Adam snapped.

"What do you think?" Cooper asked softly.

"I'm thinking you're makin' a mistake." Blue eyes blazed into blue eyes. The men were of equal height; both towered over Mary. Adam's face was an angry red beneath the shock of gray hair. Cooper's stare at the older man was a deliberate, studied insult. Adam's hand tightened on Mary's arm.

"Maybe, but it'll be your last if you don't get your hand off the lady."

"You plannin' to take us all on?"

"It won't matter to you what happens after the first shot, you'll be dead before you hit the floor."

"That good, huh?" Adam studied him for a minute, then laughed and dropped his hand from Mary's arm. "I've lived too long to get killed over a whore. Who are you?"

"Cooper Parnell."

"I've heard of you. Good with a gun, good with a knife. It's said you can ride anything on four legs. I'll pay you more in a month than you'd make on that rag-tail horse ranch of yours in a year."

"Doing what? Burning out women and kids, backshooting, chasing legal landowners off their land? I've not sunk that low." Cooper's eyes had narrowed and his nostrils flared whitely against his sun-browned skin.

"Another sanctimonious bastard! That's why you have a rag-tail horse ranch, boy, and I've got the biggest spread in the territory." Adam sneered.

"Mrs. Gregg told you to leave and take that scum with you."

"Watch yore mouth!" The cowhand who had grabbed Minnie stepped up beside Adam.

Cooper's gun leaped in his hand. It happened so fast the last word was still on the cowboy's lips. His eyes widened and color drained from his face.

"You're a second from being dead," Cooper spoke quietly.

Josh, with a shotgun in his hand, elbowed aside the two at the front door. There was a waiting silence. The grubby cowhand glanced at Adam, then backed away.

"So you're throwing in with the red ass and the whore," Adam snarled.

"I'll not kill you for that, I'll let Malone do it. It'll be just one more good reason."

Adam hesitated. Something about the man bothered him. He'd known when Cooper and his mother had bought the spread on the other side of the North Platte from a widow whose husband was killed by the Sioux. The place was a long way from his land and he'd not given it much thought. This was the first time he'd come face to face with Parnell and he had the feeling that he'd seen him someplace before. He stirred uneasily and beetled his brows while he concentrated. Then he shrugged. What the hell! It was probably in the saloon in town.

Adam walked over to the corner and picked up his hat. Then he went to the table and pocketed the coins he'd tossed there.

"Come on, boys. I know of a good little piece of ass in town you can have for two bits."

"Ya get what ya pay for!" Minnie couldn't resist throwing at them when they went out the door.

Dud Simms and Billy Hopper were the last to leave and they had apologetic looks on their faces as Josh followed them out.

Cooper sat at the table and his mother placed a plate of ham and eggs in front of him. She filled her cup from the big, blue speckled coffeepot on the cookstove and sat down opposite him.

Sylvia Parnell was a slim, pretty woman with light hair streaked with gray. She had given her son her even features and full-lipped mouth, a deep sense of responsibility, and all the love and devotion a mother could give an only son.

"I had a run-in with Clayhill at Mrs. Gregg's."

"You met him?" Sylvia's face drained of color.

"Yeah. He's what I thought he was, only worse—big, dirty talking, a bully and a blowhard. I'm taking the Indian's papers to Denver to have them recorded. Want to come with me? We can take the stage."

"No. My beans are ready to shell and I want to set out some berries. You'll make faster time by yourself."

Cooper took in the worried look on his mother's face. "You've nothing to worry about, Ma. I'll not get involved except to take the papers. Somebody ought to help the poor bastard. He bit off a hunk to chew. Being a breed would be enough, but being a breed and going against Clayhill is about as bad a deal as a man can get. I'm not only doing it to help Horn, I'm doing it 'cause Mary Gregg asked me to, and because it's time for the Clayhill rule to end in this territory if it's ever going to be settled by decent people."

"It's right that you help Mr. Horn, Cooper," Sylvia said, and looked out the window toward the mountains beyond. "Just watch yourself. Adam Clayhill is ruthless when it comes to getting what he wants."

Cooper glanced at his mother and then down at his plate. He wouldn't tell her about the Spurlocks being burned out or about the backshooter Clayhill sent out to get Case Malone. He'd tell her after he came back from Denver.

Chapter
Fourteen

"Logan, it doesn't seem possible that we've been here for more than a week." Rosalee stood on the narrow ledge in front of the cliff dwellings, the ever-present breeze that swept the valley sending her skirts billowing. "Why do you suppose Case Malone hasn't come back? Do you think the Clayhill men caught him and Ben at the ranch?"

"Malone's too smart for that," he reassured her.

"I'm worried about Ben . . . and Mr. Malone."

"Malone may be afraid he'll lead them here to us," he told her, not believing what he said, but wanting to comfort her.

"When we leave here, where will we go?" She spoke without looking around to where Logan stood behind her.

"I'd take you to Mrs. Gregg. After that I'll just have to take things as they come. I can't stay holed up forever. I've got to get this thing settled so I can start building my ranch." She glanced at him over her shoulder and he moved up to her and pulled her back against him. "There must be twenty men out there looking for us. I could have picked off a dozen if I were a backshooter."

She crossed her arms and her hands gripped the arms that were wrapped around her. She leaned against his strength and turned her face so his lips could nuzzle her cheek.

"I worried each time you went out," she whispered.

"I know you did." Her hair was fragrant and warm from the sun. He kissed the strands the wind blew against his lips.

"When will we leave?"

"Tonight. I've waited, thinking Malone would come back." His lips found the corner of her mouth. "That's not exactly true. I've been selfish, I didn't want our time together to come to an end."

She turned in his arms and her hands climbed his chest and beyond to clasp behind his neck. "It isn't the end, my love. It's the beginning. We'll be together for the rest of our lives. I'm happier right now than I've ever been in my life. The only thing that would make me happier is to know I can live with you peacefully and have Ben and Odell with us until they can strike out on their own."

Logan looked down into her face, calmly studying her. He shook his head. "Rosalee, Rosalee . . . It won't be easy. You're living in a dream world if you think we'll live peacefully. Face the reality that you'll be the wife of a breed. You'll have very few friends; you'll be snubbed and talked about worse than a whore—"

"I've lived with reality all my life, my love. The good things in life are never easy at first. We have to earn them."

"We may not find a preacher who will marry us," he said in a burst of anguish. He gazed down at her and saw the love in her eyes. The fear of losing her was more frightening than facing a hundred Clayhill men who wanted to kill him. The thought of not having her with him, never holding her again, was too painful to tolerate. He tightened his hold on her protectively.

"If it comes to that, we'll have our own ceremony. I feel that I'm already your wife. I won't feel more so because a man opens a Bible and reads a few words to make it legal in the eyes of the law. Our act of love made you my husband in my heart. The seed of our love may already be growing in my belly." Her palms moved around to glide over his cheeks. "It's unfortunate that some white people have a superior attitude toward Indians, though I'm not sure why. I also suspect *they* don't know why they think the way they do. It's what they've been taught. I sympathize with them and pity them because they are trying so desperately hard to be *above* someone."

"It's human nature, I guess," he admitted tiredly. "It's always been that way; the whites over the blacks, the rich over the poor, the strong over the weak."

"But there are changes in the wind, Logan," she said hopefully. The tips of her fingers traced his wide mouth. "There'll be hundreds of new families coming west and gradually opinions will change."

"Rosalee, Rosalee . . ." He said her name twice as he often did and hugged her so tightly her breath was cut off for a short while. "It will take a long time," he said in a distressed, husky whisper.

"I can wait," she said gently. "And I'll be happy all the while." Her inability to relieve his distress made her weak. She lifted herself on her toes. "Kiss me, then we'll get ready to go."

For a long moment he stood looking down at her, then slowly smiled. "You're good for me." His smile widened and the look of happiness on his face made him breathtakingly handsome. "I'd rather go back to bed."

"Oh, you would, would you?" she said tartly. "It's the

middle of the day. Only this morning we—" She felt oddly exhilarated and embarrassed.

"Yes? We what?" His eyes teased her.

Her face flooded with color and he laughed. From the first, his half-serious, half-teasing attacks on her modesty had fought with her time-honored inhibitions. They had bathed in the pool at night, made love in the dark. She had not yet exhibited her naked body in the light of day, nor had she looked upon his nakedness. Her mind was filled with these thoughts when he swung her up into his arms and carried her into the coolness of the stone and adobe dwelling.

"You're indecent!" she protested.

"The Cheyenne make love anytime they get the urge, day or night." He laid her down on the mattress and stretched his long length out beside her.

"What a lovely custom." Her words were breathed on his lips.

They lay quietly and kissed for a long while before Logan separated from her. He knelt at her feet, removed her shoes and stockings, then her dress and her shift. While he undressed he gazed silently into the blue-green depths of her eyes and saw there the love that he ached for.

Rosalee had never seen a man naked before, and he was more magnificent than she imagined he would be. The bronze skin on his hard-muscled shoulders and hairless chest glowed warmly. His rib cage was lean, his buttocks taut and slim. Her eyes moved down to black hair from which sprang his rod of life, throbbingly erect, and marveled at its awakening. Her gaze lingered there, then traveled down his muscled legs before moving swiftly to his face.

She stared up at him feeling none of the inhibitions she thought she would feel if a man looked at her naked body. The warmth in his dark eyes made her feel beautiful. They caressed the length of her body for countless minutes before he dropped down beside her and clasped her so tightly to his chest she couldn't tell whose heart she felt pulsing between them.

"You're beautiful, my bronze lover." She said it so softly that he felt the words on her lips. "I want you so much. Here. Now." She guided his hand to the seat of her desire.

"I love you," he said with deep emotion as he slipped a hand beneath her hips, not even realizing he had said the words.

"I love you with all my heart," she said, her voice rasping roughly. "I never dreamed love was so powerful, so wonderful."

He rose over her, his pelvis seeking, and then glided strongly into her. She sighed as he penetrated to his full length, and she locked her hands in the small of his back, arching herself against him. Tenderly, he guided her to the heights of passion, held her teetering on the brink of an all-consuming desire, and when she could bear the tension no longer, carried her with him into the blaze of fulfillment.

Their joining was wholly unlike the other times, though the same need for each other obsessed them. Now there was a strong sense of urgency that trembled on the verge of blind panic, endured endlessly, then slowly eased. They emerged, shocked and weak with spent emotions, into the reality of their separate selves.

Evening came, and they were ready to leave the valley. The wagon had been hidden among the willows and the bay team turned loose to roam and forage. They had stored the few things Rosalee had brought from home and the supplies Logan had purchased in town in a cache in the cliff dwelling he had discovered several days ago. Rosalee went down the ramp to the valley floor and Logan brushed the dust with a willow branch to erase their tracks.

Mercury, saddled, with a bedroll tied on behind, waited impatiently; stomped and snorted, anxious to be away. The mare, more docile, her reins hanging on the ground tying her as securely as if she were staked, cropped the grass, raising her head occasionally to keep an eye on her offspring. Rosalee insisted on riding astride the mare Indian fashion, with only a blanket between her and the horse because that was the way she had learned to ride. The Spurlocks had owned only one saddle and her father had used it first, then Ben, when he took over the work on the ranch.

She stood beside the mare, tall and slim, in the old split riding skirt she had yanked from the peg on the wall above her bunk, a faded blue shirt and a round-brimmed leather hat Logan had given her from his pack, and waited for him. As she looked back and saw him coming down the ramp, her heart swelled with pride. He put his arms around her for a brief embrace, joining her in a silent good-bye to their special time together.

"Ready?" She nodded. When he held his hands low, she stepped into them and he boosted her onto the mare's back. "Brutus, lead out. Rosalee will watch the baby," he told the wolf dog that came slinking out of the brush.

"I want to go to the Haywards, Logan. Odell has been there two weeks and will be wondering why I've not come for her."

"Do you want to take her with you to Mrs. Gregg's?"

"I don't know what to do. Mary's isn't the . . . place for her or for Ben, yet—"

"Is there a boardinghouse in town? I've been thinking about taking you there. You can take Ben and Odell with you."

"We can't do that," she said quickly. "We'll have to stay someplace where I can work for our keep."

"You're not to worry about that. You belong to me, now."
He placed his hand on her thigh. "I take care of my own."

"But . . ."

"That means Odell and Ben, too, my love." His tone
implied, "don't argue," and she didn't. "Stay close," he commanded. "If we run into trouble, you're to do exactly as I
tell you. Our lives will depend on it. If I put you on Mercury
and say 'go,' head for Mrs. Gregg's. There isn't a horse in
the territory that can catch him once he's reached his stride."

"I'll not leave you to face them alone! I can handle a rifle,"
she declared staunchly.

"I know that, but we won't face them in a shootout. We'll
cut and run and pick our own time, Indian fashion." He
grinned at that and was rewarded by her answering smile.
"The men working for Clayhill know only force, not tactics.
We'll outsmart them."

"You're right, my love." She leaned toward him and his
lips met hers in a brief kiss. "Don't worry," she assured him.
"I'll do exactly as you tell me." His hand squeezed her thigh
and his dark eyes loved her. He handed her the end of the
rope attached to the foal's halter and swung into the saddle.

When they left the valley Logan turned south. Rosalee
was surprised, but didn't question him. Later, they made a
deep circle and rode for a mile down a field of gray stone
over which water had run and would run again after a heavy
rain. She knew then he was doing what he could to keep the
Clayhill men from discovering the entrance to their valley.

The sky was alive with a million stars, but it was so dark
Rosalee could scarcely see the rump of Logan's horse. She
followed him, keeping close, feeling a oneness with him
although she couldn't see him. He was her man; she would
follow him to the end of the world. When they reached the
wooded bench, she shivered in the cool fresh mountain breeze
that came down through the spruce and pine trees. It was a

relief when they took an animal trail that led off the bench and rode through aspens and the cottonwood that shielded them from the wind.

Rosalee began to recognize landmarks. They passed over a draw that marked the western border of their land. A feeling of homesickness struck her. She had never been away from Odell and Ben this long before. Just thinking of Odell brought a mistiness to her eyes, and she longed to see the girl's pixie face and bright blue eyes.

Her mind was so full of these thoughts that Rosalee failed to notice that Logan had reined Mercury to a stop until she was beside him. He put his finger to his lips and then motioned toward Brutus. The dog stood stiffly at attention, his head turned at a right angle.

"He hears something we don't hear. So does Mercury," Logan murmured. The stallion's ears twitched backward and then forward, his lips quivered. Logan dismounted and put his hand over his nose. He slipped his rifle from the boot on the saddle and handed the reins to Rosalee. "Take the horses into that heavy brush, deep enough to be out of sight. Brutus and I will go down that draw." He pointed to the right. "If shooting starts, tie the mare, get on Mercury, and go. Is that understood?"

"Oh, Logan—"

"Is that understood?" he asked again.

"Yes, my . . . love," she said softly. Their eyes held for an instant, then she kneed the mare and moved away from him. Leaving him would be the last thing she'd want to do, but she knew the wisdom of his thinking. He would be more able to defend himself or get away if he didn't have her to think about.

Behind the screen of scrub and brush, Rosalee strained her ears for foreign sounds but heard nothing. The breeze couldn't reach her among the thick brush and insects buzzed around her head. Behind her a branch rubbed against another, dry leaves rustled. Something, a bird or squirrel or rabbit, scuttled into the brush. Mercury nipped at the foal and she danced to the end of the lead rope. The beating wings of an owl sweeping past almost caused Rosalee to drop the rope. She grimaced in self-disgust at the frightened fluttering of her heart and waited while the minutes went slowly by.

Logan held his rifle ready and went down through the trees, easing down into the gully, being careful of rolling stones and dry branches. Brutus moved silently ahead of him. At the bottom, close against a tree trunk, he listened. The constant rustling of trees and brush as the wind swept through the gully made it difficult for him to hear clearly, but it carried with it a faint smell of woodsmoke. Logan waved Brutus on and they followed the creek bottom until he heard the stamping and blowing of horses tied to a stringer and the low murmur of voices.

There was a small chance a sentry had been posted, so Logan proceeded with caution, moving silently as a shadow from tree to tree. When he could see the glow of the campfire through the trees he circled it until he found the horses. There were eight. He crouched low and scrutinized literally every inch of ground between him and a big windfall before he ran lightly from shadow to shadow until he reached it. He sank down amid the brush that grew around the rotting trunk and looked straight into the camp.

Logan counted eight men. Eight men, eight horses—they hadn't bothered to post a sentry. Shorty Banes was there as well as one of the young drovers who was with him the day they had attacked Logan on the trail. The men lounged around the campfire. One whittled a stick, one was tossing cards into a hat, and another was playing a game of solitaire. The rest were joshing amongst themselves and laughing.

"I ain't amindin' this a'tall. If'n the ol' man wants ta pay my wages fer lookin' fer that redskin, I'll take it. But I ain't acarin' if'n we find 'em."

"Any fool coulda figured that," Shorty growled.

He limped to the fire, crouched there, and filled a cup from the black coffeepot. Logan studied him. He was a brutal, ruthless man, utterly without regard for anyone. He was the worst of the bunch and all the more dangerous because he was stupid. Logan had had a few like him in his company during the war, and sooner or later their bad tempers and inability to cooperate with their fellow soldiers had gotten them killed. Logan knew that if he dropped Shorty the rest would scatter after firing a wild shot or two. He also knew that if the situation were reversed and Shorty Banes had him in his sights that's what he would do. The streak of decency in Logan that some men would construe as weakness caused him to hold his fire.

One of the drovers, lying propped against his saddle, brought out a harmonica and played a lonesome tune. He finished it, played a faster ditty and one of the young drovers jumped to his feet and began to jig and sing in a surprisingly good voice.

"Ole Clayhill was a fine ole man,
He washed his face in a fryin' pan.
Land is all the ole man craves,
He'll put that Injun in his grave."

Loud guffaws and cheers erupted at the end of the verse. "Give us another'n, Larson," someone shouted. "Hell! He ortta be asingin' at the saloon. Hit's better'n that fat gal what cain't git 'er legs t'gether!"

"Hell! A mule could walk atween 'em without atouchin' her."

"Ya ortta know, Larson. Ya been atween 'em enuff. How was hit?"

"Like abouncin' on a feather bed with my pecker in a bucket a lard!" The young cowhand chortled. "She ain't thar no more. I must a wore her plum out."

The harmonica player drew in and out on the instrument as if he were huffing and puffing, then played a moaning sound that ended in a long, drawn out sigh. The drovers slapped their hats against their legs and roared with laughter.

"Shut up!" Shorty shouted.

"Ah . . . c'mon, Shorty. Ya've been like a b'ar with a sore tail ever since Malone shot yore toe off. We's jest afunnin'. Go on, Larson. Give us another'n."

"Thar's a Injun on the range
     'n the boss said, kill it,
So I shot 'em in the arse
     'n he landed in the skillet.
Come'a ti yi yippi, yippi yea, yippi yea,
Come'a ti yi yippi, yippi yea."

Logan's lips twitched in a grin. Was the joke on him or on Clayhill? Finally, he came to the conclusion it was on Clayhill, because this "posse" was about as useless as tits on a bull. That included Banes, who was all fists and mouth and no brains. He backed into the solid blackness behind him and circled toward the horses again. The need to let the posse know he'd been here was on him. They could think about how dammed lucky they were to be alive on the long, hot walk back to the ranch.

Motioning for Brutus to stay back so he wouldn't spook the horses, Logan moved among them, untied each horse, and left the lead tied to the stake. Before he sprang upon the back of the last horse, he marked his name in the dirt with a stick, and dropped a couple of bullets into the "O" in Horn. Then, with gentle urging, he drove the herd into the thick pines where the soft carpet of needles muffled the sound of their passing. Away from camp, he turned them toward the draw where Rosalee was waiting. The singing and joshing going on around the campfire faded into the distance, and then the only sound was the hoofs of the Clayhill horses striking the soft earth.

Mercury let Rosalee know the horses were coming long before she could hear them. His ears twitched and he moved nervously. Strangely calm, she pulled the extra rifle from Mercury's saddle and placed it across her lap. She refused to allow her thoughts to dwell on anything except what Logan had told her to do, and the minutes paced slowly by.

Out of the shadows Brutus appeared. He walked calmly toward them and lay down. Rosalee was thinking about the significance of that when she heard the low whistle that had been the signal when Logan was returning to the cliff dwellings. Her shoulders slumped with relief and she sat hunched over for a moment before she returned the rifle to the scabbard on the saddle.

Chapter
Fifteen

The night was more than half gone by the time they drove the horses into the hills and scattered them. As they turned their mounts once more toward the valley, Rosalee couldn't hold back the giggle that bubbled up at the thought of the long, hot walk awaiting Adam Clayhill's posse.

Logan heard the soft sound and edged his mount close to hers. He raised an eyebrow. "You're downright bloodthirsty," he accused with an indolent grin.

"Yes, I am!" She laughed then, and it carried on the night wind. "I hope every one of them gets blisters on his feet the size of hen eggs!"

"Banes was wearing a boot and a moccasin. He'll have a long walk on that sore foot. Someone said Malone shot his toe off."

"Good!" Mischief brimmed from her eyes and giggles from her lips. "I think there's something wild and wicked in me after all."

Love for her rose like a hot fountain from the core of him,

rose to fill his mouth with its heat and its force. It was hard for him to tear his eyes away from her. She was his woman, he thought with a strange feeling, as if he lacked breath and could not speak, as if he were sad to the point of tears, and yet through them, like a rainbow, she was the promise of all the sweet things he'd ever dreamed of having.

He was her man, she was thinking. She didn't care whether he was Spanish, Cheyenne, Scotch or Irish. She didn't care what he had, what he'd done, or what anyone said about him—he was her man. She'd be with him for as long as he wanted her.

Although she hadn't mentioned it, Logan knew she wanted to see her home, so he took her there. They skirted the hills, approached the homestead from the north, and pulled the horses to a halt in the cedar grove. He scanned the area thoughtfully, alert for ambush. The half moon had come up over the mountains and the stark outline of the stone house was visible. The shed was a pile of burned rubble, but the posts Rosalee and Ben had sunk in the ground to build the corral were still standing, although the crossbars had been pulled down. Odell's sack swing, hanging from the big oak tree, swayed gently, moved by the restless wind. In the pale light of the moon she could see that her garden had been trampled to the ground; not even a single stalk of corn was left standing. The homestead had a sad, lonely look about it.

"I'll take a look around," Logan said. He moved Mercury over beside Rosalee. When he handed her the reins his hand squeezed hers in silent understanding of what she was feeling at the sight of the wanton destruction of her home. "If I whistle, come on in." He pressed her hand again and left her, moving swiftly, like a fleeting shadow, and she wondered how a man so large could move so lightly on his feet.

Rosalee waited far more patiently than the big horse that tugged on the bit. The stallion didn't like the smell of the charred wood, or being left behind by Brutus and Logan. When the all clear signal came he recognized it and she was forced to drop the reins or be pulled from the mare. He trotted, reins dragging, across the open space to where Logan waited beside the house, and nudged him affectionately.

Rosalee came slowly out of the woods without any of the joyous feeling of homecoming. She slid from the mare's back and went to stand in the doorway of the fire-gutted house. The inside was like a black cavern that reeked of wet, burned wood. In the dim light of the half moon she could see the grotesque shapes of what was once the trestle table, the back of her father's chair, and the shelves where she had worked and stored their foodstuffs. Her eyes sought the corner where her bunk had been. Logan's mother had died there and her father had died out here in the yard. Memories brought a mist of tears to her eyes.

The family being here had made this shell of a house a home. They had sat around the yellowstone fireplace during the long, cold winter evenings and her father had related bits of history and told them of his boyhood escapades in the mountains. By the light of the fire she had taught Ben and Odell how to read from a tattered primer and how to make their letters on a chalkboard.

"We'll rebuild it," Logan's voice came from behind her and his arms came around her waist. "If it's all right with you and Ben, we'll make this our headquarters while we build a place of our own—a place for us, and for your sister and brother for as long as they want to stay."

"Oh, Logan..." She turned and burrowed in his arms. "Adam Clayhill is so ruthless and so determined. He'll not let us stay here. He'll—"

"Remember what you said? You told me that nothing worthwhile comes easy. We'll build our home here in this valley and we'll defend our right to stay here. You hold onto that." He grasped her shoulders and put her away from him so he could look into her face. "Wait until you meet the men who are coming out from Illinois. They're battle-tested and loyal. They'll be fighting for something of their own, for I intend to buy up more range and make them full partners. Clayhill will have to come up with better than that ragtag outfit we stole the horses from to best us." He chuckled softly and drew her to him again.

"You sound so . . . sure."

"I am sure," he said with more conviction than he was feeling. "Let's find a place to bed down for awhile. We'll get some sleep. In the morning we'll go to the Haywards, get your sister, and head for town."

"Oh, no! Not town—"

"It'll be all right. Clayhill won't gun me down in town. He's got to do away with me out here on the range where his men can say I drew down on them. Trust me."

"I do, my love. I do!"

Long after Rosalee slept, Logan lay awake, looking up at the stars and thinking about what lay ahead of them. Clayhill was not foremost in his mind. He thought of the meeting with the Haywards tomorrow. It would be the first test. All his life he'd lived in the white world filled with prejudices. Never, since he was a child, had he been free of it. He had known from the moment he realized he was different from the other children that there was no easy way for him and soon ceased to look for one. He walked his own trail, fought his own battles. He'd measured himself against the land, against other men, and in battle. He was confident of his abilities and prepared to give as good as he received. What he faced now was a fight of a different kind. His arms tightened around the slim girl he held, and his lips moved in her hair. How could he protect his sweet woman from the hurt that was sure to come? He fell asleep wondering what tomorrow would bring.

When morning came again there was a cool, fresh breeze coming down the forested mountainside. It had the smell of the pines on its breath. Logan and Rosalee followed the dim track that led toward the hills and the high valley the Kentucky homesteaders had settled. The path led through the woods and then dipped to the right. They came out on a bench and saw the sunlight gleam on rushing water. Beyond the stream they climbed onto a ridge and followed it to the valley. To the east was more thick forest and then the mountains, rising boldly up, bald at their higher points, the lower portions thick and green.

It was a bright, shining morning. Rosalee, feeling refreshed after a splash wash in the spring, felt a brightness within her. This day was a new beginning.

The Hayward homestead backed to a timbered hill. That it had been built by a man who came from generations of mountain people showed in the solid log construction, trimmed with some cut boards, a wide porch that ran the width of the house, and the two stone fireplaces and the tin roof. Cut firewood was stacked in neat rows between the trees. Behind the house a large, iron washpot bubbled over a small fire. A bench with wooden tubs on it sat nearby, and to the side, in the full sunlight, a line was stretched from tree to tree to hang the wet clothes. Chickens, goats, and dogs wandered onto the porch and were prevented from going into the house by Lottie, who flapped her apron as she came out the door. The squeals of excited children announced the approach of visitors.

Mr. Hayward and his two tall sons were waiting when Rosalee and Logan rode into the yard. All were carrying their long Kentucky rifles. Rosalee had eyes only for Odell, who flew off the porch and raced toward her. She slid from the mare and held open her arms.

"Rosalee! Rosalee! I thought you wasn't comin'." Odell's voice choked as her arms wrapped around her sister and clung.

"Hello, honey. Oh, I'm so glad to see you!" Rosalee hugged the child to her, then held her away so she could look at her. "I've missed you."

"I've missed you, too." Odell's eyes went to Logan, who was still mounted on Mercury. She put her lips to Rosalee's ear. "Are you agoin' to leave me here?" Her voice was choked as if she was about to cry.

Startled by the question, Rosalee looked into her little sister's worried face. "What's wrong, honey? Do you want to stay here?"

"No!" Odell whispered urgently.

Still puzzled, Rosalee took Odell's hand and turned to greet the tall, bearded man in the round-brimmed, peaked, leather hat.

"Hello, Mr. Hayward." She held her hand out to the father and then to each of the boys. "This is Logan Horn," she said, moving over beside Logan. "He's bought the range over south of our place."

"I heard 'bout it." The mountain man's sharp blue eyes stared straight into Logan's before he turned, leaned over, and expelled a played-out chaw from his jaws. He didn't extend his hand or move from where he'd planted his heavy boots firmly in dirt yard. He stood on spread legs, his rifle cradled in his arms.

"Howdy." Logan's dark eyes stared steadily into those of the mountain man. He sat on his horse, seemingly at ease, but there was a visible tension in his hands and the half smile on his lips that did nothing to relieve the waiting soberness of his expression. From the concealing shadow of the hat brim, he surveyed the other man, his black eyes boring down on him with an intensity wholly at variance with his relaxed attitude. The two men continued to eye each other, neither speaking or moving, while the unfriendly silence built up, thicker and higher.

"Rosalee." Lottie called from the porch, breaking into the stillness.

Rosalee glanced at Lottie, then back to Logan. His eyes flicked to her, then back to Mr. Hayward. She felt a pang of bitter disappointment. It had not occurred to her the Haywards would reject Logan's offer of friendship. Holding tightly to Odell's hand, she went toward the porch and Lottie.

"Odell, why don't ya run play with the girls while I talk to yore sister?" Lottie said without greeting Rosalee.

Rosalee glanced at the older woman and then at her sister, who clung to her hand and moved slightly behind her.

"It's all right, honey. You've got to tell Polly and Sudie May good-bye. We'll be leaving soon." Rosalee loosened her hand and gave her sister a little push.

"C'mon in," Lottie said when Odell rounded the corner of the cabin. "C'mon in and tell me if'n ya've lost yore senses, or what'n the world's caused ya to go do what ya've done."

"What do you mean, Lottie?" Rosalee stood just inside the door. She saw the breakfast things were still on the table and it hit her like a blow between the eyes that she and Logan would not be invited to stay and eat, a courtesy usually extended by mountain people even to one they considered an enemy.

"We got word 'bout Clayhill aburnin' ya out. We're plumb sorry 'bout it. It's a shame it ahappenin' jest after yore pa up 'n died 'n all, but what'n the world made ya go off with that breed, Rosalee? Ya've ruint yoreself with decent folk by adoin' it."

Rosalee stared at her with stricken eyes, then her face

stiffened. "I had no choice but to leave when Adam Clayhill came to burn us out. Logan could scarcely walk from the beating his men gave him when they ambushed him on the trail. I drove his wagon into the canyons where he would be safe until he got his strength back. I love him. I'm going to marry him."

"Yore aweddin' up with that breed?" Lottie's voice squeaked with disbelief. "Rosalee! He ain't nothin' but a red nigger buck!" she burst out, and it was as if she were pleading for her to deny that it was true.

"He's a *man*, Lottie!"

"He's a breed! We heared it. Now we've put eyes on 'em, we know it! It sticks out all over 'em. Yore ma 'n yore pa'll not rest easy in their graves 'cause a what ya done!" She shook her head miserably. "I'd never a thought it a ya. Ya seemed so steady 'n all."

Rosalee was gripping the doorframe so tightly her arm shook. Now that the horror was upon her, she realized how unprepared she was for this—how defenseless. Searching for words to lay across the widening chasm between her and her friend, she heard Lottie's voice coming at her again, hesitant yet determined.

"Ya kin stay here 'n help me with the younguns fer yore keep. Ben kin work with the boys. People'll forgit in time 'n a decent man'll ask fer ya."

Rosalee knew then that Lottie would never understand, she would always condemn her for giving herself to a man she considered of inferior blood. It had been ingrained in her from birth that it was an unbreachable sin for a white woman to mate with a man who was not as white as she was.

"Logan Horn is the man I've chosen to marry," Rosalee said in the backwash of silence, feeling more anger than she had ever felt in her life and trying hard to hold it down. "He's a man of mixed blood, as most of us are. However, his mother was an Indian, his father white, and you consider him inferior. I don't see him as anything but a man, not as an Indian or a breed, but as a man. He's a good man, Lottie. If you should ever need his help, I'm sure he'd be glad to give it."

"My land agoshen! Air ya gone dosey, too? Why'd we ask help of a breed? What's turned yore head, Rosalee? I thought ya was so level-headed. Ain't ya got no pride a'tall?" Lottie spoke in a tone of deepest regret.

"Yes, I've got pride. That's about all I've got left except the love of a decent, honest man who happens to have Indian blood in his veins. His blood is red, the same as yours and mine. He eats, sleeps, loves, hates, and hurts the same as we do, Lottie." Rosalee spoke quietly, proudly, wrapped in unconscious dignity.

"Ya jest ain't agoin' to listen, air ya?" Lottie moved a chair nervously. The legs rasped loudly on the rough plank floor. Her weathered face was set in wintry lines. "Mixed blood's bad blood! There ain't no gettin' rid a the stain once ya got it. Ever'body knows it fer a fact. Well—" She seemed suddenly out of patience. "It makes me no never mind if'n yore of a mind to sink so low. I told the menfolk ya'd been tainted long ago by the book learnin' yore ma give ya. It set yore mind on the wrong track. Ain't there no way a turnin' it back to what's right 'n decent?"

"Thank you for taking care of Odell." Rosalee swallowed her anger and took a long, deep breath to steady herself before she spoke in a low, controlled voice. "Logan will take care of us, Lottie. He's starting a ranch on the range south of our place. Ben and Odell will be living there with us. You'll always be welcome." She turned to leave, but Lottie's sharp voice called her back.

"Rosalee! Ya cain't take that chile to live with that breed! Leave 'er here 'n I'll raise 'er as mine. Thar ain't no need for 'er to suffer the disgrace."

Rosalee turned, and the look she gave Lottie was incredulous. "I'll not leave my sister here so you can instill in her your warped sense of values and fill her head with the nonsense of mixed blood, bad blood, and tainted blood! I'll not have her mind filled with a false sense of self-worth because she's white! She'll stay with me and Logan where she'll learn to judge a man by his actions and not by who his parents were." She stepped out onto the porch and called, "Odell."

Odell came around the corner of the house as if she had been waiting. "I got my things." She was carrying the pillowcase that held her extra dress, nightclothes, a doll and the wooden animals her pa had carved. "Are we agoin' now?"

"Yes, we're going. Tell Mrs. Hayward good-bye and thank her for the visit," Rosalee instructed.

Odell mumbled the words without looking directly at Lottie and clung tightly to Rosalee's hand. Logan was still mounted, holding the mare and the foal close to him. Brutus stood beside him, keeping an eye on the Hayward dogs that had come out to snarl and then slink away after a warning growl. Mr. Hayward and the boys had spread out as if ready to defend their home.

Embarrassment and shame washed over Rosalee like a warm spray from the hot spring. Shame for the Kentuckians, not for herself, and certainly not for Logan. She lifted her chin a little higher than she usually carried it and smiled at him as she walked toward him. His dark eyes were on her and she was determined that he not see a speck of defeat or regret on her face or in her attitude. He dismounted and she waited beside him while he tied Odell's bundle to his saddle. Without a word, he lifted the child up onto the back of the mare and boosted Rosalee up behind her.

"Bye, Mr. Hayward. Bye, boys," Rosalee called as the mare followed Mercury out of the yard. Brutus brought up the rear, keeping a leery eye on the Hayward dogs to be sure they kept a respectful distance from the colt.

"Looka thar, Pa. She aridin' bareback 'n follerin' 'im jest like a squaw."

The boy's voice reached Rosalee and she flushed angrily. She had heard the words clearly and she knew Logan had. Her heart went out to him and she longed to turn and shout that he was a fine man, a credit to the territory, and persuade them that they were wrong to despise him because of his mixed blood. Where was the logic, she thought tiredly, that a man like Shorty Banes could be held in higher esteem than Logan because his parents were both white and one of Logan's was an Indian.

Logan worked his way north, weaving in and out of the forest, riding the crest of the hills. Under the aspens and close to their groves were stands of golden cinquefoil. Mixed with other wild flowers were the beautiful columbine Rosalee loved. She saw them, but today her mind was so busy she couldn't appreciate their beauty.

"Where's Ben?" Odell had been unusually quiet since they left the Haywards.

"He took a wagon load of our things and went to Mrs. Gregg's. Mr. Clayhill had been at our place and said he was sending his men back to burn us out. Some of his men waylaid Mr. Horn on the trail and beat him terribly. He was in terrible pain and had the fever on him. I drove his wagon and took him into the canyons to hide until he could recover."

"Where're we agoin' to live? Mrs. Hayward said we could live there, but Mr. Hayward said you was ruint, and folks'd look down on them for takin' us in. Oh, Rosalee, they said you'd not show your face again after what you did. They said you'd not come back."

"Oh, honey, I've done nothing that I'm ashamed of. I did what I had to do to help Logan and myself. I wouldn't leave you. I thought about you every day. I knew you'd be all right with Lottie. Did you have a good time with Polly and Sudie May?"

"I did . . . at first. Then some men came and talked to Mr. Hayward. After that I heard them talking about you and Mr. Horn. They said . . . they said . . . Oh, Rosalee, they said he was taintin' your blood 'n that a white woman who'd hump a breed was lower than a snake's belly! They made it sound real bad. Does it mean you'll die like Pa and Mama?"

"No, of course not! It means that they're stupid and ignorant!" Rosalee said angrily. "My blood can't be tainted by anyone, honey," she explained in a softer tone. "As for the other, I think they meant that if I should marry Mr. Horn and live with him as his wife it would make me a low-down person. That isn't true, Odell. I'm who I am, regardless of whom I marry. And I am going to marry Mr. Horn. We love each other and we want to live together for the rest of our lives. You and Ben will live with us until you grow up and find someone you want to marry."

"Oh, Rosalee! You can't!"

"Why not? You liked Mr. Horn. You told me you did." Rosalee was so angry at the Haywards she was almost ill, but sheer determination held her anger down and permitted her to speak in a calm, reasonable manner.

"I did! But I didn't know he was dirty . . . and stinkin'!"

Rosalee gasped. "Is that what Mr. Hayward said? How dare he say that about Logan! Logan is the cleanest man I've ever known!" Anger and frustration surfaced and knifed through her. She ground the words out angrily, knowing it wasn't personal filth Mr. Hayward had referred to. "I'll do my best to explain it to you, Odell," she said minutes later when she had her anger under control again. "Logan's father was a white man who went to an Indian village and married a girl who was part Indian and part Spanish. The white man later deserted the girl and her baby. You saw Logan's mother when he brought her to our house. He said she was very beautiful when she was young. How can they honestly say that Logan is 'dirty' and 'stinking' and has bad blood because that Indian woman gave birth to him? He loved his mother, just as we loved our mother. I don't understand why the Haywards and people like them feel the way they do about Indians and about those who are partly Indian. Logan is a good, kind man, Odell. He'd give his life to protect us."

"Mr. Hayward said he stole the money to buy the land, and Mr. Clayhill was right to chase him off it." Odell's voice wavered.

"Mr. Hayward knows nothing about it. Logan was raised by his father's brother in Saint Louis and his uncle left him the money when he died."

"Why did Mr. Hayward say those bad things about you and Mr. Horn? I hate Mr. Hayward!"

"No, you don't hate him. You should feel sorry for him and all people like him because they're so self-righteous and because they're so narrow-minded and stupid!"

Logan heard the low murmur of voices behind him and knew what was happening. He felt his resentment rising and cursed the day the white man came to his mother's village. He cursed his uncle for taking him away from it and raising him in the white man's ways. Here he teetered between two worlds, and the woman who was the personification of all the yearning dreams he'd had through all the years of empty waiting was being made to feel she was sinning against both God and society for mating with him. A wave of sickness rolled over Logan. The bridges were burned behind them. Come what may, there was no turning back now.

His attention was drawn to Brutus, who had stopped in the middle of the narrow animal track. He pulled Mercury to a halt, turned back to Rosalee, and held his finger to his lips. Brutus continued to stand on stiffened legs, his ears up, his tail extended. Logan's eyes scanned the area for cover and spied a large boulder through the thin stand of trees. He pointed to it. Rosalee nodded and turned the mare. Within seconds they were out of sight.

With a light hand Logan lifted the stallion in a pivot that set it squarely down on its backtrail. He moved over the tracks made when the mare and the foal turned off the trail and then moved into the trees in the opposite direction. From her position behind the boulder, Rosalee could see what he was doing and knew he was making a trail away from them.

"What'er we adoin' this for?" Odell whispered.

"Sshh . . . Someone's coming up the trail."

"But—"

"Sshh . . ."

The rhythmic sound of horse's hoofs striking the hard-packed path became louder as the rider approached. Rosalee edged the mare forward until she could peer through the brush. The man, riding a handsome, prancing buckskin, sat tall in the saddle. The brim of his hat shaded the upper part of his face, but she could see that the lower part was clean shaven. There was no bedroll tied behind his saddle, so he wasn't a drifter. He carried a rifle in a scabbard and a six-shooter lay snug against his thigh. He pulled the buckskin to an abrupt stop when he came to the place where Logan had pivoted the stallion. It was plain the man was trail-wise. He'd recognized immediately what Logan had attempted to do. He studied the tracks, then moved forward slowly and cautiously.

When Rosalee recognized the rider something like relief flowed through her. She was sure it was Cooper Parnell, although she had seen him only once or twice and always from a distance. Was he looking for Logan, or was it just a coincidence that he had met up with them on the trail?

Chapter
Sixteen

"Parnell?" At the sound of Logan's voice a gun leaped into the rider's hand and the stallion jerked to a halt. A few seconds later, Logan went slowly out of the thick pines and onto the trail ahead of Cooper.

"Howdy, Horn." Cooper slid the gun back into the holster and visibly relaxed. "I didn't think I'd come on you so soon. You're a ways from where I expected you to be."

"Where was that?"

"Malone said you'd be at the Indian houses on the cliff, or nearby."

"You know about them?"

Cooper grinned. "I know about them. Tracked a herd of wild horses in there a time or two."

"Is Malone all right?"

"Clayhill sent an addle-brained fool out to kill him when he burned the Spurlock place. Malone's shot up some."

"Sonofabitch . . . I figured something had to have come about or he'd be back by now."

"The backshooter was Shorty Bane's sidekick, Shatto. Malone blew his head off," Cooper said matter-of-factly, and pushed his hat to the back of his head. He pulled the makings of a cigarette from his shirt pocket and began to roll a smoke. "I took your papers to Denver and had them recorded. Mrs. Gregg thought it a good idea. I was going anyway."

"I'm obliged to you. They were giving me some worry," Logan said with a slow smile. He eased himself in the saddle. From the concealing shadow of his hat brim, he surveyed the fair-haired man with the sharp blue eyes. He had a sudden feeling of something familiar. It was in the way the man sat on the stallion, in the long, thin fingers that rolled the cigarette, in the slant of the eyebrows and the tilt of his head. There was something else, too. He felt strangely at ease with him. Here was a man he could stand back-to-back with in any fight.

"You going to make Miss Spurlock stay behind that boulder all morning?"

Logan's eyes flicked to the boulder and back to Cooper. "I must have done a mighty sloppy job covering the tracks if you can see them from here," he said disgustedly.

"You covered them. It's Roscoe. He's got a two-track mind; running and pleasuring mares. He can smell a mare a mile away even if she's not in heat." He held the smoke between smiling lips and took a match from a tin box.

Logan's eyes swept over the buckskin. The horse stood obediently, as if rooted to the ground, but the flesh along his flanks quivered and his nostrils were extended. He looked back at Cooper and nodded. "I should've noticed." He pursed his lips and whistled.

Rosalee came toward them leading the foal. Cooper watched her approach with appraising, narrowed eyes. He had heard about Rosalee Spurlock. It was said she was not only pretty, but spunky and capable. What he'd heard was more than true about her being pretty. She glanced at him once, then settled her eyes on Horn. Cooper saw the look and recognized it. So, that's the way the wind blew. She was in love with the Indian. Godamighty! Did she know what she was in for? He supposed so, he thought seconds later; she'd been to the Haywards to fetch her sister. He put his fingers to the brim of his hat in a polite greeting.

"Howdy, ladies."

"Is Mrs. Parnell your ma?" Odell asked with a gap-toothed grin on her face. "I talked to her once at Mr. McCloud's store. We talked a long time 'bout ribbons and dressgoods. We was there to sell Pa's birds."

"She told me," Cooper said, and Rosalee silently thanked him for the warm smile he gave her sister. "She's got a fondness for little girls. She said she was figuring on stealing you away and bringing you home, but your sister come back for you."

Odell giggled happily. "She's nice. She's 'bout as nice as Mrs. Gregg. Do you know Mrs. Gregg? She lives in a pretty white house with flowers 'n a big hitchin' rail in front."

Rosalee flushed with embarrassment. Cooper's eyes flicked to hers, then crinkled slightly at the corners.

"Sure do. Ma'll be plum glad to hear you think she's as nice as Mrs. Gregg." He pulled his hat down, pinched the fire from his smoke, and flipped it onto the dirt. "Been to Haywards." It wasn't a question and there was a dryness to his tone.

Rosalee nodded. "My sister was there." Her eyes sought Logan's and Cooper didn't miss the look that passed between them.

"My mother'd be pleased if you stopped in for a day or two. Our place is on the way to town." His eyes bored into Logan's with a silent message.

"We're going to town to be married," Rosalee said quietly, and smiled into the dark eyes that flashed to hers.

"Well, now. Ma likes nothing better than a wedding. I think they're fine, too, as long as it's not me being hitched," he said between chuckles, and kneed his horse toward Logan's. He stuck out his hand. "Congratulations, Horn. You're a lucky son-of-a-gun."

"Thank you. I realize that."

Rosalee looked from one man to the other. Their eyes were locked with a silent understanding. She blessed Cooper Parnell with all her heart. His acceptance of her relationship with Logan made up, in a small way, for the treatment they'd received from the Haywards. She turned her eyes quickly lest he see the mistiness there.

"It's a couple of hour's ride to the ranch from here. We should make it by meal time. There's a clear stream about a mile down the trail where the ladies can rest and get a cool drink." Cooper swung his horse around, keeping him well back from the mare, as the stallion's teeth were bared to nip her, and started back down the trail.

Rosalee longed to reach out and touch Logan's hand as she passed him to take a place in the middle of the procession, but she smiled into his eyes instead and mouthed the words, "I love you."

The Parnell ranch sat in a valley lush with vegetation and an inexhaustible water supply. The surrounding hills formed both a natural barrier against livestock's straying and an impregnable defense in all quarters. Logan narrowed his eyes against the bright sunlight and surveyed the homestead with appreciation. The house, of stone and log construction, backed to the hills, a natural shelter from the cold north wind. Behind it was an array of pole corrals and several low, tin-roofed stone buildings. To one side was a high, stockade-type corral full of restless, milling horses, and beside that a smaller enclosure where a man was riding a bucking horse. Further on, where the hills widened out into a large oval meadow, a herd of horses stood in belly-high grass.

Logan's high-strung mount suddenly emitted a piercing neigh and fidgeted around. A shiver racked the muscle-corded frame and he tossed his head, trying to remove the hateful bit in his mouth. Logan held the stallion in check, then moved up beside Cooper.

"You must have mares in season?"

Cooper laughed. "Your boy knows. Most of my mares have been serviced by Roscoe or a small mountain-bred stud. My aim is to breed a fast horse with heavy hind quarters. I'm still hoping to find me a good stallion among the wild horse herds. So far, no luck. I'd like to make a deal to put yours on some of my better mares."

"How many?"

"Four good ones. You get your pick of the foals."

"Fair enough. Are you breaking horses for the army?"

"The army or anybody else who's got the need and the price."

"I'll be needing work stock."

"I can supply them."

Cooper glanced over his shoulder. Rosalee and Odell were a good distance behind them, chattering away like a couple of blue jays. "I've got good news and bad. Which do you want first?" Smile lines fanned out from Cooper's eyes when he looked at the man riding beside him.

"Give me the good news, I can use some."

"While I was in Denver, I looked up your friend James Randolph. Your men, and a herd of about three thousand steers, are about a week out of Junction City."

"The hell they are!" Logan's swift laugh exploded and dissolved on the wind.

"The men were on their way when Randolph got your letter. He located them at Fort Collins. They were able to buy a small herd there and added to it when they bought out a widow over on the South Platte. He sent you a letter and I took it out to Mrs. Gregg before I went to Denver.''

"But . . . how the devil did they pay for the herd?"

Cooper laughed. "Your friend Randolph's got more contacts than hairs on a mule's tail. He sent the money with a detachment of cavalry going to the fort. I take it he's got access to your bank account."

"He does. He's been handling some investments for me He's a damn good man. We owe each other plenty. He was my lieutenant during the war. Godamighty! It'll be good to see those men again."

"It seems they needed a few extra hands to handle the herd and hired on a few of the widow's. Randolph said you'd owe them wages when they got here."

"Is that the bad news?" Logan said, grinning broadly

"No. The bad news is Clayhill."

Almost imperceptibly, the look on Logan's face altered leaving it curiously devoid of expression. "What's the bastard done now?" he muttered.

Cooper glanced out across the grassland that waved under the pressure of the wind. Goddamn! He liked this man, liked him and admired the guts it took to stand up in this territory and take what he wanted knowing he'd have an easier time of it back East where his Indian blood would be less of a problem. For the space of a minute Cooper regarded Logan in thoughtful silence, studying his powerful frame from boot to hairline, and back down to his high cheekboned face. He found the black. inscrutable eyes on him, and was struck by the power of the man's steely composure. Goddamn, he thought with unaccountably clear reason, maybe old Clayhill had met his match!

"He's had his men spreading it around that Miss Spurlock's been whoring for them out at her place. There's not a decent woman in town that'll look at her twice." There was no way to say it, Cooper thought, but straight out. "That's not all . . . he's brought in a bunch of riffraff, all wanting a piece of your ass for a bonus. There've been two killings at the saloon in a week, one of them a sixteen-year-old kid. Watch your back if you're going to town."

Logan's head turned slowly. A cold mask moved up and over his features, covering the rage sweeping up from deep inside him. His eyes, looking out from between their thick fringe of lashes, were hard and flat and completely unreadable.

"There isn't much I can do about the wrong he's done to Rosalee but kill him. I made a promise not to do it unless it was his life or mine. It puts me between a rock and a damned hard place."

"I reckon it does," Cooper said, and spurred ahead to open a gate so they could pass into the ranch yard.

Sylvia Parnell stood on the porch wiping her hands on her apron. Rosalee had spoken with Cooper's mother a time or two in town. Later, her liking for the woman grew when Mary Gregg confided to her that she and Sylvia were friends. However, the hostile treatment she and Logan had received at the Haywards had been so unexpected that, now, a sudden tension gripped her. She wanted desperately to look into Logan's eyes and reassure him of her love, but he and Cooper were riding slightly ahead. As they came closer, Sylvia stepped off the porch, a smile of greeting on her face.

"Rosalee! What a pleasure to see you!"

"Hello, Mrs. Parnell."

"Remember me? I'm Odell." Rosalee smiled in spite of her anxiety. One never had to worry about conversation with Odell around, she thought with a warm spurt of affection for her little sister.

"I certainly do remember you." Sylvia placed an arm

around the child after Logan lifted her down. "How are you Rosalee?"

"I'm fine, thank you."

"It's nice to see you again, Mr. Horn. I didn't expect Cooper back so soon. I told him to bring you for a visit if at all possible."

"Thank you, ma'am." Logan put his fingers to his hat brim in a polite gesture.

Rosalee saw the tightness in the muscles of his face and felt the tension in his hands when he lifted her from the horse.

"Thank you, my love," she murmured loud enough for all to hear and smiled sweetly into his eyes. He didn't look at her. He was afraid, she thought intuitively. He was afraid she'd be embarrassed and hurt when Mrs. Parnell found out they were going to be married. Concern for his anxiety crowded all other thoughts from her mind. It would hurt, but only because he'd be hurt. It would make no difference! He was all that mattered to her now.

She clung to his arm and turned to face Sylvia Parnell with a confident smile on her lips. "We're on our way to town to be married," she announced proudly.

Sylvia glanced at Logan and saw the flicker of apprehension in his obsidian eyes. Holding his gaze, she smiled and saw him let out a slow breath. She held out her arms and Rosalee went into them.

"My dear! I'm happy for you," Sylvia said and hugged her. She held her hand out to Logan. "You're to be congratulated, Mr. Horn."

"I'm aware of that, ma'am." He took off his hat. His dark eyes gleamed in the bright sunlight and his smile chased the fierce look from his face.

Sylvia led the way to the door opening off the porch. Odell, chattering continuously, danced along beside her. Rosalee's eyes followed Logan and Cooper as they led the horses to the corral. Logan turned to look back at her, and she lifted her hand before she went into the coolness of the house.

It wasn't until she and Sylvia were cleaning up after the evening meal that included three ranch hands that Rosalee had a chance to speak to Mrs. Parnell alone. Cooper and Logan had gone to inspect the mares and look over Cooper's latest herd of wild horses. Odell was playing with a litter of new puppies Cooper had brought from the barn and placed in a box beside the smokehouse.

"Mrs. Parnell . . ." Rosalee carefully wiped the china plate and set it on the shelf. "Odell was terribly confused after being with the Haywards. They're of the opinion that because Logan has Indian blood I'm degrading myself by marrying him. I'm rather worried about taking her into town now. I'm afraid there will be . . . unpleasantness."

"There will be unpleasantness, Rosalee. You must prepare yourself for it. People can be terribly hurtful at times."

"I don't mind for myself. I'll endure anything to be with Logan. It's Odell I'm worrying about. She's a friendly child and she loves to be with people. I don't want her hurt on my account."

"You can leave her here with me for awhile. I'd love to have the company of a little girl."

"Oh, please! I wasn't hinting for her to stay here!" Rosalee said quickly. "I just don't know what to say to her to make her understand that there are good people and bad people regardless of the color of their skin."

"I'd say it's almost impossible for a child her age to fully understand. As I see it, the Indians have been much more tolerant of us than we have been of them. They accept whites among them, intermarry, and love the half-breed children. I find it hard to blame them for raiding and scalping the white settlers after what Chivington did to them at Sand Creek."

"Logan's mother was one of the few who escaped the massacre. Her father was killed there. She and a brother went north to the Wind River country. That's where Logan found her. He was bringing her back to her birthplace when she took sick. She was very ill when he knocked on our door and asked to bring her in out of the rain."

Sylvia took the dishwater to the door and threw it out into the yard. "She must have been beautiful. Logan is a handsome man," she said while hanging the pan on a nail beside the stove.

"Her name was Morning Sun. Her mother was a Spanish captive, but she came to love her Indian husband and refused to go back to her own people." Rosalee hung the towel she'd used to dry the dishes on the back of a chair to dry and failed to notice the trembling in Sylvia's hands as she smoothed the cloth covering the necessaries in the center of the table.

They went to the porch and sat on the bench. The mountain breeze was cool but refreshing after the heat of the cookstove Rosalee looked out over the stretch of valley to the craggy peaks beyond and sighed. It was beautiful and peaceful here. It was also wonderful to be able to talk to another woman about her love. She turned to look at the quiet, calm woman beside her. Sylvia's clear, blue eyes were watching her.

"It will not be easy, you know," she said quietly, and reached out to clasp Rosalee's hand. "Following your heart is sometimes the most difficult path a woman can take."

"I know. My mother followed her heart. She married my father against the wishes of her parents. They thought she was marrying beneath her station in life, but she loved him and never regretted it no matter how many hardships she had to endure."

Sylvia looked away toward the railed enclosure where Logan and Cooper were examining the mares. "Tell me about Logan," she said in her quiet way. "He must have been very young when he left his mother."

"Yes. His white father divorced his mother in something called the Omaha Dance. It was very humiliating for his mother, but it allowed his father to leave the village without making deadly enemies of her people. His brother was more honorable and refused to leave without his Indian wife and child. He took them and Logan back to Saint Louis with him. His uncle must have loved him in his own way. I hope he did. A little boy without his mother needs love."

"Has Logan said anything about his . . . father?"

"Nothing, but I know he despises him. I heard him tell his mother he'd vowed to kill him. I'll never forget the words she spoke just before she died. She said, 'Killing is the refuge of cowards and my son is not a coward. Show your father you are the better man and he will die a thousand times.'"

"Yes," Sylvia said slowly. "It would be a bitter blow to the pride of . . . such a man to be bested by a son, and doubly so if his son had Indian blood."

"Logan was younger than Odell when he discovered he was different from the other boys," Rosalee continued, her thoughts completely involved with the story she was telling. "He couldn't understand why they refused to play with him and called him a dirty half-breed Indian. He said he ran home and asked his uncle what it meant. Later, the parents of the other boys demanded he be removed from the school, and he was tutored privately until his uncle sent him to a school back East."

Sylvia shook her head. "Poor little boy. He had a worse time of it than Cooper." She looked at Rosalee quickly and added, "I raised Cooper by myself until we met Oscar Parnell. He was a wonderful man and was everything a father could be to my boy. He died after we'd put the money down on this place and before we even got here. He would have loved this valley."

"Did you come out to the territory before the war?"

"I've lived here all my life. I was born at Bent's Fort. My

parents were missionaries sent out here to educate the 'savages,'" she said with a dry laugh. "There are times when I find it hard to tell which are the savages and which the civilized people in this country."

The vision of her burned-out home flashed into Rosalee's mind. "If Adam Clayhill and all he stands for is what's considered civilized, I'd sooner remain a savage!" she bit out bitterly.

Sylvia's shoulders stiffened. She kept her face averted and watched the two men down at the corral climb over the rails and walk toward the house. Both were tall, strong men who moved with loose-limbed ease. Logan was dark, and she was sure that the mustache that curved down the sides of his mouth and gave him such a fierce look covered gentleness, or this sweet girl could not have fallen so completely in love with him. Cooper, on the other hand, was blond, with blue, laughing eyes that gave the impression he was unconcerned about anything except the joy of living. Sylvia knew how deceptive her son's appearance was. He was steel inside; when riled to anger, when pushed to the extreme, he lashed out at a foe with deadly accuracy and didn't understand the word "quit." The two men were so alike, yet so different. How strange that fate had brought them together.

Logan was immensely relieved that his men, the remains of the trusted platoon who served with him during four years of a hellish war, were on the way. He wanted to ride out to meet them, but more than that he wanted to marry Rosalee so that if he were killed she would have financial security for herself and her brother and sister. He spoke of this to Cooper on the way to the house.

"Is there a preacher in town? I want to marry Rosalee as soon as possible." His direct, serious gaze met Cooper's amused one and the other man's smile faded. "She'd not be able to live here peacefully as my widow, but she'd have money to go East and make a new life."

"I see what you mean. There's a preacher who could do it up legal . . . that is, if he will." Cooper looked him straight in the eyes and added, "He's a hypocritical bastard." The emotion rioting through the fair-haired man when he thought of the preacher was wholly concealed behind the noncommittal expression that settled over his face. "Ma knew him years ago down around Fort Bent."

"If he can marry us and make it legal, he'll do it," Logan replied stiffly.

Cooper recognized the determination behind the words. "Will I have time to use your stallion before you go?" he asked, and grinned, bringing the conversation to a lighter vein.

"If you can get the job done tomorrow. He's ready," Logan observed pointedly and jerked his head toward the towering animal who paced the corral with shivers racking his muscle-corded frame. He paused to emit a piercing neigh. Logan raised his dark brows and grinned at Cooper. "Thank God he doesn't go around in that condition all the time! He'd have a hell of a time jumping a fence."

It was dusk when the men came to the house and dark when Sylvia went inside, lit a lamp, and showed Odell where she was to sleep. Cooper disappeared to talk to a gaunt, old man with an unkempt, gray-yellow mane that whipped around his shoulders as he turned his head from side to side, constantly surveying his surroundings. He came riding in on a small dun horse and headed straight for the bunkhouse without even a wave of his hand.

"Volney Burbank," Cooper said. "A bona fide, born and bred mountain man. He's been a big help keeping my land free of predators and spotting wild herds in the mountains. He comes by now and then for his tobacco or for bullets for that Winchester he carries. I'll go down and visit a spell, that is, if the wind's in the right direction."

As soon as Cooper rounded the corner, Logan slid down on the bench and pulled Rosalee to him. Her breathy laugh came softly to his ears and she let him draw her close. He bent his head and put his lips hard against hers. She expelled her breath and her body strained to his. Suddenly there was hunger in his kiss. Searching, healthy hunger.

With his arm still around her, he drew his shoulders back and looked into her face. Through the layers of clothing between them, she could feel the strong beat of his heart and the tautness of his muscled thigh pressed to hers. His lips were folded together, deepening the lines down his cheeks, but his eyes shone with laughter.

"Do you know what I want to do to you?"

"I can't imagine!" she exclaimed with a provocative smile

"I'd like to hurry you back to the cliff houses, take that dress off you," his voice lowered threateningly, "and the petticoats and all else women wear, and . . . love you, love you, love you."

"But we can't go back for awhile."

"No," he breathed, and leaned toward her and kissed her lips tenderly and possessively. "No," he said again, tiredly, and folded her into the crook of his arm and pressed her head to his shoulder.

"I love you," she whispered. "I'm going to tell you that everyday for the rest of my life."

"I love you, too, sweet woman, but you see how it's going to be. What happened at the Haywards will happen again and again. The day may come when you'll feel it's not worth it."

"Oh, darling! The day will never come that I don't love you and want to be with you."

"Cooper says there's a preacher in town who can marry

us. We'll go there the day after tomorrow if you're still of a mind to."

"If I'm still of a mind to! What a thing to say, Logan Horn." Sharp white teeth nipped the skin on his neck. "I want to marry you more than anything else in the world and be with you every minute of the day and night. I don't care if we live here, or in Denver, or in a Cheyenne village as long as I'm with you."

Rosalee rubbed her cheek against his shoulder and listened to the reassuring beat of his heart. If only they could have remained in the cliff houses where there were no conflicts, no day-to-day battles with ignorant prejudices, no Adam Clayhill. She lifted his hand to her face and kissed the crooked finger that fascinated her so. A sudden thought occurred to her and she pulled away from him so she could see his face.

"Logan, do you think our child will have a crooked finger like yours? Oh, I hope so!" she exclaimed before he could answer. "Our son will have it, then our grandson, and his son . . ." She laughed happily and began to quote as if reading from a book: "The crooked forefinger on the left hand is a characteristic of the famous Horn family, who were early day settlers in Colorado Territory, and whose patriarch, Logan Horn, was so adored by his wife, Rosalee Spurlock Horn, that she followed him constantly, never letting him out of her sight for the entire fifty years of their married life!" She giggled softly with her mouth open against his neck. "How does that sound to you, Mr. Horn?"

He lifted her chin and kissed her deeply before he spoke. "Perfectly wonderful, sweetheart," he whispered against her lips, and doubled the hand with the crooked finger into a tight fist.

Chapter
Seventeen

Della Clayhill stood at the head of the stairs and listened to Adam's angry voice coming from his office below.

"What the hell do the bastards think I'm paying them for?"

She had been amused at first by Adam's anger at the Indian who bought up the range he had used for twenty years, and by his plans to keep him off of it. Now, it irritated her.

"I don't have a man on this ranch with the guts I had when I drove the gawddamn redskins outta this valley and claimed it!"

Della rolled her eyes to the ceiling. Adam was back to the same old story and it was beginning to be boring.

"That red ass whipped Shorty Banes in less than a minute. The fool's name should have been Short-of-Brains!" Adam shouted.

That's right, Della thought contemptuously. When Logan Horn got through with him he didn't have the strength to pull a sick whore off a pisspot! At the thought of all that quiet strength packed in that handsome, bronze body, a thrill of excitement swept through her.

While Della waited for the man who was with Adam to leave, she thought about her relationship with her stepfather. She enjoyed her new position in Adam's life. It was exciting to have him bellow her name, take the stairs two at a time and come stomping into her room to take her roughly. Since they had become lovers he spent more and more time at the ranch. But he had become too possessive. He seemed to think he could have her whenever he wanted, as if she were his paid whore. Damn him to hell if he thought he was going to keep her here to await his pleasure whenever he wanted a piece of ass, she thought angrily. *She* was going to be the one to call the shots from now on. She'd not be subservient to any man except for as long as it took to get what she wanted.

Shortly after they had become intimate, they had discussed marriage. Adam said it was out of the question. Too many people knew her as his daughter, and he couldn't afford a breath of scandal if he was going to be a candidate for the first governor of the state of Colorado. Della lifted her carefully plucked eyebrows and smiled at the thought. Adam didn't know it, but she had no intention of marrying him if she could get what she wanted without doing so. Someday she'd be the sole owner of this cattle empire; the most powerful woman in the territory. With fifty men or more working for her, she'd not only rule sixty thousand acres but own the town as well. She wished now she had paid a little more attention to the tall Texan, Case Malone. She was sure that with a little extra *enticement* he could have been won over. When the time came for her to take over the ranch she'd need a strong man by her side.

Della's thoughts were interrupted by a bellowing oath from Adam. A cowhand came out of his office and walked rapidly to the door. Adam followed and his loud, angry voice could be heard all over the house.

"The sons of bitches ain't got the brains of a pissant! I'll not send out a wagon to pick up a bunch of jackasses who sit around with their fingers up their butts and let a fuckin' blanket ass steal their horses right out from under their noses. The bastards can walk! Hear? That's not the half of it by a long shot! They'll round up those horses on their own time. Tell 'em that!"

"Yes, sir."

The front door slammed shut with a loud bang that rattled the glass. Della heard Adam stomp back into his office. She knew he would pour himself a half-glass of whiskey, then sit down in his rolling chair behind the desk. She patted her hair in place, shifted the neckline of her dress so a little more bosom showed, and went slowly down the stairs.

At the door of his office she pulled back the heavy velvet drapery and paused to look at him. He was leaning back in the chair, as she knew he would be, with the whiskey glass in his hand. His eyes were closed and she was able to study him without him being aware of it. Had he looked this old a few weeks ago? His thick, gray hair appeared to be even grayer against his sun-browned face. The lines on each side of his mouth had deepened and his jowls had begun to sag. He was still a handsome, robust man for all his fifty years. She had a sudden desire to see him as he had been twenty-five years ago with firm young skin and a strong lithe body. The thought came to her that, then, he would have been a match for the Indian. No wonder her mother had been swept away by his ardent pursuit and allowed him to bring them to this desolate place.

"I know you're there, Della. Come on in." Adam lifted the glass and gulped the rest of the whiskey.

"How did you know it was me, Papa?" Della glided into the room and stood before the desk.

"'Cause you smell like a French whore."

Della knew he was watching her from beneath his heavy lids because they fluttered, his lips remained open, and he took in a deep breath of air into his lungs.

"How many French whores have you smelled, Papa?" she whispered huskily, and sat down on the edge of the desk.

"Hush up calling me that. You know I don't like it when we're alone . . . come over here."

Della laughed softly and moved up onto the desk so she could cross one knee over the other. "What were you ranting at that poor man about?"

"Nothing that concerns you. Come here. I've got a need for you."

Della's eyes roved over him from the top of his head to the bulge in his crotch.

"Call Cecilia, your little Mexican whore. She'll give you a quick screwing. You know I don't like a short one. It's not worth getting all messed up for."

"Gawddamnit, girl!" Adam roared. He leaned forward and banged the glass down on the desk. "You know I don't like for you to talk like a slut!"

Della's tinkling laugh filled every corner of the room. "Yes, you do! You know you do! Nothing makes you more eager to fornicate than for me to whisper all those dirty things in your ear."

"That's different, by Gawd!"

"You're afraid I'll not be able to act the perfect lady when the time comes. That's it, isn't it, Papa?" She leaned forward, knowing he could see down the front of her dress almost to her navel. "We've not been together in Denver for a long time. I can be just as hoity-toity as Mama used to be, but I've got a lot more under my skirts than she ever had. *That*,

my dear Papa, makes a world of difference. The dear ladies
of the Elite Club love me for a sweet, innocent girl; their
men love me because I can give them more—much more—
than any whore in town! And it's doubly exciting for them
because each thinks he knows something about me that no
one else knows."

Adam jumped to his feet. "Are you screwin' around with
every struttin' popinjay that comes along?" His face had taken
on an angry, red flush. Veins stood out in his neck as he
shoved his face toward hers.

"Not *all* of them, darling. Only the ones with the money
and influence. Are you jealous?" She laughed lightly, happily.
"Where do you think I learned all the tricks that make you
so happy and . . . horny? I hope you're not so old-fashioned
as to think men should have the exclusive right to all the sex
they want? Darling!" she chided softly. "You've so much to
learn—"

"I won't have it! Do you hear me, Della?" He grabbed
her shoulders and shook her. "You're mine, now. You'll not
spread your legs for anyone but me!"

Della looked at him calmly and then smiled sweetly. "I
don't belong to anyone but myself. And if you don't like me
the way I am, I'll . . . pack up and move to Denver."

"Don't threaten me, girl!" he roared. "You'll not leave
this ranch without my permission. You'll do as I say, hear?"

Della threw her head back and laughter bubbled from her
lovely mouth. She was so incredibly beautiful that Adam
couldn't even remember what he was angry about. Her eyes
shone like stars and her soft lips spread, showing perfect
white teeth. Her head was tilted back and he could see the
pink wetness inside her mouth. Anger flowed out of him as
desire flowed in. Godamighty! She was too beautiful to be
real. He silently cursed the God that had not brought her to
him when he was young and in his prime, then praised him

for having brought her to him while he was still able to give her what she wanted. She was his. Totally his! She made him feel young . . . as if he was just beginning.

He put his hands beneath her armpits and roughly dragged her across the desk. Papers, account books, pens and ink bottles scattered to the floor. He picked her up in his arms, carried her to the big leather chair, and sat down with her on his lap.

"Papa . . ."

"Shut your mouth! No, by Gawd! Open it—wide." He clamped his mouth to hers as if he were dying of thirst, and his big hand moved roughly beneath her skirts until his fingers found the damp well between her legs. The hand of his arm holding her to him slipped inside the bodice of her dress and he filled it with her breast, squeezing it tightly. Minutes passed before he lifted his head and glared down into her face. His breath came in short gasps and he could hear the thunder of his heartbeat.

"I'll kill you, girl, if I ever find you with another man. No one but me will ever touch you here—" he gripped the space between her legs with strong rough fingers. "Or here—" he squeezed her breast. "Or here—" he placed his lips so bruisingly hard against her lips that he cut them against her teeth and she tasted the blood on her tongue.

Exultant, Della knew she had raised a devil in him, that she was the one with complete control, although he wasn't yet aware of it. This was the way she liked him best; aroused, angry, rough, demanding. She wiggled against the hard lump that pressed her buttocks.

"Take me upstairs, Papa," she gasped when she tore her mouth from his.

"No, by Gawd! You'll service me here on the floor like the whore you are!" He dumped her from his lap and followed her to the floor, his knees on each side of her. He knew nothing excited her more than his cruel, masterful love-making. He opened his britches, threw her skirts over her head, and plunged the full length of his throbbing erection into her moist opening. She let out one long cry of ecstasy and wrapped her slim legs around him.

Later, Adam sat in the big chair with Della cuddled on his lap. His hands gently smoothed her hair. At times like this she could ask him anything, make him promise to do anything she wanted him to do.

"What made you so angry, Adam darling?" Her fingers played on his soft white mustache.

"It's that Indian, lovey. He and that Spurlock woman took off for the canyons, and I've had men looking for their hideout for a couple of weeks. They didn't find it, but the Indian found them and ran off their horses. One of my drovers came in to say they were walking back to the ranch and wanted a wagon sent out for them. To hell with them! It'll do them good to walk—teach them a lesson."

"Why don't you just give up and let the Indian have the land?"

"Hell, no, I'll not give up and let a gawddamn redskin have that range. I've put a bounty on the bastard's head that should draw in some—"

"You've done what?" Della asked sharply and straightened up to look him in the eye. "You've put a price on his head? That wasn't very smart of you, Adam."

Adam laughed. "Don't get all riled up, lovey. I just sent out for a few gunfighters. You know I can't afford to be connected with killing him outright. It might be that one of my men might take it on himself to ambush him. I told them to bring him in alive . . . if they could. It's got to look like a fair fight or word would get down to Denver I had him killed. It might not set too well with the Central Committee."

"Did you send someone out to kill Case Malone?"

"That dumb bastard took it on himself to backshoot Malone. He wanted to be foreman and thought it'd put him in good with me. Malone had it coming. He crippled three of my men."

"He could've killed them."

Adam chuckled. "It would've been better if he had. Then we could've lynched him—all perfectly legal."

"What if word gets to Denver about you burning out the Spurlocks?"

"Who would believe it? Accidental fires happen all the time. Why would I let them stay there two, three years, then burn them out?" His face tightened when he thought of the girl standing him off with the rifle. Goddamn her! He'd gotten his revenge.

"When are we going to Junction City?" she asked idly.

His hand slid up over her breast and cupped her chin. "I'm going in a few days, but you're not going to town till some of the riffraff clear out."

"You either take me, damn you, or I'll follow," she said softly with a sweet smile.

"You do and I'll beat your ass." His voice came out thick and unsteady.

"You do that anyway," she said saucily and jumped off his lap. At the door she turned and looked back at him. "We can stay in your rooms above the saloon. Of course, you'll have to get rid of that whore you keep there."

Adam grinned. The little devil was jealous! "Bessie's no whore. She puts on a damn good show that brings customers to the saloon."

"That cow!" Della exclaimed haughtily. "I could put on a performance that would bring men to that saloon like flies on a pile of fresh cow shit!" She flung up her head and flounced out. She could hear his roar of laughter as she went up the stairs. Let him think she was jealous, she thought with a sly smile. The old fool! If only she could be sure that brother of hers wasn't included in his will . . .

Della sat in the buggy, her folded parasol on her lap. A mile back she had thrown off the duster she wore to protect her white dress, removed the scarf from her head, set the white straw hat with the blue satin roses on the top of her high-piled hair, and secured it with a pearl-headed hatpin. They had turned the bend in the road and were coming into town.

"Sting that lazy horse with the whip, Samuel, so he'll step lively."

"Yas'm." The black man dressed in a white shirt with a high, starched collar, black coat and pants was sweating profusely. He flicked the whip out over the horse's back.

"Sit up smart!" Della commanded sharply. "Show these yokels some quality."

"Yas'm."

Early that morning, Adam and two riders had left the ranch without a word as to where they were headed. Della waited until noon, and when he hadn't returned she packed a few things in a bag and told Samuel to hitch up the buggy. A glimmer of an idea had been floating around in her head since the night Adam had bragged about Bessie. It was a reckless, mad idea, but she reasoned she needed some excitement after the boring weeks she'd spent on the ranch.

"Ya'll wants me to go the preacher's house, ma'am?" Samuel asked. Della usually stayed there overnight when she came to town because the hotel was so dirty and run-down.

"Not this time. Take me to the saloon."

"De saloon? Ah . . . missy . . . ah doan—" Samuel turned his shiny, sweat-slick face toward her and rolled his eyes.

"That's right. You don't know anything. Hush your mouth and take me to the saloon like I told you."

"Yas'm."

There was more activity in town than usual. A freight wagon was unloading boxes and crates at the mercantile. The mules, standing in their heavy harnesses, flicked off flies with their dusty tails. The fat woman who ran the eatery sat on the porch fanning herself. A drover on a mangy bronc came into town from the other end of the street stirring up a cloud of dust. The hitching rail in front of the saloon was crowded with tired, patient horses. Loud, drunken laughter floated out into the street when two dusty, whiskered men came through the swinging doors at the same time.

Samuel pulled the horse to a stop beside the board porch and Della hissed, "Not here, you fool. Move on down."

The men coming from the saloon stopped to stare at the lovely vision all in white, then bounded down the split-log steps and loped after the buggy. When it stopped they were beside it.

"Yeeee . . . doggie! Do ya see what I see?" The man's wind-burned face was split in a wide grin and his bright blue eyes were watery and red streaked.

"Whoooeee . . . We done found us a woman what looks like a dolly. Where'd ya come from, dolly? Yo're as purty a sight as I ever did set my eyes on. Yessiree bobtail! What you doin' with that dressed-up boy, purty thin'? Hee, hee, hee . . ." His laugh was a high-pitched giggle.

The other man crowded in and placed a rough brown hand on the side of the buggy. "Ya shore do smell purty. I could give ya a fine time in the saloon. I got me a whole ten dollars."

Della smiled sweetly at him while her hand groped for the whip handle. She was still smiling when she brought it sharply across his face with all the force she could put behind it. He let out a strangled cry and staggered back, his hand going to his face to cover his eye. Still smiling, Della jumped lightly from the buggy and stood on the boardwalk, the whip in her hand.

"Ya bitch!" he croaked and staggered off down the street. His companion took a step toward her, an angry scowl on his face.

"Ya had no call to do that! He was only funnin'." He eyed the smiling woman with the whip. The scowl changed to one of puzzlement as he realized she had obviously enjoyed hurting his partner. He lifted his hand to snatch the whip, then changed his mind and followed his friend down the street.

Della felt strangely elated. How wonderful to be able to have physical control. She looked up the street and saw the fat woman gawking, and down the street to where two women had paused in front of the mercantile to peer from beneath stiff-brimmed calico bonnets. A man stood on the saloon porch and spit a stream of yellow tobacco juice into the dusty road. Good, Della thought triumphantly. In five minutes everyone will know that Della Clayhill had come to town.

"There, Samuel. See how easy it is? I'll just keep this with me," she said and wrapped the thin, leather strap around her gloved hand. "Bring my valise," she ordered, and started up the wooden stairway attached to the side of the saloon building.

The door at the top of the stairs opened onto an L-shaped hallway that ended with steps going down into the saloon. There were four rooms on the upper floor; two small ones at the back, and two large rooms at the front with windows looking down onto the street.

"Go on back to the ranch," Della ordered crisply, and took her bag from Samuel. He tilted his head, his eyes large and frightened. "Do as I say. I'll tell Adam I made you go."

Samuel went to the door, turned and looked at her with a puzzled look on his black face. "Mastah ain't agoin' ta be a likin' it."

"That's no concern of yours," Della snapped. "Go on!"

"Yas'm."

She waited until he went out the door before she went down the hallway and pushed open the door to one of the front rooms. It was dark and the air was heavy with a sweet musky odor. Heavy draperies covered the two windows. Della set her valise inside the door, went to the windows, pulled back the covering, and looped it behind a metal holder attached to the frame. Light sprang into the room. It was a large room with a four-poster bed in the center of it. A naked woman with tangled, dark red hair lay on her stomach in the middle of the bed. Clothes were thrown over the backs of the two chairs and spilled out of the open chest of drawers. Beside the bed, a chinaware chamber pot, its lid askew, smelled as if it hadn't been emptied for a week.

Della grimaced. She went to the door, opened it, and slammed it shut so hard the walls shook. The only move the woman made was to turn her head. She began to snore. Della went around to the side of the bed, unwound the whip from her hand, and struck the white, bare buttocks a stinging blow. There was an instant response. The woman reared up in the bed. She brushed the hair from her face. Her wide, startled eyes looked at Della with disbelief.

"What the hell!"

"Get up and get out," Della said quietly.

"Get out? Who'n the hell are you to be tellin' me to get out? This is my room."

"Not if I want it. I'm Della Clayhill. I'll give you ten minutes to get this room cleaned up and to get out."

"This room goes with my job. Mr. Clayhill said so."

"Mr. Clayhill isn't here, but I am . . . with this little persuader." Della flicked her lightly on the thigh with the tip of the whip.

Bessie was a big-boned, handsome woman with thick,

auburn hair, large amber eyes and voluptuous breasts. She had started singing in saloons at the age of fifteen, and now, in her late twenties, she was perfectly capable of handling almost any situation that came up during the course of an evening in the saloon. This was an entirely different matter. She'd heard of Della Clayhill, the beautiful stepdaughter of the wealthiest man in the northwest territories. She'd seen her riding through town in her buggy. Dressed all in white, with her beautiful, smiling face framed with silky blond hair, she had looked like a fairy princess. Bessie had envied her. She had wondered what it would be like to be so beautiful, to have all the lovely clothes she wanted, to live in a grand house and have a nigger drive her around in a handsome buggy.

The cold, little pissant didn't look beautiful to her now. She was looking down her nose at her as if she were a wart on a mule's ass! But the bitch not only had a whip in her hand, she was the owner's stepdaughter! Bessie got off the bed. She felt big and gauche beside the woman. She didn't like the feeling. Pride forced her to hold her head high while she crossed the room to pick up a robe.

Della stood silently and watched as Bessie picked up her clothes. When she had an armful, she dropped them outside the door and came back to dump the rest of her things in a worn valise. When she went out the door, she slammed it behind her. It was flung open almost immediately.

"Take your pisspot with you."

Bessie put down the valise, walked back into the room, and picked up the half-filled chamber pot. She turned and looked down at Della with raised brows.

"Of course, your ladyship," she said in a mocking English accent heavily laced with sarcasm. "Anything else, your ladyship?" She held the pot in her hands, silently daring the other woman to insult her again.

Della flushed angrily and her hand tightened on the whip.

"Go ahead, *princess*. Touch me with that whip and you'll get this right in the face!"

The two women glared at each other. Bessie was tempted to douse her with the contents of the pot regardless of whether or not she raised her hand. Finally, it was Della who, with a superior smile, backed away and motioned with her hand for Bessie to leave.

Outside the door, Bessie paused. She was so angry, and her legs trembled so that she feared they would be unable to carry her down the hall to the small room at the rear. She'd had her share of hard knocks in this world, but never before had she been treated like so much . . . horseshit!

Bessie sat down on the sagging bed and stared at the bare floor of the room that was only used, now and then, by a drifter or a gambler who had the price. The walls were unfinished, rough plank boards, the window small and high. The air in the room was heavy and smelled of dirty feet. She clenched and unclenched her fist and gritted her teeth in frustration. That cold bitch would pay for this, she vowed. She'd see her humiliated and dragged in the dirt if it was the last thing she ever did!

Chapter
Eighteen

Logan enjoyed the day he spent in Cooper's company. For the first time since he'd come west he was companionably at ease with another man. They looked over the horses Cooper had for sale and Logan picked out twenty head, the beginning of a remuda for his ranch. Cooper promised to have the horses saddle broken, ready to work, and delivered to the Spurlock ranch in a month's time.

For several hours they discussed brands and the immediate necessity for Logan to get one on his stock and registered with the Cattlemen's Association in Denver. They traced several designs in the dirt with a stick and Logan decided on a five-pointed star. Cooper showed it to his foreman who was also the smithy on the ranch and he set to work forging the iron.

Before the day was over Logan bought a big, gentle roan gelding for Rosalee to ride, and helped Cooper select the mares suitable to put to his spotted stallion. By evening, a tired but contented Mercury had serviced each of the mares twice and they were reasonably sure some of them had caught.

Cooper was greatly interested in Logan's chestnut mare and the foal sired by Mercury. Logan discovered the tall, blond man was far more knowledgeable about good horse flesh than he was. Cooper suggested his stud, Roscoe, would make a good sire for the foal's issue and Logan agreed. As it was time for the foal to be weaned from the mare, Cooper offered to keep them at the ranch in separate corrals until Logan was settled on his own ranch.

They were at the horse trough. Cooper splashed water on his sweaty face and wiped it on his neckerchief. He grinned, friendly blue eyes catching and holding friendly dark ones. He had spent the day with this man. There was a lot about him he liked.

"I've got a thing to ask you." From the tone of Logan's voice Cooper knew it wasn't easy for this man to ask a favor of any man. He remained silent and nodded his head. Logan took a paper from his pocket. "This is a letter to Randolph. I'd be obliged if you'd see that Rosalee and her brother and sister get to him if things don't work out for me."

"If it comes to that, I'll see that it's done." Cooper nodded again solemnly, took the letter and put it in his shirt pocket. "Let's go eat. I can smell Ma's berry pie from here."

It was not until the morning Logan and Rosalee were leaving for town that Sylvia found the chance to speak with Logan alone. It was scarcely daylight when she went out to scatter grain for the chickens and saw him in the far corral with the nervous foal. She hurried through the chore and walked rapidly alongside the pole fence toward him.

"Mornin'," she called. "Breakfast will be ready soon."

"Mornin'." Logan released the fidgeting foal, and she took off on the run. "This girl is aware of that and wants her mother."

The colt, with her tail standing straight up, raced the length of the corral, wheeled, and came prancing back on slender, dancing legs. She stood at the railed fence with head and tail upflung, squealing her displeasure, her eyes fixed on her mother, who grazed with Cooper's mares in the pasture beyond the house.

"She's a pretty thing." Sylvia moved up close to the fence.

"She'll make a fine mare," Logan answered and crawled between the rails to stand beside her.

Uneasiness touched him and his stomach muscles began to tighten. There was no doubt in his mind that Mrs. Parnell had sought him out to talk about Rosalee. She was nervous. She fidgeted, shifted her feet, and her hands held the grain pan to her so tightly the edge pushed into her side. To Logan's watchful eyes these little signals betrayed her. He filled his nostrils with the fresh morning air and waited, knowing there was no polite way he could stop her from saying what she had come to say.

Sylvia's blue eyes flicked down to his feet and then moved up across his chest to his face. She stepped back so she didn't have to tilt her head so high to see him, her eyes locked with his, and in them she saw deep tension but also learned patience.

"Mr. Horn, ah . . . Logan—" She corrected herself and looked away from him and back again. Her composure was almost shattered by the quiet waiting look on his face; but with determination she tightened her trembling lips, took a deep, hurtful breath, and waited for the knot of tension in her throat to dissolve.

"Yes, ma'am?" he prompted.

"May I speak to you in . . . confidence?"

"Certainly, ma'am." He clamped his jaws shut after the words. Here it comes, he thought. Without him being aware of it, the look on his face altered, leaving it devoid of expression.

Sylvia forced herself to continue looking up into his dark face. "I tried all night to think of a way to say this——" she began in a breathless whisper, and could not go on.

"You won't embarrass me, ma'am. Say what you have to say and don't let it trouble you." He took a slow breath. His disappointment was choking him. He had been so comfortable here, so sure that his relationship with Rosalee was not offensive to her. He would let her have her say, then tell her that nothing she, or anyone else, could say to him would keep him from his love if she wanted him.

"I must say it!" Sylvia said with a sudden burst of courage. "I must know if . . . you know who your father is!"

Her unexpected words threw him completely off balance. Dismay rose in him, stopping his breath in his throat. The words on his lips died between his hard-clamped jaws. He looked down at the woman, his eyes hard.

"Why should that concern you, ma'am?"

His cold question raked through her like a jagged blade, but she met his downbearing gaze steadily, gathering strength from the thought that now it was started, it had to be finished.

"I know a man who has a crooked finger——like yours. It's a family legacy passed down to one or two of the children in each generation." She took a trembling breath when she saw the hatred flare in his eyes, and his hand resting on the rail, the one with the crooked finger, clenched into a hard fist. Sylvia spoke again before her courage left her. "He had a son by a Cheyenne woman whose name was Morning Sun." The last words came out on an expelled breath.

"Is there something you want to know, Mrs. Parnell?" he asked, and there was no mistaking the resentment in his voice.

She closed her eyes tightly. All the color drained from her

face and she moved her head from side to side. Her chest rose with her slow indrawn breath.

"No," she whispered, then, "Yes. I must know if you know who he is."

"I know," he said harshly. "Does that satisfy your curiosity, or do you want to know more of the sordid details of my life?"

"I don't mean to pry into your background, but I had to know. There's something I want *you* to know. Something that may be important to you." She hesitated, then placed her hand on his where it rested on the fence rail. "This man, the one with the crooked finger, is Cooper's father, too."

In the waiting stillness Logan uttered a word on an exploded breath. "Godamighty!"

"Cooper doesn't know," Sylvia said quickly.

"Godamighty! That means—"

"Yes. You and my son are half brothers."

"But . . . why are you telling me? And why haven't you told Cooper?"

"I want him to know . . . someday. It's his right. But I'm afraid if he knew now he'd go gunning for him. He knows his father left me unwed. He suffered taunts for being a bastard when he was young and didn't know what a bastard was. I had to explain to him what it meant."

"Does *he* know about Cooper?"

"He knows a girl by the name of Sylvia Williamson was pregnant with his child when he sneaked away in the middle of the night and left her to face the disgrace of being pregnant and unwed." A pained look came over her face as she remembered. "He came to Bent's Fort and spent several months there. He said he'd been held captive by the Cheyenne but escaped and was on his way East. I had never met a man like him—handsome, glib of tongue. He could charm the skin off a snake when he set his mind to it! One night, after he'd taken my virginity, he told me about the Indian woman, Morning Sun, and about the son born to her with the crooked finger, a legacy passed down through his bloodline to one or two offspring of each generation. He was quite proud of the fact. He was going to take me back to Saint Louis and give me the world." Although she spoke quietly, the very softness of her voice gave her words a harsh quality. "He did give me something far more precious—my son," she said finally.

Logan was stunned into silence, and Sylvia seemed compelled to tell him everything.

"Needless to say I was a disgrace to my missionary parents. I left my home and worked as a laundress at the fort. Cooper was about five years old when I married Oscar Parnell, who was everything a father could be to my son. After years of hard work we finally saved the money to buy this place. Oscar died before we got here."

"Does *he* know you're here?"

"I've heard about his crooked finger, and I've seen him from a distance; but I've not come face to face with him and I hope to God I never do."

The vein beneath the fair skin of her temple showed blue in the morning light and Logan knew what a strain on her it had been to tell her story. He took the pan from her hands.

"Thank you for telling me, ma'am. I'm sorry for all you've gone through, but I can't help but feel glad that Cooper and I have some of the same blood, sorry as it is."

Sylvia clasped his hand in both of hers. "I saw how the two of you hit it off and I was so pleased. Cooper didn't have many friends while he was growing up. People can be cruel to a small child, as I'm sure you know. If the time should ever come that he should know about his father, and I'm not here to tell him, tell him what I've told you and he'll know it's the truth."

"You can depend on it."

*   *   *

The wonder of Sylvia Parnell's words stayed with Logan all through the leave-taking. He tried to keep his eyes from straying to his newly discovered half brother, tried to keep his mind on what the women were saying.

"Don't worry about Odell. We're going to make up that pretty, yellow cloth Logan bought for her and in a few days Cooper will bring us to town." Sylvia gave Rosalee a final hug.

"After we're married Logan wants to go out to meet the men coming in with his herd," Rosalee explained. "I may go to Mary's and wait for him if he won't let me go with him." She was wearing her riding skirt, but she had a dress she wanted to be married in, a loan from Mrs. Parnell, in a bag she hung on her saddle horn.

"We'll find you. I'm sure the town will be buzzing with all the news," Sylvia laughed. "If there's anything you want me to know, leave word with Mr. McCloud."

"I might have two dresses by the time we come to town Mrs. Parnell said I'd be pretty in some green she has." Odell fairly danced with excitement and wasn't at all unhappy about being left behind.

"You be a help to Mrs. Parnell, honey." Rosalee hugged her little sister and held her hand out to Cooper. "Good-bye."

"Good-bye, Miss Spurlock. The next time we see you, you'll be Mrs. Horn." He smiled widely. "It'd be worth the ride to town to kiss the bride. I reckon I could do it now—"

"Stop teasing, Cooper," his mother scolded. "You're making Rosalee blush."

Logan watched with an amused smile. He helped Rosalee mount, then held out his hand to Sylvia. Their eyes caught and held with secret understanding; both were smiling faintly.

"Thank you for . . . everything, ma'am."

"You and Rosalee are welcome here anytime."

"We'll sure have to come back and get this young lady if we miss connections in town." He reached down and hoisted a giggling Odell in the air, then set her on her feet. "She'll be just as pretty as you thought she would be in that yellow, ma'am. I reckon we'll have to build a fence around her in a few years to keep out the suiters until she's grown."

Odell giggled and blushed and dug the toe of her shoe in the ground, but she clung to his hand and looked at him with adoring eyes.

Cooper stepped forward and held out his hand. "Now don't be so stiff-necked and proud, Logan, that you go riding right down the middle of town. Take that back trail I told you about and come in from the side. You'll see the church. The preacher's house is right beside it. You know I'd be more than glad to go along if you just say the word."

"Thanks, but I don't intend to face up to anyone with Rosalee along. We'll go to the preacher and see what he has to say. It goes against the grain to take the back way, but like Case Malone said, pride doesn't keep you from getting a hole in the head."

Cooper laughed. "Case said it right."

Logan clasped his hand warmly and his eyes lingered on his face for a long while before they flicked to Sylvia standing proudly beside her son. She knew what he was feeling and returned his smile warmly.

As they rode away from the ranch, Brutus trailing Mercury, Rosalee couldn't help thinking about the difference in this leave-taking and the one from the Haywards' when they had stopped by for her sister. Oh, bless Sylvia, her heart cried. She turned and waved happily to Sylvia and Odell, then held her hand out to Logan. He grasped it tightly.

"I just want to touch you," she said. "It seems years since we've been alone."

"To me, too. As soon as we're out of sight I'm going to kiss you."

"Let's hurry, then!" She snatched her hand back, put her heels to the roan, and raced ahead of him. In a thick stand of pines she drew up and waited.

Watching her, Logan's heart swelled with love and pride. He rode up beside her and pulled her from the saddle to sit across his thighs. Holding the reins of both horses in his hand, he held her tightly with the other. Her arms went about him and her mouth, soft and eager for his kisses, found his in mutual hunger.

"Darling!" Her mouth moved a fraction and the word came from the center of her being. Her lips sought his mouth again and conveyed the deep heat in her body which was about to flare out of control.

"My love!" His voice was hoarse and breathy, his eyes were close and flared with warmth. Little flecks of light seemed to float in their depths.

His arms, like rigid bands, held her, and she could feel the evidence of his want, firm and hard, against her. She throbbed with response, with an urgent need to be filled. He kissed the dewy sweetness of her mouth time and again.

"We'd better stop this," he moaned into her open mouth.

"Why?" she asked and giggled. "I love it, and I love you—"

His hand moved over her breast and his lips nibbled at hers. "Because . . . when I have you again it will be as my wife."

Rosalee felt her breath catch in her throat, felt her insides warm with pleasure as she looked into his dark quiet face and eyes now filled with love for her. Love and tenderness welled in her. She lifted her hand and held it to his cheek.

"Darling . . ." The whispery word sounded as if part of the wind. "I know you're worried about taking me into town.

Don't think about it and don't worry. I love you, and nothing anyone says or does will keep me from being with you always."

"It could be worse than at the Haywards'."

Her arms encircled his neck. "If it is, we'll face it together."

He kissed her again and at that moment the temptation to take her back East where they could live a more peaceful existence pressed down upon him. The thought nagged at him while he pulled her horse close so she could climb back into the saddle.

They rode side by side when the trail permitted, and at other times Logan took the lead, Brutus always a dozen yards ahead. They rode cautiously on the downward trail that ran along a narrow ridge through a stand of close-growing trees, blow-downs and large granite boulders almost hidden by thick brush. The land to the right of them sloped steeply to the river below. It seemed to Rosalee they were the only living things in all this vastness until a large brown bird glided lazily into the air, gradually circling down to the river.

Late in the morning the dog stopped and froze. Logan pulled up his reins and Rosalee moved beside him. They heard heavy crashing in the brush ahead and Logan slipped the rifle from the saddle scabbard. Crossing the trail ahead were two furry black bear cubs, an enormous black mother bear sauntering along behind them.

"The little ones are . . . adorable," Rosalee laughed softly. "The mother looks so calm and patient."

"She may look calm, but angered she's deadly. She could tear you to pieces with one mighty swipe of her paw. You notice Brutus knows enough to keep his distance and to keep quiet."

"I've seen them from a distance but never up close."

"You're lucky. These mountains are full of them."

Rosalee shivered and inched closer to Logan. They sat quietly until they could no longer hear the crackle of brush as the bears passed through. Logan waited a moment longer, then moved on down the trail and soon they left the ridge behind. The ground leveled out and the going was easier for the horses. The river moved alongside with a pleasant gurgling sound, but soon they left it to take the trail Cooper had told them to take to approach the town from the east.

As they rode down out of the hills toward the town, Logan thought about the preacher and Cooper's reaction. If he will, he'd said. He decided that he would first speak to the preacher alone and save Rosalee the unpleasantness if the man were reluctant to marry them. However reluctant, Logan thought, the preacher would do the job. If Logan had to threaten the man, and he probably would have to do so, he was determined that it not spoil Rosalee's wedding day.

They had circled to the east and now approached the back of the stores that lined the dusty street. Logan slipped the rawhide thong from the hammer of his six-shooter and freed the Winchester in its scabbard for easy use, if needed. A few horses were tied behind the stores. A slow smoke rose from the chimney of the eating house. All was quiet; the town was lazing in the noonday sun. Logan motioned Brutus back and led the way to the rear of the mercantile where they dismounted. Logan tied the horses and commanded Brutus to stay with them. He took the bag containing Rosalee's dress from the saddle horn and ushered her into the back door of the store.

They stood just inside the door and waited while Mr. McCloud escorted a woman to the front porch. Logan was sure the man knew they were there by the way he'd grasped her elbow and by the stream of flattery that fell from his lips to keep her attention. When he was rid of the woman he stuck his head out the door and looked up and down the sidewalk before he took a sign from the nail beside the door and hung it on the doorknob. He closed the door firmly and walked rapidly to the back of the store.

"Howdy, folks." He held his hand out to each of them. He didn't seem to be the least surprised to see them together.

"I was wondering, Mr. McCloud, if Rosalee could stay here for a little while. I've an errand that shouldn't take over half an hour," Logan said after he and Rosalee had exchanged greetings with the storekeeper.

"You can wait in my room, that is, if you don't mind the mess, ma'am."

"But, Logan—"

"You need someplace to change your dress and I'll not be gone long."

"I could do it at the parsonage," she protested gently. She placed her hand on his arm and smiled into his face.

His answering smile lent a fleeting warmth to his features. "I think it best if you do it here," he told her.

"I hung out the 'closed for dinner' sign. C'mon and join me for soda crackers and cheese." Mr. McCloud brought a cloth-wrapped bundle from beneath the counter and dipped his hand into the cracker barrel. "I usually noon here at the store and supper at Mable's. Have a hunk of cheese, ma'am."

"I will, and thank you. Logan and I are going to be married today." She looked at Logan and his slow smile once more altered the stern cast of his face.

"I kinda figured that—changin' your dress, goin' to the parsonage, and all. Congratulations, Horn. If I wasn't so damn old I'd a been after her myself. Help yourself to the crackers, now."

Rosalee munched the cheese slowly, trying not to gobble. It had been several years since she'd had cheese and it was so good. This was her wedding day, she thought dreamily. It wasn't at all like the day she'd dreamed about—wearing a beautiful white dress and walking into the church on her father's arm. But marrying Logan made up for everything. Her eyes lingered lovingly on his tall, buckskin-clad figure. He had removed his hat and his shiny black hair sprang back from his forehead and hung almost to his shoulders. His face was clean shaven and the soft, black mustache that hung down on each side of his mouth made him look more Spanish than Indian. But Indian he was, with those high cheekbones and fathomless black eyes. It was strange, but she already felt married to him, and the ceremony wasn't so important to her anymore.

"Young Ben was in a few days back. I tried to give him the money I got for your pa's birds, but he said leave it here and you'd take it out in trade. Sure a shame about your folks getting burned out. Some folks kinda got up in arms about it. Wasn't no call for Clayhill to do that."

"How is Ben? Did he manage to get away with some of our things? How about the cow?"

"From what I hear he did. He appears to be fine. He was chipper and seemed to think Horn, here, and Case Malone were goin' to set Clayhill back on his ear. He'd grown up some since I saw him last. I hear you've got a good sized herd comin' in," he said to Logan, and sliced off another hunk of cheese with a bowie knife.

Logan's brows described a puzzled arc. "How did you know?"

The storekeeper laughed. "Not much happens here that people don't know about. Even Adam Clayhill's gone out to look 'em over."

"The hell you say!"

"He only took a couple of men with him, so I don't figure he's ready to do nothin' yet."

Logan chuckled. "If he starts anything with the men driving that herd, he's going to think he's been tied in a poke with half a dozen wildcats. They don't back down once they've set out to do something. The Clayhill name'll mean nothing to them, and it'd make no difference if it did."

"I never saw the town so full of drifters." McCloud looked meaningfully at Logan and shook his head. "Sure a lot of trash in town."

Logan nodded, aware of what the storekeeper was trying to say without alarming Rosalee.

"Have you heard how Case Malone is doing?" Rosalee asked.

"He's doin' fine. Him and Mrs. Gregg came in and got hitched yesterday."

"They got married? I'm so glad! I told you they loved each other," she said to Logan.

"It took some persuadin' for the preacher to marry what he considered a fallen woman," McCloud said with a chuckle. "But after Case caught hold of that high stiff collar of his and threatened to choke the life outta him, he 'saw the light,' as he's so fond of sayin'. The pious fraud ought to be run out of town," he added with a disgusted snort.

"What if he doesn't want to marry us?" Rosalee's worried eyes sought Logan's. The thought had occured to her before, but she had shoved it to the back of her mind.

"It doesn't matter if he wants to or not, sweetheart. He'll do it and he'll give us a proper paper to prove it. Don't worry." He handed her the bag with her dress. "Go on into Mr. McCloud's room and get ready for your wedding. I'll be back for you in half an hour and we'll see what the preacher man has to say."

The storekeeper went out the back door with Logan. "He won't want to do it."

"I'm aware of that, but I figure to do my persuading beforehand."

"Watch yourself."

"I figured to ride the roan up to the preacher's house. Do you mind if I put my horse in your livery shed?"

"Good idea. That horse is a dead giveaway. So's the dog."

"Brutus will stay with Mercury." Logan lengthened the stirrups on the saddle and mounted the roan.

Mr. McCloud stood in the back door of his store and watched Logan lead the spotted stallion into the livery shed. He waited until he came out again and headed toward the preacher's house before he went back inside. He shook his gray head in sympathy for what Logan had to endure because of his Indian blood.

"That man's in for a bad time with that pious, sonofabitchin' preacher," he mumbled to himself. "But if anybody can scare the shit out of him, he can." He grinned. "I wish I'd gone along to see it."

Logan tied his horse to a hitching rail outside the low board fence surrounding the yard and went to the screened door. It was one of the few he'd seen since he came West. From what he could make out through the screen, the inside of the house was what would be considered luxurious in a frontier town but moderate back East. He wondered how the small congregation could afford such luxury for their preacher. He lifted his hand to knock, but before he did a man came to the door from the side of the room and Logan knew he had been watching from the window.

"What do you want here?"

Logan eyed the man for a moment before he spoke. He was a small, thin man with sparce gray hair and a hooked nose. The high stiff collar was too large for his neck and black trousers held by the suspenders were too large for his skinny frame. The upper lip of his small mouth was raised as if he were smelling something unpleasant. It's not going to be easy, Logan thought, but then he knew it wouldn't be.

"Are you the preacher?" Logan asked at last, knowing that he was, but wanting him to say it.

"I'm the Reverend Gerald Abernathy," he said haughtily. "What do you want?"

"I want to talk to you. Do you want to come out, or do you want me to come in?"

"Say what you've got to say from there. I've heard about you. I got nothin'—" The door was jerked open and the big man was crowding him away from it before he could finish the sentence. "Just what'er you tryin' to pull off here? This is a house of the Lord. It ain't for the likes of you! You can't come in—" he sputtered.

"I'm in," Logan said softly.

"Get out! You're a . . . heathen, an Indian!" he spat the word as if it were nasty in his mouth.

"Shut up or I'll wring your scrawny neck!"

If Logan had reached out and slapped the man, the effect could not have been more startling. His slack jaw dropped and he stared at him with disbelieving eyes. The Adam's apple leaped convulsively in his scrawny neck and his voice came out, high-pitched and strangled. "You dirty, stinkin' half—"

"Don't say it," Logan said in an unruffled voice, and with an easy motion fastened his hand to the man's shirt front and pulled him so close to him that his head was tilted far back. He looked him full in the face, his eyes cold. He spoke softly, but every word struck the preacher like a shower of ice chips. "You're a marrying preacher. I'm bringing my lady here in a few minutes and you're going to marry us all legal and proper. If you put your filthy tongue to one word about us while we're here, I'll make you wish to God you'd never learned how to talk. Do you understand my meaning?"

"I—I'll . . . it ain't right for you to marry a white woman . . . even if she's—"

Anger, like a white-hot heat, surged up from his toes and worked its way all through him. His powerful hands clamped onto thin shoulders and he shook the man so viciously his head flopped back and forth like a watch fob on a chain. When he realized that he could easily kill the man, he slammed him down in a chair and stood over him.

"Goddamn you, you mealy-mouthed sonofabitch!" he gritted between jaws clenched with hate. "I'm bringing Miss Spurlock here, and if you say one word to spoil her wedding day I'll see you boiled in oil! Better yet, I'll pass the word to my Cheyenne brothers. They'll come in the night and burn this place to the ground—with you in it! Or they may take you with them and burn you at the stake in a ceremonial orgy after they take the skin off you an inch at a time."

The preacher's eyes were rolled back in his head, his small mouth was open, and he gasped for breath. Logan stood looking down at the speechless man and realized that if he had finished saying what he had started to say about Rosalee he would have destroyed him. It was the first time in a long time he had allowed his iron control to slip, and the experience made him weak.

"Get yourself together," he snarled. "I'll be right back. You better remember what I said and be here." He turned on his heel and walked out the door.

Chapter
Nineteen

Della spent her first night in the room above the saloon wishing she was downstairs. She could hear the loud male laughter, smell the smoke from the cheap cigars, and hear the clinking of glasses over the scraping of bootheels on the rough plank floor. It excited her and she almost envied Bessie when she heard the pounding of whiskey bottles and beer glasses and the lewd, suggestive remarks after she finished her song.

Bessie had complained, as Della knew she would, and the bartender had rapped on her door. Instead of rebuking her for taking Bessie's room, he had asked if there was anything he could do for her. His beady eyes had danced with the knowledge he would have interesting news to tell the bar patrons. Della knew that and didn't care. She ordered him to have her meals sent over from the restaurant for the next few days. She vaguely wondered how long it would take Adam to find out she was there and how angry he would be when he came to take her home.

The next day, while waiting for her noon meal to arrive,

she pulled a chair to the window and idly watched the people go in and out of the mercantile across the street. She also had a view of the livery stable, behind and to the side of it. When she saw Logan Horn, sitting tall in the saddle of a big roan and leading his freckled stallion, she jerked to attention. There was no mistaking him; she'd seen him in her mind's eye a thousand times since she first saw him on the street. She leaned forward and waited, her eyes glued to the door, until he came out of the livery and rode behind the row of store buildings. He wasn't leaving town! He would be back to the livery for his horse and his dog.

Della hastily threw off the peignoir she had been lounging in and carefully pulled a fresh white dress over her high-piled curls. She adjusted the neckline and tied a blue satin ribbon around her waist and another with a cameo pinned to it around her neck. After applying rosewater to her arms and throat, she picked up her white umbrella and left the room.

Riding back to the livery from the preacher's house, Logan was so angry he was almost sick with it. Doubt that he and Rosalee could make a decent life together in this country touched him more strongly than ever before, but he closed his mind to it. He'd finish what he started, by God, or die trying! It was a hell of a thing for a man to be in a black mood on his wedding day, he thought grimly. He rode his horse through the big doors of the livery stable, wanting a minute or two alone before he went into the store to tell Rosalee the preacher was willing to marry them.

At first he didn't see the woman standing in the shadowed corner. If he had been as alert as he should have been, he would have noticed Brutus hunkered down beside Mercury, his eyes riveted on the far corner of the stable. Logan was dismounting, swinging his leg over the rump of the horse, when he saw her. He paused, then with both feet firmly on the ground, he looked at her over the horse's back. She stood smiling at him, a vision all in white. Her blond hair, against the rough, dark, plank wall, gleamed; her skin, milk white; her lips, red as tulips. She was beautiful. He knew immediately that she was Della Clayhill.

"Hello, Logan Horn. I've been waiting for you."

"Ma'am." He politely put his fingers to the brim of his hat. He tied the roan to the rail and walked behind the horse.

"Is that all you have to say?"

"What else is there to say?"

"You're not curious to know why I've been waiting for you?" Della hadn't moved from the corner, but her eyes had moved over him like oil on a hot skillet.

"I reckon you'll tell me if you want me to know."

Her quick laugh broke the quiet of the barn with a throaty vibrance. Her lips remained parted. A frankly appraising glint shone in her eyes as they made a leisurely examination of him. It was done, from head to toe, with painstaking care to detail, lingering deliberately on his torso below his belted overshirt. Her starkly naked gaze reflected blatant, unmistakable desire.

"I don't think I have to tell you. You're a man, aren't you?" she said finally. He'd almost forgotten what he had said to cause her to say it.

"Yes, ma'am. But I'm not starving."

She was openly amused. "Come over here and . . . we'll talk about it."

"No!" If it was possible to shout in a whisper he had done it. His mind was spinning with thoughts of getting rid of her without a fuss. She spelled nothing but trouble.

"No!" She echoed his word. "You're saying no to what I'm offering? Well, goddamn you!" Her face reddened and her mouth thinned. "Who are you to be sayin' no to . . . me!"

Knowing he had made a mistake and that this was an

explosive situation, he smiled, slowly and deliberately, although he felt as if his face would crack.

"I'm saying no to *now*. I don't want to get strung up before I finish what I start."

"That's more like it, big warrior." Her mouth curved into a smile once again and she beckoned him with a crooked finger. "I can be a help to you. I've got Adam Clayhill wrapped right around my finger."

She put her hands on her hips and threw her shoulders back so that her breast stood out against her dress. She flattened her belly and swayed. Then, without taking her eyes from his, she unbuttoned the top of her dress, showing the milky whiteness of her breasts, and taut dark nipples.

Logan breathed deeply. He grew cold, then hot. Somehow her nakedness was more than nakedness. The way she displayed herself was—obscene.

"Don't you want to kiss me, Chief? Don't you want me to touch you?" Her voice had a husky, excited tremor.

"Of course, I do." The lie came thickly from his throat.

She laughed and moved her body in such a way it made his flesh crawl! She was truly a thing of beauty nourished in filth. Cold chills dashed the anger from his veins and he wanted to get away from her as fast as he could. Beautiful as she was, he'd sooner mate with a bitch dog.

"Are you afraid of Adam Clayhill?" she asked with a taunting sound in her voice.

"I'm not afraid of any man."

"He'll kill you if he can. He says if you stay others will follow. He thinks you're dangerous. Are you?"

"I suppose I am . . . when cornered." He faced her squarely.

"Consider yourself cornered. You want me, don't you?"

"Yes, but not here where it would be hurried. Tonight. Where are you staying?" He forced the smile on his lips to reach his eyes.

"You'll come to me?"

"Do you think me a fool?"

"Nooooo . . ." She drew the word out. Her pale blue eyes were fixed on him, knowingly amused. "I'm staying above the saloon. The front room on the right."

"Is there a back door?"

"Right up those stairs, Chief. You can see them from here. I'll leave the door unlocked."

"I'll be there." He lowered his voice and the words came out thick and unsteady.

Della held out her arms. "Come kiss me. Tonight I'll make you feel things you've only dreamed about. Then we'll talk. I can be a big help to you. Together we can beat that old bastard at his own game." She laughed. It was a beautiful sound, but it fell on Logan's ears like the grating of an axle badly in need of grease.

He stepped close to her; there was no avoiding it. She grasped his arms and pushed them aside and came firmly against him. She encircled his waist in both her arms and leaned the upper part of her body back, her hips pressing against him.

"I knew you'd be like this; cautious, hard to get." Her voice came out in a throaty rush. "You're worried now— afraid we'll get caught in here. They'd kill you, string you up in a minute if I screamed rape! What a waste—" She broke off, drew a long, shuddering breath, and moved her hips demandingly against him. "Tonight I'll make it so good for you, you'll never be satisfied with another woman. I'll make you rock hard, again and again. And when you think you can't do it again, you will. Do you believe it?" she demanded softly. Her hand, gentle at first, then with persistent, skilled fingers, worked its way between them to burrow between his legs.

"Of course I do. You're . . . some woman."

"Kiss me, you . . . sweet savage!"

Her unloosed hunger rendered him momentarily at a loss. He was so repulsed that it left him trembling and constricted his chest until he thought he would suffocate. He wanted to fling her to the floor and kick her away from him and was mortified that he was forced to stand and suffer her touch. Willing himself to play out the game, he crushed her to him and put his mouth to hers with vicious impact. The pressure was hard and swift, but she managed to plunge her tongue into his mouth. He lifted his head quickly, thinking he would gag. He grabbed her shoulders and put her from him. He was breathing hard. He had the feeling he was being devoured.

"Go!" he said harshly. "I can't take much more."

"Ohhh . . . God!" she whispered breathlessly and rubbed against him. "Since that day on the street, I've thought about you and felt you inside me." Thinking he was as aroused as she, her hands moved along his narrow flanks. As they approached his sex, he grabbed them.

"No! Tonight. Go back to your room. I'll wait in here for awhile, then I must leave."

Della's eyes shone like silver stars. She buttoned her dress and picked up her parasol. "Sweet, sweet . . . savage! I've waited a long time to meet a man like you. Come to me tonight. I'll be waiting."

"It'll be midnight or later. I'll have to be careful."

"I know." She came to him and lifted her lips. He forced himself to brush them with his. "Bye, for now . . ."

After she was gone, Logan leaned on the roan horse. He was sweating profusely. The ordeal with Clayhill's stepdaughter was far worse than the one he'd been through with the so-called man of God. He felt dirty and filled with a shame that made his stomach queasy. God almighty! Would they never leave him alone? Rosalee, Rosalee, my sweet bride, that woman wasn't fit to live in the same world with you.

He stood in the shadows and looked across the street toward the saloon. From the front window she had been able to see the livery barn by looking over the small, low building beside the mercantile. He cursed silently, then moved swiftly. He was sure she hadn't had time to reach the room, so he led the horses out of the barn and tied them on the other side of the store. They could be viewed from the street, but Mercury wouldn't be so noticeable without Brutus. He had to chance it. He went to the back door of the store and called the dog to him.

"Come, Brutus." The dog came to him, glanced back toward the horses, then sat down on his haunches. He tilted his head in such a manner that Logan knew he was puzzled by the order. "I know it's not what you're used to doing, but this time you're going to have to keep out of sight." He pointed to the ground and the dog lay down. "Stay here," he commanded.

Logan slipped inside the store and paused so his eyes could adjust to the gloom after the bright sunlight. He heard voices and moved out of sight behind a thick curtain of harnesses that hung from the rafters. The man McCloud was waiting on wore an old felt hat, the wide brim rolled up on the sides to form a sharp point in front. Chaps and spurs proclaimed him a drover, but he was wearing a tied-down six-shooter that announced he was handy with a gun, or thought he was. He slouched against the counter.

"I hear tell that Injun's all horn 'n rawhide. That so?"

"He's not a man to be messed with, if that's what you mean. Is there anything else you want?" McCloud asked pleasantly. "If not you owe me two bits for the tobacco."

"I hear tell that red ass fights with his feet. I ain't never seen that done afore."

"You're *hear tellin'* a lot," McCloud said dryly.

"It's all the town's talkin' of. I reckon that Clayhill'll wrap that Injun's hide 'round a stump 'n kick the shit outta 'im when he catches up with 'im."

"I reckon he'll try."

"Mister, you sound like you're atakin' sides with the redskin."

"Is that any business of yours?" McCloud demanded loudly. "Right's right, if it's an Indian, a Mexican, or a know-it-all saddle tramp. The man bought the land, he's got a right to live on it the same as you, if you'd bought it."

"Hoo . . . ly sheeit! This country'd go straight to hell if'n the redskins owned all the land. In no time a'tall it'd not be worth doodley squat!"

"Who do you think owned the land before we got here?" McCloud snorted. "Ain't you got nothin' else to do but stand here and run off at the mouth about somethin' you know nothin' about?"

"Folks ain't goin' to like it a'tall, you takin' sides with the Injun. Folks won't do no tradin' with—"

"That'll suit me fine! Folks can do their tradin' in Longmont or Denver. It'd be no skin off my ass!" McCloud's voice boomed. "I'll burn the sonofabitchin' store down and go back to Springfield where folks have somethin' between their ears besides horseshit!"

"Now . . . looky here—"

"You looky here! I think what I please and say what I please. This here's my store and there ain't nobody tellin' me how to run it! Why don't you get the hell outta here?"

Logan couldn't help but grin at McCloud's spunk. He was relieved, however, when he heard the bootheels of the angry drover pounding on the plank floor as he made his way to the door. A moment passed before McCloud came to the back of the store.

"How'd you make out with the preacher?" he asked when Logan stepped from behind the harnesses.

"It took a threat or two, but he'll do it. Is Rosalee ready?"

The storekeeper went behind the counter and knocked softly on a door. It opened almost immediately and Rosalee, smiling radiantly, came out and hurried to the back of the store, her eyes searching its shadowed depth.

"Here she is, Horn. Can't say as I've ever seen a more beautiful bride."

Logan stepped out and she went to him, her eyes fastened on his. Her slightly flushed cheeks and the blue dress made her blue-green eyes seem all the brighter, clearer. Her hair was piled on the top of her head and a narrow blue ribbon was wrapped around the bun. She was lovely, and Logan's heart lurched painfully at the thought of the hostile minister waiting to marry them.

"Sweetheart—" His voice broke off, shaking. "Sweetheart, you're so . . . pretty!" His hands on her arms held her away from him and he looked at her with eyes that moved over her hungrily, lovingly. She gazed back at him, the ache of love in her tremulous mouth. "I wish I had been able to dress appropriately. I'm sorry I must wear these old buckskins for the most important event of my life."

"It doesn't matter what we're wearing. Sylvia wanted me to wear this dress. I would've been just as happy in my old riding skirt."

"We must go." Logan forced his eyes from her glowing face and looked at the storekeeper. "Thanks, McCloud." He extended his hand.

"No thanks are necessary. Go on with you, and get yourself hitched, legal and proper, to this pretty woman before somebody else gets her." There was a kind of rough hoarseness to his voice.

Rosalee laughed. "That would never happen in a million years, Mr. McCloud. I've waited all my life for Logan Horn."

"If you get in a tight, come on back and hole up here. I

reckon I got guns and ammunition to hold off an army, if need be."

"You'd do that?" Logan asked with a puzzled frown.

"There comes a time in a man's life when he stands up for what he thinks is right. You're doin' it, aren't you?" He held Rosalee's hand in both of his. "Happy weddin' day, Rosalee."

Her eyes misted and she reached up and kissed his cheek. "Thank you."

Logan took a quick look around before he pulled Rosalee out into the bright sunlight. Brutus still lay beside the door.

They hurried around to the side of the building where the horses waited. Logan led her to the roan, lifted her to sit in the saddle sideways, thrust a foot in the stirrups, and swung up behind her. With Mercury's reins firmly in one hand, he put his heels to the roan and they moved behind the buildings until they were at the far end of the street. When he was sure they were out of sight of the saloon window, he swung out toward the church and the preacher's house beside it.

Rosalee knew he was taking extra precautions and didn't speak. Nothing could dampen her bubbly spirit that day. The sun was shining, she was with the man she loved, and it was her wedding day. She leaned contentedly against him and her arm around his waist tightened.

A short way from the church, Logan stopped the horses behind a thick growth of wild honeysuckle and sumac. His brown fingers lifted her face and his eyes searched hers, before he lowered his head and kissed her softly, reverently. All thought left her. She closed her eyes and gave herself up to the joy of his kiss. There was no haste in it. Slow, sensuous, languid, he took his time. She kissed him back hungrily, her hand moving to the back of his neck to hold him to her. The kiss lasted endlessly, as if they each found it impossible to end it. When she felt his warm breath on her wet lips, she opened her eyes. His face was very close.

"I love you more than life," he whispered. "I'll love you with all my heart and soul and spirit until the end of time and to the hereafter. You're my bright star in a dark night, the soft touch of the restless wind, the warmth of a spring day. I'll spend the rest of my life taking care of you."

"And I you, my love," she pledged solemnly. "I give all of myself into your keeping forever."

"No man has ever received such a gift before, and no two people will ever love as we shall." The sincerity of his words brought tears to her eyes and they rolled from the corners into the soft hair at her temples. "There was never a more beautiful bride, or one who was loved and cherished more." His lips kissed the wetness from her eyes. "Don't cry, my love."

"I'm crying because I'm happy," she whispered joyously. "Happier than I ever dreamed I could be. I'll always remember this moment when we pledged our love as our true wedding."

"I wish it could have been in a more beautiful setting than behind a clump of sumac," he said in a lighter, teasing tone. He kissed her hard and quick. "I want to do more than kiss you. I can't now, but when night comes, my darling . . ." he threatened and put his heels to the horse.

Rosalee's laughter bubbled up. "You're not scaring me, Logan Horn!" Her eyes sparkled at him through the thick lashes.

"I hope not, my love." His dark eyes were alive with smile lines that fanned out from the corners.

She laughed softly and tried to tuck the stray tendrils back under the ribbon around the bun on the top of her head.

They passed the church and moved on to the preacher's house. Logan dismounted and lifted Rosalee down. She smoothed her skirt while he tied the horses, then with a hand firmly beneath her elbow, he led her up the walk to the door.

Reverend Abernathy pushed open the screen door and motioned them inside. Without saying a word, he turned his back to them and walked across the room to pick up an open Bible. When he turned to face them he kept his eyes on the book he cradled in his two hands.

Rosalee glanced at Logan, an amused smile on her face. "Hello, Reverend Abernathy," she said brightly.

His eyes flicked up and back down. "Hello, Miss Spurlock. Are you ready?" His voice was so low it was bearly audible in the quiet room.

"We're ready," Logan replied, and laced Rosalee's fingers with his in a tight knot of love.

"We are gathered here in the sight of God—"

"Just a moment," Logan said. "We need a witness."

"My wife is in the other room. She's already signed the paper—"

"Tell her to come out."

"Martha," he called and his voice squeaked.

A tall, thin woman in a black dress with a small white collar appeared in the door. Her hair was pulled back in a tight, small knot and she held her hands behind her. Rosalee glanced at her and thought she looked as if she had been sucking on a sour pickle. She had to press her lips tightly together to keep from laughing.

"We are gathered here in the sight of God and man to join this . . . man and this woman in holy matrimony." The preacher's thin mouth turned down at the corners in a grimace. "Do you take this man?" He scarcely gave Rosalee time to answer before he continued. "Do you take this woman?"

"Yes, I do." Logan's voice was firm and he looked at Rosalee with a consuming tenderness in his dark eyes.

"I now pronounce you husband and wife." The minister

said rapidly in a sing-song voice, and for the first time he looked up at them.

They had eyes only for each other. It was as if they were alone in the room. She lifted her face to his and Logan kissed her upturned lips gently. Their eyes clung, hers like bright, new stars, his, a shiny dark mirror. He held her tightly to his side and squeezed her hand so hard her fingers were white.

"Here's your paper." The cold words jarred between them. There was no mistaking the hostility in the preacher's voice. It was as if he was no longer intimidated now that the ceremony was over.

They turned back to the preacher. Logan gave him a quelling look and snatched the paper from his hand. He scanned it carefully before he tucked it inside his shirt.

"Thank you, Reverend." Rosalee smiled happily at the man despite the fact he stood stiff with disapproval. He didn't move as much as an eyelash as he stared into her eyes. She cared not a whit. She continued to smile at him while Logan dug into his money belt. She was determined to not let him dampen her spirit on this wonderful occasion.

On the way to the door, Logan flipped a coin onto the table. He held the screen open for Rosalee to pass through, then turned. His dark eyes bored into those of the man who professed to be a man of God. He stared at him for a long moment, and then coldly recited the ancient Cheyenne prayer of those about to die:

"Nothing lives long, nothing stays here,
Except the Earth and the Mountains . . ."

The preacher's jaws clenched as the color left his face. His trembling hands grabbed the back of a chair for support. "You . . . promised—" he croaked.

"If you lay your tongue to one filthy word about me or my wife, I'll forget that promise," Logan warned in a voice as cold as ice. His eyes were hard, his face stoic; he'd never looked more Indian than he did at that moment. He lingered until he was satisfied the man knew the meaning of the words before he turned and let the screen door slam shut behind him.

On the porch he grabbed Rosalee's hand and they ran down the walk to the horses. Their laughter mingled. They were like excited children: Everything was new and wonderful. Rosalee mounted the roan; her blue dress scarcely reached mid-calf, but it was of no concern to her. The big horse skittered sideways, sensing the excitement. She held him firmly in check until Logan mounted. He looked at her and the smile on his face was the most beautiful smile she'd ever seen. He put his heels to Mercury. The stallion half squatted on his powerful haunches, then launched himself into thundering flight toward the thick stand of spruce and pine beyond the town, his body stretching longer and lower to the ground with every giant stride.

In joyful abandonment, Rosalee gave the roan the necessary encouragement to follow Mercury. She was happy, so happy! There was no past, no lonely future; only Logan. She felt cleansed, enriched, newborn.

Chapter
Twenty

Two miles from town they pulled the running horses to a halt. Mercury danced on a tight rein and the roan pranced. Rosalee had forgotten about Brutus until, tongue hanging from the side of his mouth, he caught up with them and sank down on his belly in the cool grass. Her laughter rang in the quiet stillness of the woods. It had a joyous, earthy quality, like the wind; it was full of love and happiness and the sound soared, pure and sweet, right up to the tops of the giant pines.

Logan's dark intense gaze clung to her. It traveled lovingly over her thick, wind-tousled hair, over her radiant face with its passionate mouth and searching, laughing eyes, and down the tight, slim body and firm, round breasts. This was his bride, his mate forever and always. He was not a religious man, though his uncle had insisted he have religious training. He had never called on the white man's God for anything. Now, a silent prayer was in his heart, thanking God for bringing this woman into his life, and asking help to keep her safe and happy until the end of their days together.

"Oh, Logan, they were so... funny! The reverend was scared to death. I think he thought you'd... scalp him! And his wife... poor thing! She looked as if she lived in a sauerkraut barrel." Laughing words gushed out of Rosalee's mouth like water from a fountain. "But I'd look sour, too, if I were married to that dried up old prune!"

Logan edged his horse closer to hers. That she was his was a miracle of ever-expanding proportions. It increased his resolve to hold onto this intangible something hidden beyond the enjoyment of welcoming flesh. He felt a sense of awe. She loved *him*. Wanted to be with *him*. The solitary years stretched behind him. The agony of that loneliness was over.

"I didn't need him to say the words to make you mine, Mrs. Horn. I wanted the paper for legal purposes." He leaned toward her and found her soft, trembling mouth. His lips clung to hers as though he slaked a long, long thirst, and when he finally let them go, he said in a voice that quivered with emotion, "I give you my life, my eternal love."

"Oh, Logan! I'm as happy as a dog with two tails!"

He smiled deep into her eyes; her answering smile was one of startling girlish sweetness, warm with the glow of complete trust. It was fearless and honest and full of an overwhelming love that blazed like the noonday sun. With his gaze fixed on her face he felt his mind grind to a halt. The very realness of her happiness caused a lump of fear to rise and constrict his throat. To see the light go out of her eyes would cause him more pain than he would be able to endure. He swallowed audibly and forced his lips to hold the smile.

"Put on your riding skirt, sweetheart. We'll be traveling a rough trail." He handed her the canvas bag he had slung over his saddle horn.

"Where are we going?"

"To a place where we'll be welcome."

"To Mary's?"

"Yes, to Mary's."

Logan stayed mounted while Rosalee changed clothes. His eyes constantly scanned their back trail. When Rosalee remounted, he wheeled his horse so they could ride side by side until it became necessary to ride single file with Brutus leading the way. They headed south, staying among the trees. The trail they followed was seldom used. At times it was overgrown with a low-spreading shrub with hooklike thorns, making it necessary to go off the trail and into the rocks. Occasionally, through the thick brush, they could see the road below they dared not travel.

In late afternoon they came out onto a bench that overlooked Mary's house. The late afternoon sun was slipping behind the mountains to the west. When Rosalee would have ridden on, a softly spoken word from Logan held her back.

"Wait."

She pulled up sharply and turned to see him staring fixedly at a screen of scrub cedars. A quiet hung on the timbered benchland of diffused sunlight and dense shade. The plaintive song of a mourning dove seemed surprisingly loud in that impenetrable quiet. The faint scent of tobacco smoke had caused Logan to stop and cautiously study the terrain below them and above the road. He scanned it methodically, studying each rock, tree, and shrub with particular care, making allowances for light and the length of the shadows. Finally, the flick of a horse's tail, fighting the pesky flies, gave away the man's position. He was sitting on a rock among the stunted cedars and gnarled oak that clung to the hillside above the road. After a long wait Logan spoke again.

"Wait here," he said without looking at her.

Without questioning him, Rosalee quietly moved the roan back into the woods.

Logan wheeled the freckled stallion, and with the flick of

his hand signaled Brutus to stay beside him. He made a wide half-circle and swung down toward his quarry, the irregularity in the hill's outline and the thick growth of brush beneath the tall pines affording concealment. Reining in, he sat the stallion and waited.

Ghostlike, Brutus drifted down through the screening brush and rocks and sank into the grass ahead of the horse, his gaze fixed on the man seated on a flat rock, his elbows resting on his knees while he rolled a smoke.

There was another stretch of waiting silence. Logan saw the dog's hackles rise. Without a sound he rose to a half crouch, stole forward a half dozen feet, and sank into the grass.

Trained to respond to the lightest touch, Mercury stood perfectly still while Logan watched the man in hard-eyed silence. He was a small man with hair that hung over the collar of a faded flannel shirt. His boots were run-down at the heels and his pants showed signs of long wear, but the rifle he held on his lap and the six-gun in the holster were well cared for. There was a bedroll tied behind his saddle. He was a drifter, a hired gun.

In the silence Logan dropped three quiet words.

"Drop the gun."

He watched the man's back stiffen, his head suddenly thrust forward in surprise, but he made no other move. He was trailwise enough to know that if he did he was dead. Logan waited, letting his silence work on the man's nerves. Finally, as he knew he would, the man carefully lifted the rifle from his lap and began slowly to get to his feet.

"I'd be careful with that rifle if I were you."

"I ain't no fool!" He placed it on the ground and turned.

"I'm not so sure of that. Not even a half-wit greenhorn would lay himself out as open as you did." Logan couldn't resist the taunt. Anger bubbled up. The sonofabitch was waiting to ambush him! He was playing a hunch that sooner or later he'd get in touch with Case Malone and was watching the road to Mary's house.

A look of contempt came over the man's face as he realized Logan's breeding. He emitted a mirthless laugh, silently congratulating himself. He'd been right in thinking the Indian would visit the whorehouse. On the point of speaking, he detected a movement and fixed his gaze in sudden consternation on the shaggy apparition noiselessly rising from the grass and advancing on him. The dog's upper lips curled away from gleaming fangs in a blood-chilling wolf grin.

"Christ—"

"He won't attack unless I tell him to. Were you waiting for me?"

The very softness of his voice whipped the man's gaze to Logan. With brash confidence in his superiority over men of Logan's heritage, he spread his legs and his shoulders dropped. He looked Logan up and down, eyes brightly glinting. This was the half-breed they were talking about at the saloon as if he were the devil himself. Hell! He didn't look so tough. He was nothing but a dirty, stinking blanket ass, for all his size and manner. Doubt that he could take the Indian touched him for a moment; but he lifted his voice loudly against it.

"Ya'd be smart to get yore red ass back to whatever reservation it belongs on. Ya keep on ahangin' out in this country apesterin' white folks and yore apt to get yore hide shot full a holes."

"Is that what you're here to do?" The very softness of Logan's words should have been a warning, but the man on the ground was tragically incapable of gauging the full depths of the danger confronting him.

"Well, I ain't agoin' to jest stand here 'n let a stinkin' Injun shoot me," he sneered.

"That's up to you." Logan's voice was quiet and he appeared to be relaxed, as if they were having a casual conversation. "You make a wrong move and you won't have any say in the matter. Drop your gun and ride out. I don't want any trouble."

"I ain't never seen the day a nigger, a Mex, or a Injun could run me off!" he replied tartly. "Ya think a breed can—"

"Watch yourself!" Logan spoke with a voice as hard as iron. "I'm telling you again. Lift the six-shooter out of the holster and ride out. I don't want to kill you."

"That's right friendly of ya. Yore right uppity fer a breed." He gave a laugh of derision. His confidence soared. He was on his feet, the Indian was mounted. Hell! He'd shoot him out of the saddle before his hand reached that big army Colt on his thigh. Then he'd ride into town leading that speckled stallion! Folks'd sit up and take notice.

Stupid fool, Logan thought. The man saw a chance to make a name for himself and he wouldn't back down. Greed for a brief moment of recognition and a few coins would cost him his life. He forced the thoughts to the back of his mind. He couldn't afford to allow pity to distract him. He fixed his gaze on the man's face and smiled, although he had never felt less like smiling. He knew his smile confused and angered the man, so he waited, giving the anger time to stiffen him up before he gave his final jab.

"I feel sorry for you. You're nothing but a piss-poor piece of white trash sent out to do another man's killing. If you're so anxious to die, make your move."

Logan watched the man's face. When he was ready, he would know it by the look in his eyes. He caught the slight tightening of his frame and the barest movement of his eyelids. Suddenly, the man's right hand snapped down toward the gun on his thigh. Instinctively, Logan's own hand moved with the swiftness of a coiled, striking snake. The big saddle-gun bucked in his hand, its furious bellow shattering the sun-drenched stillness. The echo of the shot splattered into a thousand fragments against the rocky canyon walls and faded into nothingness.

The impact of the big slug flung the man back against the twisted trunk of a tree. He hung there, his hand raised in a futile attempt to stop the blood pouring from his chest. His hat, tilted when he struck the tree, still clung to his head at an odd angle.

"Oh! Christ!" he said in a breathless, failing voice of deepest dismay. He looked down at his chest with an expression of pure horror, and then with a faint sigh he went limp and slumped to the ground.

Brutus rose up. Sensing the man was no longer a threat, he walked to him, sniffed, then moved disdainfully away to lay belly down on the cool grass. The scent of blood rather than the bark of the gun set Mercury dancing, and Logan was forced to hold him with a strong hand. He wheeled the stallion and calmed him before he dismounted beside the lifeless body.

A wave of sickness washed up from the pit of his stomach. He'd looked into the faces of men he'd killed during the war; young, serene, unbelievably innocent faces. This man's face looked younger in death, although it was slightly haggard from not enough food and too much drink. He wanted to look away, but forced himself to look at the man who had tried to kill him and whom he had killed. It was all so . . . utterly pointless. In the backwash of emotion, nausea roiled up inside him and he turned away before he became retchingly sick.

Rosalee heard the ugly bark of the shot, and fear squeezed the air from her chest. Even in her near panic she realized the folly of moving out from the place where Logan told her to wait. She had no gun. She'd be more of a hindrance than a help to him. She made herself hold the roan motionless while she sat rigidly upright, wildly staring around. What could she do? She didn't know where he was! She gazed with growing fear in the direction from which he would come. Nothing moved. There was not even a birdsong to break the silence.

After what seemed like hours, but could have only been minutes, she heard the crackle of brush and first Brutus and then Logan and Mercury came into the clearing. She was seized with an uncontrollable trembling and clenched her teeth after she said his name.

"Logan—"

"It's all right," he said gently. "It's all right."

The hoofs of their horses loosed a rattling barrage of stones as they took the downward trail in a rush. On the level road Rosalee and Logan put their heels to their mounts and cantered into Mary's yard to find Josh and Ben, rifles cradles in their arms, cautiously emerging from the barn, and Case Malone standing beside the back door. Ben let out a shout of greeting when he recognized his sister, then rushed forward in a delirium of joy.

Rosalee slid from the saddle and hugged her brother. "Oh, Ben! I swear to goodness! Let me look at you—you've grown a foot!"

"Yo're gettin' shorter," he said with a wide grin. "Have you seen Odell? Does she know about the house bein' burnt?"

"Logan and I went by the Haywards'. Odell is with Mrs. Parnell. Ben . . . Logan and I were married today." She watched him with anxious eyes. He glanced quickly at Logan, then back to his sister.

"Well what'a ya'know. I got me a brother-'n-law." He held his hand out to Logan and quick tears spurted in Rosalee's eyes.

Logan grasped the boy's hand firmly. "I'm sorry my being at your place brought Clayhill's vengeance down on you. We'll rebuild it, Ben, and get you set up in the cattle business like your pa wanted."

"That'll take some doin'." The boy's young face creased into worried lines, and his bright blue eyes went from the tall man's face to his sister.

"It's going to be all right, Ben. Logan will take care of it," Rosalee said with a confident smile.

"Rosalee! Logan! We've been worried to death about you!" Mary came across the yard to meet them, immaculate as usual, every brown hair on her head in place. Poised and cool looking, she seemed to be immune to the heat of the late afternoon. "I'm dying to know what's happened."

"Oh, Mary! So much has happened I don't know where to start!"

Hugs, handshakes, and congratulations were exchanged after a brief exchange of news. Mary and Rosalee walked toward the house and Logan spoke quietly to Josh.

"I'd be obliged for the loan of a shovel. I left a man up there in the hills." He inclined his head toward the steep rise beyond the house.

Josh nodded. "We heard the shot."

"Fetch two shovels, Josh," Case said. "I reckon two can do the job faster 'n one."

Rosalee lay in Mary's high, soft bed and waited for Logan. Mary had insisted they spend their wedding night in her room. Now, full of the delicious meal Meta prepared for their wedding supper, Rosalee stretched her limbs and spread her shiny clean hair over the pillow. The bath in Mary's hip tub was the next best thing to bathing in the warm springs in the valley of the Indian ruins, she thought contentedly. She heard the low male voices as Logan bid

Case good night, and the creaking of the floorboards in the hall just before the door opened and he came into the room.

The flame of the single candle wavered in the draft from the open door, but steadied when it closed. Logan had bathed. He had put his shirt on his wet body and damp spots came through the cloth. His damp hair, black as midnight, was combed back from his face. His thick, dark lashes made shadows on his cheeks, and the softened lines of his half-smiling mouth touched her heart. He reminded Rosalee of a picture of a Greek statue in one of her mother's books. How had this handsome, wonderful man come to love *her*? She was so ordinary!

He came to the foot of the bed and feasted his eyes on her face. Silently, she held out her arms in welcome. Her lips tilted in a smile and her eyes sparkled with silver glints. Each time he made love to her he felt as if he were worshiping at some sacred place. He knew it was because he had never before gone into a woman with love, or wanted love returned. He felt humble and shy as he moved to the side of the bed and knelt down to pay homage to this precious woman who was his wife. She smiled at him tremulously, and with a quick indrawn breath he drew her to his chest, rocking her comfortingly for a minute before reaching for her mouth and kissing her gently.

Rosalee kissed him back, their lips barely touching. "Come love me," she whispered.

"I intend to," he said, his voice was a breathy whisper against her mouth.

He stood and removed his clothes while her eyes loved every muscled inch of his bronze body. When he was completely naked he lifted the sheet, lay down beside her, and drew her atop him. He folded her silken softness into the hardness of his body. She crossed her arms on his chest and propped her chin on them to watch his face. Her hair, like a shimmering waterfall, spilled onto his chest, and he gathered a handful. She watched as he coiled it around his fist, then drew a long strand across his mouth.

"Ah . . . Rosalee, Rosalee, my beautiful, sweet Rosalee," he murmured. "When I'm with you like this I forget there's another world out there." His voice was painfully husky. His lean hard fingers wound themselves through her hair to draw her mouth to his. "My wife, my beloved wife—"

His hands stroked her body, and as her own hunger started to pulsate, she became irritated by the nightgown that kept his hands from her flesh. She raised her head and saw the grin she adored claiming his face.

"What is this bowed and lacy thing you're wearing? It's very pretty, but it's between us." His fingers plucked at the lace that edged the high neck.

"It's a nightdress. Mary laid it out for me to wear and I didn't want to disappoint her." She giggled. "Mary can be very proper at times. I don't see any need for it. I don't need it to keep me warm and you've already seen all of me." She sat up on her heels and drew the soft gauze up over her body, baring her rounded hips, narrow waist, and the firm perfection of her breasts to his dark gaze. She flung the gown over the bed post and shook out her hair.

Logan caught her in his arms and pulled her down atop him again and rolled with her until her slender form was beneath his. In a joyous ardor, her flesh and blood, nurtured by her love for him, responded. She clung to him, lips parted, eyes closed. His kisses were soft at first, then fierce. His mouth was moist and firm and forced hers to open so his tongue could wander her soft inner lips before venturing deeper. His hands were wonderfully gentle, and it seemed that time stretched into the merest gossamer while they traced every nerve and plane of her form, touching her with the gentle

control of a lover determined to give as well as receive pleasure.

With a flurry of soft, muttered words, Logan lifted himself
between her spread thighs and placed himself on her, touching
without thrusting, allowing her impatient movements to pro-
pel him to his destination. She wiggled herself nearer to
deepen the penetration, arching her back to press her breasts
to his chest, and he drove into her steadily and strongly. They
moved in the ancient, eternal rhythm that increased in speed
and intensity. She answered him joyously, responding at once,
making the mating ritual complete. This was love. Their
bodies, their beings wordlessly expressing the depths of it
with painstaking tenderness and reverence.

The climax of their loving left her whimpering softly. She
was speared on the pinnacle of bliss. His rapture rivaled hers,
and exhausted, happy, they came reluctantly down from the
heights. Logan held her close to him, his arms making her
feel safe and cherished.

"It's not just the meeting of flesh that makes us one," he
whispered. "It's more than that; our souls, our spirits meet
as well as our bodies. We belong together, my love."

"Yes." She wiggled free of his arms and pulled his head
to her chest. His half open mouth turned to her skin, moist
and warm. "This is a small part of eternity that will forever
belong only to us," she told him.

His face was damp. She smoothed the black hair from his
forehead in a caressing motion. Gradually, his taut body relaxed, and his mouth nuzzled the rigid nipples on her breasts.
She held him like a tired child, clutching him fiercely as if
to protect him from all the problems that plagued him. She
stroked his head in the maternal motion of a soothing mother
and wished she could keep him safe and secure here in her
arms forever.

They floated on a lazy cloud of fulfillment. He sought for,

and found, her hand, then held it against his cheek. He had not cried since he was a small child, yet he felt something deep within him that could only be tears.

"My sweet love," he said helplessly. "I hope to God I can keep you safe and happy."

She heard the anguish in his voice and her arms tightened. "And I you, my love." Her mouth searched and found his.

He could taste the clean sweetness of her flesh under his lips. Gently, with infinite tenderness, his kiss deepened and she opened her mouth to receive it. Once again, a tide of passion bore them far from reality. Her fingers curved around his hard shaft and guided it into the dark, heated cavity of her body. He felt himself throbbing inside her and delighted in the uninhibited pleasure she took in their sweet coupling. She brought to it all the wild joy of aroused womanhood. Some would have called her wanton and utterly shameless, but he knew only searing happiness as each caress lit fresh fires within him. Rosalee reached her peak; and when he felt her incredible contractions encompass him firmly, he soared inexorably to his own heights of ecstasy.

Afterward, they lay in each other's arms, sated and happy, whispering together. Logan pinched out the candle and nothing existed beyond the charmed circle of their closeness. Her hand caressed his soft, nestled manhood and his hand rested between the warmth of her love-wet thighs. It seemed incredible that there was a shred of desire left in either of them, and yet . . .

Bessie at the saloon in Junction City finished her song, and with a flounce of her skirts made her way between the tightly packed tables, dodging the pinching fingers that reached for her. She glanced at the clock that sat on the backbar in front of the mirror. It was almost midnight.

"Where 'n the hell did they all come from?" she asked the bartender crossly. "And where 'n the hell are they goin'?"

"They come from where they come from, 'n while they're here it's our job to git their money." He set a bottle on the bar. "Take it to that big, black Irishman in the corner 'n collect his coin.

Bessie picked up the bottle and the bartender swabbed the bar with his grimy cloth and watched her as the Irishman pulled her down on his lap. He grinned and shook his head. Bessie was one woman who could take care of herself.

"Ye be truly a thing of beauty," the Irishman crooned with his lips to her ear. His voice was slurred, but he was far from drunk. He rubbed his whiskered cheek against hers. He was a huge man with broad shoulders, a deep chest, a glib tongue and a hot temper. "There be not a bird in all Killarney that'd match his song with your'n. I be tellin' the truth, now."

"Colin McCarthy, you're as full of shit as a young robin! Let go of me 'n drink your whiskey."

His powerful hand tightened on her arms painfully. "That ain't all I'm full of! Me balls is 'bout to bust. I tain't had me no wench in nigh on a month."

"I'm no whore!" she hissed. "I told you that before."

"Well, now, so ye did." His voice softened. "Fergive a blatherin' Irishman. I tain't got no sores or nothin'. Jest horny as a ruttin' stag, I be. Ye be soft 'n smell like a Irish rose. I kin show ye a fine time, me darlin'."

A glimmer of an idea wiggled into Bessie's mind. "Are ya sure ya ain't got not the clap, Colin?"

"Why no, luv," he protested venomously. "I be clean as a newborn bairn." His rugged face creased in an innocent smile.

"Well " Bessie drew the word out. She tilted her head and looked at him. She'd spent the last ten years in saloons and prided herself on being able to judge a man. She'd be a month's pay he had the clap . . . if not something worse. There was vermin in his hair, and she knew it would be in the hair on his body as well. If he'd had a bath during the last five years, she'd be surprised. He smelled as if he'd been lying with something dead! "Well . . ." she said again. "I like you, Colin—"

"Ah . . . Bessie—"

"Ya'd have to be awful quiet. I don't want no one to know I'm favorin' you over the others who've been after me."

"Ach, I kin be quiet, lassie. Quiet as a bird on the wing," he said in a raspy, excited whisper.

"Wait here. I'll go up and unlatch the upstairs door." She trailed her fingers across his chest and up to tickle his neck. "My room is in the front next to the stairs. The walls are paper thin up there, so be real quiet; and don't say a word even when you come in my room. I'll be on the bed all spread and . . . waitin'," she whispered huskily. "Go outside. Give me five minutes, then come up and plow me, my ruttin' bull!" She blew her warm breath in his ear when she slipped off his lap.

Bessie gradually worked her way across the crowded room to the stairs. She could scarcely keep the grin off her face. The means to get even with the uppity bitch had fallen right in her lap! The Irishman would scare the hell out of her if he didn't give her a dose of clap. Her only worry was that the poor fool could be hanged for rape. But she pushed that thought aside. Miss High-and-Mighty wouldn't want the stink of being raped tagging her for the rest of her life. She'd keep it quiet, if she could.

There was no light beneath the door of her old room. She tiptoed past it, hugging the opposite wall, and suppressed a giggle. There was no way the Piss-Queen could have locked her door. The doors to the rooms opened out in the hall. The only way to lock them was with a key, and her room had never had one. She went to the outside door at the top of the stairway that clung to the side of the building and was surprised to find it open.

Bessie hurried back to the cubbyhole she'd used since Della had taken her room at the front of the building. She went inside, closed the door, and pressed her ear to it. Soon she heard the click of the outside door as Colin closed it behind him. She marveled that the big man could move so soundlessly. The creaking of the floorboards told her when he passed, and she opened the door a crack to see the dark form pause at the door to her old room, then open it quietly and disappear inside.

Bessie ran lightly down the hallway and then walked slowly down the stairs and into the noisy saloon.

Chapter
Twenty-One

Della sat beside the window of her darkened room and looked down on the street, anxious for the time to pass. The moon had been swallowed by clouds, and darkness was thick outside the circle of light that came from the swinging doors of the saloon below. Occasionally, a drunk staggered from the board porch and, after a try or two, would manage to mount his horse and ride off into the darkness.

Thoughts of Logan Horn had occupied every corner of Della's mind since their meeting in the livery barn. She recalled again and again every word that passed between them. He had been exactly as she thought he would be; reserved and suspicious of her motives. A sly smile spread across her face. Adam would be furious when he found out she was here; and if he discovered she had taken the Indian to bed, he would be wild with anger. He could be a dangerous man when aroused, but no more so, she thought, than that magnificent savage. Her heart began to pound with excitement.

If she were careful, she reasoned, she could have both of them.

A half hour before midnight, she left the chair beside the window and removed her clothes. When she was completely naked she took the pins from her hair and placed them on the table beside the bed. She considered lighting a candle, but decided against it. There was a crack beneath the door and cracks in the board walls. She'd not put it past the saloon woman to spy on her if she had the chance. This was the most dangerously exciting encounter of her life, and she was determined to enjoy it to the fullest. She had never bedded an Indian. In Denver she had enjoyed the diversion of sleeping with a Mexican and a Frenchman, but until now the opportunity to experience the rutting technique of an Indian had not presented itself. Her nerve ends tingled with anticipation.

Della lay down and stretched with her arms high over her head. The cool mountain breeze from the open window fanned her hot body. The sound of singing drifted up from below. The saloon woman was singing a Civil War ballad. Her voice was really quite good, Della thought begrudgingly. When the soft ballad was finished, Bessie raised her voice and sang a lusty tune, much to the delight of the male audience.

"He placed his hand upon my knee.
I said, young man, get next to me.
It's the hole beneath the naval hole—
Rinky-dinky, dumb-de-dee-o. Oh! Rinky-dinky,
    dumb-de-dee-o!"

The men whooped, stomped their feet, and pounded on the tables with glasses and whiskey bottles when she finished the song that contained numerous verses, each one more raunchy than the last. Della felt a sharp stab of envy at the male attention being directed toward the big, brassy woman. Someday, she vowed, she'd have her own saloon. She would

be the entertainer and give the men something to really stomp
and shout about.

The sound of someone coming up the stairs just outside
her bedroom window drew her attention. He was coming!
She had had no doubt in her mind that he would keep his
promise to come to her. Because of the noise drifting up from
below she heard nothing more, but she kept her eyes on the
door. There was a soft scratching sound, then it opened quietly. A huge dark shadow filled it.

"I'm here," she whispered, and the door closed.

He came quickly toward her and before she had time to
catch her breath or speak again he threw himself on top of
her. The air exploded from her lungs just before his mouth
covered hers. His beard scratched her face and he sucked at
her mouth like an animal. He was fully dressed. The buttons
on his shirt cut into her breast and his boots jarred against
her shins. Anger welled up inside her. Damn him! She tried
to push him off her, but couldn't budge him. He lifted his
mouth and grunted, then found hers again. His breath was
foul! She tried to bite him, but he pried her jaws apart with
this thumb and forefinger. His tongue plunged into her mouth
and swirled. Disappointment knifed through her. She liked
to be mastered, but not *mauled*!

Della twisted her body and tried to draw her knees up in
an attempt to get out from under him. Her frenzy excited him
more. He worked his hand down between them and into the
opening of his britches. He pulled out his huge, rock-hard
tool. She felt it at the opening between her thighs an instant
before he plunged it into her. The feeling was surprisingly
exquisite!

"Ah . . . ah . . . ah—" The sound burst from her and lost
itself in his mouth. She had never been filled so completely.
With each movement it felt as if he would split her asunder.
His sex was huge; even larger than the thing she'd made out

of a bone and covered with layers of soft doeskin to use on
herself for temporary relief. She forgot her disappointment,
forgot to be angry because he hadn't undressed. She forgot
the sickening odor of his body, forgot everything except the
weapon she was speared with. Bucking beneath him, she
wrapped her legs around him and her hungry body pressed
upward. He pounded at her furiously, pounded and grinded.
She drummed her feet against him, increasing the urgency
of her movements, wanting more and more, yet wanting to
hold onto this incredible feeling for as long as possible. He
gushed into her just before she jerked convulsively and wave
after wave of intense pleasure washed over her.

Della came out of a near swoon aware of the heavy body
pressing her into the lumpy mattress. She gave him a shove
and he rolled to the side. He was gasping for air, as she was.

"Bessie, Bessie, me . . . darlin'."

Della heard the words. Awareness hit her like a dash of
cold water. She sprang out of bed. Good God! The thick
body! The beard! The odor! This man wasn't the man she
had kissed in the livery barn!

"Who are you?" she gasped. "What the hell—"

"Ye be a good whore, gal. The best I e'er . . . had . . ." His
voice trailed off as he fell into a drunken sleep.

Whore! He'd said whore! Her mind spun crazily. She fum-
bled on the table for the stick matches and drew the head
along the rough boards until it flared. She held it to the
candlewick and light washed over the room.

Della batted her lids against the sudden glare, then turned
to look at the man on the bed. She stared and then shrank
back as a shudder of revulsion passed through her. He was
so big the side of the bed sagged. The hand on his arm that
hung over the side looked like a giant, worn claw. He was
dressed in the clothes of a mule skinner or a miner; his pants
tucked into the tops of heavy, laced boots. He had a month's

accumulation of dirt and beard on his face. His mouth was agape and she could see stubs of rotten teeth.

Della's stomach did a slow roll. Then her eyes moved to the large, wet, limp piece of flesh hanging from the front of his open britches. There were several large sores on it ranging from the tip to the base where they disappeared into a thick mat of hair. Her hands flew to her cheeks as realization dawned. A half gasp, half shriek escaped her.

"My God!" She shook her head in agony. "Oh, my God!" She stood frozen in terror for a full moment before she ran to her valise and grabbed the jar of vinegar she carried with her. Before sex she always soaked a small sponge in the vinegar and poked it up into her vagina as a preventive against pregnancy. Half sobbing, she saturated a cloth and washed herself, again and again. In her panic to clean herself she pushed the vinegar-soaked cloth as far into her as she could.

A loud, snorting snore followed by a whistle brought her attention back to the man who had done this to her. A high rage started in the pit of her stomach and rose to her brain in a red wave. She grabbed the buggy whip from the nail on the wall and brought the thin leather down on him with all the force of her anger behind it. She aimed for the still elongated piece of limp flesh, but missed and the skin laid bare by his open shirt felt the biting sting. He came up out of the bed with a roar.

"Goddamn ye, Bessie! What'd ye—" The whip came down across his face and neck and cut off the words. He looked with disbelief at the blond, naked woman wielding the whip. Her face was contorted with rage, and her hair whipped wildly about as she spun around to get more leverage on the whip. "Who be ye?" Utterly confused, he danced around the end of the bed in an attempt to escape the lash. Finally, he stood his ground and tried to catch the leather she swung at him.

"You bastard!" she screamed. "You goddamn, dirty, fucking, sore-infested bastard! I'll kill you!"

"Ye ain't . . . I don't . . . Ye goddamn . . . whore! Stop it!" He yelped as the whip laid a trail of blood across his cheek and he bolted for the door. "Ah . . . shit!" he yelled and fell against it. It yielded to his weight. He staggered into the hall and ran for the back door.

Della slammed the door shut behind him and fell on the bed in a storm of weeping.

Morning came and Della packed her valise. She was in a cold fury. In the course of one night she had been "raped" by a filthy clod who had more than likely given her the highly contagious clap, if not the incurable pox, and she had been left waiting like a cheap floozy by a half-breed. She almost choked on her anger. She would get even! She sure as *hell* would get even!

Looking calm, cool, and beautiful, just as she had when she arrived, Della left the room above the saloon and walked the short distance to the stage coach ticket office. Her main concern, now, was to get to Denver and see a doctor.

"Hello, Miss Clayhill. Nice to see ya, Miss Clayhill." The fawning ticket agent hurried toward her and took the valise from her hand.

"Is this the day the stage to Denver comes through?"

"Shore is, Miss Clayhill." The man took a heavy watch from his pocket and made a big show of studying it. "Now . . . let me see—" He pursed his mouth and looked at the ceiling. "It ortta be here by two o'clock, if'n it's on time."

"May I wait in your office?"

"Course ya can, Miss Clayhill. With all the toughs in town it ain't safe fer a pretty gal ta be sittin' on the street. It just beats all how one redskin kin get things stirred up. The sooner yore pa runs that Injun outta the territory the better. Then things kin get settled down agin. One a them bastards . . . I'm beggin' your pardon, ma'am, can get them savages riled till they break off the reservation. Then there'll be hell to pay. Why . . . that 'n is so brazen he come right into town in broad daylight and . . ."

The agent continued to rattle on. Della heard only half of what he said until the word "married" caught her attention.

"What was that you said?"

"I said that Indian sneaked in here yesterday 'n married that Spurlock woman. Why . . . I never heard of a decent white woman doin' such. Preacher Abernathy said the redskin threatened to scalp him and burn the church. He said that after he said the words they rode off to the south with her aridin' astride with her skirts pulled up to her knees. It's disgraceful, is what it is!"

Della drew in a quivering breath. The sonofabitch! He was on his way to be married when he met her in the livery and he had no intention of going to her room. The knowledge cut into her pride like the sharp edge of a knife. The blow was so acute that her chest tightened so that she could scarcely breathe, but her mind leaped into gear. They went south, he said. South could only mean to Mary Gregg's. She walked out the door, stood on the walk, and looked up the street. Hatred bubbled up inside her, the hatred of a woman scorned.

Adam Clayhill rode down the dusty street trailed by a dozen ranch hands. He had left the ranch at dawn in a foul mood. He was still in one. Goddamn that girl, he cursed silently. He should have whipped that nigger to within an inch of his life for taking her to the saloon and leaving her there. But then he knew how stubborn the little devil could be once she set her mind on doing something. Goddamnit! He had enough on his mind without having to corral that headstrong girl! By God! He'd chew her rump when he found her.

He pulled up at the saloon, dismounted, and threw the reins to one of his men. He stomped up onto the board porch and looked up and down the street. It was then that he saw her standing in front of the stage office.

"Stay here," he snarled to his men.

Della saw him as soon as he rode into town; by the time he reached her, she had an expression of distress on her face and her eyes were swimming with tears.

"What the hell have you been up to?" Adam grabbed her arm and jerked her to him.

"Don't, Adam. Please don't!" she whispered. I've got to talk to you . . . but not here—" Her words ended with a sob. "Oh, Papa! Something terrible has happened!"

"What do you mean?" he growled.

"It was . . . awful—" she sobbed and tugged on his arm. He moved with her to the end of the porch and around to the side of the building. Della sniffed and drew a lacy, perfumed, bit of cloth from the sleeve of her dress and dabbed at her nose.

"Gawddamnit, girl!" he snarled impatiently.

"Please don't be mad at me, Adam," she said tearfully and leaned against him weakly. "I'm sorry I worried you. I . . . just wanted a little excitement. I was so . . . bored at the ranch. You didn't pay any a—attention to me . . ."

"I'm mad as hell and I'll beat your butt when I get you home." His voice softened. "But . . . don't cry." He folded her in his arms and patted her back.

Della squeezed her eyes so the tears would come again and looked up into his hard, craggy face. "I love you . . . Papa Adam . . ."

"There, there, girl . . ."

"But . . . I've got to tell you . . ."

Adam grasped her arms and held her away from him. "Tell me what?" he demanded. "If someone's hurt you, I'll—kill 'im!"

"*He* . . . came to my room last night." Her lips trembled. She held the lower one between her teeth in a pitiful attempt to still it before she blurted, "He attacked me! He threw me on the bed and—and—"

Adam drew a deep breath into his lungs and his nostrils flared as rage consumed him. "Who?" he bellowed.

"Sshh . . ." she whispered frantically. "I don't want anyone to know. I'm so ashamed!"

"Gawddamnit! Who was it?" Adam gritted.

"The . . . Indian! He did it because of you, Papa. He was getting even because you burned out the Spurlocks!"

"The Indian?" Adam said in disbelief. Then, "The Indian! Did he put his red pecker in you? Tell me, gawddamnit!"

"He . . . he forced me. He's so strong." She blinked her eyes rapidly and the tears rolled again.

"The sonofabitchin' bastard!" Adam cursed. "I'll tie a rope around his red pecker and drag him to death! I'll split his gullet and spill his guts from here to Denver! Gawddamn his red heart! I'll—"

"He's out at Mary Gregg's. I don't want to be here when he comes back!" Her voice raised in panic.

Adam grasped her upper arms and shook her. "He's at the whorehouse?"

"He went there yesterday. It was . . . after midnight when he came back to town. I . . . was asleep—"

"I'll get 'im! I'll make the bastard wish he'd never seen the light of day!" Anger had turned his face a mottled crimson. "And you're not goin' nowhere till I can go with you. You're goin' to the preacher's house and you'll stay there until I can take you home." Adam's hard gaze fixed on her face. When she opened her mouth to protest, he snarled, "Don't give me backtalk, girl. If you had stayed home where you belong, this wouldn't have happened."

"No, Papa! No! I want to go to Denver."

"You'll do as I say!" he thundered. "You'll stay with the preacher! Hear?" With his hand firmly attached to her arm he moved her to the front of the stage coach office and down the boardwalk.

Della fumed. It had gone so well . . . up to now. She was rather pleased with her performance. But she didn't want to go to the damned preacher's! The man made her want to puke. And his wife, creeping around the house, reminded her of a black spider. She wanted to go to Denver, had to go to Denver and see a doctor! She'd play along for now because she had no choice, but when the stage left this afternoon she'd be on it.

Adam walked into the saloon a half an hour later. Although it was mid-morning, there were more than a dozen men beside his own drovers drinking and playing cards. All heads turned in his direction.

"Any man here who wants to earn ten dollars for a day's work come with me," he announced in his bellowing voice.

Several men, to whom ten dollars seemed a fortune, stood immediately. Others, more cautious, but needing the money, shoved back their chairs and stood slowly.

"Who'er ya wantin' ta hang?" The voice came from the back of the room.

"You want the money or don't you?" Adam asked irritably.

"I don't sign on without knowin' the job."

"We're hangin' a gawddamned, fuckin' redskin!" Adam roared.

"Now yo're talkin', boss." Shorty Banes chortled gleefully, slammed his empty beer mug down on the bar, and headed for the door.

Henry McCloud stood in the doorway of his store and

watched the men led by Adam Clayhill speed through their own dust cloud as they rode out of town. He shook his head in frustration. He knew Clayhill was after Logan Horn and there wasn't a damn thing he could do about it.

Logan and Case Malone stood leaning against the rail fence of the far corral and watched Brutus take off in hot and hopeless pursuit of a pronghorn antelope buck who had appeared on the edge of the grove. It had stamped its feet and released a blast to emphasize its disapproval of this invasion of its domain and then whirled back through the trees with a white signaling of its rump hairs. With lips pursed to whistle the dog back, Logan decided to let him go. The chase would end, he knew, as all such similar ones had ended—with victory for the pursued; and Brutus, after enjoying the chase, would return.

"Not knowin' when ya was acomin' in, I sent Frank out to meet yore herd a couple days back. I figured they'd need directions to your range," Case said.

"I'm obliged. It was a load off my mind when Cooper told me they were coming."

"Grass can be mighty poor down along the South Platte." Case sprinkled some tobacco in a thin brown paper, rolled it, twisted both ends, and put one of them in his mouth. He struck a match with his thumb nail and held the flame in his cupped hands while he drew on the smoke. "There's open range not ten miles northeast a here. I told Frank to take 'em there. Would a done it myself, but I wanted to stick close to Mary in case Clayhill shows up agin."

Logan started to speak, but Mercury suddenly emitted a shattering squeal. Logan looked around and saw him frozen at attention, his eyes searching the woods beyond the house; but when he followed the direction of his gaze he saw only the empty timbered bench on the hillside. And then, some bit of motion in the timber caused him to go on watching. Uneasiness touched him and he glanced at Case with a puzzled frown.

"Somebody's up there," Case said, then dropped his smoke to the ground and stepped on it.

Logan searched the thick screen for several minutes before he saw the head of a horse, then another. Uneasiness mounted and then escalated when riders came into view and wound swiftly down out of the timber. Then he heard the sound of pounding hoofbeats coming down the road toward the house. They were descending on them from two sides.

"Josh! Ben! Stay in the barn," Logan yelled as he and Case broke into a run for the house which to Logan, at that moment, seemed a million miles away. He cursed himself soundly for drifting into culpable negligence. He sprinted far ahead of Case, trying desperately to reach the house before the riders. He made it to within a dozen yards and was stopped by a harsh voice.

"Hold it right thar, Injun!" A man with a florid face and a fringe of red hair showing from under a battered hat brim stepped from the back door. He held a pistol in his hand. "Don't try nothin', redskin, er yore white squaw'll get gut-shot shore as shootin'."

Logan skidded to a halt, his frantic eyes searching for Rosalee, stubbornly hoping for some miracle that would give him a chance to defend himself, his wife, and his friends. Mary was pushed out the door as were Meta and the three girls.

"Stop pushin', ya ... warthog!" Minnie snapped.

Mary's eyes clung to Case and she would have gone to him, but the man with the gun motioned her back. A man came through the door with Rosalee held tightly against him. His forearm was around her neck, pressing into her windpipe, and the end of his gun barrel was pressed to her side.

Fear, like a numbing coldness rising from the ground, worked its way through Logan. Rosalee's tormented eyes locked with his. He fixed his gaze on the red-haired man with the gun.

"Let them go. It's me you want."

"Make a move, Injun, and he'll kill 'er. Drop yore gun ... careful like." Logan lifted his gun from the holster with his forefinger and dropped it to the ground. "Now you," the man said to Case, and Case obliged.

The foremost of the riders were now at the edge of the yard and the rest closely following. Adam Clayhill moved his head back and forth to scan the yard, then halted within half a dozen yards of the group beside the back door.

"I tol' ya it'd work, boss. We sneaked in pretty as ya please." The redheaded man was so pleased with what he'd accomplished that he felt compelled to make certain the big, monied man was aware of it. "This here's the white squaw!" He jerked his head toward Rosalee.

"I know who she is," Adam snarled.

Logan kept his eyes on Rosalee, refusing to look at the big man on the horse. He was quivering with rage, sick with rage.

"What are you doing here?" Mary demanded. She spoke then, realizing even as she heard the sound of her own voice how completely inane the question was. Adam ignored her.

"Tie 'em up," he ordered. "Malone, too. We'll call a town meeting and have a trial. When we hang 'em it'll be within the law."

Mary gasped. "You can't have a *trial*! You're not the law. Besides, they've not broken any law."

"Malone killed one of my men, and the Indian raped a white woman. A trial's more than they deserve."

"You ... lying bastard!" Mary looked pleadingly at the men in the tight circle behind Adam Clayhill. "He's lying and you men know it. He sent a man to kill Case. Case was only defending himself. And . . . Logan and Rosalee are married! Don't you see, he's using you to get rid of his enemies." She searched each face. The only men who met her eyes were the drifters who had wandered into town and needed the money Adam offered. The rest of the men kept their eyes averted. Their faces were cast in hangdog looks.

"You're a bunch of cowards," she screamed. "Haven't you got any backbone? Are you going to let this arrogant bully push you into doing something you'll regret all your lives? Logan Horn bought the land Clayhill wants. Case shot the man who shot him first!"

"Shut up, whore!" Adam roared. "Shut up or I'll slap a gag in your mouth."

Case's hands were bound, and when he jumped at Clayhill he was jerked roughly, his arms pulled back. He stumbled against Shorty Banes's horse. With a violent curse, Shorty put his foot against Case's back and shoved him to the ground.

"Ya friggin' bastard! Ya ruined my foot! I said I'd see ya hang 'n I will!"

Logan kept his eyes on Rosalee's face. He knew if he looked at Clayhill he would explode in a rage and be shot on the spot. He couldn't let that happen. He'd live. Somehow he'd live to make this man die a thousand times.

"He ain't no full-blood." The red-haired man's pale green eyes flicked insolently over Logan. "I betcha he had 'im a white daddy 'n thinks that sets 'im up high as a white man."

Logan's voice was hoarse with impotent rage. "As high as you? I'd rather be dead!"

Shorty Banes laughed. "Ya will be, Injun."

"Put 'em on a horse. Put that one belly down." Adam spit into the dirt at Logan's feet. His face was flushed with suppressed fury. He wanted to swing the bastard from the nearest tree, but he didn't dare or word would get out he'd been in on a lynching. If there were a trial, and Della, without going into detail, were to say that he put his hands on her, he could hang him and the matter would be dropped. He was sure the deed to the south range hadn't been recorded. With the Indian dead the land would be his."

"What about the women?"

"Bring the *squaw*. The boy and hired man are in the barn. If they make trouble, shoot her. Sorry we ain't got time for you to pleasure the *whores*, boys," Adam said with a loud laugh. "We got business in town."

"If'n ya come back here, I'll piss in yore face," Minnie shouted. "That means you, Dud Simms. And you, Billy Hopper, and Oscar the big prick Duncan! Ya'll ain't nothin' but a bunch a pricks. I hope them little, twiddly things yo're so proud of rot 'n fall off'n ya! Bastards! Sons a bitches! Shitheads! Put ya all together 'n yo're not half the man the Injun is. That goes for you, too, Mister shit fer brains Clayhill what thinks his shit don't stink! Ya kin take yore money 'n shove it up yore ass!"

"Watch your mouth, whore, or I'll shove it up yours!" Adam gritted and wheeled his horse.

"Sure I'm a whore! I'm good 'n proud a it. I earn my money." Once Minnie's mouth was in gear she never knew when to stop, so she shouted after him, "What'a ya think that prissy, hot-twat out at yore ranch is? Ever'body in the territory knows she'll shuck her drawers at the drop of a hat! What she's got atween her legs ain't no better'n what I got. Ain't that right, boys?"

"Shut yore mouth!" With a roar of rage, Adam jerked his horse around and charged the girl. Minnie sped for the doorway and slipped inside. He pulled cruelly on the reins and the horse reared, front hooves flailing the air.

"Got ya where the hair's short, didn't I, ol' man?" Minnie called daringly from inside the house.

Her taunts brought grins of admiration from many of the riders who sat waiting to move out. At one time or another each of them had wished to cut the boss down but hadn't the courage. The skinny whore from Mary's place had hit the nail square on the head, and, secretly, they enjoyed hearing her blast him.

Rosalee had eyes and ears only for Logan. He was lying belly down on the sorrel mare one of the men fetched from the corral. A rope going beneath the horse's belly connected his hands and feet. She sat on the rump of the red-headed man's horse, her hands tied together in front of him. She had not said a word. Somehow she knew Logan would not want her to beg on his behalf. She clenched her teeth and strained to hold back the growing panic as they moved away from the house.

She looked back at Mary, Meta, and the two girls standing in the yard. As she watched, Mary lifted her skirts and started running for the barn. Josh and Ben came out with rifles cradled in their arms. Ben shaded his eyes with his hand and looked in her direction. He looked so young and helpless standing there in the morning sun in britches that were too short for his lanky frame and in his pa's old hat.

When they were lost from sight, Rosalee turned back to stare at the back of her captor. She was keenly aware that this could very well be the last day of her husband's life. But she clung to the hope that if they had any chance at all it would be in town.

Chapter Twenty-Two

'Ain't no sense fartin' 'round with a trial," Shorty snorted. "He ain't nothin' but a goddamn breed, 'n Malone crippled me 'n killed ole Shatto."

"You've got no say in this," Adam growled. "Get 'em up here on the porch and watch 'em like I told you, or get the hell out of the way and let a man do the job."

The harshness of that voice slapped Logan across the face. It penetrated to his flagging consciousness and stung him to life. The ride to town, belly down on the horse, had been one of the most painful experiences of his life. There was a roaring in his head and a pain in his side. Somewhere along the way his stomach had been unable to stand the constant jarring and the contents had come spewing out of his mouth. He opened his eyes and saw dusty boots, then he felt his wrist come free from his feet and he fell backward off the horse. He landed hard and lay there while an enveloping dizziness tipped the world end over end around him. He'd kill the *Wasicun*! He'd kill the *Wasicun*! The thought repeated itself again and again in his mind.

Logan waited until the world ceased to roll and pitch under him, then inhaled deeply and pushed himself upright. Immediately, dizziness threatened to capsize him again, but he leaned against the horse until it passed and willed his legs to stiffen to hold his weight."

"Move."

The sharp command was accompanied with a prod in his side by a gun barrel. The very fact that Logan centered all his attention on the almost insurmountable task of staying on his feet kept his mind from the anguished thought of what this was doing to Rosalee. He stepped up on the board porch of the saloon and immediately a rope was looped about his neck. He felt a moment of panic. He was going to die without seeing her again! Then the rope was thrown up over a porch beam and tied. Case Malone stood beside him, his hands tied behind his back, a loop about his neck.

Logan's wavering vision began to clear. Men and horses mingled in front of them. He searched frantically for a sight of Rosalee and finally saw her in the back of the crowd astraddle the rump of a horse. He was never more proud of her than at that moment. She held her head high and looked at him over the heads of the men and horses.

"We got ourselves in one hell of a mess," Case said softly.

Logan looked at the tall Texan for a moment before he spoke. His face was expressionless, his dark eyes flat. "My mother's people say that hate and greed are like maggots eating into the soul of the *Wasicun*." He turned back, spread his feet to balance himself, and stared straight ahead.

Case vaguely wondered what that had to do with anything. He'd been in tight places before, but this was the tightest. He was pinning his hopes on Mary and Josh. His Mary wouldn't take this sitting on her backside. She'd be here fighting till the end. The only comfort he could find was in the fact that men were generally protective of women, even this rough bunch.

He doubted any physical harm would come to Mary or Rosalee. If they managed to hang him and Logan, they'd be run out of town. On the other hand, they'd not want to stay here anyway.

The instant Rosalee's hands were free she slid off the horse. She had to get help! She looked at the hostile faces of the men and took a backward step. Terror held her in its icy grip. How could this be happening? Her mind screamed for her to do something.

"What'er we to do with 'er?"

"I say haul her up thar with the Injun," Shorty said. "She ain't nothin' but trash. Injun lover!" he sneered and spat in the dust at her feet.

"Ah . . . leave 'er 'lone," someone said crossly. "She ain't done nothin'."

"Ain't done nothin'?" Shorty snorted. "She's humped the Injun, is what she done!"

"She ain't agoin' nowhere," the red-haired man said with an ugly laugh. "If'n the boss wants her tarred 'n feathered, it'll cost him more 'n ten dollars."

"I ain't got no stomach fer tarrin' a woman."

Rosalee's eyes sought the man who spoke. It was Pete, the young drover who was with Shorty Banes when they came to the ranch and caused her father's death. He was standing beside another young drover, the one Minnie had called Dud Simms. They turned away when they saw her looking at them, and the small hope that they would in some way help her died.

Determined to not cower in the face of the male hostility, Rosalee smoothed her hair, then her skirt down over her hips, tilted her chin a mite higher than she usually carried it, and walked purposefully through the crowd. She mounted the saloon porch and went to Logan.

"I love you," she whispered for his ears alone, and lifted her two hands to push the tangled hair back from his face. "Tell me what to do."

"I love you," he answered so softly that only she could hear. "Go to McCloud and stay with him."

"If they try to hang you, someone will die. Mary and Josh are coming—"

The sound of two rapidly fired shots cut off her words.

"What the hell's goin' on here?" McCloud stood on the boardwalk, a rifle in one hand, a pistol in the other.

Adam came out of the saloon. "We're havin' a trial," he bellowed.

"What's the charges?" McCloud demanded.

"Malone killed one of my men, crippled three more. The Indian attacked my stepdaughter."

The shocking words hung in the air, wavered there, then a murmur from the men rolled crushingly over the silence.

"That's a lie!" Rosalee shouted. "I've been with him every minute."

"Can you prove the charges?" McCloud yelled.

"Your gawddamn right I can prove both of them or I wouldn't be here." Adam walked down the steps and stuck his finger in McCloud's face. "You better back off, store-keeper. I'm not goin' to stand for meddlin' from you."

"If you're agoin' to have a trial you're agoin' to wait until every man, woman, and child in this town is here. You ain't agoin' to have ever'thing your way, Clayhill." McCloud turned and fired his pistol in the air. "Get them horses off the street," he yelled. "Doolie, get on that horse and spread the word fer ever'body to come, 'n if'n they can't walk, crawl! That means that horse's ass of a preacher and Della Clayhill, too."

"Logan!" Rosalee whispered frantically. "What does it mean?"

"It means he's determined to see the end of me . . . one way or the other." Logan looked at Rosalee or kept his eyes straight ahead. He'd not yet looked at the *Wasicun*. Even the sound of his voice caused such implacable hatred to knife through him that droplets of sweat broke out on his forehead and made him gasp for air.

"Get away from the prisoners," Shorty Banes growled and nudged Rosalee.

She glanced quickly at Logan and he moved his head slightly. She understood. She would be no help to him here. Their help would come from Mr. McCloud, or from others in the crowd that was gathering. She stepped off the porch before Shorty pushed her again and made her way to the storekeeper.

"He didn't do it, Mr. McCloud. And Case only killed in self-defense."

"Gawd! I know that, girl. I'm just stallin' for time. He's got thirty men or more and I've never been up against such odds."

"Mary and Josh and Ben are on the way. I can handle a rifle. That would make five of us."

"If we start anything he'd not wait for a trial. He'd shoot 'em on the spot. Let's hold tight and see what happens. Gawd, but I wish Cooper Parnell was here."

"I wish Logan's men had gotten here," Rosalee moaned, then added, "There's no use wishing. Wishing doesn't do anything but waste time. Will you lend me a gun? I can hide it in my dress pocket."

"Come to the store. I've got to lock it up anyway. In all the excitement I forgot."

Rosalee came out of the store as Mary's buggy came careening into town. She pulled the lathered horse to a stop in front of the store. The wind had blown some of the pins from her hair and it floated around her face and stuck to her wet cheeks. Her anxious eyes searched the streets. Minnie sat on the seat beside her and Ben and Josh pulled up beside the buggy. Mary jumped down and ran the few steps to the walk.

"What's happened?" she asked breathlessly.

"Nothing yet. Mr. McCloud is helping us all he can. He

insisted that Clayhill not start anything until everyone in town is here."

"I'm going to see Case and no one had better try and stop me," Mary said. She put her hand in the pocket of her heavy skirt and marched down the walk.

"Ya better stay here, Minnie," Josh said gently. "From what I hear you stirred Clayhill's temper. Ain't no use in gettin' it riled more."

"I ain't 'fraid a that old bastard. He don't dare lay no hands to me here in front of ever'body," she answered saucily. "He'd better not lay no hands on Mary, neither. I got me my Colt right here under my skirt and I'll blow his pecker off!"

"What'er we agoin' to do, Rosalee?" Ben's worried eyes found his sister's. Charlie, panting from the run, fell at his feet, his tongue lolling. The dog's eyes rolled up to gaze at Rosalee, and he wagged his tired tail; but she was too worried to notice him.

"I don't know, Ben. I don't know. It looks like they're getting ready to do something." Rosalee went down the walk, being careful to not let herself get boxed in by the crowd of people that had gathered in front of the saloon. It seemed to her that every person in town was there; women still with their work aprons tied around their waists and men who had stopped their work when the call came. Children, wide-eyed and shy, held on to their mother's skirts.

Two men carried a table from the saloon and set it on the porch in front of Case and Logan. They placed a single chair at the end of it. Adam Clayhill came out, removed his hat, and flung it down on the table. His white hair was a startling contrast to his ruddy face. He was angry, but holding himself in check as he'd not done in years. He wasn't as concerned with Malone as he was with the Indian. He was determined that he would swing. He'd not yet let himself really think about what the savage had done to Della. If he did, he would pull his gun and put a bullet square between the bastard's eyes. However, the act had given him an excuse to get rid of him legally. Della would be as mad as a hornet if she had to face the crowd and tell her story, but she was tough and she'd get over it. Adam sat down at the table and motioned for one of the men to fire their gun to signal the start of the proceedings.

"You all know what we're here for. We'll try Malone first." Adam held up his hand to still the murmur of voices that followed. "I'll say what I know first. Malone was my foreman. He refused to obey orders and I fired him. He sneaked up on a bunch of my men and shot three of 'em in the foot. Another one of my men tried to get the drop on him before he killed someone and Malone shot him down. It's a clear case of murder."

"Adam Clayhill, you're the biggest liar God ever let live!" Mary stood in front of the porch with her hands on her hips.

"I stated the facts. You weren't there, so stay out of it."

"Neither were you. Tell these people what your men were doing at the Spurlocks' in the middle of the night."

"They had spent the day looking for strays and had camped there." Adam's face flushed even more and his hamlike fists clenched and unclenched.

"That ain't so!" The squeaky young voice was Ben's. He pushed his way through the crowd. "That ain't so," he repeated. "They was aburnin' us out, like you told 'em to do."

"You hush up! Yo're just a wet-eared kid!"

"I got eyes same's anybody else. I got ears, too. You told my sister you was agoin' to come back 'n burn us out fer helpin' Mr. Horn." Ben stood his ground and Rosalee wished her mother and father could hear him speaking up against the biggest landowner in the Colorado Territory. They would be as proud as she was.

"I never said any such thing!" Adam shouted. "You're not old enough to testify, so hush up."

"I'm old enough to have a say." Mary turned her back on

him and looked at the people in the street. "All you men who were at the Spurlock place know Case was only trying to keep you from burning it to the ground. You also heard Adam Clayhill tell Rosalee that if she didn't let him have Logan Horn he would burn her out. Shatto was a troublemaker who turned backshooter. He shot Case first and Case almost died. Is there a man here who wouldn't have shot back?"

There was a lot of foot shuffling and low murmurs, but no one spoke up.

"Is there a man here who thinks Case Malone should die for killing the man who shot him?" Mary insisted.

"Yo're gawddamned right there is!" Shorty Banes swaggered forward, hitching up his britches. He came to within a few feet of Mary and shoved his face close to hers, then looked back at the crowd. "You agoin' to stand here 'n let a whore talk ya outta hangin' a man what ortta be hung?"

"This ignorant piece of horse dung has already been the cause of one good man's death. When Rosalee Spurlock resisted his vile attention, his friend Shatto grabbed her. Her blind father tried to help her and was kicked to death by Shorty Banes's horse. His opinion is less than nothing," she said with contempt. "Is there anyone else that thinks Case is guilty?"

"Look here, by Gawd!" Adam roared. "You're not taking over this trial!"

Mary tossed a look of defiance over her shoulder. "How many here think Case should be freed?" she shouted.

At first there was silence, then, "Let him go!" Voices rose from the back of the crowd and rolled forward.

"He ain't guilty of nothin'."

"He done what any man would a done."

"What'er ya tryin' to do, Clayhill? Railroad 'im cause he bucked ya some?" McCloud called out.

Adam looked out over the sea of faces and knew he'd have to back down on Malone. The case was weak, and he should have thought about it before he had him tressed up and brought to town. When this was over he'd figure out a way to get him out of the territory.

"All right. I'm a fair man. I may have been wrong about him. But I'm here to tell you that if any of my men were in on burning out the Spurlocks they'll hear from me. Turn Malone loose and we'll get on with the trial."

"No, by Gawd!" Shorty shouted. "He ortta pay fer ruinin' my foot."

Adam turned on him in fury. "Shut your mouth! You can settle with him any way you please, but not here."

Someone stepped forward and cut the rope that bound Case's hands. When they were free, he lifted the loop from his neck. Mary was beside him and together they moved to the side of the porch.

"I'm athinkin' we better be hangin' ya out a shingle," he whispered, and hugged her to him. "Ya argue a good case, sweetheart."

"Oh, Case! I was so scared. How are we going to help Logan?"

"By stayin' right here and waitin' our chance. I hope that gun that's weighin' down yore skirt is mine."

"All right. All right. Let's get on with the trial," Adam was saying. "I tell you, folks, I came close to killin' this redskin outright." His voice was calm and serious. "You all know I was put out when the Indian sneaked in and bought the land I've been using and was set to buy. Any one of you would have been the same. We don't want the redskins movin' in on us and takin' up the good land. I was going to go to Denver to see what could be done about it. This mornin' my girl came to me in distress and told me what this stinkin' red savage had done to her. He's a viper who's come in among us, is what he is, and he isn't fit to live!"

Rosalee, standing on the edge of the crowd, caught her breath.

She began to work her way to the front. Out of the corner of her eye she saw something bright yellow and turned her head to see Odell, in her new yellow dress, clutching Mrs. Parnell's hand. Hope rose in Rosalee's heart that Cooper was also here.

"Now, folks, I can have my girl come up here and tell you what he did to her if I have to. It's not easy for a woman to talk about such." Adam was feeling good about the way the people were reacting. The women were terrified and the men outraged. "First I'll ask the Indian what he's got to say for himself," Adam said with an exaggerated air of fairness.

Logan's blood boiled in an agony he thought he couldn't endure. He had the sensation of floating not in water but in a vacuum of utter loathing. He looked out over the crowd that had gathered to watch his humiliation. Most of them stared back in stony-eyed hostility. It was an old and familiar scene magnified a hundred times. He'd learned to steel himself against the animosity, but facing it with the *Wasicun* as witness caused the air to burn in his mouth and his eyes to blur with helpless rage.

In the corner of his mind that could function outside the hate Logan noted that Cooper now stood beside McCloud. Thank God, he was here. He'd be a help to Rosalee. The Clayhill woman, in her white dress, was with the preacher and his wife down by the Land Office. He couldn't imagine what story she would make out of their meeting in the livery. It hadn't lasted more than five minutes. Josh, Ben, and Minnie were at the back of the crowd. Mrs. Parnell and Odell had edged closer so that Odell could see. Rosalee was coming through the crowd toward him. He drank in the sight of her like a thirsty man long deprived. "Oh, my sweet woman! What have I done to you?" he groaned.

To the crowd Logan appeared stoic and unrelenting in his attitude. He stood with his feet spread, his shoulders back, and his head up. He was taller than most of the men, and from the porch he looked down on everything and everyone with an air of detachment that seemed to render him wholly untouchable.

"What do you have to say for yourself, redskin?"

For the first time Logan turned his mirror-black eyes on the *Wasicun*. Points of light flared in their depth. Inward, silent red rage pushed him beyond reason and he spat full into the face of the man he despised.

"Gawddamn you!" Adam's fist lashed out and only the quick, instinctive movement of Logan's head prevented it from hitting him squarely on the mouth. Instead it glanced his cheek. Adam wiped his face with his sleeve. "You son-ofabitch," he muttered so low that only those standing near-by could hear. "Your red ass'll hang before night and the buzzards'll have your eyes before morning."

Adam turned to the crowd. "You see how savage the Indian is? I don't see any need for puttin' my girl up here—"

"I do," Rosalee shouted. "If she's accusing my husband I want to hear it from her own mouth. And stop calling him the savage and the Indian. His name is Logan Horn."

"Yeah! Put 'er up there, Mr. Moneybags. Let's hear what the twitchy-twat's got to say," Minnie called, and then laughed. A few of the men laughed with her.

Adam's face was beet-red with anger. He shook his fist at Minnie and shouted, "I've taken all I'm goin' to take from you. Get back to the whorehouse or you'll be flaggin' your skinny ass out of the territory before mornin'."

"You don't scare me, bugger man!" Minnie made an obscene gesture and grinned saucily. Some of the men threw her admiring glances.

"Clayhill," McCloud called. "Horn's entitled to hear the charges against him. If you don't want your girl to testify, turn him loose."

"No, by Gawd!" Adam shouted. "My word ought to stand in this town. I say he forced himself on her and he should hang!"

"No man should hang on your say. Put the woman up there to tell it." A man with a cut down the side of his face spoke up for the first time.

Adam turned to see who was taking sides against him. The man and his partner had refused to ride with him this morning, and now he wondered what part they had to play in this.

"All right. Come on up here, Della. Come on, honey. Don't be afraid. Just tell the folks what you told me and you can go on down to Denver and try and forget the wrong done you." Adam's voice gentled as if he were talking to a child.

People craned their necks to see Della as she came down the walk to the saloon porch. She tilted her parasol to shield her face from the crowd and held the skirt of her white dress back to keep it from brushing against the rough boards of the building. She looked cool and innocent and beautiful. Mable, the fat woman from the restaurant, watched her, rolled her eyes in disgust, and fanned her sweating face with a turkey wing.

While the crowd waited for Della, Bessie pushed her way through the double doors of the saloon and came out to lean against a porch post. Her dress of kelly green satin made her hair look as red as a sunset and her skin as white as milk. Her hair was piled on the top of her head and a green satin rose was pinned to the side. Bessie knew she looked good. She watched Della Clayhill with a half sneer, half smile on her lips. She'd heard Colin stomp down the stairs last night, but not before she'd heard the squeaky bedsprings dance their song of love. The Piss-Queen had been thoroughly screwed by the railroader, Colin McCarthy, and she'd put up no fight a'tall.

Chapter
Twenty-Three

Rosalee watched Della Clayhill step up on the porch of the saloon. She was stunningly poised and beautiful. Every head turned toward her, every eye focused on her lovely face, framed in silvery blond hair. A quietness settled over the crowd; men gawked, women gazed at her with envy.

Rosalee felt a slow dread begin to build in the pit of her stomach. Had she made a mistake when she insisted that Della tell what happened between her and Logan? Somehow, she had thought the crowd would know that she was lying. Now, she wasn't so sure.

Adam got up from the table and went to meet her. He took her arm and ushered her to the other side, away from where Logan stood, head up, dark eyes gazing out over the heads of the people gathered in front of the porch. He seemed to be unconcerned with his immediate surroundings.

Della closed her parasol and carefully snapped the holder in place before she looped the handle over her arm. She drew the bit of cloth from her sleeve and let it flutter in her hand.

"You don't have to be afraid, honey. You just tell the folks what happened," Adam coaxed.

"Oh, Papa—"

"Now, now, don't cry."

"Do I have to tell . . . it all?" Della let her voice drop to a murmur and the crowd leaned forward to try and catch the words.

"Tell just enough so we'll know what happened."

Della dabbed at her eyes with her scented handkerchief, took a deep sobbing breath, and visibly straightened her shoulders. She looked into the faces of the crowd. Almost a hundred pairs of eyes were looking at *her*. She was on stage and suddenly began to enjoy herself. She'd give the yokels something to talk about while she was getting even with Logan Horn. She glanced at him and then quickly away. He was ignoring her. Damn him! She would have given him everything, and he had turned her down for a silly nester's daughter.

"I came to town to wait for you, Papa—"

"You'll have to speak up, honey, so the folks can hear you," Adam said gently.

Della cleared her throat and began again. "I came to town to wait for you, Papa. I thought I'd be here several days. I didn't want to bother the Reverend Abernathy and his wife, so I took a room here." She lifted her hands toward the building behind her. "Mr. Boline was kind enough to bring me my meals so I didn't have to go down on the streets alone. It was so stuffy in that room and so . . . lonesome. I sat beside the window and watched for you." She threw another frightened glance at Logan. "I saw the . . . Indian come out of the livery and sneak off behind the buildings. He must have . . . seen me in the window—" Her voice broke off pitifully and she dabbed at her eyes again.

Watching her, Rosalee was almost sure the crowd was

convinced she was telling the truth. The sickness in the pit of her stomach grew more acute as she realized Della Clayhill was laying the foundation for her big lie. She was holding the attention of the people and they were drinking in every word. Mentally, Rosalee counted the ones here who would help Logan. How could seven or eight, she thought desperately, stand against thirty or forty armed men!

"I thought I should tell someone the Indian was in town, but I didn't know who to tell, so I just waited for you, Papa. Then, well . . . there was so much noise downstairs I couldn't sleep, so I sat by the window until almost midnight before I went to bed. A little later I heard someone come up the outside stairs. I never dreamed I was in . . . danger." She clasped her hands tightly together and moved closer to Adam. "He came into my room. He just opened the door, came in and . . . threw himself down on . . . me. I didn't have time to scream or anything—"

"It couldn't have been Logan! He was with me at Mary's!" Rosalee shoved her way to the porch and stood within a few feet of Della. "You're lying if you say it was Logan," she accused.

"Why would I lie?" Della asked pitifully. "I didn't want to tell anything so embarrassing. I'm ashamed. I wanted to get out of town, but Papa thought the people of Junction City should know—"

"It wasn't Logan," Rosalee insisted venomously. "He was with me all night."

"Didn't you . . . sleep?" Della asked hesitantly.

"Not much!" Rosalee said proudly. "It was our wedding night."

This brought some loud guffaws from the men.

"Have you heard enough, folks?" Adam's booming voice carried over the murmur that rose from the crowd. "What would you do in my place? Would you want a man—redskin or not—to live after forcing himself on your daughter?"

"Noooo . . ." The shout was led by Shorty Banes and taken up by dozens of men in the crowd.

"She's lying!" Rosalee shouted, her face red with anger. She turned on Adam Clayhill. "She's lying so you can get rid of Logan and get the land he bought. That's what you've been trying to do for weeks! You're a vicious, mean man, Adam Clayhill!"

"And you're trash!" Adam snarled. "No decent white woman would take up with a redskin buck." He was losing his temper again, and Della intervened quickly before he ruined everything.

"I'm not lying!" she cried out. "He . . . came to my room and attacked me! What kind of town is this that would stand for an Indian to attack a white woman in her bed?"

Rosalee looked wildly around her. Case Malone was leaning casually against the building. His empty holster now held a gun. She couldn't see Mr. McCloud or Cooper, but over the heads of the people she could see Josh and Minnie standing in the buggy. Rosalee put her hand in the pocket of her dress and her fingers closed around the butt of the pistol. She moved over to stand in front of Logan. She'd kill, if need be, to protect her man!

"I've heard enough!" Adam slammed his fist down on the table.

"Let's hear the Indian's side of it," the man with the slashed face shouted. "Did you rape the woman?"

Logan looked down at the man coolly. "Why would any man want her when he's got a woman like mine?"

Stung by the remark and not wanting her anger to show, Della turned away and began to sob. Adam put his arms around her, drew her head to his chest, and patted her back.

A prickling sense of fear ran up Rosalee's spine and raised

the small hairs on the nape of her neck. She leaned back against Logan and felt him nuzzle her hair with his lips.

"Stay steady, my love," he whispered. "It isn't over yet. Our time will come."

There was a loud clapping of hands and a peal of feminine laughter rang out from the end of the porch.

"That's the best show I've seen since a fat woman danced bare naked on the bar in Abilene!" Bessie's loud voice reached every person on the street. "Your little gal sure puts on a good show, Mr. Clayhill. Did you screw the Indian before or after Colin McCarthy, honey?" she called sweetly. What the hell, she thought. It's time I was moving on anyway. Old Clayhill can take his piddly job and shove it up his ass!

Heavy silence followed her words, and Adam turned to her with a murderous look on his face. "Shut yore filthy mouth," he snarled.

"You want me to hush up and let her lie stand? I'll not keep my mouth shut. I'd speak up for this man or any man that's about to be hung for somethin' he didn't do." Bessie turned to the men lined up in front of her and smiled. She knew she was popular with the men. "I've been square with you, boys. I told ya right off I wasn't a whore, and not a one of you come to my room. I'm obliged to you for it. Speakin' out like this'll mean I'll be movin' on. Clayhill owns this town, lock, stock, and barrel. Well . . . maybe lock and stock, but not the barrel. Ain't that so, Mable?"

"He don't own my eatin' place, and that's the spittin' truth! I ain't beholden to nobody!" The fat lady fanned her face furiously with the dried turkey wing. Things were getting interesting. She made a mental note to give Bessie a free send-off meal.

"What you're sayin' ain't got nothin' to do with nothin'," Shorty Banes yelled. "That half-breed needs hangin' 'n ya know it."

"Shorty's right, folks—"

"I'm not done talkin', Adam Clayhill," Bessie said firmly. "Shorty ain't right. He's just sayin' what he thinks'll please you, and he's got a grudge against the Indian 'cause he kicked him in the balls!" Bessie waited for the laughter to die down, then continued. "Last night, about midnight, Colin McCarthy, the railroader that's been hangin' around here off and on, went upstairs. You boys know that nobody goes upstairs in this saloon without an invite. He and this *poor, little innocent girl* must a had a rompin' good time. I could hear the bedsprings squeakin' all the way downstairs. Ain't that right, Albert?" she asked the partly bald man in the front row. He bobbed his head up and down in agreement and tried to keep the silly grin off his face. "Albert Olson and I stood on the stairs and laughed about it. I even danced a jig to the rhythm." There were horrified gasps from the women in the crowd and laughter from the men. "It sure didn't sound to me like she was being *forced*."

"You lying bitch," Adam shouted over the laughter. "Where's this McCarthy? We'll hang him, too."

"He rode out this mornin'. He got a bad case of clap and wanted to get down to Denver to get some medicine," Bessie said matter-of-factly. "He did some braggin' before he left."

"He shore did," the man with the slashed face spoke up. He grinned at Della, who suddenly recognized him as the man she had cut with the whip the day she arrived. "He said she was the best piece a ass he'd got this side of the Mississippi. Ole Colin gave 'er a good recommend, and I'm thinkin' he give her the clap, too. I'd give 'er a try, but I ain't got no need of the clap."

Uncontrollable anger swept over Della, and unthinking, she swung on Bessie and blurted, "You sent that filthy, sore-infested varmint—" Della cut off her words, horrified at what she'd revealed.

Bessie laughed.

Adam blurted an oath.

Rosalee held her breath.

The crowd gaped in open-mouthed astonishment.

Adam collected himself first. "We'll find the bastard and hang him with the Indian!"

"The Indian didn't go up those stairs before or after midnight. I was goin' up after Colin come down, but then he told me 'bout the clap." The man looked at Della with icy blue eyes.

"Papa! He . . . forced me!" Della cried.

"I didn't hear nobody hollerin' for help," Bessie said dryly. "Did you, Albert?" The bald man swung his head back and forth.

Adam stood stock-still. Della's words had shaken him to the very roots. They had knocked all his illusions out of him. His lips beneath the white mustache thinned and his heart seemed to stop, then leaped into a mad gallop. Snatches of words raced through his brain. Sore-infested . . . squeaking bedsprings . . . best piece of ass . . . He knew how hot-blooded she was. It was true! He'd thought she was wholly his. "I love you, Adam!" she'd said. The goddamn lying little bitch! He stared unseeingly back at the people staring at him. A sudden, unprecedented fury tore through him. He turned, lifted a hamlike fist, and slapped Della with such force she staggered into Bessie.

"Ohh. . . . Papa—"

"There, there, girl," Bessie said gleefully, and steadied her. "If the old man throws you out you might get on out at Mary's. She runs a good clean whorehouse."

"Get out of my sight," Adam roared. "Get out of my house! Take your hot little ass down to Denver and stay there!" He sat down heavily in the chair beside the table. Humiliation was crushing him.

Della burst into real tears and stumbled down the walk

toward the stage office. Adam had turned on her! He had actually slapped her in front of these people! The crowd opened up so she could pass through. Some of the people were stunned, but some of them enjoyed her humiliation.

"Uppity whore's lorded it over all of us."

"Serves 'er right."

"The bitch had no time fer us. Always alookin' down her nose, she was."

"She got the clap! Hee, hee, hee."

Della heard the hissed words, dropped her parasol, and began to run.

Rosalee was equally stunned. Things had suddenly been taken out of Clayhill's hands. Della Clayhill had been discredited. She looked at the big, brassy saloon woman. Bessie grinned at her and winked. Rosalee smiled back.

Case came forward, slipped a knife between Logan's bound hands, and cut the rope. Rosalee reached up and lifted the loop from her husband's neck and then put her arms around him.

"Oh, darling. It's over!"

"Not yet, it ain't!" The hoarse, angry voice came from the street.

Logan put Rosalee firmly aside and faced Shorty Banes. The heavily built man stood on spread feet, his gun in his hand.

"Ain't neither one a ya agoin' ta git off!" His small, bright eyes flicked constantly from Logan to Case. The crowd behind Shorty scattered. "Don't move!" he shouted to Case. "Don't move a gawddamned muscle. Ya ruin't my foot."

Three things seem to happen simultaneously. Rosalee saw a flash of yellow behind Case, Shorty lurched forward to shoot, and Logan's foot lashed out and struck his arm. The sound of the shot echoed down the street and dissolved in the far distance.

A woman screamed and Rosalee saw Odell's small body

lying in the dirt beside the steps. With a cry of anguish she ran to her sister and dropped down on her knees beside her. Bright red blood poured down from the side of the child's head and splotched the new yellow dress.

"Odell! Oh, God! She's been shot!"

Logan saw Odell fall, heard Rosalee scream, and a furious, unearthly cry tore from his throat. He lunged toward Shorty, whirled and kicked. The blow landed beneath the shorter man's chin and snapped his head back. Logan spun on his toe. His foot lashed out again and he kicked him in the groin. Before Shorty could double up, Logan delivered a powerful blow to his windpipe with the side of his hand and Shorty dropped dead at his feet. It was over in less than a minute.

The crowd was stunned again. They'd never seen such a display of killer strength used in such a vicious way. Frightened by what they'd seen and not understanding it, the men surged forward. The redhead, who had sneaked into Mary's and had taken pride in taunting Logan, jumped on his back and a dozen others followed to bear him to the ground under their tremendous weight.

"He's a killer!"

"He killed Shorty with his feet and hands!"

"Hang 'im!"

The words penetrated Rosalee's dazed senses. She was torn with the decision of whether or not to stay with Odell or go to her husband. Bessie knelt beside her and Mrs. Parnell hovered over them.

"It's just a crease," Bessie said. "Look." She lifted the hair from Odell's temple. "She'll be all right. I'll take her down to Mable's and take care of her. Scotty," she called. "Come over here and carry this youngun. Go on," she said to Rosalee. "Go to your man. There's more trouble brewin' for him."

Rosalee jumped to her feet and looked frantically for Logan. Mary stood helplessly nearby and Case stood against

the wall with a gun pressed to his side. Cooper Parnell was
on the edge of the porch beside his mother. Adam Clayhill
was shouting to the men.

"Shoot him. Shoot the murderin' sonofabitch."

"No!" Rosalee screamed, but her voice was lost in a volley
of shots that came from the back of the crowd.

"Let 'im up," Josh shouted. "Let Horn up, or by Gawd,
we'll open up on ya."

Men peeled off the pile holding Logan. The last man off
was the redheaded man. He held a gun to Logan's back and
a man hung onto each of his arms.

The crowd was ringed by six mounted, armed men, and
Josh and Minnie stood in the buggy with guns in their hands.
Ben and McCloud stood on the walk with rifles pointed toward
the porch. Five of the mounted men were strangers, the other
one was Frank, the drover who had worked for Clayhill.

"Are you goin' to let a bunch of strangers and a wet-eared
kid come in here and back us off from our duty?" Adam
shouted. "The Indian killed Shorty. You all saw it."

"Shorty had it comin'," Case said. "He drew on my back
'n shot a little girl who was arunnin' to her sister."

"We're not givin' him up." Adam shook his fist at the
newcomers. "Ride on out of here. This is none of your affair."

"I'm athinkin' it is. Mr. Horn's our boss. I ain't alikin' to
have my boss shot down by a piss-poor outfit like I see here."
The lanky man let go with a stream of yellow tobacco juice.
"You be all right, captain? Me'n the boys here'll do a bit of
turkey shootin' if'n you say the word. I'd not have no trouble
a'tall pluckin' the tail feathers of that big'n with the snow on
top."

"We'll give you as good as you give." Adam's aroused
voice quivered. "Back off, or I'll shoot him myself."

"It'll be the last shot you'll fire." Cooper spoke from the
side.

Adam looked at him and his lips curled in a sneer. "You again? Get on back to that piddly ranch of yours and tend your own business."

Sylvia took off her stiff-brimmed bonnet and moved stiffly out into the street between the two groups lined up against each other.

"Ma . . ." Cooper said and started after her.

She turned to look at her son. "Stay back, Cooper. I'll handle this." She walked up to within a few feet of where Adam stood beside the red-haired man who was holding the gun on Logan. "Adam Clayhill, put a stop to this," she said softly.

Adam had been watching the mounted men, and he beetled his brows and looked at her. "Get out of the way. This isn't a woman's business."

It suddenly occurred to Logan what was happening. "No, Mrs. Parnell! Cooper," he yelled. "Come get your ma!"

Sylvia ignored him and looked Adam in the eye. She was a tall, slender woman, her blue skirt flapping in the wind, standing between two groups of armed men. She stood firmly in front of the man she'd hoped never to face, determined that there would be no more killing. Adam looked closely at Sylvia and his mouth sagged.

"Sylvia?"

"Yes. Sylvia Williamson."

"What the hell are you doing here?"

"Your sins have caught up with you, Adam Clayhill. You're a poor excuse for a man, and I'll not let you get innocent people killed and grind this man down in the dirt as you have so many before him. You've treated Logan Horn as if he were less than human. You don't know or care who he is. You'll just kill him in order to get his land."

"Mrs. Parnell! I forbid you—" Logan almost choked. "You're Mrs. Parnell?"

"I'm Cooper Parnell's mother. Logan Horn's mother was

Morning Sun, a beautiful Cheyenne woman. Look at Logan's finger. It's crooked. Like yours. You deserted a little boy with a crooked finger years ago. That little boy has grown into a man. He's ten times the man you are, Adam Clayhill. You left Morning Sun in disgrace and ruined her life. You left me, but I survived because a good man loved me. You had your way with both of us and then sneaked off to escape your responsibility."

Sylvia drew back and struck his cheek with the palm of her hand. "I'd just as soon kill you, but this will have to do." The sound of the slap resounded in the hushed silence. Adam staggered back, not from the blow, but from the realization of what she was saying.

Excited voices passed the news.

"My Gawd! Did ya hear that? The Injun's old Clayhill's son! Folks, did ya hear that?"

"If that ain't the damndest thin' I ever heard of!"

"I thought there was more to it than him just wantin' to run off a blanket ass."

"It ain't no wonder he was tryin' to run him off! He didn't want nobody to know he'd been a *squaw* man!"

Snatches of the talk reached Adam. He was stung to action. He grabbed Logan's wrist and stared at the crooked forefinger before Logan could jerk his hand away. Adam looked into his eyes—eyes that looked back unflinchingly, as venomous as those of a rattler. Logan shook free of the hands holding him. The men stepped away from him as if an invisible hand had pushed them. He took a step forward and thrust his face close to Adam's.

"If you ever put your hands on me again, I'll kill you!" he warned in a tone that quivered with hate.

The men moved farther back, leaving Logan and Adam Clayhill facing each other.

"It was Henry! Henry sent you to bedevil me," Adam accused and stumbled back a step.

"You're not fit to say his name!" Logan's hand flashed out and hooked into the front of Adam's shirt. The other hand lifted of its own accord, and he had to restrain himself to keep from chopping the life out of this man he had hated all his life. He was shaking with fury and took a long, slow breath to steady himself. He spoke in a low, controlled voice, but every word came out and found its mark with the exactitude of an artfully placed arrow. "I'll say this one time: I never want to look on your face again. If you see me coming, get out of my way. Cross my path, and it'll be the last path you cross, *Wasicun*! And you'd goddamned well better believe it." Logan spat the words out as if they were something nasty in his mouth. He stood for a long moment, his muscles tense, his mind fighting his desire to kill. His face was filled with lethal hatred. The cords in his neck stood out, and it clearly required all his self-restraint to hold himself in check. His mouth opened and closed as if strangling. "If I see you again, I'll kill you. So help me God, I'll kill you!"

"Logan—" Rosalee's voice reached into his mind. Her hand was on his arm. He shoved the big man from him contemptuously, turned his back, and put his arm around her.

Adam Clayhill had turned dead white. For an endless moment he had thought the Indian was going to kill him as he had Shorty Banes. "Damn you to hell," he whispered in a shaking voice. He swiveled his head and saw the men staring at him. It jarred him back to the present.

"What'a ya want us to do, Mr. Clayhill?"

"Nothin', you fool!" he growled. "Shorty drew down on Malone's back." Then, "Get Shorty out of the street!"

"Yes, sir. Ah, Mr. Clayhill, about our pay—"

"Tell the bartender to pay ya. And you men get on back to the ranch."

Rosalee stood in the street with her arms around Logan's waist. "Oh, Logan! Oh, my love!"

"How is Odell?"

"She's going to be all right. The bullet just creased her scalp. Bessie and Mable are taking care of her."

"Thank God!" He grinned at her. "Either your God or mine, sweetheart, I don't care which." He stretched his neck to see his men who sat patiently waiting.

"Logan . . ." Rosalee tugged on his arm to bring his attention back to Cooper. He was standing beside his mother. His puzzled eyes were going from her to Adam Clayhill.

"Come on, son. Let's see about Odell." Sylvia took his arm.

"Ma? I've got to know if—I heard what you said!" There was a paleness beneath Cooper's sun-browned skin and determination in every line of his face.

"It's not important, son. Nothing has changed. You and I are the same as we've always been."

"Is he my . . . pa?" Cooper demanded.

"No, son. Oscar Parnell nurtured a seed that was sown in the wind. He was your pa in every sense of the word except for a minor one."

Cooper looked deeply into his mother's eyes and finally, after a long hesitation, he said, "I see what you mean, Ma."

Adam stood stone still and stared at Cooper Parnell. His bushy brows drew together as his mind tried to absorb the fact that this was his son. He felt sudden pride. Goddamn! He could've made a real man out of him if he'd gotten hold of him in time.

The eyes Cooper turned on Adam Clayhill were as blue as a cloudless sky reflected in an icy pool. Slowly and deliberately, he drew back his fist and smashed it into Adam's nose, knocking him off his feet. He looked down at him sitting in the dirt, blood spurting down over his white mustache. He spat on him, as Logan had done. "I promised myself that if I ever found the man who caused my mother so much pain I would kill him," he said. "And someday, I probably will." His mother pulled on his arm and they moved away.

"Don't be angry with me, Logan," Sylvia said when they were away from where Adam was picking himself up out of the dust. "He wouldn't have backed down and there would have been killing." She put her hand on his arm and he covered it with his.

"I know. My men wouldn't have backed down either." His dark eyes looked over her head and met Cooper's. He waited.

Cooper held out his hand. "You knew?"

"About him?" He jerked his head toward Adam, who was dabbing at his nose with a handkerchief. "I've always known who he was. His brother raised me. They were as different as night and day."

"I guess it's something we've got to live with."

"You get used to it after awhile."

"Did you know about me?"

"Your ma told me a few days ago. How does it sit with you having a brother of mixed blood?"

Cooper's face broke into a smile. "Pretty goddamn good, brother! Pretty goddamn good!"

The two tall men stood grinning at each other. The miracle of having a brother was so new. Cooper slapped Logan on the shoulder with one hand and clasped his hand with the other. For a long moment dark eyes looked into blue ones. The respect and growing affection they had for each other glowed in unspoken communication.

Tears slipped from Sylvia's eyes and rolled down her cheeks as she watched her son and his newly found brother.

Chapter
Twenty-Four

Adam Clayhill, followed by his drovers, rode out of Junction City with his back ramrod straight and his head high. He had just suffered the most humiliating defeat of his life, but damned if he'd let anyone think he cared. It had taken a few minutes to get himself together after being knocked off his feet, but he had a lifetime of experience in turning defeat into victory. He would do it again.

He tried to shut his mind against thoughts that plagued him. He hadn't thought of Morning Sun or Sylvia Williamson, the skinny, little daughter of the missionary down at Fort Bent, for years. God, he thought now, Preacher Abernathy came from Fort Bent, but he wouldn't have known that he was connected in any way with the Williamson girl.

And . . . goddamn Henry! That interfering, sanctimonious Indian-loving bastard! That's where the redskin got the money. He got it from my own brother! He wondered if Henry had left him everything. If he had, Horn had enough money to buy half the territory. Then he remembered Henry's practical side. It wasn't likely he'd turn a fortune over to a breed. He'd want to be sure the money wouldn't be squandered. Goddamn! If he'd left the snot-nosed kid with the Indians where he belonged, none of this would have happened.

"Jesus!" he muttered. "I've got two boys and they both hate my guts." He laughed a mirthless laugh. "Hell! Who needs 'em? I've still got the biggest and best ranch in the territory, and own most of the town besides. I can't do anything about the Indian right now, but he isn't going to come waltzing in here getting everything his own way. I didn't get to where I am by sitting on my ass!"

Adam had an instant of regret about Cooper Parnell. "Big, like me," he muttered to himself. "Blond hair, where mine was more red. By God, he came from my seed; there's got to be something of me in him somewhere . . . It'll take him a little time to get over the shock of finding out I'm his pa, but then he'll come around. It might not be a bad idea to have him on my side. He'll knuckle under quick if he thinks he'll get a piece of the ranch when I'm gone. Hmmm . . . That boy might be some real use to me."

His thoughts turned to Della and he spoke them aloud. "Damn her little twat! What the hell did she tell me that cock-and-bull story for? Why did she want the Indian hung? I'd bet my bottom dollar he turned her down for the Spurlock woman. If that's what he did, she'd have been furious. She's ruined herself before the whole town. But she's like a cat, she'll land on her feet. She can live down there in Denver. She isn't cut out for ranch life anyway. After awhile, after we've both had time to cool off, I'll go down and see her. Hell, she needs me more than I need her. I've still got Cecilia."

Logan carried Odell out to Sylvia's open buggy and laid her down on the covered straw that had been brought from the livery. Rosalee adjusted a pillow under her sister's bandaged head.

"Sylvia will take real good care of you, honey. Logan and I will come for you as soon as we get a place ready. We're going to rebuild our house and stay in it until Logan can build on his land. His men are going to bring their families out as soon as we can build a place for them to live. We'll have our own little town out there and there'll be children for you to play with. We'll even start our own school. What do you think of that?"

"Did my dress get ruined?"

"Sylvia says she can soak out the stain. You sure looked pretty in that dress."

"I didn't thank you for the dress, Mr. Horn—"

"If you keep on calling me Mr. Horn, I'm going to have to start calling you Miss Spurlock. I'd rather call you Odell."

Odell smiled weakly. "I forget about you and Rosalee bein' married."

"I'll keep reminding you," he said with a full, rare smile.

Cooper helped his mother into the buggy after she'd hugged both Rosalee and Logan. "Don't worry about Odell. We get along just fine together, don't we, punkin'?" She smiled and wrinkled her nose at Odell.

"I can't thank you enough—"

"We don't want your thanks." Cooper handed his mother the reins. "We're family now. That makes Odell almost ours. By the way, Logan, I'm going to kiss your bride." He glanced at him with a crooked-mouthed grin. His arm went around Rosalee and he kissed her firmly on the lips. When he lifted his head he was smiling broadly. "Doggee, brother! You did all right for yourself."

Logan reached out and drew Rosalee into the circle of his arm. "Damnit, Cooper! You're taking this brother thing too far!"

Cooper whooped with laughter.

"Come on, Cooper," Sylvia called laughingly. "Stop your horsing around. We've got to get this child home and in bed."

"Head on out, Ma. I'll be right behind you." He held his hand out to Logan. "Let me know if I can be of any help to you."

"We'll be out to pick up some horses."

The two men clasped hands, nodded, and smiled. Cooper mounted his horse and rode after the buggy.

Rosalee and Logan stood in the street and watched him ride away, then turned to each other.

"I'm still dazed," Rosalee said. "If I could have chosen any man in the world to be your brother, he would have been Cooper."

"Yes," Logan said very quietly. Then, "I killed a man today with my bare hands."

"Yes," Rosalee said very quietly, as he had.

"I lost control when I saw Odell fall. I thought of your father's death and I heard you cry out—"

"He would have killed Case."

"I never thought of Case after the shot was fired," Logan admitted. "Rage at what had been done to us tore through me. I *wanted* to kill him. I can't promise that I won't kill .. Clayhill."

"I know." Rosalee put her fingers to his lips. "Do you remember what your mother said? She said, 'Show the *Wascun* you are the better man and he will die a thousand times.' He died a little today for all his big bluff when he rode out of town."

"Rosalee, Rosalee—"

"God was really looking out for us today, Logan. I was so relieved I thought I would faint when your men rode in with Frank, although at first I didn't know who they were."

"Case sent Frank out a few days ago to guide them in.

Those men mean a lot to me. We've been through tough times together. Our affection and loyalty runs deep."

"I could see that." She smiled. "Are you going to ride with them to take the cattle out to your range?"

"You mean *our* range, sweetheart. I thought you and I would take Ben and ride out to your place tomorrow and see what has to be done to the house. We need to fix it up so we can live in it. We'll make that our headquarters for awhile. The men should be there with the cattle tomorrow or the next day."

"So much has happened," Rosalee said. "Did you ever think we'd be able to stand here in the middle of the street in Junction City and not be afraid someone would see us?"

"Some good people stood by us today. More than I thought possible when we got here this morning. I must admit I thought it almost hopeless, although I knew McCloud would do what he could. I was surprised at Mary's spunk. You're a fighter, too, sweetheart. But it's going to be a long pull. They may tolerate us, but that's all." His hand went to the back of her head and caressed the thick braid that hung down her back.

"I'll be satisfied with that." She smiled at him with adoration in her eyes.

They walked, hand in hand, to where Mary, Minnie, and Case stood beside the buggy.

Mary called to her, "Are you riding back with us, Rosalee? Josh has gone to look for the sorrel Logan came in on and Ben went to the store with Mr. McCloud."

"I'd like to talk to Bessie first and thank her for what she did. She'll be out of a job, now."

"She's acomin' with us. That mean old bastard throwed her plumb out 'n told the bartender to toss her stuff outta the window. She's gettin' it now." Minnie tilted her chin and posed saucily with her hand on her hip. "I like 'er 'cause she's gutsy. Maybe me 'n her could start us up a business now that Mary's shuttin' down."

"I think I know where I can find you a silent partner." Mary looked up at Case with a twinkle in her eye.

"Ya mean it?" Minnie fairly danced with excitement. "Bessie could do what you do. She said she warn't no whore."

Case groaned. "Mary Malone, yo're goin' ta be the death a me, 'n that's a fact!"

"Look at it this 'a way, Mr. Malone," Minnie said brightly. "There ain't agoin' to be no draggy times 'round yore house."

Logan, standing apart, searched the faces of the men on the street. He found the one he was looking for and went toward the group lounging beside the watering trough. He stopped in front of the man with the slash down the side of his face. His dark eyes looked directly into the man's eyes.

"I'm obliged to you for speaking up for me today." He waited, half expecting stony-eyed hostility to greet his words, but he was compelled to say them.

"No more 'n no less than I'd a done for anybody." The man held out his hand. "Name's Lige Freeman."

"Logan Horn." Logan grasped his hand.

"This here's my partner, Tom Spink. We rode in a few days ago from Kansas 'n stopped to wet down our whistles."

"Howdy." Logan shook the other man's hand. "Looking for work?"

"Can't eat grass," he said, and grinned.

"Talk to Malone. He's that tall man over there by the buggy. He can tell you what we're planning on; and if it suits you, we'd be glad to have you."

"We're obliged."

Logan walked back toward Rosalee. He felt good about his talk with the men. It was a beginning.

* * *

It wasn't until they were in bed at Mary's that Logan had a chance to tell Rosalee about his meeting with Della at the livery and how he had promised to meet her at midnight.

"She was angry and jealous because you didn't come to her room. I could scratch her eyes out!"

Logan laughed softly, wrapped his arms tightly around her warm, naked body, and hugged her tightly. "Would you do that?"

"You can bet your life on it! Any woman who sets her sights on my man will think she's got a bobcat by the tail!"

"Rosalee, Rosalee," he said her name twice as he sometimes did when his emotions made his throat tight and his voice husky. He kissed her ear, kissed it again and again, loving kisses, dipping into his never-ending love for her. "There's something I want to tell you. I've thought about it a lot and I want to share it with you. My spirits were at the lowest ebb of my life the night I came to your door. My mother was dying and I couldn't find a place to get her in out of the rain. Then I saw the light, so faint it was a mere pinprick in the darkness." He paused and buried his face in her neck, then continued in a husky whisper. "The night wind was at my back, and it seemed to be pushing me toward that light. It was as if I were going through a dark tunnel, and if I could only reach the light I would find peace. Does this make any sense to you?"

"Darling . . ." Rosalee stroked his head. "I had wakened out of a sound sleep. I heard the wind rippling the tin on the roof and the drip of water on the floor. I lit the lamp so I could see to put a bucket under the drip. I was wide awake, and now that I think about it, I was waiting."

"I hurried toward the light, but when I reached it, I was afraid I'd be turned away." His mouth was open against the rise of her breast and she felt wet lashes against her skin. "Oh, my sweet Rosalee. I waited too long to go look for her." There was anguish in his voice. "I put duty to my country and my uncle before her."

Rosalee cradled his head in her arms and put her kisses along his brow. "You were just a little boy when you left her."

"But she was my mother and she had no one—"

"She had you," Rosalee whispered, her lips against his brow, the smell of him in her nostrils, the brush of his hair on her face. "She had you in her heart, just as you're in mine."

Her kissing lips went along his forehead, along the heavy brush of dark lashes, and she pulled his face into her breasts, pressed it to them and felt his lips take up the kissing. His arms clamped her to him, hurting her, and he lifted his mouth to hers, covered it, his body quivering. His hands on her were huge and seeking, his mouth open, exploring, caressing, and hers answered it.

He was covering her, there was the quick, sharp entry, and she wanted him, all of him, body, lips, mind, and she was trying to get into him. There was bigness and hardness that moved her in rhythm, the singing of his breath and her breath, a blending of music that accompanied his moans and her moans. They entered the far distant world together, the world of blinding light, and rose to its peak on a brilliant crescendo.

They fell apart and panted. She lay beside him and gasped. Mere seconds passed before he gathered her tenderly and naked into his arms, as if he were not whole without her there. He held her to his strong, relaxed body and stroked her breasts with his palm until they gradually quietened. He smoothed the sun-streaked hair from her face and traced her eyebrows with his fingertips.

The restless wind blew down the mountains and into the open window. He stroked her breasts again, gently, kissed her mouth, kissed her breast, reverently kissed her belly where his child could already be springing to life. There was the motion and the music again.

A long time later, he turned on his back and pressed her head to his chest. They relaxed contentedly against each other with the sense of a hunger fed, and with the sureness that there would be another time like this. In between these precious times would be a sweet, deep companionship. They would work and share the joy and the grief. They were twined in love, in flesh, in heart and soul.

"Rosalee—"

"Hmmm," she murmured into his ear, kissing and murmuring and kissing all at the same time.

"I just like to say your name." He swallowed several times before he whispered, "Rosalee . . . Rosalee . . . oh, my sweet woman."

Dear Reader,

I thank you for buying my book and hope it has given you a few hours of enjoyment, allowing you to forget the problems of everyday living while becoming involved in the lives of a pioneer hero and heroine.

I am grateful for the reception my stories of the frontier have received from you, the final critic. Please write and let me know the locale and time period in our American history you most like to read about. I would be pleased to know which characters of mine you find the most interesting.

You can write to me: Dorothy Garlock, c/o Warner Books, Inc., 1271 Avenue of the Americas, New York, NY 10020. Your letters will be forwarded to me immediately. I will answer each letter as quickly as possible and add your name to my mailing list so that you will receive a newsletter telling about my new releases.

Dorothy Garlock
Clear Lake, Iowa